30 THINGS I LOVE ABOUT MYSELF

30 THINGS I LOVE ABOUT MYSELF

RADHIKA SANGHANI

THORNDIKE PRESS
A part of Gale, a Cengage Company

Copyright © 2022 by Radhika Sanghani Ltd.
Thorndike Press, a part of Gale, a Cengage Company.

Thorndike Press® Large Print Softcover Romance and Women's Fiction.
The text of this Large Print edition is unabridged.
Other aspects of the book may vary from the original edition.
Set in 16 pt. Plantin.

LIBRARY OF CONGRESS CIP DATA ON FILE.
CATALOGUING IN PUBLICATION FOR THIS BOOK
IS AVAILABLE FROM THE LIBRARY OF CONGRESS.

ISBN-13: 978-1-4328-9834-2 (softcover alk. paper)

Published in 2022 by arrangement with Berkley, an imprint of Penguin Publishing Group, a division of Penguin Random House, LLC

Printed in the United States of America
1 2 3 4 5   26 25 24 23 22

To me. I'll always love you.

Dear Reader,

I am so excited for you to read *30 Things I Love About Myself.* This book means so much to me. I wrote it because self-love is a topic that sums up my entire outlook on life — something you'll probably guess from the dedication in this book — but is often dismissed, or even criticized, in our society today. When I tell people I love myself, they either assume I'm an arrogant narcissist, or they look at me like I've just managed to climb Mount Everest in flip-flops. It is very rare for me to meet someone who answers "yes" when I ask them if they love themselves. (Something I do a lot. I actually went through a phase of doing it on first dates. It didn't go well.)

I used to be like that too: I found the idea of loving yourself profoundly uncomfortable and definitely not for me. It was only when I realized that I was quite unhappy, in both my life and in myself, that I set off on my own self-love journey. It was messy, complicated, and incredibly hard — but it was also hilarious, beautiful, and the best thing I've ever done. It changed my life.

The more I loved myself, the more I stopped judging myself or being mean to myself; instead, I accepted myself. Just the way I am. Imperfections and all. I am aware of my faults and try to work toward being a better person, but now I do it out of love, not self-hatred. It is infinitely more pleasant.

This book is complete fiction. Nina's story is very much hers, not mine. But it is inspired by my decision to actively love myself. And, like Nina, I do have a crumpled-up list of "Things I Love About Myself" in my wallet — something I started at age twenty-one on my first trip to New York, hoping it would make me feel like Carrie Bradshaw. Back then, my list was a bit tragic. It did not have many things on it. But as the years have gone on, my list — and my inner confidence — have grown. I now try to make everyone I know do their own list, because why would you not want a piece of paper telling you how amazing you are?

Unlike my previous novels, this book focuses on a British Indian family and it is set in Leicester, a diverse city I used to call "mini India" when I'd visit from London as a child to see my extended family. I am also British Indian (my family is from Gujarat, by way of Uganda) and I wanted to write about people who look like me. I'm not trying to represent an entire race or even a community here; I'm just writing about fictional characters who are believable to me. They aren't always perfect and, like all of us, they make mistakes, but that's a realistic portrayal that I wanted to convey.

This book touches on a lot of topics that can be difficult to talk about, like racism and mental health. I'm writing about specific experiences that I think are vital and important to talk about. They're not the stories of any particular real-life individuals, rather a collation of experiences I've read about, talked about, and witnessed firsthand from my personal life as well as in my job as a journalist. I hope I have achieved my goal in writing about them with kindness and understanding.

Thank you so much for reading Nina's story. I hope you enjoy it as much as I enjoyed writing it.

Love,
Radhika

CHAPTER 1

TAURUS SEASON

TAURUS
Season: April 20–May 20
Element: Earth
Themes: Self-care. Sensuality. Pleasure.
Best time to: Set goals to make your dreams
  come true.

Nina did not want to spend her thirtieth birthday in a prison cell. But unfortunately, it looked like that was exactly what was about to happen.

"Here we are." The fiftysomething police officer who'd been in charge of Nina ever since she'd been led into Leicester police station with handcuffs around her wrists and mascara down her cheeks stopped abruptly outside a heavy metal door. "Not quite the Ritz, but at least you'll be alone."

"Alone?" Nina looked up at him in alarm. "No, no, I don't need to be alone. I'll be fine in one of those group cells with the bars."

The police officer laughed at Nina's lack of knowledge. "Those only exist in America. In Her Majesty's police stations, you get your own cell."

"But I thought that being in isolation was a punishment?" asked Nina. She was trying not to panic, and up until now, she'd been fine. She'd barely made any drug smuggling jokes when the female police officer had seen her washing out her menstrual cup in the toilet, she'd handed over her shoelaces without pointing out just how difficult it would be to hang herself with them, and she'd only made one reference to the last time she'd worn handcuffs. But that had been before Nina realized she'd actually have to spend the night in a cell. Alone.

"It's normal procedure when someone has been arrested at night," said the police officer, struggling with the key to the cell.

"Not on *Orange Is the New Black*," muttered Nina.

"This isn't TV," he replied, pushing the door open. "It's Leicester."

"Please," said Nina, in one last futile attempt to avoid her fate. She looked at the name on his shirt. "Look, DC Spencer, you know I'm innocent. I didn't do anything wrong. Is it really necessary for me to stay the night? Can't I just come in tomorrow morning for the interview?"

DC Spencer sighed impatiently. "You're under arrest," he said. "Which means you're going to have to spend the night in this cell. So get in there."

He moved aside and jabbed his thumb toward the tiny room behind him. The whole thing was made of concrete and painted to look like faux marble. It hadn't worked. There was a ledge built into the wall with what looked — and smelled — like a blue plastic gym mattress placed on top of it, as well as a much smaller blue plastic lump that Nina presumed was the pillow. There was no bed linen.

"That's the toilet," said DC Spencer, pointing to a hole in a smaller faux-marble ledge. "But also where the water comes out to wash your hands."

"Oh good," said Nina faintly, trying not to inhale the musty odor. "An eco-friendly ensuite."

"If you like. At least you're dressed for it." He looked at her oversized jumper, checkered pajama bottoms, and large puffer coat.

"I only popped out of the house to get a falafel," she said, crossing her arms. "I didn't expect to get arrested."

They both looked down at a series of white stains on her pajama bottoms.

"Hummus," explained Nina. "It's not easy to eat a falafel wrap when you've got handcuffs on."

"Oh good, so you won't be wanting dinner," he said. "Right, well, that's it, then."

"Wait," cried Nina. "Is there anything I can do? I'm guessing there's no TV. But do you have any magazines? Books? A guidance leaflet? I'll read anything."

"God, I don't remember the last time anyone asked for books," said DC Spencer.

"Do you . . . think you'd be able to find something?" asked Nina. "Honestly, I don't mind what it is. I just know I won't sleep, so anything to keep me distracted would be great."

"I think all the books got ruined by a stag do."

Nina opened her mouth to speak, but DC Spencer shook his head. "Don't ask," he said, as he walked out of the cell.

"Hang on, before you go, would it be possible to get a hot drink or something?" she asked.

"Will tea do?"

"Oh, an Earl Grey would be amazing," said Nina gratefully. "Or a chamomile actually. I guess it's a bit late for caffeine."

14

DC Spencer barked with laughter. "Chamomile! The tea comes from a machine. It's powdered." At the sight of Nina's horrified face, his voice softened. "They have a hot chocolate that isn't so bad."

"My mum keeps saying I should eat less refined sugar," said Nina. "Apparently it's why my life is so bad."

DC Spencer raised his eyes to the concrete ceiling. "You're about to spend your birthday under arrest. You can have a hot chocolate."

"Oh all right," said Nina. "I'll take two."

Nina sat in the cell and cried. Ever since she'd broken up with the man who'd been planning her not-so-surprise thirtieth, she'd lost all hopes of celebrating her birthday in style. But it had never occurred to her that she'd turn thirty alone in a cold cell with watery hot chocolate and not even a bedsheet for company. Nina wasn't big on symbolism, but she couldn't ignore the fact that this was not a very good sign. Her twenty-ninth year had not gone as planned, so she'd been desperately hoping — no, she'd *needed* — for her thirtieth to be an improvement. Only, so far, it looked like it was going to be her worst year yet.

She really had just popped out for some

15

emotional comfort food when she'd been arrested. It had been her last evening in the flat that she'd shared with Nikhil until a month ago, and she'd felt depressed being there with her stacked-up boxes piled high against all the IKEA furniture he'd painstakingly built — and thus claimed as his own. She'd felt so lonely. Lonelier than she had in years, and it hurt. She'd tried to fill up the empty pit inside of her, eating everything she could find in the flat, even Nikhil's tasteless protein bars. But it wasn't enough to plug the gaping, raw pain. So she'd done what any sane woman in the final hours of her twenties would have done: stuck a coat on over her pajamas to go and buy a takeaway falafel wrap with a side of cheesy chips.

The drama had started when she came across the activists on her way home, a group of loud, jovial women walking with flasks and placards. Nina had been staring enviously because she'd never been to a protest before, even though she'd seen *Billy Elliot* four times (even once in the West End), and she'd always felt it was something she needed to tick off her bucket list. So when one of the women had asked her to hold her placard for a minute, assuming Nina was also marching against the council's unfair closure of a local center to help refugee women, Nina had decided this was her miners' moment. The cause was perfect — as a brown woman, supporting refugees was basically in her blood — and the demonstration was conveniently going past her flat. It was time for her to make a stand.

Within minutes, Nina was sharing tea from their flasks and agreeing heartily that the council had their priorities wrong. She was so inspired by the convivial atmosphere that she'd even started up a "Save our center" chant, barely taking in the fact that a bunch of angry-looking men had joined their march. For the first time in a month, surrounded by her new friends, with a bag of cheesy chips in her hand, Nina had forgotten how miserable she was.

Until suddenly, plastic bottles were flying in the air, her chips were thrown to the ground, and people were screaming. Nina was left clutching onto her falafel wrap for dear life. By the time she had processed that she was in the middle of a fight, the police had arrived and arrested anyone who hadn't realized they were meant to run. Which meant that Nina was the only one they managed to arrest.

The cell door opened. It was DC Spencer. "You can have your phone call now," he said, pointedly looking away from Nina's sodden, teary face.

She rubbed her sleeve across her eyes and eagerly stood up to follow him into the corridor. "Oh, thank you. Hopefully I've got enough battery left."

He snorted with laughter. "Oh, you won't be using your phone. That's gone into evidence. You use the phone here in reception" — he pointed to a gray plastic desk at the end of the corridor — "and Jim will dial the number for you."

An elderly police officer pushed his glasses up with the tip of his finger and beckoned to Nina. "What's the number you want to dial, then, love?"

Did she even know any numbers by heart except for Nikhil's?

"Um. Okay." She recited his number slowly.

"Very good," said Jim, slowly tapping on the keyboard. "And what's the name of the person you're calling?"

"Nikhil Tripathi." She spelled it out for him before he even had to ask and thanked god for her Indian-enough-but-not-so-Indian-nobody-can-say-it-let-alone-spell-it name of Nina Mistry.

"Very good. And what relation is this man to you?"

18

"Well, he was my fiancé. I guess ex-fiancé. We still love each other though." Jim blinked in response. "Sorry," said Nina. "Can you just put . . . friend?"

Jim took his glasses off and rubbed his eyes, while DC Spencer let out another snort of laughter. "I'm not sure it's the best idea for you to call this man," said Jim, looking up at her kindly.

"No, it's fine," said Nina. "I know it sounds strange. But we only broke up a month ago, and we were together for three years. He'll definitely still help me."

Jim looked worried. "Is there anyone else you can call? Anyone at all?"

Nina sighed. Maybe he was right. She knew Nikhil would help her if she called, because he always did. It was one of the reasons she'd fallen in love with him. But they had promised to not speak after the breakup, and considering she was the one who'd broken his heart, that was probably the least she could do.

She tried to think of who else she could call instead.

She knew her mum's phone number, but having to deal with her critical judgment was not an option. "Typical," she'd say, even though being locked in a cell was actually very atypical behavior for Nina. "It's always one thing after another with you. You bring shame on me by insisting on living with your fiancé before marriage, and then, after I *finally* come around and admit to Auntie Hetal you've been cohabiting, you end it! Do you know how humiliating it was to take back the invitation I sent my friends? Oh yes, I know you didn't want me to invite anyone to the wedding before you had a date, but *this is how our community works, Nina.* You have no respect for any of it. And now this; arrested! I'm embarrassed to call you my daughter."

They'd had variations of this conversation so many times before — "Writing about your personal life for these websites and calling it journalism! Do you have no shame?" — that Nina could recite it word for word. There was no way she was going to voluntarily put herself through it whilst having one of the worst nights of her life.

But the sad truth slowly dawning on her was that she wasn't sure who else she could call. While she had scattered friends who were free for a quick drink on a Tuesday, none of them was ever around on a Saturday night, let alone for a "Help, I'm in prison" phone call. Everyone was always so busy — putting in long hours at work, on a romantic weekend away with their partner, or going to yet another wedding. Nina didn't get it; even when she'd been with Nikhil, she'd never been that busy, and even if she had been, she would have dropped it all for her friends. But it seemed that while Nina's priorities hadn't changed, everyone else's had.

She ran through the options of who she might call. Most of her university friends had stayed in London, and when she'd left to go back to Leicester, she'd fallen out of touch with them. She did have some work friends, but even after countless boozy Friday night drinks, she didn't feel close enough to them to reach out in a moment of crisis. The only one she'd even been truly close to was Elsie, who'd spent hours crying with Nina in the work toilets at their first job at a magazine they both hated, but now that she'd been promoted to features director at that same magazine, she was always too busy to hang. Which left Nina's school friends.

Jo had been her best friend ever since they'd bonded over *Angus, Thongs and Full-Frontal Snogging* in Year Seven. They'd spent most of the 2000s racking up huge phone bills, discussing everything from what happened on Saturday night to how unfair it was that they both had such dysfunctional families, laughingly competing for the title of Most Fucked-Up Family. And when Nina unequivocally and tragically won that title in Year Nine, Jo — and her therapist mother — had been the main reason she hadn't had a total breakdown.

They'd admittedly been drifting for a while now, and Nina was slightly annoyed at her for only sending a string of broken-heart emoji after she'd told her about ending things with Nikhil, but Jo was Jo. And Nina was running out of options.

With a slightly despondent sigh, Nina turned to Jim and recited the phone number she'd known by heart for fifteen years.

"Hello?" Jo answered instantly, her voice echoing through the station on loudspeaker.

"Oh my god, Jo. It's so good to hear your voice."

"Who is this?"

"Oh sorry! It's me, Nina."

"How come you're calling me on my private number so late? Were you out? *Anyway,* it's amazing you're calling."

"Um, I'm not sure it is," said Nina. "Because I'm actually in —"

"GUESS what just happened?"

"What?" she asked, very aware that this one-sided conversation was not going the way it should.

"I'm engaged!!! Jaz just proposed!!!"

"Oh my god, wow," said Nina weakly, turning away from both the police officers so they wouldn't see her face. "Congrats! That is super exciting for you. Look, I don't want to —"

"Thanks!" cried Jo. "I'll fill you in on all the deets later. Obvs you're going to be a bridesmaid."

Nina tried again. "Jo, sorry, I don't want to make —"

"OH MY GOD, I'm the worst!" screeched Jo. "I forgot it's your birthday tomorrow. That's why you're calling, right? I'm so, so sorry but I can't do brunch anymore — we're having a family celebration for the engagement. But I *promise* I'll make it up to you."

"Thanks, Jo, but that's not really —"

"Nins, I need to go and call more people. It *literally* just happened. My ring is IN-SANE, you're going to die! I just Insta-grammed it, if you want to like it on there. Love you — and oh my god, happy birthday! Bye."

Jo hung up, and Nina was left standing over the phone in silence. Jim looked at her with obvious pity in his eyes. DC Spencer was looking at the floor, clearly trying not

23

to laugh.

"I'm afraid that's your one phone call," said Jim. "Sorry."

"It's fine," sighed Nina, pulling her coat tight around her. "It's not like I have anyone else to call anyway."

Nina went back to her cell and cried. Again. Or maybe it didn't count as a separate cry if she hadn't really stopped. She'd been crying since she ended things with Nikhil a month ago. But she'd been having weekly Sunday evening "what the fuck am I doing with my life and why don't I feel okay" cries for longer than that. She wasn't sure if they'd started when Nikhil had told her he didn't like giving oral sex or when she'd found his five-year plan in the kitchen and realized how little they had in common. It wasn't that she had anything *against* buying a three-bedroom house in Derby in three years' time, especially if it came with the border collie that Nikhil foresaw for the following year. But it just felt so grown-up and, if Nina was honest, a little dull. She wasn't ready to spend the next five years preparing for the children she knew he wanted to fill the house with.

She'd always imagined she'd spend her thirties living a glamorous life back in

London as she climbed the career ladder and wore heels to work, or traveling around the world, making love to her boyfriend in a Goan beach hut at sunrise. But the only travel on Nikhil's plan had been a FIFA World Cup trip that Nina had zero interest in joining.

For the last year of their relationship, she'd been plagued by doubts about how different they were, and how they wanted different things. But because she didn't know exactly what it *was* she wanted, she'd become even more confused. And she loved Nikhil. She really did. So she'd stayed with him, hoping that eventually her doubts would disappear and love would conquer all. It was why she'd said yes to his marriage proposal. She'd thought that making a concrete decision about their relationship would kick-start her into finally wanting the same things as Nikhil — the things you were *supposed* to want. But when reality dawned on her that she'd just signed up to spend the rest of her life with a man she wasn't fully compatible with, she'd felt worse. Two months after the proposal, she'd eventually broken up with him — and broken her own heart in the process.

It turned out that breaking up with someone you still loved was pure agony. Nina almost wished Nikhil had cheated on her, or that she had a reason to hate him. But she didn't, because he was practically perfect. Just not perfect for her. She missed him so much that it physically hurt. The only consolation was that she knew she'd done the right thing; the wave of relief that had flooded her body the moment she'd managed to say "I love you so much, but I'm starting to realize love isn't enough" had proved that to her. Unfortunately, the relief had disappeared a split second later, when a tear slid down Nikhil's face. It had been replaced by a constant, crushing pain in her gut that hadn't left her since. Sometimes it was so intense that Nina wondered if it would have been better to just stay with him. Was it *really* that bad to marry someone you were pretty sure you'd end up divorcing one day if they were your best friend and you loved them?

The Nina who'd been raised on a diet of Disney couldn't believe she was even asking herself this, but adult Nina wasn't so sure it was that bad — especially when the other option meant living like she was now. Her life was just so *empty.* It wasn't just the fact that all her friends were too busy with couples' dinner parties to hang with her; she didn't even feel fulfilled by her career.

She pretended to Jo, Gayatri, and the others that she loved working flexible hours, but the truth was that she was going crazy spending all day at home alone. Sometimes she was busy writing, but most of the time she was scrabbling around for work, and it was making her lose the passion she'd always had for journalism. Especially because the pop culture articles she was writing now couldn't be further away from the idealistic career she'd always dreamed of: giving a voice to the underrepresented and making a difference.

Nina had just about managed to pay her bills since going freelance a couple of years ago, but now that she wouldn't be splitting rent with Nikhil anymore, she knew she had no choice but to go back home. To her "don't air your dirty laundry in public" mother and her clinically depressed brother.

Nina closed her eyes and sobbed out her pain. It came out in a wild animal howl that sounded like something from *The Jungle Book,* but she didn't care. She hadn't cried like this in years. Normally she didn't let herself get to this point. She'd watch a TV show, or check her Instagram, or have a snack. Sometimes several. In extreme circumstances, she'd pour herself a glass of wine to go with her side of carbs. But here, alone in this cell, with no Internet, no carbs, and no wine, there was nothing at all to distract Nina from just how sad she really was. So she cried, and cried, and cried.

Two hours later, she was still sobbing desperately when the grate on her cell door slid open and a book landed on the floor in front of her.

She stared at it in surprise and then looked up through her tears at DC Spencer's eyes shifting awkwardly in the grate. "I found a book," he said. "It's the only one that wasn't ruined by the stag do."

Nina gingerly went over to pick it up. It was a slim, white, contemporary-looking book. The back was covered in quotes from people saying things like "This book changed my life" and "The best gift anyone can ever give you." There was no author name, but a line on the back explained it was published by a collective called the "Self-Love Club." Nina turned it over. The front cover was filled with bright red letters that read: "How to Love Yourself (and Fix Your Shitty Life in the Process)."

"Happy birthday," said DC Spencer.

CHAPTER 2

"You're free to go," said Jim, smiling at Nina, who imagined she was looking even more bedraggled than before. After all her tears, her eyes must be swollen and red, all traces of mascara washed away, and her hair plastered in greasy chunks on top of her head. "But I have a small surprise for you. To make up for your lack of a phone call last night."

"You bought some Earl Grey?" asked Nina hopefully.

"Uh . . . no, sorry," he said, fidgeting with his glasses. "No, I know you didn't have anyone you could call last night. So I looked up your 'in case of emergency' contact number, and I managed to get through to your mum. She's coming to get you!"

Nina stared at Jim in horror. "My mum? You can't be serious?"

The smile slowly dropped off his face. "Uh, yes?"

Nina closed her eyes and focused on summoning every grain of her strength. She was going to need it.

"Are you, um, all right?" asked Jim. "Don't forget your, uh . . ."

Nina opened her eyes to see him gesturing toward a plastic bag on the desk containing all her belongings: her phone, a credit card, the half-eaten falafel wrap clumsily wrapped in paper napkins, and her house keys. With a loud sigh and a dirty look aimed at Jim, Nina picked up the transparent bag and slowly walked out of the station — praying that the book she'd stolen wouldn't fall out of her pajamas.

The silver BMW pulled up outside the police station. Nina shoved the rest of the falafel wrap in her mouth and wiped her hands on her pajama bottoms.

"Oh my god," said Rupa, as Nina opened the car door and slid into the passenger seat. "You look awful."

"Thanks, Mum," said Nina. "Good to see you too."

"I'm going to have to open a window," muttered Rupa, as she drove out of the station, opening both car windows. "You smell musty."

She turned to look at her daughter. "You

know, I cannot believe what you have put me through, Nina. I have been worried sick. Why didn't you call me? What kind of daughter doesn't let her mother know she's been arrested?"

"I'm sorry. It was late, and I didn't think there was any point. It wasn't like you could have gotten me out. They told me I'd be free to go home in the morning."

"That's not the point," cried Rupa, her blow-dried hair swinging angrily around her immaculately made-up face. "How do you think I felt when a police officer called me this morning and I found out you'd spent the night there without telling me? It's so mortifying that he called me and you didn't. He said you called Jo. JO. A friend over your own family. You know that blood is thicker than water."

Nina sighed. She was too tired to navigate her mum's circular arguments. Instead she pulled out her phone to distract herself by reading all the messages she'd missed whilst in jail. There weren't any.

"Are you even listening to me?" asked Rupa.

"Yes," said Nina, as she checked Instagram. "You're angry I called Jo, not you. I'm sorry. Next time I'm in jail, I promise I'll call." No new notifications, but seven

31

hundred likes under the photos of Jo's ring. She pressed "like," then flung her phone back into the plastic bag.

"Nina," cried her mum. "Can you please treat your belongings with more respect? No wonder you ended up in jail. Honestly. I hope you know how lucky you are that they let you go with no consequences; there was an article in the *Daily Mail* recently about an innocent Indian man who *died* in a jail cell." She paused, then shook her head angrily. "It's just not right that you wouldn't tell me. Any other daughter would call their parents, but not you. Oh no, you have to be Miss Independent and try to go it alone. It's about time you acted like an adult, now you're thirty." She sniffed. "I suppose you expect me to wish you a happy birthday, though really, I can't see anything happy about this."

"It's fine, Mum," said Nina wearily. "And I'm sorry. I thought I was doing the right thing by not telling you. I just know you've got a lot going on with Kal, and I didn't want to add to your stress. I was trying to be considerate so you wouldn't worry."

"I'm your mother; it's my job to worry. I'll worry till the day you die. I'm not a white mother, forgetting her children and leaving them in jail."

"What does that —" started Nina.

"Don't try and blame this on Kal either," snapped Rupa. "You know it's not his fault he's not well. And stop changing the radio station. I want to listen to Asian Network."

Nina breathed deeply. She could do this. She'd survived jail. She could survive a fifteen-minute car ride with her mother. "Okay. Sorry. I'm just really tired and I don't feel great. Can you just drop me at Nikhil's place?"

Rupa shrieked and slammed the brakes on. "Nikhil's?! You are not going back there. Not after you broke his heart. You are going to leave that boy alone and move out of his flat once and for all. I can't believe what you've put us all through. His parents didn't even look at me at the bhajans last week. Do you know how that feels? Do you?"

Nina closed her eyes and tried to drown out her mum's lecture as they drove through the city center, into the suburbs, and finally to the picture-perfect village of Newton Linford, pulling up outside a modest detached house with symmetrical shrubs lining the driveway.

"I hope you're getting straight in the shower," said Rupa, looking her daughter up and down as she got out of the car. "You look like you haven't washed in days. And make sure you take your coat off outside. If that smell comes inside, it'll get every-where."

Nina stepped out of her shoes and coat in the driveway as her mum punched the code into the high-tech keypad on the door. "Would you like me to strip to my under-wear, or is this enough?" she asked.

"There's no need to be so dramatic," said Rupa, ushering her daughter into the cream-on-cream hallway while simultaneously spritzing mandarin and grapefruit spray into the air. "You can strip here in the hallway."

Nina sighed and peeled off her jumper and pajama bottoms to reveal a black cotton bralette and hot pink knickers. "Do you even want to know why I spent a night in a cell?"

"The police told me," said Rupa, slipping out of her cream cashmere wool coat and placing her keys on the wooden console table. "Refugee protests. I don't want to talk about it. I can't believe you'd risk everything just to support these people coming into our country to take our jobs. They're prob-ably ISIS in disguise."

Nina stared at her mother. "Mum, you were one of those. Your dad literally came here to get work."

"Because we were kicked out of Uganda

by Idi Amin and there was nowhere else to go," retorted Rupa, picking up Nina's clothes. "These refugees have no idea how lucky they are. They can stay in their countries, but they choose not to."

A half-dressed Nina followed her into the glaringly bright kitchen, with its white marble counters and freshly painted white cupboards. She wrinkled her nose at the smell of disinfectant and immediately started tugging at the bespoke porcelain door handles in search of carbs and refined sugar, hoping to distract herself from getting into the same fight she'd been having since she was thirteen. "I'm guessing there's not a surprise birthday cake hidden in here somewhere?"

"Oh for god's sake, Nina," cried Rupa. "I spent *weeks* asking you what you wanted for your birthday, and you said you were too heartbroken to celebrate so could we please cancel it — and now it turns out you were expecting a cake! Honestly, there is no pleasing you."

"Okay, sorry, forget I asked," said Nina, crouching down next to her mum's legs to open a wide drawer beneath the oven. "I just wanted some sugar . . . Ooh, here we go." She pushed aside the vegan gluten-free cereal bars and raw energy balls, triumphantly pulling out a slab of dark chocolate. At least it had sea salt in it.

"Are you going to eat that entire chocolate bar?" asked Rupa, peering down at her daughter. "It'll go straight to your thighs. And can you please put some clothes on? Your brother's upstairs, and you're far too old to walk around like that."

Nina took a deep breath, ignoring the inner teenager inside her raging with the injustice, and shoved a large chunk of chocolate in her mouth. Now was not the time to enter into a fight with her mum; she'd barely eaten any carbs in twenty-four hours. Besides, she had some self-love to work on.

When Nina, alone in her cell, had first read the title of the book DC Spencer had given her, she'd been offended. It was true that her life was shitty. But loving herself wasn't going to fix it. There were lots of things she already loved about herself. Like her long legs. Her thick hair. And, okay, she didn't love the crooked Indian nose she'd inherited from her dad, but she didn't think she was hideous. Sure, she was failing at a lot of big life things right now, like her career, relationship, friendships, family life — but she liked her personality. She was fun, honest, and . . .

a lot of things. She had her flaws, but who didn't?

She'd started reading the book purely to prove to herself that she didn't need it. The introduction spoke about how its aim was to help a lost soul (Nina inferred this was meant to be her) find true happiness by accepting themself. The goal was self-love, and by the end of the book, the reader would be able to clearly see all the things they loved about themself. In getting there, they'd also realize their life wasn't as much of a shitstorm as they thought. Instead of focusing on negative situations they couldn't change, they'd be busy living in the present, connecting with their true selves, and experiencing the indescribable joy of being their own best friend.

Nina had rolled her eyes in response. There was obviously no need for her to read this basic self-help book with its cliché advice; she already knew what she loved about herself. If anything, that was the one thing she *didn't* have to worry about right now. But there were still five hours till morning, so she pressed the buzzer to ask DC Spencer for a piece of paper and a pen — he gave her a wax crayon, because apparently pens were a self-harm risk — and sat down to write a list.

Things I Love About Myself
BY NINA MISTRY

1. Good legs. I am very lucky to have them and will not take them for granted.
2. Also my hair. (But not the fact that I also have it on my arms, other unwanted places, etc.)
3. Sense of humor. I can laugh at a lot of things — including every single one of my many flaws — and that is no easy feat.
4. I love how honest I am. Yes, I over-share a lot, but that's a positive thing. Well, not to my family, but it is to me.
5. Even when life has been shit, I haven't given in to my DNA and tried to end it all.
6. I'm a Taurus, which means I'm stubborn and strong.

That's when Nina had stopped. She'd reread the list that had taken her fifty minutes to compile and realized that two of the things she loved about herself were her date of birth and the fact that she hadn't tried to kill herself. It was so depressing that she'd almost started crying again. But after an hour of staring at her list and failing to fall asleep on the rock-hard gym mattress, she decided to give the book another shot. It wasn't like she'd be sleeping anyway; the lack of bed linen made sure of that.

Instead, Nina spent the whole night maniacally reading the book.

She couldn't put it down.

Every chapter felt like it had been written just for her — especially "How to Get Through the Agony of Loneliness" — and it made her realize that she didn't love herself at all; she didn't even know herself. She'd spent so long just doing things — being with Nikhil, working on articles for a deadline, trying to escape her family, getting drunk, eating her feelings — that she had no idea who she was beneath it all. She'd turned into "a human doing, not a human being" (direct quote from the book), and this first experience of just "being" — i.e., sitting in a prison cell with fuck all to do — was showing her that she was not okay.

If the book was right, she didn't need to marry Nikhil or get a new job to fix her life. What she needed was to go inward and do a lot of meditative breathing, and eventually, she would be able to fully accept herself. Just the way she was. Like Bridget

Jones with Mark Darcy, only *she'd be her own Mark Darcy.*

This realization was so intense that all Nina had wanted to do was post an Insta story about her *Eat Pray Love* moment on the floor of a prison cell in Leicester. But given that she no longer had a phone, Nina had instead forced herself to breathe through the urges, as instructed by the book, and let the possible Instagram captions drift through her head like passing clouds. Om.

Now, finally showering for the first time in over forty-eight hours — and yes, she'd only been in the cell for twelve — Nina felt good. On the surface, her life had ostensibly never been worse. But she couldn't remember the last time she had felt so peaceful, and it was because of the book. She knew it was weird that this anonymous self-help book had suddenly become her personal savior, but it had come when she needed it the most, and it seemed to know exactly how to help her. Because it was now very obvious that her biggest problem wasn't any of the external stuff; that was just a natural consequence of the fact that she could barely list six things she liked about herself, let alone loved.

If she wanted to sort it out, then she'd

have to get to a place where she loved herself so much that it wasn't hard to write ten things on a list. Fuck it, she should aim higher. She should try to write thirty things she loved about herself. One for each of the very long years she'd lived. How hard could it be to find thirty things she loved about herself?

While her leave-in conditioner was doing its thing — the high-end toiletries were one of the few benefits to being in her mum's house — Nina started to get excited about her self-love mission. She had many flaws, but as her secondary school netball teacher knew, she'd always loved a challenge. If she was going to do this, she'd have to do it properly. She couldn't cheat with the list by lying or exaggerating. She wanted this to be a real self-love list she could turn to whenever she felt low. Which was why she needed to pick thirty qualities about herself she *really* liked, not just things she was born with. She already had two proper ones — her sense of humor and ability to be un-flinchingly honest. That was a good, workable start; she just needed to add to it.

But as her comb got caught in a tangled-up knot, Nina felt her stomach start to churn with anxiety. What if she couldn't find thirty things she truly loved about

41

herself? She wasn't sure she could cope with failing at this task. She'd always feared failure more than anything — ironic, considering the last few months of her life had been a series of nonstop failures — so maybe she should just donate the book to charity and try to forget all about her first and hopefully last night in a cell.

Except as the knot came unstuck, Nina knew she couldn't do that. There was something about this goal that felt right in a way many of her previous life choices, if she was honest, just hadn't. She *needed* to do this. Besides, she'd always been good at homework and studying; self-love was just another subject she needed to get an A in. And it wasn't like she'd never fallen in love before. Since age thirteen she'd been an expert at falling for boys, regardless of whether they felt the same way about her. Now she just had to do the same with herself. How hard could it be?

Nina, wrapped in a huge cream towel, padded into her bedroom. Only, as she looked around, she realized it was no longer her bedroom. It was still cream, but all traces of her blue-tacked *Breakfast at Tiffany's* posters were gone. Instead, there were dumbbells in the corner and piles of political books towering on the desk, and her tall, scrawny older brother was lying topless on the bed with his laptop resting on his boxers.

"What happened to my room?" she asked as her wet hair dripped onto the new bamboo-colored carpet.

"My room now, sorry," said Kal apologetically. "I thought Mum would have told you. When you and Nikhil got engaged, she celebrated by redecorating. She said I could have your room because it's bigger."

Nina sighed and pushed her brother's legs away so there was space for her to sit on the bed. "Where's all my stuff?"

"She called it 'childhood crap' and donated it to charity," said Kal.

Nina's face scrunched up as she tried to remember how much she'd left in her old room when she'd moved in with Nikhil. It was a lot. "Typical," she said. "Guess I'll be sleeping in your old room, then?"

"It's called the guest room now," said Kal. "But yeah. How are you doing? Mum told me about jail. I never had you down as a protester; I thought you didn't care about politics."

"I care about women who have been abandoned by the government," retorted Nina. "And I was anti-Brexit. Just because I don't follow every single parliamentary decision like you do . . ."

"I'm impressed you even know what Brexit is."

Nina threw a pillow at him. "You're an idiot. Is Mum really pissed at me?"

"The usual," said Kal. "Though, weirdly, I think she was more furious about you breaking off the engagement than getting arrested. She cleaned for eight hours solid when that happened."

"Oh god. That's worse than when you quit your job and came back to Leicester."

"Yep. An unmarried thirty-year-old daughter is way worse than a former City high-flying thirty-two-year-old son who got depressed and quit his job. Got to love a bit of Indian sexism."

"It's only because she's still holding out hope you'll go back to the six-figure salary," Nina said with a shrug. "As am I, to be honest. I could do with a loan."

"Sorry, Nins. I'm not going back. That lifestyle isn't for me."

"Do you know what you're going to do instead?" asked Nina. "Not that I'm trying to do a Mum and pressure you to get a job or anything. Promise."

"You'd better not be," said Kal. "I feel like I spend so much energy trying to make my depression more palatable for her that I don't have any left to actually try and get better. So no, I have no idea what I'm going to do. And I don't think I will until I'm in a better place."

"Hey, that's okay," said Nina, pulling her towel tighter. "There's time to figure it out. Thirty-two is not old, no matter what Mum says." She paused. "I do feel a bit sorry for her. She thought we'd both be married by now with decent careers. Only we're both in our thirties, living at home, and neither of us have stable jobs. It's not exactly great material for boasting at dinner parties."

"Tell me about it," sighed Kal. "This is not how I imagined my life would turn out. I'm back in Leicester congratulating myself for managing to have a shower in the morning, while all my mates are in London, getting married and promoted."

"I know what you mean," agreed Nina. "And I have no idea how either of us is going to survive living back here with Mum. You know all the fruit tastes of vinegar because she scrubs them in it? And the only junk food I can find is covered in chia seeds. This is going to be hell."

Kal grinned at her. "Mate, I'm clinically depressed; I'm already in hell."

CHAPTER 3

"Why are you wearing my Whistles jump-suit?" asked Rupa, as Nina walked down-stairs into the hallway.

"Because all my clothes are at Nikhil's and you threw my other stuff away," replied Nina, trying not to let her mum's negative energy ruin her positive vibes. Tonight was a big deal. Not only was it the first night of her thirties, but she was going to celebrate it by following the book's advice and doing her very first self-love mission: go out on a first date. With herself.

"I hope you've put deodorant on," said Rupa. "I don't want you to make it smell."

"What? Of course I have. Mum, I don't smell. Why would you say that?"

"You ruined my blue dress when you bor-rowed it once," replied Rupa. "I had to throw it away because it smelled so awful."

"Oh my god, Mum, I was thirteen," cried Nina. "I was going through puberty. Anyway, I'm going out tonight. So I'll be back later."

"Who with?" Rupa peered at her daughter over her leopard-print reading glasses and let her glossy magazine rest on the cream sofa. "I thought we'd have a birthday dinner for you. Though it's too late to get you a cake."

"Thanks, Mum, but don't worry about it," said Nina breezily, putting her mum's leather jacket on over the green silk jumpsuit. It was a warm April evening, so she hadn't bothered to dry her still-damp hair, but she had put on red lipstick and big gold hoops. Dating herself already seemed more fun than dating a guy — she'd never go for such a statement look on a first date with a man, for fear of scaring him off (everyone knew men hated jumpsuits), but she could wear whatever she wanted to impress herself. "I've got new plans to celebrate."

"Who with?" repeated Rupa.

"Does it really matter?"

"If you're living under my roof, then yes, it matters," said Rupa. "I want to know where you're going, who with, and what time you'll be back."

Nina closed her eyes and repeated the book's first mantra to herself: *I love myself and everyone around me.* "Okay. I am going

47

for dinner and drinks with myself. I'll be back by eleven at the very latest."

Her mum stood up so quickly that the magazine slid onto the floor. "On your own? On your birthday? Oh, Nina. That's so sad."

"No, it's not. It's empowering. I'm spending time with someone I love — well, want to love."

Her mum shook her head and went over to the kitchen. She pulled out a cloth and started cleaning the already clean white marble counters. "I think it's strange. People will talk. They'll think you've been stood up. Or that you're loose."

"Loose? Who even says that anymore?" said Nina, grabbing the plastic bag with her keys and credit card in it. It wasn't the most environmentally friendly option, but it was the only handbag she had right now.

"Can you at least try not to go somewhere my friends will be?" asked Rupa as Nina walked out of the door. "Go to an English pub if you have to. Not an Indian restaurant. And you shouldn't wear those trainers with the jumpsuit. It doesn't go."

"Well, I'm sorry for the added shame that my dining alone in an outfit you disapprove of is going to bring you, Mum," said Nina defiantly. "But I am not a teenager anymore. I'm thirty years old, and if I want to go for dinner alone, then that's exactly what I'm going to do." She slammed the door shut behind her.

"Yes, a table for one, please," said Nina to the young Indian waiter at her favorite Indian restaurant. "Just one."

"Okay," he said, guiding her toward a table right by the entrance.

"Typical," muttered Nina. "The solo diners get the worst table in the restaurant."

"Um, it's the only free one," he said, scratching his diamanté earring. "You can wait for another one if you'd rather."

"No, it's fine. I'm too hungry to wait. And I already know what I want. I'll take the thali of the day, please. With an extra Peshwari naan. And a side of chili paneer. And raita, obviously. With a carafe of house white."

"Shall I bring another glass?"

Nina sighed loudly. "I knew this would happen. Society just can't handle the thought of a single woman with a healthy appetite dining alone. But I can actually eat and drink all that. You really don't need to assume someone is joining me. It's kind of sexist."

The waiter smirked. "No, it's just there's this man standing here. I thought he was joining you."

Nina turned around and froze.

Nikhil.

He looked as handsome as always: tall, broad, clear brown skin, soft black jumper, and jeans. But there were dark circles around his eyes, and he looked sad. She felt a pang of love in her chest.

"Nikhil!" she cried.

"Uh, hey, Nina," he said, running his hand through his hair awkwardly. "I, um, saw you walking in and came over to say hi. Also, happy birthday."

She gave him a small smile. "Thanks. What are you doing here?"

He gestured to a table where two middle-aged Indian couples and two young Indian women were all staring right at Nina with undisguised disgust. "Family dinner. Well, with mine, and my sister's best friend's family. I think it's a setup."

"Ah. I guess I shouldn't go over to say hi to your parents, then."

He let out a short laugh. "Yeah, definitely don't do that. They kind of hate you right now."

"Do . . . you?" she asked.

"Obviously not," he said softly. "I want to, but well, you know how I feel about you."

"I'm really sorry, Nikhil, about everything," said Nina. "You know I wished that we'd worked out. And I still love you. I just can't be —"

"With me," he said flatly. "Yeah, I know, I get it. I mean, I hate it. But it's fine. I'm going to be fine." He paused. "Anyway, you've moved out of the flat, right? I heard you're back at your mum's. It's on the grapevine."

"I've literally been there about five hours," cried Nina. "How do people already know?"

"Your mum told Auntie P who called my mum who told my sister who somehow organized this dinner in less than an hour."

"I really need to get out of this city," sighed Nina. "But they're right. I was going to message you to say you can move back into the flat whenever you want now. I still need to pick up my stuff, but I think my mum and Auntie Trish are on it."

"Okay," said Nikhil. "Shit, it's going to be weird being in the flat without you. I'll miss you. And your overpriced mattress topper."

Nina laughed through the tears pricking her eyelids. "I told you it's important to invest in your sleep. And I miss you too. I can't even explain how much it all hurts. I know we're not right as a couple, but you're still my best friend, Nikhil."

"Hey," he said gently. "I'm not really ready to be friends again, Nina. But maybe with time. We'll see."

"Okay," said Nina, dabbing under her eyelids to stop the mascara smudging. "Sure. Well, you should get back to . . . that." She gestured to the table where Nikhil's sister's best friend was now holding up her phone as though she was trying to take a not-so-subtle photo of Nina crying.

"Yep. Hey, are you eating alone?"

She lifted her chin. "Yes, and what?"

"No, nothing." He shrugged. "I just thought you hated being alone. It was always the thing that confused me most about you. You seemed so independent, but then you could also be kind of . . . needy."

"Okay, ow. An unsolicited home truth on my birthday. But maybe you're right. I did get a bit needy. I'm trying to change though. I spent a bit of time alone last night, and . . . I think I'm going to be all right at it."

Nikhil smiled at her. "Good to hear. Maybe if you get really good at it, you can give me a call and I'll consider taking you back."

"Uh, dream on, I'm the one who's meant to be considering taking you back!" She paused when she saw the look on his face. "Okay, sorry, that was too soon, right? You know I'm not so great at knowing when it's okay to joke about things."

Nikhil shook his head and leaned in to hug her. Nina let her eyes shut for a moment as she savored the feeling of being held in his arms, trying to ignore the pang in her chest as he broke away. "Enjoy your alone time, Nins. And happy birthday."

Nina finished her third glass of wine. She was drunk. And full. She shouldn't have eaten the entire Peshwari naan, but she couldn't cope with the satisfaction of the annoying waiter seeing her unable to finish her meal. Meeting Nikhil had thrown her. She'd felt so strong coming for dinner alone, but he'd reminded her how good it felt to be around someone who loved her. A good, kind, solid presence.

Was she making the biggest mistake of her life, throwing away a lifetime with her best friend? And for what? A life of solo dinners and house whites.

She ate the last chunk of the chili paneer slowly and closed her eyes. Although, on second thought, was there really anything wrong with a life of solo dinners all to herself? It was really, really nice not having to share her favorite dish with Nikhil, or listen to his complaints about how her eyes were bigger than her stomach and she needed to stop ordering food she wouldn't finish. Maybe she was being too hard on herself and her solo self-love life. This was only her first dinner with herself; it was natural that she wasn't going to fall head over heels instantly, especially with her ex gate-crashing.

She'd need to give it some time.

At least she approved of her date's food choices, and her outfit. Nina snorted with laughter. Thinking about herself in the third person was hilarious. In fact, so was the fact that she'd seen Nikhil and his entire family on her date. Or maybe she was just drunk.

She couldn't help laughing aloud as she remembered the expression on Nikhil's mum's face and the whole setup with his sister's friend. Karina, that was it. She didn't even blame Karina for trying to move in on Nikhil so quickly. He was one of the few Indian men in Leicester above six feet who was diamanté earring–free and could actually talk about his feelings — all of which made him an official catch. It wouldn't be long before there was a line of Leicester's finest single ladies lining up outside his flat like a scene in a nineties Bollywood movie. She started laughing at the image. God, she really did have a great sense of humor. Maybe it wouldn't be so hard to fall in love with herself.

"Are you all right?"

Nina looked up and saw a different waiter looking at her. She blinked at him to make sure it wasn't the same one as before. He looked handsome and older. "I'm very all right, thank you," she said. "Just laughing, at a . . . joke. I said something funny. To myself."

"Oh-kay," said the waiter. "I just wanted to check. And, um, can I get you anything else?"

"I think I've got enough food," she said.

He grinned as he looked at the pile of plates on the table. "How about . . . tap water?"

"Sure," said Nina. "Thank you."

As he left, Nina smiled. She was having fun alone. And the universe had just sent over a hot waiter. For the first time in months, things felt positive.

Her phone vibrated and she looked at the screen. It was a message from her mum. Stop laughing, Nina. The Lakhanis think you're having a breakdown. They've sent over the owner to check on you. Next time you need to embarrass yourself like this, do it in Nandos — not Veeraswamy's.

Nina tried to smile sexily at the owner as she paid for the meal.

"Thanks for everything," she said. "It was delicious."

"Glad you enjoyed it."

"And thanks for checking up on me. It was, um, sweet of the Lakhanis to ask you to do that."

The owner blushed. "They were just concerned."

"Mm," said Nina, smiling at how cute he looked. "I guess it's not every day they get provided with a big fat slice of gossip during a Sunday night dinner."

"Ah, I wouldn't worry about it," he said, giving Nina back her card and looking straight into her eyes. "I can't imagine their gossip was anywhere near as fun as the conversation you were having with yourself."

He was *definitely* flirting with her. "Oh, I can be a lot of fun," she said.

"I don't doubt it. Have a good night."

Nina felt a twinge of disappointment as he left. He was hot. And he seemed to like her. He hadn't asked her out — but maybe she could ask him out? She'd never done anything like that before, but it felt very *Sex and the City.* She took a quick look around the restaurant and noticed most of the tables had gone. There was no one left to witness anything else shameful she might do.

"Excuse me," she said to the young waiter with the diamanté. "Where did the owner go?"

"He's just gone out back, innit. Why?"

"Oh, never mind. I'll leave a note. Do you have a pen?"

The waiter sighed at the inconvenience and produced a biro. Nina grabbed it and started scribbling on the back of the receipt. Her heart was beating loudly as she handed it to the waiter. She felt like a brown Samantha. "Okay, can you give this to him, please?"

The waiter took it and started reading it. "Um, can you not?" said Nina, but it was too late. He snorted with laughter. "You've given him your number? Oh wow. Everyone is going to die when I tell them about this."

Nina's face flushed. "What? Why's that so funny?"

"Uh, he's married, blad. He's like, thirty, you know. Most people are married by then."

Nina blushed deeper. "Oh, right. Fine. Well, don't give him that, then. No need."

She grabbed her plastic bag of belongings, threw on her coat, and walked out of the restaurant as the waiter stood there still clutching her receipt and laughing. It really wasn't that funny. Nor was it that big a deal.

It wasn't like he'd personally rejected her. He just already had someone in his life. It was fine. She wasn't going to let this ruin her very first date with herself.

At the bus stop her phone vibrated again.

Nina, a MARRIED man? You met Gita at Nitin Mama's 50th. How could you make a move on her husband? Have you NO shame?

In her mum's guest room bed, flushed from two orgasms, Nina breathed out heavily. Her first date hadn't gone as planned. But it had ended in sex with someone who knew exactly what she liked. Surely this was a success in self-love? The last forty-eight hours had been . . . a journey. She'd gone from being arrested mid-falafel to having a spiritual revelation to talking to Nikhil for the first time since the breakup — to being indirectly rejected via receipt. So much had happened that she didn't even know how to feel.

But amidst all the confusion and misery, a tiny part of her felt proud of herself. She'd done something scary, and she'd put herself out there. Okay, so it had ended in humiliation and rejection, but that wasn't important; what mattered was that she'd done it.

In a rush of realization, she put down her vibrator and reached to her drawer, scrabbling for her list of things she loved about herself. She had something to add beneath 1) honesty and 2) sense of humor.

3. Brave as hell.

CHAPTER 4

GEMINI SEASON

GEMINI
Season: May 21–June 21
Element: Air
Themes: Socializing. Communication. Ideas.
Best time to: Enjoy intellectual freedom.

"Nina Mistry, get your unwashed hair off my Laura Ashley sofa," cried Rupa.

The laptop slid off Nina's lap as she jumped up in shock. "What's wrong? I was just sitting here."

"You're leaning back," said Rupa, crossing her arms over her indigo wrap dress and glaring at her daughter. "And I know you haven't washed your hair, Nina, so don't even think about lying to me. I can see the grease. I don't want it transferring onto the velvet. You know the sofas are new and the guarantee runs out in sixteen days. I might decide to return them."

Nina closed her eyes and took a long, deep breath. She counted to four, held it in, then released it for four. This was an unforeseen upside to living with her mum: she constantly had opportunities to practice the yogic breathing the book recommended. The idea was to return your focus to your breath as much as possible — like a kind of meditation — to help you live in the present. "The only time we have is the now," said the book. "As in, right now. And in the now, everything is okay. So in moments of stress, breathe deeply as many times as you need and come back to the present."

After six deep breaths, Nina was ready to respond. "But sofas are made for leaning back on. That is literally their only purpose."

"Not in this house," said Rupa, straightening the soft taupe cushions her daughter had been leaning on. "And can you put some real clothes on please, Nina. The sight of you in those leggings and Nikhil's jumper just depresses me. You're worse than Kal, and at least he has an excuse. I've got to go do some house viewings now, because *someone* in this house needs to bring in an income, but I'll be back by three." She paused. "Also, uh, can you check on Kal? Maybe try to get him to wake up before lunch. There's stuffed butternut squash in the oven for you both, if he'll eat it." Her face was creased in worry.

"Of course," said Nina. "And if he doesn't eat it, then there'll be more for me. Don't look at me like that — I'm obviously kidding!"

Rupa rolled her eyes and picked up her pale gray leather handbag. "By the time I get back, I really would like to see you with your hair washed, looking smarter, Nina. The way you look has an impact on how you feel — and on how people treat you — you know."

Nina zoned out as her mum launched into the same speech she'd been reciting for the last couple of weeks. Nina needed to wear smarter clothes, not just lounge around in athleisure. Appearances mattered. She needed to get a real job instead of writing articles no one read; Madhuri Auntie's daughter was being published in the *Daily Mail,* which *everyone* reads, while no one had even ever heard of this online magazine *Raze.* What kind of name was that, anyway? Were they even paying her a real salary or was it some sort of extended internship? And if it was a real salary, then why exactly was she lying on the sofa in holey leggings?

When Rupa finally ran out of steam and

left for work, Nina pulled her laptop back onto her legs and returned to the article she was writing on the enviable fashion in the *Hermione Granger and the Philosopher's Stone* remake. When she'd first gone into journalism, Nina had hoped to tell stories that would inspire, educate, and help people across the world. But within a year into her degree, she'd realized just how naive her dream was; if she wanted to make money, she needed to lower her standards and write about anything that paid. So she'd graduated with an envy-inducing job as a junior entertainment writer for a big glossy magazine. But even though it sounded cool, she got freebies, and she spent most of her days gossiping with Elsie, Nina was bored stiff. Not to mention how much she hated the backstabbing atmosphere. When she was made redundant a few years in, she'd been secretly relieved and had hoped a freelance career would bring her closer to her original goal of writing about things that she cared about.

Only it seemed being freelance was even worse. Nina was now a full-blown media whore, writing about everything from the hot priest in the TV show everyone loved to oversharing about her personal life in the name of journalism ("Why ARE Women

Breaking off Engagements Before They Turn 30?"). Nina had tried to pitch more interesting articles about things that mattered to her, like the unexpected racism between people of color or the anniversary of Idi Amin kicking all the Asians out of Uganda, but none of her (mainly white) editors seemed to care. Which was why she was now writing articles about how cloaks were back en vogue.

Nina closed the laptop shut and rooted around in her tote bag for her stolen book — or, as she was now thinking of it, her personal bible. The next exercise was to speak to her nearest and dearest to find out what they loved most about her, specifically family members. Only this was not something Nina was looking forward to. Her mum did not do declarations of love, her brother was clinically depressed, and her dad was dead.

"If you don't shower now, I'm going to turn the hot water off," said Rupa, walking into the living room wearing a pair of hot pink leggings and a matching exercise top, holding a mug in her hand. "It's been five hours and you're exactly where I left you. You really need to work faster, Nina. I sold a £1.2 million house *and* cleaned Kal's bedroom while he showered."

"Well, I got Kal to eat the squash," said Nina. "Not the oat crumble though. I ate all of that."

"I know, I found the empty plates in his room," tutted Rupa, sitting down on the sofa. "I've asked you both not to take food out of the kitchen."

"So how come you get to bring hot drinks in the living room? And lounge around in athleisure?"

"Because I own this house, and I'm going to Pilates," snapped Rupa, sitting on the edge of the sofa sipping her green tea. "When was the last time you used your leggings to exercise in?"

"Actually, Mother, I was thinking of starting yoga. There's a class in town that's only five pounds an hour."

"I know," said Rupa. "It's Deepa's class. You know, Deepa Padhwari?" Nina shook her head. "Her parents are so disappointed. She's quit banking to teach yoga. Thank god her fiancé works for Deloitte. He's just gotten a promotion in the Nottingham branch." She sipped her green tea, then leaned in conspiratorially toward Nina with a smile. "To be honest, I think the yoga's worth the pay cut. She's lost two stone, so maybe now her fiancé will stop messaging twenty-one-year-olds on Snapchat."

"I really don't want to know how you know what her fiancé does on Snapchat," said Nina. "But I think it's cool she's doing her own thing. Maybe I'll end up falling in love with yoga too."

Rupa snorted. "I'll believe that when I see it. Though it would do you good to lose a little bit of weight."

"Oh my god," cried Nina. "You have got to stop saying these things to me. It is honestly a miracle I don't have an eating disorder."

"Oh, calm down," said Rupa, briskly. "I'm not saying you're fat. I just think you should know that all the comfort carbs you're eating are starting to show. If I don't tell you as your mother, then who will?"

Nina closed her eyes and started her breathing. Om. She was thirty years old. Om. She did not need to fight with her mother. Om. She was over this. Om. She was a grown woman. Om. She was working on herself. Om. She just needed to ask her mum this one question, and then she could move on with her self-love exercises and sorting her life out. Om.

"Mum," asked Nina, opening one eye, "can I just ask you something quickly? It's for . . . an article I'm doing."

Rupa sighed and leaned back onto the sofa. "What is it this time? Are you going to shame me for not breastfeeding you again? It wasn't my fault you didn't latch on. We didn't have midwives who came over every day back then; they just shoved a bottle of formula into your hands."

"Okay, I really don't care that you didn't breastfeed me. I was just researching for an article. And actually" — she took a deep breath in and out again — "I just wanted to ask you if you can tell me something you love about me. Or, I don't know, like about me."

"What?" Rupa looked at her daughter blankly.

"Something that you like about me," repeated Nina slowly, and added after a long moment, "Anything at all."

"Well, don't get angry, honey, but it's very hard to think of something when you're lying there with greasy hair in old leggings on my new sofa," said Rupa, smiling apologetically.

Nina sat up straight. "Mum, can you please just try and take this seriously. I'm your daughter. You like me. Right?"

"Well, I'm not sure."

Nina's mouth dropped open. "Are you joking?"

Rupa took another sip of her tea. "Nina, don't be so dramatic. I'm your mother, and I will always love you. But I don't have to *like* you. I'm not your best friend. Jo can like things about you."

Nina wasn't actually sure if Jo did like her for any other reason bar the fact they'd known each other for almost twenty years — but now was not the time to dwell on that.

"Okay, Mum, I find that quite hurtful," said Nina. This was good. Admitting vulnerability was very Brené Brown of her (quoted in chapter three of the book), and certainly better than screaming at her mum like the hormonal teenager she should have stopped being over a decade ago. "I don't need you to be my friend, but surely there's something you like about me? Not even something you love about me, if that's too challenging, but just something you have vaguely positive feelings toward, regarding my personality."

"Oh, Nina, you were always so much needier than your brother," sighed Rupa. "But fine. I can tell you something I like about you. I like . . ."

Nina waited expectantly as her mum looked around the room, as though she was searching for inspiration.

"I've got it," said Rupa. "I like that you're

a doer."

"A doer?" echoed Nina.

"Yes," said Rupa. "You're not one of those people who sit around talking about doing things; you go ahead and do them. Which is a good thing. Well, when you do the right things, of course."

Nina stared at her mum in disbelief. But she was still going. "Like, for example, I cannot condone the way you've handled the Nikhil scenario. You know his parents are trying to set him up with Karina? What a waste, Nina. He loves you. You could have had security. And I could have finally been able to stop worrying about you."

"But you don't have to worry about me, Mum," said Nina. "I never asked you to. I'm fine." And she was. Kind of.

"You'll understand when you have your own children," said Rupa, ignoring Nina mouthing *If, not when.* "A mother never stops worrying about her children — until they get married. Then I'll be able to relax, because you won't be my responsibility anymore." Rupa's face visibly relaxed as she looked away, clearly imagining a future where her daughter was happily married and no longer compromising her new sofa.

"Well, I'm sorry, Mum. But it looks like your daughter is too busy *doing things* to get married, so you're just going to have to wait. I'm off to yoga. I'll let Deepa know she should check her fiancé's Snapchat."

"Don't you dare," cried Rupa. "He got a first from Cambridge. Where else is she going to find someone like that? Nina . . . Nina, do not even think about it."

4. A doer. Thanks, Mum.

Nina walked into the yoga studio still replaying her conversation with her mum in her mind. She knew that she shouldn't let it bother her and she should be grateful her mum loved her. But most mums liked their kids as well as loving them, didn't they? Was she really so awful that it was such a struggle for her mum to find something she liked about her? God. It was so ridiculous it was almost funny. She could imagine having laughed it over with Nikhil, sitting on the kitchen counter swinging her legs and sipping a glass of red while he chopped vegetables (he cooked; she washed up). But without him there to listen to her vent and then make her laugh by doing his uncanny impression of her mum, she just felt a bit sad.

A woman who she presumed was the two-stone-lighter Deepa was sitting at the front of the studio with her eyes closed and her legs crossed so that the soles of her feet were resting on her thighs. Her body was impressively toned — maybe if Nina did enough yoga, she'd also get a six-pack? — and she looked like she was deep into her meditation. Everyone else was in the process of unrolling the free mats and getting out towels. Nina hadn't brought a towel.

She stood in the corner of the class trying to figure out what to do. A man in front of her, whose rippling muscles were very visible in his short Umbro shorts and tight tank top, put a £5 note in a wooden bowl at the front of the class, next to some burning sage. Right. Money. Nina pulled out a £10 note from her bag and went over to the bowl. As she took £5 back, Deepa opened her eyes and looked straight at Nina. "Oh, I'm not . . . it's change," she said. But Deepa closed her eyes again, and Nina rushed to the back of the room, mortified that her new yoga teacher now thought she was a thief.

"Please, all be seated," announced Deepa from the front of the class, her eyes still closed. Nina quickly grabbed a mat from the pile at the back and joined the twenty or so participants all sitting cross-legged on the floor. She looked around at the women

71

in their vibrant, strappy crop tops with matching leggings and the men in their black yoga pants. It pained her to admit it, but she wished she'd taken her mum's advice and worn something other than plain black leggings with holes and a faded gray university T-shirt with a semi-visible pasta stain.

"Namaste, all," said Deepa, finally opening her eyes, then making a prayer gesture with her hands. "Thank you for coming here today. Today's class is going to focus on letting go. We're going to allow ourselves to feel everything that we truly need to feel, and we're going to let go of old energy to make way for the new. I want everyone here to set an intention. It can be anything you want, but I recommend that you all focus on letting go. Of resentment, of negativity, of betrayal. That person might have hurt you. They might have betrayed you and broken your trust. But you need to remember that we are all human, we are all one, and we all make mistakes. If they haven't actually cheated, then it's okay. We're going to breathe through it, let go, accept, and forgive."

Nina peeked an eye open and looked at Deepa. It seemed like she didn't need to break the Snapchat news to her after all.

"So if everyone would like to please stand up, we're going to begin with surya namaskar — the sun salutation, for those of you who have yet to learn Sanskrit. Which I really recommend you do if you want to get the maximum effect from yoga. Now, let's begin." Deepa leaped up in one smooth, elegant movement. "Come on, people, why are you still sitting there comfortably? Up! Now!"

Nina's body was trembling. She wanted to collapse into child pose, but she still had two more breaths to get through, and Deepa was standing above her. "Breathe through it," she demanded. "The trembling is your body's way of tackling old negative energy. It is leaving your body. The more you tremble, the more you're letting go of the past."

Oh god. Nina had so much past to let go of that she'd need to be in downward dog for a full twenty-four hours to tremble away even half of it. She collapsed facedown onto the mat, panting. She'd thought yoga was all about lying down, going slow, and taking breaks when you needed it, but Deepa was apparently not that kind of teacher. "Stick with it," she'd actually shouted when Nina had sneakily straightened her legs in warrior two. "The poses you don't want to do are the ones your body needs. Come on. Persevere. You can do this. YOU CAN DO THIS, TEAM." It felt more like being in a spinning class than a relaxing yoga session, but Nina had to hand it to Deepa: her intensity meant that it was impossible for her mind to be anywhere but the class. Nina was so focused on not passing out that she hadn't once thought about Nikhil, or Kal not leaving his bedroom for three days, or how lonely she felt. Instead, she was fully in the present. Namaste, bitches.

"And now it's time for the most important pose of the class," said Deepa. "Shavasana." Nina sent out a silent prayer of gratitude as she followed Deepa's instructions: lie down on the mat, open out your legs and arms, and let Mother Earth take your pain away. "Just let all the weight — the worries, the struggles, the strife, the heartbreak, the failures, the misery — just let it soak into the earth," said Deepa in the calm, yoga teacher–appropriate voice that Nina had been craving for the past hour. "Let Mother Earth carry that load for you. Let it all seep into the ground."

Nina felt her eyes watering as she absorbed Deepa's words. She had so much weight on her shoulders. The thought of letting it go

74

into the ground felt amazing. She felt tears flooding out of her eyes as she visualized all her stress seeping into her mat and the earth beneath her.

"Let it all go," said Deepa softly. "Let it go. Breathe in and out. Let. Go. Let. Go."

Nina started sobbing silently. Her body trembled more than it had in downward dog, and she felt a wave of sadness roll through her. The loneliness. The massive, massive hole of missing Nikhil. Her body physically yearned to be curled up safe inside his arms as they lay on the sofa watching Pixar movies — the only genre they could agree on — eating pad Thai out of takeaway containers. Nina's face scrunched up tight as she cried silently, the minutes passing by as she refused to let her body make a single sound.

"And now, bring awareness back into the body," said Deepa. "Keep your eyes closed, roll to the right, give yourself a hug, and come to sitting so we can close with three oms." Nina frantically dried her eyes and tried to wipe her running nose on her T-shirt. She was missing the oms, but at least she'd look presentable by the time they finished. When Deepa told the class to open their eyes — not before telling them to think kind thoughts, speak kind words, and have kind intentions — Nina was confident she'd wiped away the evidence of her tears.

"It normally happens to me in pigeon," said a voice behind her. Nina turned around to see a tiny five-feet-tall girl with bright purple hair and a nose ring looking up at her. "They say that women carry their emotions in their hips. So I always cry in pigeon. To be honest, it's my favorite part of the class."

"Oh god," Nina said, blushing. "Was it really obvious? I tried to silent cry."

"I'm not sure it worked," said the girl brightly. "But don't worry. We've all been there. I'm Meera, by the way."

"Hey, I'm Nina." She reached out to offer a hand, but Meera had already opened up her arms to embrace her.

"We've already cried in front of each other. Well, you did. I think we can hug."

"Thanks," said Nina. "So what do you normally cry about? Sorry, is that weird of me to ask?"

Meera laughed. "Yep, but luckily you for, I'm also an oversharer. I normally cry about feeling distanced from my girlfriend. Or feeling stressed about owning my own business. Often both. You?"

"Relationship stuff as well," said Nina. "Well, a breakup." She waved a hand as

Meera looked at her sympathetically. "I'm fine, don't worry. Tell me about your business! What do you do?"

"I'm an astrologer. And I have a crystal shop."

"No way," cried Nina. "That's so cool. I had no idea that was a full-time job, but I love star signs. Almost as much as I love food."

"Mmm," said Meera. "I'm guessing you're a Taurus or Virgo. Something earthy."

"Taurus," said Nina, suitably impressed. "You?"

"Gemini with Libra rising. Very airy. But I have a lot of Jupiter. Hence the dry humor. And I have my Venus in Taurus, so you and I are very compatible."

"I'm so sorry, but I have no idea what you just said."

"Follow me on Insta," said Meera, rummaging around her canvas bag and pulling out a navy card designed to look like the night sky with her name written on it like a constellation. "We can organize a time for me to read your chart; I think you need it."

"Uh, okay, thanks," said Nina, slipping the card into her pocket. She hadn't even finished putting her yoga mat away and she already had an astrologer. Maybe the stars were finally aligning for her. "I think a bit of direction from the universe would actually be amazing for me. I've been feeling a bit . . . Well, things have been a bit hard lately."

Meera nodded sagely. "Uranus is in Taurus right now. There's a lot of change going on in your life. It's going to be hard for you, considering you love stability. But don't give up. There'll be even more changes over the next few months, but you'll feel better for it. Eventually."

"Okay, how do you know so much about my life right now?" asked Nina.

"Welcome to astrology," said Meera. "DM me and we'll sort out a session. I'm not cheap. But I'll give you a discount. I've got an offer for Tauruses right now because of the whole Uranus thing."

CHAPTER 5

Nina knocked on her former bedroom door. There was a grunt in response. She took that as an invitation and gingerly pushed the door open.

The curtains were drawn even though it was almost midday, and Kal was lying in bed with the duvet pulled up over him. Nina wrinkled her nose at the distinct smell of male sweat, but forced herself to stay silent. The last time she'd suggested he open a window, Kal had taken it so badly he'd refused to speak to her for two days.

He spoke without looking at her. "What is it?"

"I just wanted to ask a favor," said Nina brightly. "It won't take long."

"I'll do it later."

Nina sighed to herself. Living with her brother meant constantly having to walk on eggshells as she tried not to upset him or accidentally damage his already fragile mental health. It was exhausting, but she knew that it wasn't Kal's fault. She shivered as she thought about how much his goddamn depression had taken from her brother already. His life in London, his successful finance career, the fancy flat he lived in with his two best mates, his laughing smile . . . It was all gone, leaving in its place a listless, tense, and very, very sad version of her older brother.

"Fuck depression," cried Nina.

Kal gave her a small smile. "Yeah. It's shit."

"Sorry. I just . . . it makes me angry that you have to go through this. Can I, uh, sit for a bit?"

He rolled over in the bed to make space for his sister. "Oh, why not?"

She took up her customary space at the end of the bed. "Thanks, Kal. How are you doing?"

"Ah, you know." He shrugged. "Today's not the best of days. But what's going on with you?"

"I'm sorry," said Nina. "Is there anything I can do to help? And we don't have to talk about my thing, don't worry."

"Oh go on, you're here now." He shifted onto his forearms and sat up. "In fact, it might help. Distract me from my pain and all that."

"Well, if you're sure," said Nina. "It's for a self-improvement thing I'm working on."

Kal narrowed his eyes. "You sound like my therapist."

"Does your therapist also ask you if there's anything you love about her? Because this is me asking you."

Kal groaned loudly. "Seriously? What is this? We're nowhere near Raksha Bandhan."

"What's that got to do with it?"

"I don't know, sibling bonds." He shrugged. "It's the only time I really think about our relationship."

Nina looked at him blankly. "Why? All I do is tie a string around your wrist, you give me twenty pounds, and we eat chocolate."

"I like it," protested Kal. "It's about a sister's love and protection for her brother."

"Well, if you want me to renew my sisterly protection this year, tell me something you love about me," Nina said with a grin. "Go on. Just one thing."

"Can I have a think about it?" asked Kal.

Nina's jaw dropped open. "Are you kidding me? What is wrong with our family? I do not understand how hard it is to say something you love about me. I could do you easily. Funny. Kind. Caring. Good laugh. Insanely long eyelashes. I still don't get why you got all the genes that the girl is supposed to get. I get these stumpy lashes and you get big wide eyes, basically no body hair, and lovely soft skin."

"That's what happens when you're the firstborn; you get the best genes," he said. "But hey, thanks, Nina. That's nice to hear. I do love you. You know that. But my brain is so fucked these days. I need time."

"Okay," sighed Nina. "No worries." She stood up, disappointed, and walked slowly to the door. She turned the knob, extra slowly, and looked back to Kal. "Do you . . . still need more time?"

He laughed. "Oh my god, fine. You are annoyingly stubborn, which I guess also means you're . . . determined. There you go. That's something I love about you. Your relentless determination. Or obstinacy. You can pick which noun you prefer."

Nina rushed over to hug her older brother. "Thanks. I love you too."

"Get off me, Nina! You're hurting my lovely soft skin."

5. My relentless determination.

Nina stood on Loughborough Road, unsure if she should go inside the tiny, dusty shop. She peered through the windows and saw rows of crystals, silver, and large lumps of pink rock. This was not very Nina of her. Her normal bank holiday activity consisted of either lying on the sofa binge-watching Netflix with chocolate or trying to convince Nikhil to go to Chai Pani for the hundredth time. But seeing as she no longer had Nikhil, or even a sofa she was allowed to lie on, going to see an astrologer she'd met in yoga class seemed like the next best option. She just wished she also had some chocolate.

"Hello?" called Nina as she pushed open the door and was greeted by a gentle scent of incense.

"Here!" replied Meera's voice from behind a purple curtain. Nina walked past the trays of crystals, trying not to knock any to the ground, and pushed the curtain back. She saw Meera sitting at a table grinning at her. Her purple hair was tied up in a ponytail, she was wearing a long, flowing, multicolored kaftan robe over pink dungarees, and her iPad was on the table. Nina looked down at her own outfit — a bright red jumper over straight black jeans with Converse — and felt incredibly boring.

"Welcome to your very first reading," said Meera. "Please, sit down." She made an exaggerated gesture to the plump velvet armchair opposite her and winked at Nina. "Don't worry. I promise it won't be as weird as you think it will. All you need to do is give me your date of birth and the location and exact time you were born."

Nina looked at her blankly. "Uh . . . I think maybe afternoon? I know my brother was born at one a.m. My mum always goes on about how prompt he was."

"Can you call your mum to find out yours?"

"Uh . . . is there no way to do it without?"

Meera shook her head. "Sor-ry."

Nina pulled out her phone in quiet resignation. She had a feeling this was not going to be as simple as she hoped.

"Hello?"

"Hey, Mum," replied Nina, ignoring the urge to ask her mum why she always answered the phone as if she didn't know it was her daughter calling. "Quick question — do you know what time I was born? Like, the hour and minute?"

Rupa sighed audibly. "Oh, Nina, why are you asking me about this? You know I don't like to talk about that day."

"Yes, I know, it's your worst memory; my big head broke you and you were in a wheelchair for weeks. I am still sorry. But do you happen to know at exactly what time

84

my head shattered your pubic bone?"

"It was in the afternoon," said Rupa vaguely. "I don't know any more than that; I've tried to block it out of my mind."

"But I need to know," cried Nina. "I can't get my astrology reading without the exact time."

Rupa tutted. "You don't care about astrology when I talk about Hindu astrology and using the stars to find you a husband. But the second a white person does it, you want to know."

"My astrologer is actually brown, Mum. Although she can't *do* any astrology unless you remember exactly when you pushed me out of your vagina."

"Don't be so vulgar," said Rupa. "It was probably four p.m. Or seven p.m. No, four. Let's do four."

Nina hung up the phone and looked directly at Meera. "She has no idea, but she's guessing four p.m."

Meera smiled serenely as though she hadn't just heard the entire conversation. "Great."

"I guess that happens a lot, right?" asked Nina. "Parents not remembering when their kids were born?"

"Um, a lot of them write it down in a special place. You know, along with their first word, first step," explained Meera as she pressed buttons on her iPad. "But, obviously, everyone's different. Let's find out what your chart says about it all."

She showed Nina her screen. It was filled with a large circle covered in lines and illegible symbols. "You've got a lot of earth. You are very, very Taurus. So I'm guessing you're practical, you like nature, you're stubborn, and you like good-quality materials. High-thread-count bedsheets? Chocolate?"

Nina nodded enthusiastically. "Yes. To all of these things."

"And I feel like you're very sensual. Venus is the ruling planet of Taurus, so she's important to you. And you have her in Pisces, which is where she's really exalted. So basically, you're good at sex."

"Oh my god, thank you," said Nina. "That's nicer than anything a man has ever said to me."

"You're a journalist, right?" asked Meera. "Well, that's because Mercury is here, which means communication is important for you, and you're a very social person, good at making friends. You like breaking taboos, you love helping people, and you can really realize your dreams if you work hard."

As Meera carried on complimenting her,

Nina wondered why on earth she'd never had an astrology consultation before. It seemed to just consist of listing her best attributes or using the planets to explain away her flaws. Nina was an official convert. Especially when her chart led Meera to say they were compatible and should hang out.

"I could always do with another soul friend," said Meera. "It's so hard to make connections these days, when everyone's on their phone all the time. It's a gift from the universe when one lands on your doorstep. Or your yoga mat, in our case."

Nina forced herself to look relaxed about the fact her insanely cool astrologer had just offered to *be her friend* and pushed away the inconvenient truth that it was two p.m. and her phone battery was already on 5 percent. Instead, she nodded in what she hoped was a soulful manner. "Totally agree. New connections are really important to me. I actually had a bridal brunch with a few of my oldest friends the other day, and I think I'm realizing they're no longer my, uh, soul friends anymore."

"That's hard," said Meera sympathetically. "But you're going through your Saturn return now — oh, that's a big life moment that happens every thirty years, where you move closer to what you actually want in life — so it's to be expected. You'll make new friends though, don't worry. Have you and these friends been drifting apart for a while?"

If Nina was being honest with herself, things had started to change in Sixth Form when Jo befriended the new student, Gayatri — or, as Nina miserably thought of her, Nina 2.0. Like Nina, she was Indian and smart, but unlike Nina, she was also super confident, sexually active, and just like Jo, set on becoming a lawyer. They'd always included Nina in their plans, but over the years, when they both went to Nottingham together to do law while she studied journalism in London, and they both got well-paid jobs in the same law firm with well-paid boyfriends to match while she struggled on a junior journalist's salary, dating a string of disappointing men, Nina had felt more and more like a third wheel.

When she'd finally got a well-paid boyfriend of her own (Nikhil wasn't a lawyer but had a very stable job as a dentist), she'd thought she'd have more in common with the girls again. But it hadn't happened. Maybe it was the fact she still didn't have a well-paid job, or even a proper job. Or maybe it was because her relationship was filled with constant bickering and disagreements, while theirs seemed flawless. Whatever the reason, Nina would leave their monthly pizza and wine nights feeling more and more deflated, wondering why they cared so much about risotto and house prices — and why she didn't.

Nina sighed as she thought back to the pitying expressions Jo and Gayatri had given her when she turned up to celebrate Jo's engagement at her bridal bunch recently in her favorite denim skirt and a striped Breton top. It transpired there was an unofficial dress code she didn't know about; Jo, Gayatri, and the eight other bridesmaids had all been wearing floral dresses.

"I was in denial for a while," Nina admitted to Meera. "But now it's becoming very obvious how different we are. They spent the whole time at this brunch talking about caterers and wedding dresses, when we could have been talking about, I don't know, our careers, or our favorite TV shows, or literally *anything* else!"

"In my nonprofessional opinion," Meera said, shuddering, "a bridal brunch sounds fucking horrendous."

"Thank you!" cried Nina. "I swear I was never like that when I was engaged."

"You were engaged?" asked Meera in surprise.

The only thing that had made the ever-growing distance between Nina and Jo bearable had been knowing she had Nikhil. He was the one she'd confided in for the last three years, whether it was about her brother's illness, her latest argument with her mum, or how she felt about her drifting friendships. He was the one she shared her work anxieties with, and the only one who'd supported her in her plans to pursue a freelance career. He was her best friend, and had been ever since he'd synced his phone to her period app so he could ensure he bought her favorite brownies for her PMS days.

But Nina's periods had been depressingly brownie-free ever since she'd broken off their engagement and lost her best friend in the process.

She looked down at her ringless finger. Nikhil had said she could keep the gold and emerald ring, but Nina's conscience — and her mother — had refused.

"Not for long," she answered Meera. "We broke up at the end of March. So . . . just a couple of months ago. He's an Aries."

"Wow. Aries and Taurus is a pretty tough combination. They very rarely have things in common. It's unusual you were together for so long — did you fight a lot?"

90

"Yes, but we still loved each other," said Nina defensively. "He was my best friend; we always supported each other — and okay, fine, we didn't see eye to eye on *everything,* but we were always honest with each other. We even discussed our worst flaws on our first date — my impatience, his rigidity. Surely that counts for something?"

"Of course," said Meera soothingly. "I'm sure you have lots of complementary planets in your charts; maybe he has some water too. But it doesn't surprise me you broke up right around your Saturn return. When people hit twenty-nine or thirty and they're in relationships, they tend to either get engaged — or have awful breakups." She paused. "I guess you did both."

Nina fingered the purple silk tablecloth glumly. "My mum does say I'm a doer."

"Yes, because your numerology life path number is a twenty-two," agreed Meera. "It's a master number — there's only two of them — and it means you're quite capable of amazing things. You share it with Bill Gates and Donald Trump." Nina looked up at Meera in worry, but Meera shook her head. "It's about the power you share with them, not the politics. You have a lot of energy, and you have the power to change people's minds. I imagine you use your journalism to break taboos and write controversial things to shake stuff up?"

"Not exactly," said Nina, feeling the spark of something in her stomach. "But I could start. Like . . . now."

"You should. With the power of a twenty-two, you could reach a lot of people. I mean, you have to be careful with what you say, obviously. But you can make a difference. Is there anything you've been thinking of writing? What are you really passionate about?"

"Well . . . I really want to write more about race," said Nina, slowly warming up to her topic. "Like, I write a lot about TV, and things are getting more diverse, but I'm so sick of Asian characters only ever being the token stereotype. I want to see more brown people as rom-com heroes and heroines, so we start to see brown as beautiful. You know?"

"That's so true," agreed Meera. "The hot person in a movie, or a model in a big campaign, is hardly ever brown. And if they are, they're really light-skinned."

"Yes!" cried Nina. "I hate it. I . . . don't know if this ever happened to you, but the school I went to was like the whitest school in Leicester. And people always made comments about my skin color and my Indian features, like my big nose. As in, mean comments." Meera's face widened in outrage and Nina quickly continued. "It wasn't on purpose or anything. They'd say things like, 'Oh, Nins, you'd be so pretty if you had a smaller nose' or 'You're so pretty for an Indian.' You know?"

"Um, no, I don't know. That's *awful.* It's racism."

"Oh, it's fine. It was forever ago."

"But still," said Meera. "It's not okay."

Nina nodded slowly. "Yeah. It did make me feel I wasn't attractive and never could be, because of my skin color. Also, white boys never fancied me. Until I met Gareth at uni — he was a Libra, so that didn't last long." Meera nodded in sympathetic understanding. "But since then, I've realized I get way less matches on dating apps than my white friends. And the only attractive guys who match with me are brown. That's how I ended up with Nikhil. It just annoys me so much when people say they don't fancy an entire race and Indians 'aren't their type.' It's bullshit."

"One hundred percent. You need to write about it," said Meera firmly. "And the astros have your back, girl."

Nina felt a tingle go up her spine. Even on her saddest days, she had been thinking

93

of mixing up what she wrote for *Raze,* but she hadn't acted on it so far out of a total, all-encompassing, and petrifying fear of failing — the same fear that had been holding her back since 1990. Only if it was written in the stars, then maybe she wouldn't fail. Maybe her words really could reach people and make a difference.

She needed to email her boss.

CHAPTER 6

Nina felt positively charged with excitement, and it wasn't just down to the rose quartz crystal Meera had put in her bra. Her latest article for *Raze,* "Why aren't there any hot brown rom-com heroes?," had been shared more than a hundred thousand times — a record for the website — and for the first time in her life, people were messaging her about her work. Jo had sent a string of fire emoji, Nikhil had texted her Well done, and there were over a thousand comments under her article. "Yes girl," said one. "Brown love from Pakistan." She had international fans. "Fuck you, you big-nosed bitch. I can see your nose all the way here in Wisconsin." And international trolls!

It was all down to her astrology session with Meera; it had given her the confidence to write about something she actually cared about. Nina had detailed her own personal experiences in the article of growing up as a

British Indian who rarely saw anyone who looked like her on TV or in movies. Even in Bollywood, the actors were light-skinned with green eyes and European features. ("Plastic surgery," Rupa claimed. "Look at their noses; they all have the exact same one.") To give her article gravitas, she'd interviewed an expert who agreed this lack of diversity would lead to generations of young women of color growing up with body image issues. She'd even managed to speak to her former media studies professor, who not only congratulated Nina on her job but quoted her statistics showing seventeen out of Hollywood's top one hundred highest-grossing films that year had no Black speaking characters, while over forty had no Asian speaking characters. It was no wonder, as Nina wrote in the final sentence of her article, that she'd grown up convinced brown wasn't good enough.

Her editor, Mark, had loved her article so much he'd given her the title of Diversity Correspondent, meaning she could write articles like this weekly, and her pitiful amount of Twitter followers now had an extra zero at the end of it. There were more comments than she had time to read, but Nina scrolled through as many as she could, ignoring the ones that called her an ugly bitch and pausing on the ones that called her an icon.

Of course she knew that journalists received online abuse like this. But this was her first time experiencing it, and truth be told, she felt like she was handling it pretty well. It wasn't really that big a deal. In a way, it was kind of funny. These were obviously just weird teens in their parents' basements, getting their daily angst out by writing awful comments. One guy had written "I want to rape you xxx." Nina wondered mildly at the kind of troll etiquette that put kisses at the end of a rape threat, but she wasn't going to give it her attention. The only thing she cared about right now was that people were reading and sharing her work. She was saying things other people were too scared to say. At last she was using her journalism to make a difference.

6. I'm not afraid to break taboos.

"Why do you look so happy?" sniffed Rupa, walking into the living room and looking her daughter up and down. Nina was wearing freshly washed clothes, and her hair was so clean it was still dripping wet. Which meant her khaki sleeveless top was now soaked through.

"Oh, hello, Mother," said Nina airily. "Probably because my boss just emailed me to say how much he likes my latest article. He said, quote unquote, that it's an incredibly strong piece the Internet needs more of."

"Mmm," said Rupa, putting on her leopard-print reading glasses as she took out her iPad. "Very good. Though I'm not sure the Internet does need more opinions."

"Don't you want to know what it's about?"

"Send me a link," said Rupa, without looking up.

"Well, seeing as you asked," said Nina, "it's about the fact that there aren't enough brown people with leading roles in movies, and it's causing generations to grow up feeling inadequate. Also, where's *Bend It Like Beckham 2*?"

"Do people really want to read that?" asked Rupa, still glued to her screen.

"Uh, yes, they do. Unlike you, people like to read my work."

Rupa finally looked up, clearly offended. "Nina, honestly, you have a very low opinion of me. Have I ever criticized your work? Have I ever told you not to be a journalist? I've supported you all the way through. I'm supporting you right now. I haven't once asked you for rent money."

"Um." Nina raised an eyebrow at her mum, who was now innocently scrolling through her iPad again. "When I told you Jo's parents asked her brother for rent, you went on a rant about how white parents don't treat their kids properly and Indian parents would never demand money from their offspring."

Rupa shrugged and smiled breezily at her daughter. "Well, the point remains that you don't pay rent. And did I tell you that it's Sunil Mama's surprise sixtieth tonight? I hope you're coming."

"Okay, fine, but you could have given me some advance warning," said Nina, even though as she currently had no foreseeable social plans, spending an evening with her extended family would actually be a very welcome distraction. She made a mental note to text Jo, Gayatri, Elsie, and anyone else she could think of to make plans; it was about time she started filling the massive Nikhil-shaped hole in her social calendar.

"Well, seeing as all you do is lie on the sofa — and yes, I've seen you put your head on the cushions and not the throw I specifically left there for you, Nina — I assumed you were free. Honestly, anyone would think *you're* the depressed child in the family. At least Kal is prepared to spend his evenings coming to community events with me."

"I think that might be because he's so vulnerable right now that he doesn't have the energy to argue with you. Is he coming tonight?"

"He's not feeling up to it," said Rupa, frowning. "So we're going to tell everyone that he has an interview for a new job. In London."

Nina sighed. "Mum, you really don't need to lie. Kal doesn't care if people know. He lets me tell my friends."

Rupa stared at Nina in angry shock. "Don't tell me you've been telling people about him, Nina. How dare you? It's his private business. Who knows? Tell me. Tell me now."

"Okay, calm down, Mum. I guess it's only Nikhil who knows. And obviously he wouldn't tell anyone. I just . . . I don't think it needs to be such a taboo. The royal family talks about it these days. And so many of my friends' brothers have gone through similar stuff. It's really common. Especially with guys Kal's age."

"I don't care," said Rupa firmly. "Let white families talk about it to all and sundry if they want to. But I won't. No one we know ever discusses it; it's different for us.

Look at Pritesh Uncle. We all know he's in jail for fraud, but do we talk about it? No. Because it's *just not done.*"

"I really do think things are changing, Mum. It's not like it was back when . . . everything happened with Dad."

"Oh, because you're the expert on our community, are you, Nina?" asked Rupa angrily, still distractedly scrolling through her emails. "You with your white attitudes, and your cohabiting before marriage, and then breaking it off for no reason at all. I don't know what your grandparents would have said if they'd been around today."

As Rupa began ranting about how she wished Nina was more like her cousins, she slipped into her mother tongue of Gujarati. Nina took this as her cue to silently pad out of the living room. She'd learned over the years that when her mum started her wounded-Indian-mother routine, it was best to just walk away. Otherwise she'd be stuck listening to a monologue she didn't fully understand, and the second she did speak, her mum would start a second rant all about how much of a disappointment Nina was for never learning Gujarati.

"Nina, hurry up and try this blouse on," said Rupa, standing in the doorway of her bedroom holding a pile of brightly colored saris. "I don't want the same disaster we had before Shriya's wedding where your sari blouse wouldn't do up because you'd put on weight."

Nina ignored her mum and looked past her to the smiling middle-aged redhead standing behind her wearing a black and purple sari that looked like it had been designed by Jackson Pollock.

"Auntie Trish!" Nina cried out, rushing straight to her faux auntie. "It's been ages. I miss you. You look amazing. This sari is gorgeous."

Auntie Trish enveloped Nina in a warm, powdery hug that smelled of Dior. "Thanks, my love. I had it modeled on one Deepika Padukone wore." She broke away to do a twirl, then suddenly grabbed Nina's shoulders. "Oh, and don't think I've forgotten about the arrest. What are you like? Plastic bottles, honestly. Protesting isn't worth it."

"I didn't throw them!" cried Nina indignantly. "You know I have bad hand-eye coordination. And I just wanted to support something I care about."

"Well, you need to care from a distance next time," said Auntie Trish, perching on Nina's bed as Rupa walked out of the room. "You know your mum will have a meltdown

102

if the masis and mamas find out about your jail time. But don't worry — I'm very proud of you for surviving."

Nina smiled at Auntie Trish, who had now pulled out a compact mirror and was putting on lip gloss. She was so different from her uptight mum, but ever since Rupa had sold Trish a detached three-bed two-bath after her divorce from "that bloody bastard" over ten years ago, they'd become best friends. Nina assumed it was due to the fact that both of them had been heavily disappointed by their husbands and children — and that Auntie Trish was basically the most Indian person she knew. The fact that she was white was irrelevant; she'd seen every Bollywood movie at least twice and could speak more Gujarati than Nina.

"Come on, Rups," called Auntie Trish. "Get these saris out, then. We need to make sure Nins looks stunning."

"Yes, yes," said Rupa, coming back into the room with even more fabric weighing her down. "This is the one I picked out for you, Nina." She pulled out a dark red and green sari. "Earth tones to bring out the gold in your skin."

"No," said Auntie Trish immediately. "She'll blend in. You need her to stand out. What about that one?" She pointed to a bright pink sari covered in diamantés.

"Okay, guys, calm down," said Nina. "I'll just wear the same dark turquoise one I always wear. It's not like I need to make an effort for Sunil Mama."

"Rupa, don't tell me you haven't told her," cried Auntie Trish.

Rupa looked down at the floor, and Nina wondered why Auntie Trish had the power to turn her mum into a normal human being in a way that no one else could. "I didn't want to make it a big deal," said Rupa defensively. "It's not official they're a couple yet."

"What? Who?"

Rupa sat down on the edge of the bed next to Auntie Trish and sighed. "Nikhil is coming. And he's bringing Karina."

"What the fuck," cried Nina.

"Language, Nina," said Rupa.

"Oh, let the poor girl swear," interjected Auntie Trish, crawling over the saris on the bed to come and put an arm around her. Both of them ignored Rupa's squeals and attempts to protect the saris from creasing. "She's just found out her former fiancé is dating a total bimbo."

Nina felt a tear slide down her cheek and burrowed her head in Auntie Trish's sari. She loved Nikhil, and if he was happy with someone new, then she was happy for him. She really was. But she also felt inexplicably sad. The arrival of Karina felt like confirmation that her and Nikhil's love together was really, truly over. And even if it was the right thing, it was still a loss. A really painful loss that no amount of cheesy chips could fill.

"Oh, sweetheart," said Auntie Trish, stroking her hair. "It's okay to be sad. It's always hard when your ex finds someone new."

"I just miss him," sniffed Nina. "I miss sending him funny links. I miss arguing with him in the dessert aisle, and I even miss his stupid dental tips. You know, normal relationship things."

"I know, baby," said Auntie Trish. "But that's what you've got your friends for."

Nina thought back to the last message she'd sent to Jo and Gayatri asking if they were free for drinks next Friday. Jo was busy with wedding stuff, and Gayatri was doing dry June so she'd fit into her maid of honor dress. Nina had immediately fallen into a slump of self-pity. She hadn't known Jo had chosen a maid of honor, and a quick Google had proved that dry June was not a thing.

"I just can't believe he's already moved on," said Nina quietly, looking up into her aunt's concerned face. "It hasn't even been four months."

"Well, you are all getting on, age-wise," said Rupa as she folded the saris. "People tend to move faster once they hit thirty. Though Karina is only twenty-eight."

Nina wiped her eyes. She knew her mum was right. Nikhil was thirty-five, and he often talked about wanting kids. He and Nina used to spend hours mock-arguing about the names they'd give their future children (he liked the traditional Ravi and Radhika; Nina preferred Kylo and Skye). But whereas the reality had always seemed like a very distant blur for Nina, Nikhil's five-year plan had proved he was already preparing for it. Of course he was going to find someone else who was ready to settle down. She just couldn't believe that it had happened already. It didn't make sense. She'd been the one to end it, and she was still sobbing over him every Sunday night. But he — who'd been so heartbreakingly devastated — was already happy with someone new.

"Oh, Nins, you're going to find someone one day too," said Auntie Trish, putting her arm around her again.

"I can only dream," muttered Rupa.

"It's not even about that," said Nina sadly. "It just . . . It feels like the end of an era. He was my best friend for so long, and now

he's someone I haven't spoken to in two months."

"Well, you did break up with him," said Rupa. "His moving on was always inevitable."

"I know, I know," said Nina. "But do I really have to see them together? Since when is it okay to bring a plus-one you've just started dating to an Indian thing?"

"Nina, don't be so old-fashioned; you know that things are changing," said Rupa. "People are bringing their boyfriends and girlfriends into the fold earlier than ever. Look at Auntie P's twins — they brought their fiancées to Sona's wedding!"

Nina sighed. For the last three years, she'd been Nikhil's plus-one. But now she was going to have to see him with another woman holding his hand, whispering inappropriate jokes into his ear at family gatherings, and sharing plates of paneer with him. She had no idea how she was going to bear it.

"Don't worry, darling," said Auntie Trish. "We're going to choose you the most gorgeous sari so you can show that Karina bitch that she's got nothing on you. Here, dry your eyes and try this on."

107

Nina was fine.

Absolutely fine.

Her heart hurt, sure, but that was to be expected when her ex-boyfriend, ex-fiancé, and ex–best friend had his arm around Karina fucking Gupta. She took a deep breath. The swearing was unnecessary. She didn't actually have anything against Karina; she was probably great. Nina was just sad. Really sad. It hurt to look at Nikhil standing next to the buffet, loading up on crispy bhajia, and knowing that she couldn't just take one off his plate and give him a kiss.

She missed him. His strong arms holding her tight, his sparkly eyes, his cheerful smile, his smooth skin that never failed to surprise her with its unexpected softness. She didn't miss his growing beer belly though. Or the way he'd withdraw into himself like a sulky child when he was tired from a long day dealing with difficult patients at work and take his grumpiness out on her.

This was good. Nina needed to keep remembering all of Nikhil's annoying qualities. Maybe she should write a list: "Things I No Longer Love About Nikhil." Most of them were silly and small, but there were some big ones too. Like the way he just couldn't understand Nina's love of travel and got frustrated whenever she made "rash" decisions (Nina personally labeled them "spontaneous"). Or how he'd roll his eyes when she'd start crying during an argument, which made Nina feel like he was undermining her feelings. And then there was the fact that his family was so normal that he never really knew how to respond to any of the Mistrys' melodrama. Nina seriously hoped the next love of her life had a family as dysfunctional as her own.

"Hey, Nins," said Nikhil. She'd been so lost in her thoughts that she hadn't noticed him walk straight toward her and her giant polystyrene plate filled with chili paneer. Her mum had already come over to hiss at her that she was taking too much food and should put some back so there was enough for everyone — even though it was just as much as every man in the room had taken. Nina had pretended she hadn't heard her.

"Nikhil, how's it going?" They hugged awkwardly, trying not to spill their food.

"Good," he said. "I hope it's not weird that I brought Karina. Sorry. I feel like I should have texted you to warn you that we've started dating."

"No need." Nina smiled brightly. "The

auntie grapevine brought it to me in advance. Why do you think they've trusted me not to spill food on my mum's best silk sari?"

"It's pretty," he said, looking admiringly at her bright orange sari with gold trimmings. "So, how's life? Is your brother here?"

The smile dropped off Nina's face and she shook her head. "He's still . . . you know. Good days and bad days. But anyway — how are, uh, things at work?"

"Well, it's peak root canal season," Nikhil said with a grin. "So, pretty shit, really. How's your work going?"

He'd barely finished his question when Karina and three friends who looked scarily similar to her swooped in with a waft of perfume, hair spray, and diamantés. "Hey, babe," said Karina, putting her arm on Nikhil's shoulder. "How's it going?"

"All good," he said. "You and Nina know each other, right?"

Karina lazily leaned an inch toward Nina, and the two air-kissed at a distance, while the three friends surrounded them like protective — and very glamorous — bodyguards. "Sure. How are things?"

"Good, thanks," said Nina. "What about you?"

"You got made redundant, right?" asked one of the friends, chewing loudly on gum. "From that magazine?"

"Well, yeah," said Nina. "But that was a while ago. I've been freelancing a lot since. For *Raze,* mainly. I got a promotion, actually!"

Nikhil's face creased into a warm smile. "Hey, that's amazing. Well done."

Another of the friends, wearing electric blue with matching eyeshadow, crossed her arms. "Oh yeah, I heard about that piece you wrote. They were discussing it on BBC Asian Network the other day."

"Oh my god, no way," cried Nina. "What were they saying?"

Karina looked at her in faux pity. "I mean, people think it's a bit awkward that you're writing about race. Like, the Indian community is kind of private, and now you're acting like you're speaking for everyone? Also, you're, like, trying to break taboos that no one wants to break."

"Oh," said Nina, feeling her stomach sink. "Well, I'm really just speaking for myself. And I think it's important to break taboos."

"Yeah . . ." said the gum-chewing girl. "It's just that on the radio, they were debating your article, and the ladies' panel felt that it was a bit . . . under-researched? And

111

kind of desperate? Like, your point about how Indians wear Topshop and eat Halloumi. It's kind of . . . embarrassing."

"Yeah," chimed in the girl in blue. "We don't need you to speak on our behalf. People *already* fancy us. And my mum actually does wear a sari at home and cook curries, so it's kind of rude of you to call that outdated."

Nina's mouth dropped open. "I didn't! I just want more people to be represented on TV. It's just . . . representation," she finished off lamely. "It's a good thing."

"Don't worry, Nins," said Nikhil. "Some people really like it too. Besides, it's good to cause a bit of controversy. No such thing as bad publicity, right?"

Nina smiled brightly. "Yes, you're right. Anyway, it looks like my mum and Auntie Trish need me, so I'm going to . . . Bye."

She didn't know why she was so bothered by Karina and her friends' comments. She hadn't written the article to please everyone. But she'd imagined that breaking taboos would only irritate racists and white people, not her own community.

"Nina, beta," said her mum, beckoning to her with a bright, slightly manic smile as she stood next to a guilty-looking Auntie Trish and a tall, skinny guy in a shiny black

112

shirt. "Come and meet Sunil Mama's best friend's son, Milan. Look how tall he is! And he's just finished a PhD at Oxford . . ."

CHAPTER 7

CANCER SEASON

CANCER
Season: June 22–July 22
Element: Water
Themes: Feelings. Home. Family.
Best time to: Hang out in water.

Nina peeked one eye open. She was supposed to have both her eyes closed as she focused on visualizing herself walking through a forest, but she was distracted by the sight in front of her. Alejandro was the most beautiful man she'd ever seen in Leicester. Probably because he wasn't from Leicester; he was from Colombia. His skin was as brown as hers, but in a more golden way, and with his chiseled bone structure and salt-and-pepper hair, he was scarily good-looking. Nina assumed this was why 99 percent of his meditation students were female and most of them were wearing crop tops even though the session involved zero exercise or movement (Nina really needed to invest in one of these yoga-esque tops; her faded T-shirts were clearly not part of the spiritual self-love uniform).

She couldn't believe that Meera hadn't mentioned how attractive he was when she'd recommended this meditation class to her. If she had, Nina definitely would have worn mascara. She sighed audibly as she took in his toned body, every muscle clearly visible in his tight black shorts and baggy undershirt. The knowing way he looked at his female students and murmured their names suggested that Alejandro had slept with the entire class, but she didn't care. She wanted to put herself down on the waiting list. And if she wasn't mistaken, they had chemistry. They'd only spoken for all of 2.5 seconds, but when Alejandro had put his hand on her forearm and looked straight into her eyes as he'd said, "Welcome," Nina had felt a shiver run through her body. She didn't need Meera to tell her that her Venus was very, very exalted right now.

"Thank you so much for that powerful class," said Nina, looking deeply into Alejandro's crinkled brown eyes. She'd deliberately spent the last ten minutes in the toilet, hoping that by the time she came out, everyone else would have left — and her scheming had paid off. They were now alone in the room together, and she was making full use of her one opportunity to hit on Alejandro. "It was my first time, and I really enjoyed it."

"Namaste," he said, clasping his hands to his chest and looking back at her sincerely. "Thank you for your presence."

"Namaste," replied Nina, quickly mimicking his prayer gesture. "So, um, how long have you been teaching?"

"Over twenty years," said Alejandro, his brown eyes creasing in the corners as he smiled. Nina wondered how old he was. His forties? Fifties? Not that it mattered either way — he was hotter than any man she'd ever met her own age. "Long before it was fashionable."

Nina laughed. "Yeah, I guess it's changed a lot."

"It has," he agreed. "And what about you? What do you do?"

"I'm a journalist."

"Really?" He looked at her with interest. "What sorts of things do you write about?"

"I spent a long time writing about TV shows," said Nina. "But now I'm trying to write more about diversity and race."

"That sounds really interesting."

"It can be. Though being a meditation teacher sounds far more interesting to me."

Alejandro locked his eyes onto hers, and for an intense moment they just looked at each other. Nina did everything she could to hold his gaze. "Hey, what are you doing now? Are you free?" he said, leaning to speak quietly in her ear.

"Um, yeah, I guess so," said Nina, her mind whirring quickly. If she wasn't mistaken, he was about to ask her out.

"Okay, well, how about we spend some time together?" he asked. "I really like your energy and I feel like . . . you might be as attracted to me as I am to you."

Nina's mouth fell open. She had never come across a man that direct. It took most guys at least six dates to say even half of what he'd just told her. She was into it — but also slightly terrified. How could she, one of the most basic people she knew, go on a date with someone so . . . spiritual? Sexy? Old? Nina wasn't sure what the right adjective was, but as she looked into Alejandro's magnetic eyes, she realized it didn't matter. It was time for her to leave her comfort zone and finally let her Venus run free.

"Yes," she said hoarsely. "I am."

"Let's get out of here, then," Alejandro said, grinning and sliding into motion as he grabbed a woven tote bag and tied a jumper round his waist. "I don't know about you, but I haven't had my nature fix today. How about we go to a river?"

"Uh, okay. A river walk sounds nice."

"Good," replied Alejandro. "And seeing as it's so hot, maybe we could even cool down with a little swim in some natural water."

"Um, this is Leicester," said Nina, feeling a little deflated. "We don't have natural waters to swim in. And even if we did, I don't have a swimsuit with me."

"Oh, do not worry," said Alejandro. "You won't need a swimsuit."

The old Nina would have flat-out refused to get into a middle-aged stranger's hippie white van, but she was trying to live in the present and go with the flow. Alejandro told her the van was ideal for storing yoga mats and cymbals for his gong baths, and the mattress in the back was perfect for spontaneous road trips. She was kind of into the wafting aroma of sweet incense and sage. As the self-love book said, "The past is but an interpretation and the future is an illusion. All we have is the present." Which was why Nina was now sitting next to a man she'd

118

just met, on her way to a secluded river to swim with no swimsuit, like the free spirit she'd never been before. She couldn't decide if she was more likely to die from pneumonia — it was a very sunny July day, but this was still England — or from being murdered by her meditation teacher. She pulled out her phone to share her live GPS location with Jo, explaining, On a rebound date with a hot, spiritual 52yo Colombian. Living my best life! (but also being safe in case of murder, etc).

Even just writing that made Nina want to laugh out loud. The third entry on her self-love list was right; she *was* brave as hell. She couldn't remember the last time she'd done something so spur-of-the-moment and wild as this (possibly Jo's twenty-fifth birthday, when she'd made out with the DJ, the bouncer, and two barmen — or as Gayatri had said, "all the help"), but it felt good. She'd spent the last year with Nikhil desperately trying to coax him into being more spontaneous — particularly in the bedroom. But he'd always wrinkled his brow at every one of Nina's tentative suggestions, until she'd quietly resigned herself to a life of vanilla sex and predictable climaxes. Nina had no idea if this alfresco date with Alejandro was going to end in the

119

kind of climax she was secretly hoping for, but if it did, she knew that it definitely wouldn't be vanilla.

"So," said Alejandro, turning to smile at her as he pulled up to a red light in the city center, "tell me about you."

Nina never knew how to answer open-ended questions like that. Should she talk about her job? Her hobbies? Did she even have any hobbies? "Um, what do you want to know?" she asked hesitantly.

"What are you into? Are you a traveler?"

"I'd like to be," answered Nina honestly. "I've visited a lot of Europe, but the farthest away I've been is Bali, with my ex, and Thailand, with my best friend before uni."

"Southeast Asia calls me as well," said Alejandro. "I had a life-changing experience at a silent retreat in Indonesia."

"Wow," sighed Nina. "I'd love to see more of the world. But my friends, and my ex, weren't that keen on the backpacking vibe."

"Why couldn't you go alone?"

"I could have," said Nina, temporarily distracted by the sight of his tanned arms changing the gearshift. Forearms were her favorite part of the male physique, and Alejandro's were no disappointment. "But I always thought I'd get lonely. And, you know, money."

"Ah, but loneliness can't be eased by external distractions," said Alejandro. "Only by internal reflection."

Nina looked at him, impressed. "That sounds very wise."

He smiled at her. "A lot of people travel to escape their feelings, but of course, the feelings go with them."

"Isn't it helpful to get away and have perspective though?"

"Sure," he said. "Travel can bring you stillness, which helps the healing. But you've got to want to do the work. And a lot of people prefer the parties."

Nina grinned to herself as she remembered being eighteen and getting drunk on the beach with Jo, dancing till dawn, and waking up with sand in her hair. She missed those carefree days before Jo met Jaz and swapped three a.m. partying for three-course dinner parties.

"What are you thinking about, hermosa?" asked Alejandro.

"Oh, just what you said about loneliness," said Nina, deciding not to share her hazy hedonistic memories. She'd never been with someone as spiritual as Alejandro before — he was actually wearing a beaded necklace under his shirt — and she didn't want to ruin things by revealing her basicness just yet. Especially not before he revealed his abs.

The last time Nina had been to this part of Leicestershire, her dad had still been alive. Her parents fought the entire drive there — Nina and Kal had their Discmans firmly plugged in, as they'd learned to do for every car journey to drown out their parents' nonstop bickering — and they had a picnic by the river surrounded by dozens of other families doing the same. Nina spent the whole time wishing she could be with any other family but her own.

Two years later, her dad had succumbed to the depression that had been underlying his life for as long as she could remember. They'd never gone back.

Nina shook her head, trying to shake the memory away. Now was not the time to think about her fucked-up family.

Alejandro parked the van on a small dirt road hidden by trees from the main road. They made their way along a precarious path twisting downhill through more trees toward a small river, with Alejandro sprightly leading the way and Nina wincing as nettles stung her bare legs.

Now they were standing alone in the shallow, clear water. In their underwear.

It was the first time that Nina had been so physically exposed on a first date, and as much as she was trying to stay in the present, she was finding the present very, very uncomfortable. Alejandro's body looked like a work of art, and hers definitely did not. She was squishy, her legs were unwaxed, and her black cotton underwear was not sexy. She was currently trying to subtly hide behind a rock, but Alejandro was having none of it. He took her hand and pulled her out into the middle of the river. Or stream. Nina was unclear what the difference was.

"You have a beautiful body," he said. "It's so natural."

"Thanks," said Nina, trying to sound more confident than she felt. "Though yours is much more beautiful."

He smiled. "We can swim to warm up if you want. Or if you would like, I'd love to do a special breathing meditation with you."

Nina decided the day couldn't get any weirder. "Sure, why not?"

"Okay, great. So just start by holding my hands, and let's breathe deeply together."

Nina obeyed him stiffly, trying not to think about how strange this all was. The water lapping around her feet was freezing cold, there were pebbles and twigs in between her toes, and she knew the sun was shining brightly on the smattering of hormonal acne on her jawline.

"Let's close our eyes," he suggested.

Nina nodded gratefully, waiting for his to shut before she followed suit. Now she knew he couldn't stare at her, she relaxed and let her breathing become as deep and steady as his. With his rough hands gripping onto hers, she started to feel a wave of desire run through her body. Who knew breathing could be such a turn-on?

Alejandro took a step closer to Nina. She could feel the heat of his body near hers. Her heartbeat started to quicken, especially when he wrapped his hands around her body and moved hers onto his. Nina was now very excited — his shoulders were so strong, his skin so soft — but her eyes were still closed. She didn't know if she was allowed to open them or not. Just as she was deciding whether to sneak one open, she felt his stubble graze her cheek. Then his lips. And then his lips were on hers. He was kissing her. And it felt like actual magic.

"Que rico," he murmured. "Que rico."

Nina had no idea what he was saying, but it was making her wrap her arms around him even tighter as they kissed deeper and deeper.

"Espera un momento," he said gently, breaking away. "Wait."

"Is something wrong?" she asked in confusion.

"No, no. It's just good to go slow."

"But . . . why?"

"It's tantra," he said, surprised. "You've never had tantric sex?"

Nina shook her head. She didn't even really know what it was. "Is that the one where you don't orgasm?"

"Oh, you'll orgasm." He smiled. "The difference is that it takes longer to get there. It's all about the breathing and the connection. As I breathe in, you breathe out. We share our breath as one, and it heightens the sexual experience."

Nina bit her bottom lip, suddenly feeling self-conscious again. What if she wasn't good at tantra? What if Alejandro thought she was too intense in the bedroom, like Nikhil did? What if it would be weird having sex with someone who wasn't Nikhil? And someone she had only properly met two hours ago? Nina's mind slipped into overdrive as she officially began to freak out. What was she even doing? What if someone saw them? What if she got arrested again?!

"I . . . can't," she said, before asking the

least intense of her questions. "What if someone walks past?"

"Trust me, no one comes here," said Alejandro, immediately making Nina seethe with irrational jealousy at the thought of him having been to this exact spot with other women. "We'll be fine."

Nina looked at him uncertainly, but Alejandro just smiled at her, took her face into his hands, and gently kissed her again. Nina felt every single nerve ending in her body come to life, and it wasn't because of the freezing water lapping around her ankles. This was already so, so much better than normal sex — and they hadn't even taken their underwear off yet.

"You . . . are . . . perfect," said Alejandro, running his hands over her body.

Nina made a strangled sound. He was saying *positive affirmations* to her. The self-love book would be so proud. With renewed confidence, she lifted her gaze to meet Alejandro's and let herself feel the full brunt of his desire. Her breathing synced with his without even trying, and as Nina stared into Alejandro's intense brown eyes, she realized she was officially doing tantra. And, judging by the feel of Alejandro pressed against her, it was definitely going to be worth risking another night in a jail cell.

7. My spontaneity.

CHAPTER 8

The worst part about being lonely meant Nina had no one to call to say she'd just had tantric sex in a river. Or stream. Things like this did not happen often in her life. She'd never gone on an alfresco date before, nor a date that didn't involve some form of drinking. Nor had she ever let an incredibly attractive older man undress her in running water, carry her naked body in his strong arms over a bunch of rocks, lay her down on a sunny bed of moss, and give her the most magical experience of her life — all while an actual butterfly fluttered by.

Lying in bed wearing a sheep-covered nightie her dad had given her when she was twelve, Nina still couldn't believe that any of this had really happened. But it had. Her postcoital glow and the ridiculous smile lingering on her face proved it. It had been so much fun throwing caution — and her underwear — to the wind. After years of having sex that ranged from quite good to below average, she'd finally hit "fucking incredible." And the best part was that just as she'd started to feel hangry and tired, Alejandro had produced a cheese baguette from his rucksack. It was exactly the kind of date she wanted to retell in inappropriate detail to her closest girlfriends over bottles of pinot. But, rather concerningly, she no longer seemed to have any close girlfriends she could call.

This week she'd been added to a WhatsApp group to organize Jo's hen do, and every single one of her cost-effective suggestions — including an astrology night with Meera — had been dismissed in favor of expensive European minibreaks complete with spa treatments and cocktail-making classes. Even Gayatri, who knew her financial situation, had vetoed her ideas, and then taken it one step further by mocking Nina's love of star signs. It was classic Virgo behavior, but Nina was still hurt by it.

It was all just extra proof that she was trying to cling on to friendships that no longer made her happy. She'd tried to tell Jo about Alejandro in more detail, but Jo's response — Ew, he's in his 50s? And doesn't have a proper job? Pls tell me you didn't shag him —

was so far away from what Nina had hoped for that it had left her feeling flat with disappointment. Even Elsie, the ultimate Hufflepuff, had been more worried about diseases Nina could have picked up from the water.

The self-love book had a theory she couldn't ignore about people being $+2$s, -2s, or 0s. A $+2$ was someone you spent time with who made you feel positive and uplifted afterward. A -2 did the opposite and left you feeling drained. A 0 didn't really impact you either way. Nina opened up the book and reread the chapter on connection. It was all about the importance of spending time with as many plus people as possible, though obviously it was hard to completely avoid zeros and minuses — especially if, as in Nina's case, you were related to them.

"True $+2$ connection is a gift from the universe. If you come across it, don't let it go. Treasure it, nurture it, and help it grow."

Nina closed the book thoughtfully. According to this, most of her (wine-fueled) friendships were not based on real connections. If Nina was honest, she couldn't remember the last time she'd had a real, emotional, vulnerable chat with a friend where they spoke about the shitty stuff in their lives and not just the glowing, airbrushed anecdotes — or wedding planning. It had been something she'd done all the time with Nikhil, but that was no longer an option, and she was definitely not there with Alejandro. The only time she'd truly been close to it in the last few weeks was with Meera.

It felt weird to think of someone she'd met twice in her life as being a true +2 connection, but then Nina remembered it was "a gift from the universe." She couldn't reject a gift like this — the book said it was "important to always say yes to any form of blessing; otherwise, you send the wrong message to the universe" — so she reached for her phone.

Eight minutes and five drafts later, Nina had composed a message asking Meera out on a friendship date for drinks after yoga the following week. She changed the emoji one last time, opting for a prayer hands followed by a cocktail emoji, and pressed send. Ten seconds later, she reached for her phone to see if Meera had read her message. She hadn't. This was more nerve-racking than asking out a guy. Nina put her phone down again. And then reached for it again. Still nothing. This was going to be a long morning.

■ ■ ■ ■

"Why are you grinning at your phone?"

Kal was standing in the doorway wearing a threadbare navy sweater with gray tracksuit bottoms, an eyebrow raised.

Nina sat up, indignant at being interrupted whilst repeatedly rereading Meera's text saying Hell yes followed by two clinking-glasses emoji. "You could have knocked."

"I did. But you were too busy doing — sorry, what are you doing?" asked Kal, walking in and sitting on the edge of Nina's bed.

"Being vulnerable and fostering connections," she said, lifting her chin into the air. "And you?"

"I just made some toast," replied Kal.

"Um, and you didn't think to bring me some?"

"You can make your own. Well, later. Mum's in the kitchen now and she's pissed off because I used the same knife for peanut butter and jam."

"Shouldn't have let her see you do it," said Nina, shaking her head. "Rookie error. So what's up? You don't come into my room just to hang. Though you're very welcome to. Oh my god, do you remember when we

132

used to lie in my room just watching *Die Hard* movies on repeat? We should so do that again."

"Yeah, I was the one who introduced you to them," he said. "Maybe we can watch them again, when I feel better. I can't concentrate on anything for more than ten minutes right now. But, actually, I came to talk about your latest article. The one on how it's racist to say you don't date Asians."

"Ah, that's so sweet," cried Nina. "How did you find it?"

"You've shared it on every single social media platform. I couldn't not find it."

"So, what did you think of it?" she asked excitedly. "How crazy was that poll I conducted? I can't believe 54 percent of people would never date an Asian!"

"Yeah, it's fucked up. And it's really cool you're writing about racism, but — I just feel like you need to be a bit careful. There are a lot of negative comments on the article."

A look of worry flashed across Nina's face. "There's more? I mean, yeah, I saw some. They're getting kind of intense. But it's normal, right?"

"Nins, they're a lot more than intense," said Kal gently. "There are thousands of messages on your articles. People . . . people are saying they want to murder you. They're talking about trying to find your address and come round to your home."

"What? They can't do that, can they?"

"If they really wanted to, they could," said Kal. "They could dox you." He rolled his eyes at Nina's blank face. "They find out your private information and put it online. So then your address and everything is public. They might even hack you."

"Fuck," breathed out Nina. "Well, if that happens, I'll call the police. DC Spencer will sort it."

"I know you care about what you're writing, but is it worth taking this level of abuse?"

Nina crossed her arms. "I'm not letting these racist psychos stop me from writing my truth. Then they'll have won."

"Look, I just . . . I'm not really okay with people talking about wanting to kill and rape my younger sister. These people are properly vile, Nina."

"And I really appreciate you caring so much," said Nina, reaching out to place her hand on her brother's arm. "But, Kal, I'm not going to stop doing this. It's the first time in my entire career that I'm saying something important. And people are listening to what I have to say." Kal opened his mouth to interrupt, but Nina shook her head. "Honestly, I need to keep going. If we're too scared to talk about difficult topics, nothing will ever change. I know people saying they don't want to date Asians isn't as bad as that time those guys called you the P-word, or Mum and Dad getting a brick through the window when they moved into this house. But it's all part of the same thing."

"Okay, fine," said Kal, putting his hands into the air. "Just so long as you know what you're getting yourself into."

"Of course, I'm fine. In fact, I actually have another article to write. So, if you don't mind closing the door on your way out . . . Thanks!"

Her brother walked out of the room shaking his head as Nina pretended to busy herself on her laptop. She felt guilty for ignoring Kal's advice, especially as it had been months since he'd last shown such an interest in her life. And she was a bit scared of this new wave of threatening comments. But Nina was finally living her dream of being a Proper Journalist writing about things she cared about. There was no way she was going to let these basement-dwelling losers scare her back into lying on the sofa writing about *Buffy the Homophobic Slayer.*

■ ■ ■ ■

"I am actually dead," said Meera, following Nina out of the yoga studio toward the nearest pub for their first friend date.

"We definitely deserve a midday drink," said Nina.

"Agreed," said Meera. "I keep vowing to myself I'll find a different yoga class to go to. Something a bit more focused on breathing and going slow. But then I'm like, it's five pounds. Where else am I going to get such cheap yoga? And at least she's Indian."

"What's that got to do with it?" asked Nina.

"Well, it just makes a change from another white yoga teacher pronouncing 'namaste' wrong."

"Huh, I never really thought about it that way," said Nina. "I actually forgot yoga's an Indian thing."

"That's exactly my point," said Meera, as they navigated their way past an elderly couple with a shopping trolley. "I mean, I was bullied the whole way through school for my smelly curries and my yellow teeth from drinking turmeric with milk, and everyone thought yoga was weird. Now everyone drinks turmeric lattes, there are queues outside Indian restaurants, and yoga's fashionable. But everyone's forgotten where it all came from."

"You're so right. I never thought of that. Being brown is officially en vogue."

"Right?" said Meera. "But it's kind of bullshit too. It's like society's taken all the 'best bits' of our culture, whilst keeping the discrimination and unconscious bias. It's cool that things like Ayurveda are everywhere now, but I just wish we could retain the respect. Like people turning yoga into an Insta sport. Deepa's completely mad, but at least her classes still have the Indian spirituality and discipline."

"Oh my god, you've just given me the best idea for my next column," cried Nina. "About cultural appropriation — with the yoga thing, but also people wearing bindis at Glastonbury. I mean, we're not in the empire anymore. The Brits need to get their own culture."

Meera laughed. "Sounds like you're already writing your piece. Love it. Okay, G and Ts?"

Two drinks and two hours of oversharing later, Meera was gasping with laughter as Nina finally found herself with a willing audience for her wild sexual story. "I can't breathe. It's a spiritual porno. Do the breathing exercise he made you do again."

Nina obeyed and imitated Alejandro holding her tummy and telling her to breathe in and out slowly. "Más profundo," she said in her shitty Spanish accent, and they both cracked up laughing again.

"So, what about you?" asked Nina. "What's your love life like?"

"I used to have stories to rival yours, but I've spent the last year in a serious relationship."

"What's she like? Is she into astrology too?"

"Sarah's an accountant," sighed Meera. "We have very different interests, which is hard sometimes. But we're just such a part of each other's lives now. I know all her friends; she knows mine. I can't imagine not being with her. And I love her, obviously."

"I know exactly what you mean," said Nina quietly. "Hey, show me a photo of her. I need visual context."

Meera pulled out her phone to show Nina a photo of a woman who looked like a younger Gwyneth Paltrow. "Wow," said Nina. "She's *hot*. Hey, how are your parents about it all? I mean, you're breaking two taboos there — you're dating women, and

138

you've gone white."

"I know, I just need to have a kid out of wedlock, and then that's the holy trinity of taboos!" Meera said, grinning. "But I'm actually very lucky and have quite chilled-out parents. Well, my mum and stepdad. My actual dad's insanely conservative, but I barely see him. He's remarried some Gujarati woman from India who he met online. They've moved to Preston."

"Oh my god, like a mail-order bride?"

"Yup," said Meera. "I reckon she just wanted a visa. But weirdly, they seem kind of happy. My dad never really knew what to do with my mum and me, but now he's found someone as traditional as him."

"Wow. Are you close with him?"

Meera shook her head. "No. I have to hide a lot of my life from him when I go visit. He doesn't even know I'm queer, or in a long-term relationship. I know it's easiest that way, but it makes me a bit sad I can't be my authentic self with him. I know he'll never accept me."

"Oh, Meera," said Nina. "I'm sorry, that's such a shame. What about your mum though? She accepts you, right?"

"Yes, thank god. It's mainly down to my stepdad; he's the best. He's also Gujarati, but he's lived here most of his life, and he's hilarious. He's a corporate lawyer, but he's also one of those people who's permanently smiling, takes nothing seriously, and laughs everything off. He's so relaxed that he's helped my mum be really cool with" — she gestured toward her purple hair, multiple piercings, and the huge constellation tattoo on her arm — "all this."

Nina sighed wistfully. "I can barely get my mum to accept the fact I eat refined sugar. I wish she'd meet a chilled-out guy, but she's too uptight to date."

"What about your dad?"

Nina paused. "He's actually dead."

"Oh my god, I'm sorry. How did it . . ."

"It's fine," said Nina. "He killed himself. When I was fifteen."

"Fuck. Depression?"

Nina nodded. "Yep. It was awful. Obviously."

"Shit. Were you close?"

Nina looked down at her chipped lilac nail polish. "Not really," she admitted. "I loved him, of course. But I didn't really know him. He was always working — he did something in finance — and when he was at home, he just . . . wasn't present. He barely ever spoke to me or Kal, unless we got an A on the latest exam — then he'd congratulate us. So, I spent a lot of time trying to get As."

"That must have been hard. How did your mum handle it?"

"Uh, not so well," said Nina cautiously. "She's kind of a perfectionist, so she couldn't help herself constantly making little comments to my dad to get out of the house, to start being a better father, to shave his beard. But all that happened was that she'd get under his skin, and he'd eventually snap and start yelling back. It was shit."

"Fuck, it sounds it," said Meera, putting a hand on her friend's arm. "How did you cope?"

"Well, I didn't know he was depressed; I just thought he didn't like me. So I learned to stay out of his way."

"That makes sense. You were so young."

"In a way, I think that protected me from some of the worst of it," said Nina slowly. "But my older brother, Kal, he'd try and get involved a lot when Mum and Dad were arguing. And now he has depression too. I feel like it has to be genetically linked."

"Shit, your poor brother. Did you guys get therapy after your dad died?"

Nina shook her head. "Mum didn't believe in it back then. Dad wasn't even diagnosed with depression — I mean, it's pretty obvious now in hindsight, but back then you didn't go to the doctor unless you had physical symptoms. I was really lucky though, because my best friend's mum was a therapist, so she helped me work through a lot of it after Dad died, and obviously Jo and I talked about it all the time." She paused. "I don't think my brother really had anyone he could talk to in the same way."

"That's a real shame," said Meera softly. "But I'm glad you had support. And if ever you want to talk about it, I'm always here."

"Thanks," said Nina. "And thank you for getting it. Not everyone does. At school I think people used to believe my tragedy was contagious. And my . . . Nikhil never really knew what to say about my dad."

"Probably because it's not a nice, neat family disaster," said Meera, shaking her head. "Like an amicable divorce or cancer."

"That's exactly it," agreed Nina. "People either shut down and go really cold when I tell them, or have really over-the-top re-actions. It's why it's so refreshing that you're just being normal about it."

"It's probably because my family is crazy too." Meera shrugged. "That's the one bonus of having a dysfunctional family; you can handle anything your friends tell you about theirs."

"Well," said Nina, "in that case, I am so

very grateful that your life has been as fucked-up as mine." She raised her glass. "Here's to dysfunctional families."

8. I can put myself out there and be vulnerable enough to make new connections.

CHAPTER 9

"Nina Mistry," declared Mark Camberwell with a flamboyant flourish of his arms. "The woman of the moment."

Nina smiled awkwardly at her editor as he ignored her outstretched hand and kissed her cheeks twice.

"So nice to see you again," he said. "You should come to the office more."

This was officially Nina's second time to the office — an open-plan area in a coworking building in Birmingham ("It's just so nice to be somewhere authentic that isn't gentrified yet," Mark had mused) filled with wooden tables, metal chairs covered in bright cushions, and twelve members of staff all wearing trainers. It had the young start-up vibe that every office run by millennials was duty-bound to succumb to, complete with bowls of free fruit and a state-of-the-art coffee machine. But it was an hour's train ride away from Nina's mum's house, which meant it was too far to commute regularly. Plus, no one had ever actually suggested she work in the office. She was only there now because Mark wanted to discuss her career as *Raze*'s first and only diversity correspondent.

She followed Mark and his baseball cap to a brightly patterned window seat, accepting his offer of an oat milk flat white. "So," he said, "we are *loving* your columns. Who knew you were hiding a talent like that?"

"Ah, thanks," said Nina, shifting in her chair. Even though she'd tried to prepare herself for this meeting — she'd paired an oversized bright orange blazer with black jeans and a white T-shirt for a "capable but cool" vibe, combined with half an hour of internally repeating self-confidence affirmations to herself in the mirror — she still didn't feel fully comfortable. It was partly because she had no idea what to expect from the meeting, but also because Mark was two years younger than her, the CEO of "the most innovative media outlet this century," according to Forbes, and her boss.

"Okay. So, basically we love everything you're doing," he said. "And we just want to make sure your work is seen by more and more people. So, we were thinking, we need to get you doing more social media. Maybe some videos? Of you sharing your opinions? And you need to be messaging more people, Nina. Like, getting in debates and things. Okay?"

"Uh, on social media?"

"Obvs," he said. "Is there . . . a problem?"

"No, I mean, I love raising awareness of topics that aren't being covered elsewhere, and I really want the messages to get out there," she said, fidgeting uncomfortably in her chair. It was one thing being vulnerable in the pub with a friend, and another thing entirely to do it with your boss. She took a deep breath. "The thing is, Mark, I'm just not sure about doing more on social media, because I am getting a lot of abusive comments online. Like . . . more than I ever imagined. It's really increased in the last few weeks."

"Ugh, trolls, right?" said Mark, sipping his coffee. Nina noticed his nails were painted black. "They're the actual worst."

Nina nodded in relief. She hadn't been sure if she should tell Mark or not. But the volume of messages she received kept rising, and they were no longer confined to her Twitter feed; scathing remarks about her physical appearance and her lack of intelligence were now appearing under her Instagram photos, in her Facebook messages,

146

and even straight into her Gmail. It was all getting to her more than before. With each nasty new post, it was harder to brush off comments telling her how ugly she was. Especially when she was already emotional from PMS. Not to mention how fucking creepy it was to read about people describing what machete they'd use to kill her.

"I'm so glad you get it," she exclaimed. "It's gotten quite bad lately. There's a lot of death and rape threats."

"They're just insecure kids in their bedrooms." Mark shrugged. "You've got to ignore them. Or laugh it off."

"Well, no, I am. I mean, I've been trying. A lot. But sometimes they make really cruel comments that can be quite" — she took another deep breath — "hurtful."

Mark raised his eyebrows. "A lot of our writers get those sorts of comments. Look at Ellen — she's, like, the most hated woman ever."

"Oh, I know it's not just me," Nina hastened to say. "But Ellen's also, well, she's blonde. And really pretty. I don't want to complain, but I feel like I'm getting more personal abuse than most people."

He stared at her blankly, and Nina realized she needed to speak his language. "Mark, it's racist, sexist, and intersectional. I get the typical 'ugly' comments, but they also relate it to my heritage, saying that there's no way 'a big-nosed Indian like me will ever get laid.' They don't understand how a man would ever want to touch my 'dirt-colored skin.' And they want me to 'go back home,' even though I was born here."

Mark's face dropped into a serious expression. "Oh my god. As a white man, even a pansexual one, I just don't even feel I can comment on this." He nodded sagely. And then his eyes lit up. "But it is such good column material. Why don't you write on this? It could be really therapeutic for you. Or I also had an idea for you for your next one."

He pulled out a notebook and turned to a page filled with a long list. It had "NINA" scrawled at the top of it. "I really love your stuff so far, but I thought it might be good to give you some more direction for the next ones. So I've come up with some topics. What do you think of saying, 'Stop assuming all people of color are left wing'?"

"I . . . don't know. I've never thought about that before. But, going back to the online abuse, is there something we can do? Like, take comments off my articles?"

"Oh, Nina, you know that's not who we are. It's just not *Raze* policy. Our whole ethos is about being the voice of the people by the people. You know?"

Nina nodded. "Okay. I'll just . . . stop reading my notifications for a bit, then."

"Oooh, I wouldn't do that," said Mark. "Engage, Nina. Stand up to them. You know you need to be active on social so that your articles get more reach. And we are all about reach." He pointed to a sign on the wall that said *RAZE = REACH.*

Nina sighed and focused on trying to make the most of the meeting that had already cost her £9.50 in travel. "Okay, fine. Well, before we discuss ideas, there was just one more thing I wanted to remind you about. I really appreciate the promotion, like, a lot, but I haven't actually been paid for the last few months?"

"Oh my god, I know, I am so, so sorry. It's mortifying. But we swapped accountants recently, so they have a huge backlog to get through. Don't worry. They've promised they'll get it sorted by the end of the month."

"Oh, okay," said Nina. "If you're sure. Can you maybe put it in an email to me as well, just so I have it all in writing?"

"Of course. So. Back to my ideas. What do you think of doing a piece in defense of brownface? I know it sounds controversial,

149

so bear with, but is it really that big a deal to put on some fake tan to dress up as Pocahontas?"

Nina lay on her bedroom floor in shavasana. Though she wasn't really sure it counted as shavasana if she hadn't done any yoga poses beforehand. Her meeting with Mark had left her feeling confused. She knew the site needed clicks — she wasn't naive about why they were so excited by her articles lately; she'd single-handedly boosted their unique views by 35 percent, and every column she did became the site's most read in under twenty-four hours — but she also wasn't fully comfortable with the way *Raze* was going about it. Her article on yoga and culture appropriation had been published word for word as she'd written it, but with the highly exaggerated headline of "Yoga isn't for white people." That wasn't what she was saying, and it wasn't really a surprise that the angry, racist abuse had increased threefold since it had been published.

She knew that Mark was right and this was just a part of the business she had to get used to. But she wasn't sure she could keep brushing off the comments as if they weren't hitting home. She knew it was pathetic to care about people calling her fat and ugly. Feminists did not let people's opinions about their looks get to them. She was more than her body. Etc., etc. But none of these facts stopped it from physically hurting when she saw that someone had found an awful photo of her online and annotated all of her flaws. "Oily skin," "big Indian nose," and "vile acne scars" might all be true, but that didn't make them any less soul-destroying to read.

Nina had tried to be open about her vulnerability to Mark, but it hadn't felt courageous like it had with Meera. He'd made her feel even more exposed. And now she wasn't sure what to do. Thank god she had plans with Alejandro at the end of the week. Some chakra-unblocking meditation followed by some chakra-stimulating sex would sort her out. She reached over for her phone to message him — lately they'd been sending each other slightly erotic voice notes; something Nikhil had always refused to do because he hated the sound of his own voice — when she saw that she had a new email. The subject line was "TV appearance," and it was an offer for *her* to go on TV. Nina stared at her phone in shock and reread the email. Twice. She couldn't believe it. But ITV — *ITV* — had seen her recent

151

articles on race, thought they were "fascinating," and wanted to invite her to go on prime-time breakfast television to "raise awareness about representation and everyday racism." For a fee. Of £200.

Nina screamed out loud in excitement. This was her chance to finally present herself in the mainstream media as a serious journalist who cared about actual issues, and if she played it right, it could lead to more opportunities just like this. Meera and the stars had been right; she was destined to have an impact on the world. Or she would when she got off the bedroom floor.

"First," said Alejandro to the dozens of women eagerly awaiting his next words, "you have to practice the anal."

Nina snorted and then stopped abruptly as she realized everyone else was focusing on silently trying to lock their chakras. Or something like that. Nina hadn't fully understood what practicing the anal actually was.

"The anal lock is the moola bandha," continued Alejandro, standing at the front of the room in a tight white T-shirt and baggy black trousers. Or was it a skirt? Either way, he looked good. "And that is the one we're going to work on first. So, please tighten the muscles you'd use for excretion and urination."

Nina had thought it would be sexier than this to hear Alejandro talking about kundalini energy in his South American accent (it was the main reason she'd agreed to come to the class — as well as the fact that she wanted to show off her new galaxy-patterned crop top and matching leggings), but it felt more like being in a science lesson. Still, as the class practiced channeling their sexual energy, she got to do it knowing that hers would be channeled directly by the teacher after class.

"Breathe deeper, Nina," said Alejandro, coming up behind her. He placed a hand over her stomach, and Nina breathed in deeply, forcing herself to stay calm. Alejandro knew exactly what she looked like naked and had seen her stomach at a variety of angles, so there was no need for her to sit there feeling anxious about him touching her rolls. "I want to see your belly stick out even more when you inhale. Come on, inhale deeper . . . Good," he said encouragingly. "Can you feel the energy?"

"I think it will probably kick in for me a bit later," she said. "Like . . . after class."

"That was magical," said Alejandro, stroking Nina's hair as he lay next to her on the mattress in his van. "I felt a connection with you before, but this time it was . . . sublime."

"Thanks," said Nina shyly. "I think it's because I've been working on some stuff. Like being in the present more."

"Oh?" he asked, leaning on his side to look directly into her eyes again.

Nina had always hated the thought of having eye contact — before, during, or after sex. Her inner British prude found it embarrassing, so she always closed her eyes. But she was slowly realizing that she may have wasted every sexual experience she'd ever had by keeping them shut. Because having a pair of deep brown eyes gazing infinitely into hers while their owner lay on top of her was apparently just what her body needed to orgasm. Repeatedly.

"It's from this book I'm reading," she explained. "It's kind of . . . self-help." She looked at Alejandro to gauge his reaction, but he nodded encouragingly. "Well, there's a really interesting chapter on how you can use your breath to stay in the present, and seeing as how we were doing tantric breathing anyway, I figured I'd just add in the present thing. To try and focus on every single physical sensation, and not have any thoughts in my head. You know?"

Up until now, Nina had always had a fantasy in her head during sex. With Nikhil, the main way she'd been able to orgasm had been if she'd floated above the scene and watched over them. Or imagined herself as Cleopatra with Mark Antony and Julius Caesar fighting over her. But this was the first time, probably ever, that her mind had been fully focused on the present moment. And it turned out that this was way more conducive to her orgasms than having imaginary sex with ancient Romans.

"The present is so important," said Alejandro. "And as you can see, it makes such a difference to intimacy. I really felt I was with you today, and that you let me in."

Nina smiled awkwardly. "Thanks." She wasn't used to discussing emotional connections during postcoital chats — Nikhil had normally just fallen asleep — but she was kind of into it. So much so that she decided to share too. Not to the point of telling Alejandro that she'd daydreamed about how gorgeous their child would be, but just a little more vulnerability than usual.

"I felt the same," she said hesitantly. "I think the first few times with you, I was maybe a bit nervous, so I couldn't be 100 percent myself. But now I know you more, it's easier."

"I understand," said Alejandro sincerely. "We're creating a connection. And it's not just sexual."

"It's not?"

"Of course not. Everything's linked. Our souls are getting to know each other."

As he leaned in to kiss her, Nina laughed happily. Fuck the Internet haters who thought she was going to die alone; she was building a sacral soul connection with a hot spiritual healer.

9. Living my life fully in the present.

CHAPTER 10

LEO SEASON

LEO
Season: July 23–August 22
Element: Fire
Themes: Action. Drama. Attention.
Best time to: Work on your confidence.

Nina was nervous. It was seven a.m., and she'd barely slept all night. She'd been so anxious about her upcoming TV appearance that she hadn't even enjoyed the free toiletries in the central London hotel they'd put her up in. And now she was meant to be live on air in thirty-five minutes, breaking taboos around race and diversity. She felt so sick that she was starting to wonder if she'd made the right choice in saying yes. But then again, how was she supposed to reject her first-ever offer to go on national TV and start making a difference? As Meera had said, this was her destiny.

"What color lip do you want?" asked the makeup artist, who had apparently given up trying to hide the bags under Nina's eyes.

"Anything," whispered Nina. "You choose."

"Okay," she responded cheerfully. "I'll do a nice subtle pink. It'll look lovely, don't worry."

Nina nodded mutely. She was worried — but not about her lipstick. She'd written down a list of all her main points, but even so, she wasn't really sure what she wanted to say. She wasn't even fully sure what the conversation was going to be about. The producer had said he didn't want to over-prepare her so she could be "nice and natural." Nina was just praying that no one she knew would be up at 7:35 a.m. to see her on TV. Especially her mother.

"Nina Mistry?" A sound technician walked into the room. "We're ready for you."

Nina stood up, her legs barely supporting her. She was sick with nerves. But she could do this. She'd survived a night in jail, a breakup with the man she thought she'd marry, *and* living with her mum. What was a five-minute TV appearance in comparison? She allowed the technician to thread her mic through her mum's blue silk shirt and stared at the woman she'd be debating against. She was also Indian.

This was not ideal, considering one of Nina's backup "save the debate" points was that she was just expressing her personal opinion as an Indian woman. That would not work if there were two of them. Especially if the other one was wearing a killer red trouser suit with heels and looked like she won debates in her sleep. Nina looked down at her old white trainers and wished she'd thought to clean them.

Both women were introduced, then quietly led through the set and shown their seats next to the presenters. There were five massive cameras pointing straight at them. Nina's heart was beating so loudly she thought she was going to throw up. She tried to breathe her way through her nerves, like the book had taught her, but before she'd even finished one deep inhale, the presenters were introducing her.

"So, is it cultural appropriation to wear bindis? And should white people not be allowed to do yoga? We're going to speak to Nina Mistry, a writer for *Raze* magazine, who says yes, while Entertainment Films CEO Parvati Graham will be telling us why she's wrong."

A CEO?! Nina tried to keep focusing on

her breathing. This was fine. Totally fine. She just had to stay true to her points.

"So, Nina," asked the male presenter known for hating everyone, "you're against white people doing yoga?"

"Um, no, not exactly," she said, temporarily thrown by his blunt question. "I think it's great that yoga is so popular, with all people, but to me it is a real shame to see every yoga class taught by someone white. I just think we need to connect more with the Indian roots of it, and if possible, I'd love to see more Indian yoga teachers."

"Mmmm, interesting point," said the female presenter. "And what do you think, Par-var-ti?"

"Well, I think Nina's point is lacking," she said, sounding just like every report card Nina had received through secondary school. "Yoga came from the East, yes, but that doesn't mean it isn't for everyone. We adopt things from all cultures; that's just part of the way we live in an international era. It's absurd to think you can't do yoga or say 'namaste' because you're white."

"No, that's not what I meant," said Nina. "I'm just saying that people aren't crediting Indian culture. My point is actually —"

"To be honest," interrupted the male presenter. "I think I'm with you on this."

He winked at the TV. "It gives me another perfect excuse to ignore my girlfriend and stay as far away from yoga classes as possible. No downward dog from me, as you viewers will be glad to know."

"Thank god for that," laughed the female presenter. "But Nina, you've also written quite strong articles about wanting to see more brown people on TV. How do you feel about the new remake of *Sex and the City* featuring an all-Black cast?"

Nina smiled brightly, hoping to cover up the fact she wanted to crawl under the table and never leave. "So, I think it's amazing to see more diversity and representation with people of color on TV. But, to me, it's also a shame they didn't choose any brown or Asian actors. There've been quite a few remakes starring Black actors lately, which is obviously really great, but, like, where are the brown ones? Or East Asian ones?"

The female presenter nodded at Nina encouragingly, and she continued, warming to her topic. "I mean, I love #BlackGirlMagic, but, where's the #BrownGirlMagic in the entertainment industry? I feel like Hollywood's making a big effort to work with Black actors, which is amazing, but the number of brown actors they use is half that. To me, this just shows it's time to put the 'aim' back into 'BAME' . . . You know, because BAME means Black, Asian, and Minority Ethnic. So, the aim is great, but let's not forget the Asian and Minority Ethnic."

"I think we get it," jumped in the male presenter gleefully. "You've had enough with Black representation on TV, and now you want Asian people to have their turn."

Before Nina could take in what he had just said and correct him, the CEO began shaking her head aggressively. "I'm sorry, but this is just shocking," she said. "Like Nina, I'm also a British Indian, but I'm thrilled to see people of color on TV — whether they're Black or brown. We all need to stand together, and I really strongly disagree with divisive comments like these. Of course BAME is a problematic term, but if anything, it should be all about #BAME GirlMagic. Any progress should be celebrated, and we shouldn't dismiss, compromise, or stop fighting for the rising number of Black actors in the mainstream at all."

"I completely agree with you," cried Nina. "I love the progress, but I'm just saying that we should make sure other races aren't forgotten and —"

"Well, there you have it," said the male presenter, raising an eyebrow as he interrupted Nina mid-flow. "A diversity correspondent — and who even knew that's a job title these days — is saying there are too many Black people on TV."

10. I always try to speak my truth. Even when people don't listen.

Nina sat on her hotel bed in a daze. That had been a full-blown disaster. She had publicly humiliated herself on TV. Or rather, the presenters had publicly humiliated her on TV. Why, why, why had she ever thought it would be a good idea to try to express her views live on air? She could feel her phone vibrating, and she bit her lip as she thought of the inevitable comments on Twitter. Unless . . . there was a tiny 1 percent chance that it hadn't been as bad as she thought? That people had understood what she was trying to say?

She pulled out her phone. She had a message from her mum. I hope you're happy. That was a disaster. They're calling you racist on BBC Asian Network. A *racist,* Nina. How could you do this to us? After everything we've been through. And couldn't you have cleaned your trainers? They looked filthy.

Nina closed her eyes and moaned out loud. This was her worst nightmare. She was no longer someone giving an insightful opinion on something controversial; she *was* the controversy. And she'd officially gone viral, for being *racist.* It was unimaginably bad. Her phone vibrated with another text. Oh, thank god, it was Meera. Nina eagerly opened it up, hoping Meera would tell her she hadn't done as badly as she thought.

That presenter is a complete dick. Sorry if my yoga comments sparked this. I knew what you were trying to say. Ignore Twitter. Call if you want to chat xxx.

Nina's stomach plummeted. It was worse than she'd thought. She'd fucked up. Properly. Her phone vibrated again. What was she going to find now? A barrage of messages from her masis and mamas disowning her for bringing shame on the community? An invitation from the far-right British National Party welcoming her to their racist ranks? A message from Deepa banning her from future yoga classes?

It was Mark. Well done!!!! Can't believe you didn't tell us you had a TV appearance. All so proud of you in the office. Great points. Totes agree. He'd signed off with five thumbsups. Was he fucking kidding? He was an asshole, and Nina was never writing for him

164

again. God, why hadn't she just stuck to writing about pop culture? She wasn't the kind of person who could write insightful, society-changing articles about race, and she never had been; she'd lost every single debating competition at school, even the one about not wearing uniforms. This TV debate was exactly the same but with way higher stakes and a much harsher audience than a uniform-hating Year Eight. How had she ever thought that she could pull it off?

Her phone vibrated again. Nina stared at it in fear. There was a message from Jo, and it was really long. This was not a good sign.

Nina, what was that interview? I don't want you to get upset by this, but after watching you on TV, I've had a long and considered think, and I feel it's for the best if you aren't my bridesmaid anymore. I'm so sorry if it sounds dramatic. But as an ally to people of color, I just don't feel comfortable with your comments. And if I'm honest, I actually feel a bit triggered by your suggestion that white people like myself shouldn't do yoga. I'm hoping you didn't really mean it, and I don't want it to affect our friendship. But I don't have the headspace to engage with you on this right now. I mean, what were you thinking? Obviously you can still come to the wedding. But I just think you being bridesmaid will generate too much negative attention, and I don't feel comfortable with it. Hope you understand. X

Nina wished her response to this whole mess could be having a shower, putting on some red lipstick, and coming up with a clever comeback scheme where no one would ever misquote or misunderstand her again — like a sassy heroine in a post #MeToo movie. Instead, she was lying under the duvet with TV makeup running down her face, incurring late check-out fees she couldn't afford to pay, and obsessively reading the constant stream of online abuse flooding her social media accounts. This time it wasn't just anonymous right-wing accounts labeling her a stupid, ugly feminazi; left-wing people *she already followed on Twitter* were calling out her divisive racism.

One of the comments from a prominent left-wing MP — an actual MP — had over a thousand likes. What had she done? Nina stared in total shock as hot, sticky shame spread through her veins until she was numb with agony. It hurt so much she could barely even breathe. She didn't understand how to even process just how big this had all become. She'd managed to fuck up on a scale she hadn't known was possible — and it was getting worse by the second.

Her appearance had already been written about on every major tabloid website in the UK, and it was fast making its way across to American news sites too.

"Brown girl magic is over before it began," screamed one headline. "This brown woman thinks there are too many Black people on TV," said another. Even the *Guardian* had published a column titled "It's time to wake up to everyday racism — even when the perpetrators are of color." The author was a woman of color in her fifties whose career was so inspiring to Nina that she'd referenced her in every job interview. She'd almost reached out to her for help, then had reread the last line of the article — "More than anything, it's just the disappointment of someone on our own side letting us down like this" — and burst into disconsolate tears again.

It seemed like the entire Internet was against her. Everywhere she looked there were comments by people "astounded someone as thick and unattractive" as she could exist, and Nina couldn't stop reading them. How could she when they were expressing things that made perfect sense?

Like the Black journalist who said she'd "ridiculed the urgent need for better representation and more" and the blogger who didn't understand why she'd "wasted her platform and opportunity to make an actual difference at a time when every word and every action counts more than ever"; Nina was wondering the exact same thing. There were even tweets from prominent Black celebrities — including Nina's favorite-ever actress — condemning her comments.

#BAMEGirlMagic was trending, while the only comments about #BrownGirlMagic were negative. Nina's misguided attempt to make life better for brown people had completely backfired, and the more messages she read, the more she couldn't help but agree that she was "an ignorant waste of space who never should have been allowed a platform to spread hatred from."

She'd been so pathetic and stupid. She hadn't even fought back against the male presenter who'd misrepresented her views. And why hadn't she thought to quote any of the stats she'd put in her article or mention the experts she'd interviewed? That could have clarified her argument and helped get Parvati onto her side. But no, obviously Nina had failed to say anything intelligent or well-informed during her first and last TV appearance. Instead she'd actively offended millions of people around the world and "taken a step backward in the fight for equality."

Nina let out a ragged sob as the magnitude of what was happening to her sank in. She'd gone viral for the truly despicable act of promulgating prejudicial views that hurt people and had alienated her friends and family along the way. She'd failed as a journalist, a girlfriend, a bridesmaid, a daughter, a sister. How could she face any of her friends and family again? Nina choked on her grief as she realized she had no idea how she was going to bounce back from this.

Well. Maybe she didn't have to.

Nina suddenly pushed the duvet off her and started scrabbling wildly around the room until she found the £200 check the TV producer had given her for her appearance. The post-#MeToo heroine she wanted to be would rip up the check for the humiliation it had caused. But the real Nina was too poor and sad to do that. Instead she would squander what could be her very last journalistic paycheck on an extended hotel stay, room service chips, and as much alcohol as she could afford.

She switched off her phone and shoved it

under the bed.

It was time to numb the pain.

CHAPTER 11

The front door opened before Nina could even turn the key. "Oh my god, you're back," cried Auntie Trish, pulling the door open. "Thank god you're okay, beta." She crushed Nina in her arms, hugging her. "We spent all of yesterday waiting for you. We've been worried sick. Why was your phone going to voice mail?"

"I turned it off," said Nina, her voice muffled by Auntie Trish's pink chiffon scarf. "I wasn't exactly getting the nicest messages."

"Oh, don't worry about that," said Auntie Trish. "That presenter is a complete dickhead. He was putting words into your mouth. He barely even let you speak. He's awful."

Rupa appeared in the hallway in a widelegged denim jumpsuit. She looked coldly at her daughter. "I cannot believe you thought this would be a good idea, Nina."

Nina bowed her head. "I know. It was a really big mistake."

"Well," said Rupa, crossing her arms, "I imagine you've seen the coverage." She pointed to the kitchen. "It's in there."

Nina slipped off her trainers and followed her mum and Auntie Trish into the kitchen. There was a pile of newspapers on the table, all conveniently laid open on pages where she could see unflattering screenshots of her face on TV, mouth wide open, with various headlines about her abhorrent racist views. She slowly sat down, ready for her mum's lecture, and looked humbly at her hands. But her mum was silent. Nina looked up and was shocked to see that she was crying. "Mum, what's wrong?"

Auntie Trish had her arm around her. "Oh Rupa, it's okay. It'll all be fine."

"It's not fine," sobbed Rupa loudly. "It's everywhere. Everyone's talking about it. Everyone. My *boss* wants to know where you got those views from. All my friends have called to say they've seen it and to send their condolences. The man in the mithai shop brought it up when I went to buy gatya."

"Condolences?" asked Nina. "Isn't that a bit extreme?"

Her mum's eyes flashed. "Extreme? Like

your views? You don't know what this is like for me, Nina. I've worked for years to build up a reputation here after you-know-what happened. My family always makes comments about how I've brought you and your brother up alone, and all the mistakes I've made. It's hard enough trying to handle everything with Kal, without you making it worse by doing things like this, and then driving through town in a van with an old hippie wearing *beads.*"

Nina's mouth dropped open.

"After everything I've told you about dating spiritual men," cried Rupa. "Who can trust a man in wooden beads?" She shook her head vehemently. "Auntie Hetal has been gossiping about it for weeks, ever since she spotted you. Good timing, considering she'd just run out of things to say about you abandoning Nikhil. I *protected* you from that, but do you care? Oh no, you go on, making your disastrous mistakes everywhere, and now you've given them this TV nightmare to talk about. But what you don't realize is that by ruining your life, you're ruining mine. They all say it's my fault you've turned out like this. They blame me, Nina. They blame my poor mothering skills for you becoming a loose . . . mess."

Nina felt her own eyes watering. "But,

Mum, that's not fair. I'm sorry my mistakes are impacting you like this, but — I'm thirty. I'm a grown woman. My mistakes don't have anything to do with you."

Her mum laughed maniacally as Auntie Trish sent Nina a warning look. "Try telling that to your mamas. In our culture, your children are your children for life. They represent you, and as their parents, you're responsible for their successes and their failures. That's just how it works, whether you like it or not. So thank you, Nina. For ruining my reputation just as much as you're ruining yours."

Nina's face crumpled with emotion. "Mum, I'm really sorry. I didn't mean to."

"Oh, you never do, do you," her mum said, turning around to pat her face dry with a crisp white napkin. "It's never your fault."

"I'm sorry," said Nina helplessly. "I'm really sorry."

"It'll all blow over soon," said Auntie Trish kindly. "You know what it's like. Next week they'll be talking about how Pushpa-Ben turned up at the mandir in a sleeveless sari blouse with her fifty-year-old second husband. You know she's almost seventy."

Nina gave Auntie Trish a small smile as Rupa put the towel away and started tidying up the newspapers. She paused on the

Daily Mail, which had a headline above a photo of Nina's face reading: "Is this the face of millennial racism?" Rupa started to shake her head again. "I'm going upstairs. I need to rest. I haven't slept all night."

"Because you were worried?" asked Nina. "I'm sorry, I should have let you know where I was before I turned my phone off."

"Because I was heartbroken," said Rupa flatly. "I still am."

As her mum walked out of the room, Nina turned to look at Auntie Trish, tears sliding down her face. "This is really bad, isn't it?"

"Oh, sweetie, it'll be okay," said Auntie Trish, coming over to hug Nina. "You've learned your lesson now. And the TV thing wasn't so bad, really. You didn't say anything wrong. It just got taken out of context."

"No, it's all my fault," said Nina, collapsing her head onto the table. "I can't believe I said that stupid thing about putting the 'aim' back into BAME. I was just trying to sound clever, but I fucked up so badly. And why was I even trying to make it about brown people when I could have just celebrated the progress for Black people? God, I feel so awful, Auntie Trish. What have I done?"

"It's okay, sweetie," said Auntie Trish, sitting down next to Nina and patting her back. "I know what you were trying to say. Racism doesn't 'belong' to one group. It's as nuanced as the communities it affects, and there are ways to be sensitive without denying other valid experiences of it."

"Yeah, and I chose the most insensitive way," said Nina glumly. "No wonder everyone thinks I'm racist."

"I don't," said Auntie Trish.

"Really?" asked Nina looking up with red eyes. "You believe I'm not racist?"

"Of course, you numpty," said Auntie Trish. "You've got a police record for protesting against inequality."

Nina gave her a watery smile. "I guess so. I just . . . really hate myself right now."

"Don't say that. It was one mistake, and it'll blow ever. And at least you looked gorgeous." Nina scoffed, but Auntie Trish continued, "No, really, you did. I love what they did to your hair, curling it like that. I forget how lovely it is when you have it scrunched up in that messy bun all the time."

"Well, I look disgusting in the screenshots the newspapers have chosen," said Nina. "As the trolls are already telling me. In detail."

"Ignore them," said Auntie Trish sternly. "Promise me you will delete your social media, at least until this dies down. Nina. It will do you no good reading what those evil bastards write. Okay?"

"Jo doesn't want me to be her bridesmaid anymore. She feels 'triggered.' "

"Oh that bitch," cried Auntie Trish. "Triggered? How does she think her poor fiancé feels every time she vetoes another Hindu wedding tradition because she thinks the guests will find it boring? You know she's cut the ceremony part of the wedding so it's only thirty minutes. The priest is so shocked he almost canceled. Everyone knows it's an hour minimum — and the guests like it that way. It's the perfect time to gossip."

Nina put her head into her hands. "I've ruined everything."

"Stop with the self-pity now, Nina," said Auntie Trish. She stood up and started rooting around the cupboards. "You need some food. Does your mum have anything here that isn't birdseed?"

"I've hidden a stash of chocolate Hobnobs in the corner under the flaxseed. They should still be there."

"Bingo!" said Auntie Trish. "I'll put the kettle on."

Kal walked into the kitchen in his boxers and a maroon T-shirt. "I saw your TV thing on Catch Up."

"And?" asked Nina, as Auntie Trish tact-fully busied herself with the tea. "You may as well be honest. Everyone else has."

Kal sighed. "I know you care about what you're saying, but it does look a bit like you did it for five minutes of fame."

"That's not why I did it at all," cried Nina in shock. "You know it was about me trying to raise awareness of equal representation and, well, start difficult conversations. It just . . . backfired."

"Yeah, but Nins, you've got to think about what it's like for Mum," he said. "It's not easy for her."

"I know. But . . . don't I have to live my own life?"

"To an extent, but she's our *mum,*" replied Kal. "And for all her flaws, she's taking care of her two thirtysomething kids when she should be retired, traveling the world or whatever it is single women with grown-up kids do." He looked at Nina's crestfallen face. "It's not the end of the world, and I'm sure it'll blow over, but I just think you've maybe been a bit selfish about it all."

"Selfish?" cried Nina. "Me? I'm sorry, but that's a bit rich, considering the fact you're the one who barely leaves his bed while Mum does everything for you." She winced at the wounded expression on Kal's face, already regretting her words.

"Seriously, Nina? You're really going to go there?"

"No, Kal, wait —"

But her brother ignored her and walked out of the kitchen shaking his head. Nina stared after him, winded.

Auntie Trish quietly slipped a cup of tea in front of her, followed by the pack of Hobnobs. "Have some of these, love. Everything looks a lot better after a cuppa and a chocolate cookie. Promise."

Nina let the hot water of the bath soothe her muscles and her stress. She was so tired. The day had felt never-ending. She couldn't believe she had another one to get through tomorrow. It was normal for her mum to be furious with her, but she hadn't seen her this broken since she first heard about Kal's breakdown and had driven over to London to take care of him while he lay in bed, unable to get out of it to go to work. Nina felt awful to think that she'd been responsible for making her mum cry. And the fact that Kal actually agreed just made it all a hundred times worse. They'd always been there for each other when their mum was angry at them — they'd figured out as kids that the best way to beat Rupa was to join forces and make jokes until she rolled her eyes and gave in — but this was different. Kal was disappointed in Nina. So was her mum. And even though Auntie Trish hadn't said it, she knew she was too.

Nina slid down into the bath, and her tears dissolved into the soapy water. It all felt so surreal. She wished there was someone she could talk to. She wanted to call Meera, but she was scared of ruining her new friendship with her by being too needy — and what if she judged Nina too? She couldn't afford to lose the only +2 friend she had right now. Maybe she could call Jo; she'd been so amazing when Nina's family's life had fallen apart in Year Nine, patiently letting her cry until her tears ran out and knowing exactly when to break the tension with a joke. But then Nina remembered the message Jo had just sent her. Jo obviously didn't want to speak to her, not when the thought of her being a bridesmaid made her feel "uncomfortable."

Nina lowered herself farther down so her head was fully submerged under the water. She wanted to stay down there, where the sound was muffled and nothing felt real. Everything hurt. It was too much. When her breath ran out, she resurfaced with a gasp. The pain was too much. She couldn't stay here, bathing in her own shame. She had to get away. She needed to keep numbing the pain. She might not have the minibar of the Holiday Inn anymore, but she did have another source of distraction nearby. Nina reached over for her phone and dialed Alejandro's number.

"Come here, guapa," said Alejandro, gesturing across the van mattress for Nina to nestle up against his naked chest.

She breathed in the strong smell of his raw sweat. "Mm, thank you for today. I . . . really needed this."

"My pleasure," he said, bowing his head. "How are you feeling about the, uh . . ."

"Horrific fuckup I caused?" Nina sighed. "I don't know. It doesn't feel real. I just want to hide away till it all dies down."

"You know hiding isn't the best way to deal with things."

"I know, I know," she said, as she guiltily thought about all the lessons in the self-love book she was currently avoiding. "But I think I do need some space to . . . process it all. And then I'll go back to reality."

He nodded. "Well, like I said, you're welcome to stay with me for a night or two."

"Thanks," said Nina. "But I think that will just make my mum even angrier. And she's

181

already pretty angry." She rolled over to look at him. "She thinks I've ruined our family's reputation in the community by being self-centered."

"Self-centered? In what way?"

"I don't really know." She shrugged. "That I didn't think about how my TV appearance would affect them. Even my brother agrees with her. I guess they're right in a way — I was so caught up in trying to spread my message that I didn't think about the consequences for my family."

Alejandro nodded thoughtfully. "What about your father?"

"Um, well, he died when I was fifteen."

"I'm so sorry. What happened?"

"It's a bit *EastEnders* Christmas special," replied Nina.

"Whatever it is, you can tell me," he said openly. "I have a lot of family drama myself. My uncle is in jail for murder."

"What?" cried Nina. "Okay, that beats me. Is he in Colombia?"

Alejandro nodded. "And my father was a — how do you say? — womanizer. And abusive. So my mum brought me and my brother up alone."

"Oh my god. That sounds really tough."

"It was," said Alejandro, looking out of the van window. "But tell me your story."

Nina paused. Her mum would be furious if she knew Nina was confiding in the white beaded man. But Alejandro was proving himself to be a surprisingly good listener, and the more they connected with tantra, the more she felt she could open up to him.

"Suicide," she said quietly.

"That must have been very hard," said Alejandro, resting a hand on her arm.

Nina felt something inside her melt at his touch. She wrapped the blanket around her and looked up at him. "It was. After she . . . they . . . found him, my mum was hysterical; I'd never seen her like that. My brother was like this . . . pale ghost wandering around the house. Auntie Trish came over to help arrange things. And then, by the time we had the funeral — very quiet, with no one mentioning the S-word to our faces and very obviously gossiping about it behind our backs — Mum was in full-on organizing, capable mode. And she kind of has been ever since."

"Wow," said Alejandro, shaking his head. "And how were you? While your brother was lost and your mother was organizing her way through her grief?"

"Me?" asked Nina. She hesitated. "Do you want to know the truth? It's pretty bad."

Alejandro nodded.

"I was obviously devastated. I cried for months, but . . . a tiny bit of me also felt relieved. I know it sounds awful. But he was always so absent, and we couldn't run around or laugh or be silly when he was there. There was no lightness, ever. It was like living with a . . . Dementor."

Alejandro looked at her in confusion.

"Oh, it's a Harry Potter thing," she explained. "They suck the happiness out of everything."

"You . . . didn't miss him at all?" asked Alejandro, taking his hand off her arm to sit up straight.

"Of course I missed him . . . and the good moments. Like, when I was young, he used to set up a barbecue in the garden and grill plantains on there. It was so fun, and Mum didn't care about us making a mess because we were outside. And he'd take me for McDonald's sometimes, when Mum was getting Kal from football. He always let me get a Happy Meal and ice cream. Also, there's non-food-related stuff, like . . . oh, when we'd watch Leicester City matches. That was fun. Well, when they won. If they lost, he'd get all . . . distant again. I just . . . I don't know. I was glad the Dementor wasn't in our house anymore. But I was still heartbroken that he'd been that ill, that he'd gone."

She suddenly shook her head, sat up straight, and looked at Alejandro with an embarrassed smile. "Oh my god, I am so sorry. You did not need to know all of that in so much detail. I *really* need to remember that dead dads are not suitable postcoital chat."

"It's okay," said Alejandro slowly. "It's good to talk about things with honesty."

"I wasn't . . . too honest?" asked Nina, biting her bottom lip with a smile. "I know it's a lot."

Alejandro didn't return her smile. "I am a little surprised you make lighthearted comments about something so tragic."

"Oh, black humor. My very British way of trying to process the worst thing that ever happened to me." She smiled and shrugged. "Anyway, I've taken up enough of your afternoon with my tragic story, so I should head off. But thank you so much for all this. I really appreciate you listening."

"You're leaving?"

"Yep, got to be home for dinner. I feel like it's the least I can do after bringing so much shame on my family." Nina leaned over to kiss him. "But I've had a great time. It's so cool we can connect on so many levels.

You've really helped me take my mind off everything."

Alejandro frowned and turned away from her.

"Hey, is something wrong?" Nina asked uncertainly.

"I've done my job in distracting you," he said coolly, "and now you're going."

"Wait, what?" she asked, as Alejandro stood up, almost hitting his head on the van roof. He scowled and lifted up the blanket, looking for his clothes. "Hey, I didn't mean to offend you. I thought I'd said earlier that I couldn't stay long."

"I get it. You said it yourself — you need me to take your mind off everything. And that's it. I'm your Colombian distraction."

Nina's mouth dropped open in surprise. "No. That's not . . . it's not true. You're not just a distraction. I really like spending time with you."

"Well, it doesn't come across," he said flatly. "I've been making an effort with you. Whether it's making food for you or messaging you to share and hear about your life. But you never get in touch unless you want a distraction or your astrologer tells you it's a good time to orgasm."

"I'm so sorry," said Nina, trying to understand how everything had changed so drastically. "I just . . . I thought we were keeping it casual."

"Casual?" he asked in disbelief. "We've opened ourselves up to each other with tantra. Can you really just do that with someone it's casual with?"

"I . . . don't know," said Nina, suddenly feeling very exposed. "I thought you wanted casual; I mean, we had sex outside on the first date. And I'm not the only person in class you've slept with, am I? We only ever meet in the van or do stuff outside. We've never, like, gone to the cinema."

"So because we don't support capitalist and restrictive monogamous structures, we're not in a relationship?"

Nina pulled the blanket tight around her. "But we never spoke about us or the future. I mean, I've not been with anyone else, if that's what you're worried about."

"It's not," said Alejandro, pulling his hoodie over his head. "I didn't think we needed to spell it out. But it's okay, I'm not angry. In a way, you remind me of a younger me. I used to use people too. Being with you has taught me something. It is making me realize how I hurt all those women."

Nina blinked in confusion. She had no idea what was happening. Alejandro continued. "You're . . . immature. Because you're young. You treat men like toys because you can. It's obvious from everything you've just told me about your family. You're just a little girl searching for a new daddy. But I'm not going to be your daddy."

Nina felt like she'd been stabbed in the stomach. "Are you kidding?" she asked, finally finding her voice. "You can't say that. You barely know me."

He shrugged. "It's clear to me. You're selfish. Your mum and brother said the same."

Nina could barely speak. "But — I — no, I'm not."

"You just said you were glad when your father, your own flesh and blood, took his own life," said Alejandro. "That's not normal."

"What?" cried Nina. "No, no, it's not like that. You don't know what it was like."

"And you even make jokes about it," continued Alejandro, his voice icy. "I can't believe how cold you are, Nina."

She stared at him in shock, tears pricking her eyelids. "That's not fair. I must have explained it wrong." She thought back to what Jo's mum had said to her during their informal therapy sessions together. "It's my way of discussing trauma. It's a coping mechanism."

He raised an eyebrow. "To me, it sounds

like you just care about yourself. Even this incident on the television, you're only thinking about how it's affected you, and not the Black community, when they're the real victims of your comments."

Nina felt a sob rise up in her chest. "I'm sorry, I . . . I have to go," she said, shoving on her T-shirt and searching desperately for her Levi's. She pulled them out from underneath the driver's seat.

"You don't need to be sorry," said Alejandro, watching her calmly. "The truth is, you've been a gift to me. This whole experience. I'm so, so grateful for it. You've helped me learn a lesson about my younger self, so thank you." He looked at her with an apologetic smile on his face and brought his hands together in a prayer position at his chest. "But unfortunately, Nina, nothing like love for you has surged in me during this time that I've known you. I could never be in a relationship with you."

Nina's eyes were glazed with tears, but she managed to get up off the mattress and pull her jeans on. She had no idea what was happening, or how this had happened. All she knew was that she had to get out of there.

11. Nothing

~~11. I'm a fuckup and everyone hates me~~
11. *I keep going.*

CHAPTER 12

Nina lay listlessly in bed, the self-love book crumpled on the floor beneath her, wrapped up in the pajama bottoms she'd stolen it in. She no longer felt anything, and it wasn't just because she'd secretly been taking her brother's diazepam for the last six days. She'd cried so much lately that she was now fully numb. The entire Internet thought she was an ugly, poisonous idiot. Her family thought she was a self-centered, embarrassing child. While Alejandro thought all of the above and then some.

Meera had been incensed at the way Alejandro had spoken to Nina and said that he was a full-blown psychopath. She'd told her that he was just projecting all of his feelings about himself onto her. "He has zero right to tell you how you should feel about anything, let alone your own father's suicide," Meera had fumed down the phone. But Nina wasn't sure. Alejandro had been cruel to her, but it was because he'd been hurt by Nina's behavior. She'd been so wrapped up in her own life that she'd had no idea he'd even started to have feelings for her, and by the time it was clear, he was already breaking up with her. He was right — she was naive. And self-centered.

If he was right about that, he was probably right about it all. She'd never thought of herself as a little girl searching for a daddy before, but she *was* drawn toward men who made her feel secure. The thing she'd loved most about being with Nikhil was how safe she'd felt in his arms. And it was the same with Alejandro. Maybe she was just another basic bitch with daddy issues.

It felt weirdly good to focus on how awful she was. Instead of constantly trying to block out the negative voices in her head telling her she wasn't good enough, she could just sink into them. Because they were clearly right. It couldn't be a coincidence that every member of her family had told her she'd disappointed them at some point in her life and that she could count the people who currently liked her on one hand. She was the problem and always had been.

It was why she kept scrolling through the horrible comments about her on social media; she agreed that she was as pathetic and nasty as the *Guardian* readers said she was. It was kind of like self-harm — even though it hurt, there was something perversely calming about it too. Meera kept telling her to never read the comments, but that was advice Nina just couldn't follow. She needed to hear what they were saying about her, and she liked reading it. Besides, the hate had become so normalized to her that she was almost numb to it all now. Although that could be because of the packet of Kal's pills that she'd pilfered from the medicine cupboard.

She'd never taken meds for her mental health before, but when Nina had seen that Kal had been prescribed benzos alongside his antidepressants, she'd decided it was time for that to change. Her friends had taken benzos recreationally at university and raved about how they were the ultimate relaxation drug that made all problems go away. Nina had never seen the appeal — she'd much rather relax by eating a chocolate brownie; they were way less dangerous and so much more delicious — until now. She was in so much pain that she couldn't bear it. She just needed it to stop. She knew there were ways she could try and work through it, like meditation or whatever, but they seemed too difficult. And she was sick of trying so hard all the time. If her brother was allowed to take these beautiful, delicious pills that made all pain disappear until she was left with pure, calm nothingness, then why couldn't she?

Nina popped her second benzo of the day into her mouth — the packet said she could take up to two a day if symptoms were extreme — and waited for the next dose of numbness to kick in. The pills couldn't stop any of the thoughts going round in her head — "nothing like love for you has surged in me," the *Daily Mail* headlines, Jo's message, her brother's words, her mum's tears, and her loss of Nikhil, all interspersed with the incessant online abuse — but they could take away the feelings intrinsically attached to them. She was still aware of her humiliation and betrayals. But when the drug kicked in, she could no longer feel the shame and pain behind them all.

A knock on the door woke Nina up. "Come in," she said groggily.

Her mum walked in wearing a crisp linen shirt and indigo jeans. "Nina, I've let you have your week of self-pity. But this has gone on long enough. You need to get a proper job. It's four p.m. and you're in bed.

I already have one depressed, unemployed child living here; I can't deal with another one."

Nina looked at her mum blankly. These pills were amazing; she didn't even feel the urge to yell. "Sorry."

Her mum sighed. "Nina, please. If I can continue to show my face at work and with my friends after my daughter was shamed in the *Daily Mail,* then you can move on from this too. Don't you have some work to get on with?"

Nina shook her head. "I told Mark I'm not writing for *Raze* anymore."

"And what about the other places you used to write for?"

"They're not replying to me."

"Oh, Nina, it'll get better soon," said Rupa, hovering near her daughter's bed. "And if you can't get journalism work, then why don't you look for something else? There are always options."

"Like what?"

"I don't know, you're the one that wanted to do an English degree," said Rupa. "Why don't you try getting a nice, stable job in London? That'll be good for you. I don't think this freelancing is healthy. All this time alone in pajamas would make anyone depressed."

"I will find new work, Mum. I'm just a bit . . . tired now."

Rupa sighed, and Nina noticed wrinkles showing beneath her concealer. "Nina, please. This isn't the daughter I raised."

"Who's she?"

"Determined, hard-working, ambitious." Rupa put her hand on Nina's shoulder. "I want that daughter to come back. I know she's in there somewhere."

Nina looked at her mum's hand, and then the bedspread. "I just didn't expect any of this to happen. The work stuff. Alejandro. And I *still* miss Nikhil."

Rupa's eyes narrowed. "The man with beads? What's happened?"

Nina shrugged. "He got angry at me and ended things. He said I'm selfish. That I have daddy issues. I'm immature. Cold. Un-affectionate. Unemotional. I can't remember what else. There was a list."

"Well, you can be quite selfish and im-mature," said Rupa, sitting down gingerly on the bedspread. "But I wouldn't call you cold. Sometimes I wish you could be less emotional, to be honest. You seem to always have so many feelings."

"Thanks."

"Look, it's for the best. It wouldn't have worked out with someone like him anyway.

He's so much older than you. Not to mention the beads."

"I know," said Nina. "But it still hurts. It was my fault it ended too. I didn't . . . think about his feelings."

"Well, it sounds like it was his fault too. If he could list all your flaws to you like that."

"The trolls do it as well," said Nina flatly. "They keep telling me how stupid and ugly I am. They think my nose is disgusting. As is my skin. Hair. Face. People keep telling me they want to hurt me."

Rupa's face creased in worry. "Oh dear. You can't read those comments, Nina. It isn't healthy."

Nina shrugged. "I don't need to anymore. They're all the same. I can basically predict them now."

"You know, I did offer you plastic surgery when you were seventeen," said Rupa. "It's not too late, if you —"

"Oh my god, Mum! I'm not saying I want a nose job." She felt her eyes tearing up again. The drugs must be wearing off already. Maybe her tolerance was increasing.

"Oh, Nina, I didn't mean it like that. You know I think you're lovely. Especially when you make an effort."

"I just wish it had worked with Nikhil. I miss him. So much."

"He's moved on. He's with Karina. And it was your —"

"Decision, I know," said Nina. "But we were together for three years. How is he over me already when I still spend so much time missing him?"

"Just focus on your career. On . . . getting one."

Nina looked into her mum's worried eyes, trying to ignore the voices in her head loudly repeating the comments on her Twitter saying her career was over, she was a failure, and she would never ever succeed. "I'll try. Sorry."

Nina woke up in the middle of the night with a start. Only when she looked at her phone, she realized it was just eleven p.m. The drugs were making her lose all concept of time. She scrolled listlessly through her messages and emails. There was nothing new. Just more of the same. Meera had tried to call again a few days before, but Nina still hadn't gotten back to her. She knew she should, but the only person she really wanted to speak to was Nikhil. She couldn't call him. Or . . . could she?

She dialed his number before her rational mind could stop her.

He answered straightaway. "Hello?"

"Hey. Sorry to call so late. I just . . . are you busy?"

"Uh, no," he replied. "I'm just about to go to sleep. What's up? Are you okay?"

"I've just had a bit of an awful week. I guess you saw the whole me going viral thing?"

"Yeah . . . my mum sent me about a hundred links. She was loving it. Sorry."

Nina sighed. "Doesn't surprise me; she always hated me."

"She didn't hate you. She just . . . Okay, yeah, I guess she did. What happened though, Nins? Why did you say all that?"

"I didn't mean to," said Nina in a small voice. "I thought I was making an important point, but they twisted it. I meant to sound witty, not racist."

Nikhil let out a laugh. "Oh, mate. I liked your pun, if it's any consolation."

"It kind of is," Nina said, grinning. "I just . . . It's really good to hear your voice, Nikhil. I really miss you."

"Hey. It's good to talk to you too."

"Things have been a bit hard lately," admitted Nina. "My mum cried."

"Wow."

"Yup. And, I'm not sure if it's weird for me to tell you about this, but I also had a breakup with a guy. Well, not a breakup, because we weren't together. Or at least I didn't realize we were. But — he ended it, and it was messy."

"Shit, that sucks," said Nikhil. "It's probably for the best though."

"I guess. Sorry. I shouldn't be telling you all this."

"It's okay," said Nikhil, his voice softening. "Just try to ignore it all."

"There's just so much of it though," sighed Nina. "And the worst part is that I've been working on loving myself. And I was doing really well. Until Alejandro — and the entire Internet — told me all my flaws. Now I feel like I've taken a hundred steps back."

"I'm sure you haven't," replied Nikhil. "Everyone has lapses, but it doesn't mean you're not still going in the right direction."

"But I don't know how to keep going when everyone keeps telling me everything they hate about me," said Nina quietly. "How can I love myself when no one else does?"

"I don't know, Nina. I guess that's just life."

"Life," she echoed. "You're right. Anyway. Sorry. I shouldn't have called. I just . . . really missed you."

"I miss you too sometimes," he said

gently. "But, Nins, you know I am happy with Karina."

"No, I know, and I'm glad. Honestly. But . . ." She knew she should stop talking, but she kept going. "Does that mean you definitely think we made the right choice by breaking up? And that we won't ever, I don't know, get back together one day?"

Nikhil breathed in sharply. "Nina, I know you're going through a hard time right now, but this really isn't fair of you to say. I'm with Karina now, and you were right; you and I don't work as a couple. We're too different."

"No, I know. Sorry. I shouldn't have asked."

"Look, it's okay," he said. "I just think you need to work out what you want. Why don't you reach out to Jo or someone?"

"She de-bridesmaided me. But it's fine. Honestly. It was just a hypothetical. I'd better go. Thanks for chatting."

"Okay. Well, I hope things get a bit better for you," said Nikhil. "Bye, Nina."

Nina pulled the duvet over her head. She was just as pathetic as the comments on her social media said she was. An ugly loser who no man would ever want to touch. What had she thought Nikhil would say? Declare his

201

undying love for her and leave Karina? Then what — they'd get back together, and all their problems from the last three years would magically have disappeared? She might be drugged up on benzos, but she was still self-aware enough to realize that she was just reaching out to the last person she truly loved because she felt lonely.

It certainly wasn't fair to Nikhil, or to herself. She needed to stop acting like such a disaster. She was thirty years old; this just wasn't acceptable anymore. So a man (well, two) had broken her heart, and she'd possibly ruined her career by going viral with an opinion that was the exact opposite of what she believed. It wasn't the end of the world. She still had her health, a roof over her head, and a family who semi-loved her. Besides, like the self-love book always said, everyone was going to die. This had sounded depressing the first time Nina had read it, but then it made sense to her. If something wouldn't matter to her on her deathbed, then why should it bother her now? Yes, it was pretty fucking horrible that the world thought she was racist, but if she was about to die, she'd be thinking about her family and her loved ones — not the *Daily Mail.*

She got out of bed and start rummaging through the dirty clothes on her bedroom floor until she found the self-love book.

"The whole reason you're reading this is because you feel like your life is shitty," it said, as Nina nodded in desolate agreement. "But the truth is that often situations just happen, and we're the ones who decide whether to see them as shitty or amazing. Stuff happens to us and we see it as negative or positive. You get dumped — you see it as negative. You get complimented — you see it as positive. But when we label stuff all the time and see it through that lens, it affects our mood. The key is to just accept everything. Because, as the old man in Japan says, good bad who knows?"

Nina followed the footnote to the bottom of the page to read about said old man in Japan. It was a parable. The old man let his old horse go one day, and all the villagers told him they were sorry for his bad news. He said, good bad who knows? We need to wait and see. Then the horse came back, with twenty new young horses as well. The villagers said, well done on the good news! He said, good bad who knows? His son fell off one of the new horses and hurt himself. Villagers said sorry for the bad news. He said, good bad who knows? Then it turned out by hurting himself, the son escaped being conscripted in the war. Good news, said villagers. But this wise old man refused to see anything as good news or bad news; he just accepted it all as news, end of.

Nina read this several times. It seemed uncannily apt for her current situation. Everyone, including herself, was viewing her TV appearance as a massive disaster, akin to all the old man's horses running away. But what if it was a case of "good bad who knows" and something positive would come of this? Lying in her bed, wide-awake at one a.m., Nina wasn't fully convinced about the thought of a positive outcome coming anytime soon. But she did like the idea of not labeling everything in her life as good or bad. It appealed to her current semi-numb state. She didn't have to overanalyze and react emotionally to every little thing in her life. It didn't have to be a bad or a good thing. It could just be a thing. Life.

12. I'm learning to accept things just the way they are — good or bad.

CHAPTER 13

VIRGO SEASON

VIRGO
Season: August 23–September 22
Element: Earth
Themes: Organizing. Detail. Helping others.
Best time to: Sort things out and take action.

Nina had managed to climb out of both her self-pity and her pajamas. It was progress that no one in the Mistry family was taking lightly. Rupa didn't make a single comment about Nina not using a coaster for her Earl Grey on the glass table, instead silently placing one beneath the mug herself. Kal tactfully avoided mentioning his missing packet of diazepam. And Nina repaid them both by finally washing her hair.

"How's the job search going, then?" asked Rupa, as she hovered around the kitchen island where Nina was sitting with her laptop.

Nina raised an eyebrow. "Mum, I've been doing it for all of five minutes. And you can sit down if you want."

"Okay," said Rupa, perching on the high chrome stool opposite Nina with her *Daily Mail* in hand. "I just don't want to distract you."

"You're not. I'm just updating my CV. I've seen a few jobs I think I might apply for. And judging by the specs, I think I've got a good chance of getting them."

"Oh thank god," cried Rupa. "I was terrified you'd be living here forever. So what are they? Magazine jobs in London?"

"Um, they're actually mainly freelance opportunities," said Nina. "To edit websites and things. So . . . I'd still be living here."

"Oh well," sighed Rupa. "At least you'd have regular work again. Which is more than I can say for Kal."

"He'll get there, Mum. Is he . . . still in bed?"

Rupa nodded, and they both exchanged a sympathetic glance. "I don't understand how he can stay there for so long," said Rupa. "I just wish he'd get up, shower, go for a walk, call his old friends . . . He'd feel so much better doing something normal."

"I know, but it's not as simple as that. We have to just give him time."

"Time," said Rupa flatly. "It's been over eighteen months of *waiting.*" She cleared her throat and sat up straight. "But you're right. He'll get better. Of course he will."

The two sat in silence as Rupa flicked through her newspaper and Nina sent off job applications. She was trying to keep an open mind and apply for anything she was remotely qualified for. She couldn't afford to be picky now she wasn't working for *Raze;* she needed the money. Nina paused. *Raze still* hadn't paid her the money they owed her. It was ridiculous how long they were taking. She hoped it didn't have anything to do with the fact she'd stopped writing for them. Quickly, she typed up an email to Mark asking when she'd receive the money and pressed "send." But seconds later it bounced back. His email address wasn't working.

Her heart quickened. She wasn't sure why, but her gut knew something wasn't right. She opened up Twitter to Mark's profile and froze in shock. "So sorry to see such an amazing publication having to close. Thank you to all of *Raze*'s staff and freelancers. We couldn't have done it without you." Wait, *Raze* was closing down? How had nobody thought to tell her? She'd been working there for the last two years. In growing panic, Nina scrolled through Twitter until she found a link to a *Guardian* article. It explained *Raze* was going into administration, because it couldn't pay all its staff, and it was officially bankrupt. There were several quotes in the piece from panicked writers like herself wondering when they'd be paid. A comment from *Raze* suggested they wouldn't.

With a sick feeling in her stomach, Nina opened up her freelance spreadsheet to see how much money they owed her. It was £6,000.

"Oh god," she cried out.

"What is it?" asked Rupa, looking at her daughter hopefully. "You haven't got a job already, have you?"

Nina stared at her mum in panic. She couldn't tell her. Not after all the recent drama. Her mum would be so worried — and, worse, disappointed. "How could you continue working for a publication that wasn't paying you?" she'd ask. "And then let them exploit you by writing articles just to get cheap hits to their site? What were you thinking, and how are you going to pay your credit card debts now? Oh, Nina, you really need to grow up and start acting your age. You are thirty — how can you keep making mistakes like this?"

They would all be legitimate questions that Nina knew she'd have no answer to, because she was currently asking them of herself. How could she have been so stupid, to trust Mark's lies about the accountant? And how could Mark have let her keep on writing, all whilst knowing he couldn't pay her?

"Nina? What is it?"

"Uh, nothing," said Nina. "I'm just going to go out and take a walk. You know, fresh air. Good for the brain."

Rupa gave an approving nod. "Very good. You can pick up some almond milk on the way home. We're out."

Nina walked slowly through the tree-lined paths of Bradgate Park. She'd spent years of teenage angst roaming around these fields, ignoring her mum's *Crimewatch*-based warnings to not "ask for trouble by spending time in a park alone at night." But being in nature had always soothed her Taurean spirit, and today was no exception. It was her first time outside in a week, and in spite of the circumstances, it felt good to feel the warm breeze on her face.

Losing £6,000 was not a small issue. It was quite the opposite, especially for someone with a bank balance as low as Nina's.

Thank god she was living at home. But after so many days of crying and misery, Nina couldn't find it in herself to start sobbing or panicking hysterically. There didn't seem to be any point. When she'd left the house, she'd called Meera, who'd messaged her stepdad, and he'd done some digging. It had taken him less than half an hour to confirm that *Raze* had gone into liquidation and that Nina wouldn't be receiving any of her money. There was no point in trying to sue them or take legal action; they literally had no money to pay her with. And there was nothing Nina could do to change that.

Nina suddenly thought of the old man in Japan. It felt completely crazy to not see this as a bad thing, but she knew she needed to follow his advice and see it as just a thing. Ignoring the voice in her head shouting that this was a major fucking disaster — and so was she, having been so naive — Nina sat down on a park bench and began inhaling and exhaling deeply. After a while, she felt the tension from her shoulders dissipate. This was just a thing that had happened to her, and while it was unjust, and it would be hard to earn back the money, she could lessen the blow of it all by not reacting like the emotional disaster she used to be. Instead, she could just . . . breathe.

Sitting on that park bench, breathing and meditating her way through this latest in a long line of crises, Nina couldn't help but smile. Who could have ever predicted that she'd end up here, trying to channel a random old man in Japan? Ever since she'd picked up that book — in a jail cell, no less — her life had turned into the kind of bizarre sitcom that only got commissioned for one season. The book had brought her multiple orgasms and tangible capital-lettered Career Success — only to take it all away, with a bill of £6,000.

Nina let out a snort of laughter. She knew she wasn't meant to find this funny, but it was all so absurd. Meera had told her the universe liked to force people repeatedly into difficult situations until they finally learned their lessons, but this was next level. The way she'd been annihilated in the media, dumped by Alejandro, humiliated herself in front of Nikhil on the phone, used by *Raze* . . . The rejections were endless, but Nina still didn't know exactly what her lesson was. To love herself? Live in the present? Embrace her vulnerability? The universe was going to have to be a little more specific.

Nina shook her head and started laughing again. A woman walking past with a dog gave her a strange look. It made Nina laugh even harder. She knew she looked mad, but she didn't care. Everything was just so hilariously ironic. She, a brown woman who had finally found her journalistic voice when writing about racism, had gone viral for being racist. She was pining after the ex *she'd* broken up with. She'd been rejected by her lover for not being into him enough — when all along she'd been trying to stop herself from falling for him because she'd thought he wasn't into her. She, an A-grade student who'd never even got a detention, was out on bail. Alanis Morrissette had nothing on the irony in Nina's life.

Sitting on that park bench on a sunny afternoon in late August, Nina suddenly realized she felt calmer than she had in weeks — and it was all down to the book's advice. Instead of losing her mind about *Raze*'s closure, she'd managed to embrace chapter ten of the book, "Don't Resist Life; Accept It." When she'd first read it, none of it had made sense. You didn't accept rejections from your dream job; you used them to stoke your inner fire and blaze on with ambition. That was what her parents, teachers, and Hollywood movies had all taught her, and Nina had accepted it as a blind truth — until the book had preached the opposite.

But now she got it. She didn't need to try so hard to go against the tide; she could just let things be and learn to love her reality as though she'd chosen it. If she wasn't going to have success as a controversial columnist, she could just do something else. If it was truly over with Nikhil, then so be it. If she'd lost a whole load of money, then she'd start figuring out how to earn more. She could stop obsessing over fixing everything, and just move on. That was what the Keats quote in the book meant: "Receive the truth, and let it be your balm."

In that moment of mild post-benzo-comedown euphoria, on a park bench at eleven thirty a.m., Nina Mistry made a decision. She was done hating herself. She'd spent so long beating herself up for her flaws, but now it was time for her to stop resisting them. Instead she needed to accept them, to fucking *love* them.

Because if she didn't, who the hell else was going to?

When Nina arrived back home, her mum had gone to work and Kal was watching YouTube videos in his bedroom. She heated up an emergency frozen pizza in the oven, pulled out the chocolate cookie stash for dessert, and went up to her room to do some work. Lately she'd been half-hearted about adding to her list of things she loved about herself, and she had let weeks pass by without doing any exercises. But those days were over; it was time to stop neglecting her homework. If it wasn't for the book, she never would have managed to survive any of the recent events in her life. And she wouldn't have a slowly growing list of twelve things she loved about herself.

She pulled out the crumpled list from her wallet and beamed. It was all just so true. Like one of the first things she'd written on the list: *Sense of humor. I can laugh at a lot of things — including every single one of my many flaws.* It was uncannily appropriate for the situation she was currently in, meaning that the Nina who'd written it all those months ago was clearly a future-predicting genius.

Then there was number two: *I love how honest I am.* Nina clutched the list to her heart as she repeated the words to herself. She *did* love how honest she was, and reading this list — complete with its slightly naive and, yes, self-centered tone — she felt protective of herself. Her flaws and failures made her who she was, but this list proved it wasn't all negative. She had twelve very solid reasons for why Nina Mistry was lovable, and they weren't just bullshit things people had said to placate her. They were all real, all evidenced by her life, all chosen by her. Now she could add in a new one.

13. I'm stronger than I ever realized.

Nina spent the rest of the day alternately reading through the book and feeling guilty about her financial situation and madly applying for more jobs. But she still found the time to complete her favorite exercise in the book so far. It was all about gratitude, which was apparently the key to happiness. Instead of whining and focusing on the negativity in life, you needed to focus on the positive. Nina felt this was slightly contradictory to the idea of not labeling things as positive or negative, but she got the point; be grateful for what you do have and focus on that rather than on what you don't have. Her list of "Things I'm Grateful For" was two pages long. It ranged from detailed descriptions of her favorite food to her family — she'd listed them individually, even her mother — to things she'd previously labeled as negative, like her jail stay and the all-consuming abyss of heartbreak.

The next chapters were all about compas-

215

sion and generosity. Nina had reread them three times, because she knew this was something she had to focus on. The universe had made it crystal clear with the amount of people who'd been calling her selfish lately, and Nina was done ignoring her lessons. She needed to do more for other people.

"Helping others is the best way to fix your life when you're in a crisis," said the book. "It gets you out of your head and brings you the purest joy a human can reach: the satisfaction of helping a fellow being. Don't sit there dwelling on how shit your life is. Go find someone else with a shit life and help make theirs better. It doesn't matter if it's volunteering in an old people's home or just helping friends and family. No excuses; just do it."

It had made Nina realize, with a twinge of guilt, that she'd already had plenty of chances to do this right in her very home. But there was no point berating herself for that now. Instead, she was going to start rectifying her mistakes by helping the two people she loved most in the world.

CHAPTER 14

"Sorry, what are we doing here?" asked Kal, looking suspiciously at the shelves of blank pottery and tables of brightly colored paints all around him.

"We're painting pottery," said Nina happily. "Surprise!"

"This is really not what I thought you meant when you said you were taking me out for a surprise treat," sighed Kal. "I was hoping we were going to go to Chai Pani for lunch."

"Hey, this is going to be more fun than eating chili paneer, and you know I don't say that lightly. So what are you going to paint? I think I'm going to do a mug. Maybe with an inspirational quote."

Kal looked around at the plain crockery and then walked over to a dusty-looking shelf filled with figurines. "I like this one," he said, holding up a tiny dragon with a £3 sticker beneath it.

"Um, you know I'm paying for this. You don't need to pick the cheapest thing. You can do a bowl or a mug or something useful."

"I want to paint this one," said Kal simply. "It's nice."

Nina tried to hide her smile as her brother walked over to the assistant and very seriously began asking for recommendations on painting techniques. She had no idea if this was going to help him at all, but there was a section in her book all about mental health that explained the importance of play in battling depression — and he already seemed much more into it than she'd expected. It had a quote from someone called Andrew Solomon, who said, "The opposite of depression is not happiness but vitality, and my life, as I write this, is vital, even when sad." Nina had decided this was her new mission: to bring vitality and play to her brother's life. The book hadn't specified any exercises in particular, so she'd decided to start with the healing, therapeutic powers of arts and crafts. Specifically, pottery.

"This is kind of calming, right?" asked Nina hopefully.

"Mmm," replied Kal. He was engrossed in intricately painting his two-inch dragon.

They'd been there for an hour and Nina had almost finished her pint-sized mug — painted midnight blue with "Love What Is" stenciled onto it in white — but Kal had barely painted half of his.

"What's your dragon called?" asked Nina.

Kal looked up at his sister with raised eyebrows. "Nina, I know you want this to be some kind of art therapy, but it's not easy when you keep trying to check if it's working."

Nina bit her bottom lip. "Sorry. I didn't realize I was being so obvious. Or annoying. I'll shut up and let you paint."

"Oh, it's fine," Kal said, relenting. "I need to wait a few minutes for this layer to dry before I can add in the detail."

Nina smiled. "Okay. So . . . how are things?"

"As good as they can be when you don't feel like you'll ever be yourself again." Kal shrugged. Nina looked at her older brother with obvious concern, and he responded by pulling a face. "Nins, it's depressing enough being depressed. Let's not let it depress you too."

Nina made a face back. "Kal, I feel like you're always joking about everything, so I have no idea how you're actually doing. You know you can talk to me properly."

There was a moment's silence, then Kal looked up at Nina with a small smile. "Not great," he said, quietly. "I don't want to kill myself. I don't want to leave you and Mum. But sometimes, god, Nina, those urges are so strong. I just — it's not even rational. It's not about you guys. It's just so, so painful to feel this way that it seems like the only option."

Nina reached out to touch Kal's arm. "But what about the help you're getting? Your pills? Aren't they helping?"

He shrugged. "Sometimes. But sometimes I feel like they just make me so tired. Or angry. I don't know."

"Fuck, we need to get you better ones. What about therapy?"

Kal shrugged. "Sometimes it helps. Sometimes not. My therapist is really hung up on Dad."

"Really?" asked Nina. "What does she say?"

"Well, just the obvious. That your dad killing himself is bound to give you some issues," said Kal, looking down at his dragon. "She finds it weird that we never discuss it as a family. She thinks it's made it harder for me to actually process it, which means I have to do it now, all these years later."

Nina looked down guiltily at her mug. She

knew this was partly her fault; she hated remembering how gray and sad everything had been back then, so she avoided the topic as much as possible. But she hadn't thought about the effect her silence could have on Kal. "I'm sorry," she said softly. "I guess I just don't like thinking about it all."

"I know," he replied. "But it's not just you. Mum hated talking about him — she still does. She had that period of crying all the time after he died, then she just . . . clammed up, and that was it."

Nina nodded in agreement, then looked around the café, sparsely scattered with families and young kids painting pottery. "Well, you and I can talk about it now if you want?"

Kal shrugged. "I don't really know what to say."

"Do you miss him?"

"Yeah," said Kal. "I do. I know he wasn't that involved. But he was our dad. Do you remember how he used to take us to the park to play football when Mum was making dinner? And how we'd make him watch *The Jungle Book* with us all the time?"

Nina looked at her brother. "I'm not sure. I have some blurry memories of being in the park, but it's all so vague. Most of my memories are of tiptoeing around the house so we didn't bother him. I remember being sad when he didn't get excited about the Father's Day cards I'd make him. Huh, I guess that's why I stopped getting him cards."

"I guess you were younger, so you missed more of the good times," said Kal sadly. "He used to love football. And food."

"All right, I do remember some of it! The barbecues. The time Leicester did really well that season and he danced around the living room with Mum."

Kal laughed, then his expression became serious. "I know he stopped being that dad a long time before he died, but Nins, I hate that he's not here. Obviously I miss him, but also, I just . . . I wish we had a dad."

"What do you mean?"

"I've talked a bit about it in therapy. Basically the hardest thing for me wasn't even his actual suicide. It was afterward. I felt I had this pressure to be the man of the household, and not disappoint Mum, and go into this high-earning career to support her. But I didn't ever do it for me; it was to try to fit into this masculine ideal."

"Wow," breathed Nina. "I never knew you thought that. That must have been so hard. But you know Mum's never been desperate for your money. She's basically the queen of

Leicester real estate."

"It's not about the money. It was the man stuff. It wasn't even Mum who made me feel that way. I guess it was the uncles. They'd take me for an after-dinner whiskey and come up with all this stuff about stepping up and taking responsibility."

"Bloody hell," said Nina. "It sounds like something out of *Goodfellas.* You were only seventeen."

"You won't get it because you didn't have that pressure," Kal said dismissively. "You're the younger sibling, and you're a girl, so you got to study books and journalism and go into a low-paid career. No one cares that much if you don't do well."

"Um, seriously?" said Nina, with raised eyebrows. "I've felt pressure my entire life, Kal. To not disturb Dad when he was 'having a hard time.' To follow in your hallowed footsteps and get all As. To prove I could make it as a journalist. To be a daughter Mum can boast to her friends about. Non. Stop. Pressure."

"Huh. I didn't think about that side of things . . . Yeah, I guess we both had a lot of pressure."

"And still do," Nina pointed out. "Though the one good thing about me getting canceled by the Internet is that I've hit rock bottom. It's kind of liberating, in a way."

"I know what you mean, actually. I feel like that being so ill right now. Only at least yours is public; hardly anyone knows what I'm going through, because Mum keeps hiding it and pretending I'm still a big City success."

Nina sighed. "I know, it's so annoying. But it's just her way, Kal. It's the way she was raised; 'don't air your dirty laundry in public,' etc. I don't think she'll ever change."

Kal raised an eyebrow. "And I'm the dirty laundry? Nice."

"So am I, don't worry," said Nina. "But you know how you and I feel so much pressure? She must feel it too, trying to be perfect in everyone's eyes — to her friends, to the family. Everyone."

"It's true," agreed Kal. "Fucking hell. All of us need therapy."

Nina smiled. "Hey, I'm glad we spoke about this. Even if we probably should have done it, like, a decade ago."

"Yeah, but that was before men talking about their feelings was acceptable," said Kal. "Oh cool, my dragon's dry!"

"Wait a second. I have a favor to ask you. About Mum."

"Okay?"

"I think it's time to get her a boyfriend.

And I need your help."

Kal stared at his sister. "*What?* Have you asked Mum?"

"Not yet. That's why I need you."

"Uh, I'm going to stay out of this," said Kal, turning to his dragon.

"No, no," cried Nina. "You can't. She likes you more than me — you need to convince her to date."

"But she doesn't need to. She's fine. And we don't exactly need a stepdad. I'm thirty-two."

"I know, but it isn't for you — or me. It's for her. She's lonely, Kal. And she deserves someone great after everything with Dad. She's been single for fifteen years. But she won't do anything about it, because she's scared . . . and proud. Which is where we come in."

"Oh god. It's like *The Parent Trap.* But worse."

"I know." Nina grinned. "Can you pass me the glitter pen?"

Rupa looked at her two adult children proudly showing her their painted pottery and plastered on the bright smile she'd last used when they were ten. "Lovely. Very . . . sparkly, Nina. Make sure you put it in a separate cupboard from the Cath Kidston

225

mugs though. I wouldn't want a guest to have to use it by mistake."

Nina exchanged a glance with Kal. They'd had a bet that Rupa would tell them to hide their creations from any visitors within twenty seconds of seeing them. Rupa put on her glasses to peer closely at the dragon. "Oh, Kal, it's lovely. So intricate. It will look lovely in your room."

Nina rolled her eyes. It was typical of her mum to compliment Kal's work more than hers. But it was also true. Somehow, it turned out that her older former-banker brother had a knack for painting small fantasy animals. She elbowed him and gave him a pointed look. It was time.

"Hey, Mum," asked Nina, sitting up on the marble counter like she used to as a kid, swinging her legs, "how come you never dated after Dad died?"

"Because of you two," responded Rupa, turning back to the sweet potato and coconut dhal on the stove. She placed a lid onto it to stop the strong garlic and masala smell from escaping and turned the extractor fan on full. "I didn't have time, did I? And can you please get down. You're too old to sit up there."

Nina slid down onto a stool next to Kal and raised her voice to be heard over the fan. "Okay, but what about once we were older? It's not like either of us would have minded, right, Kal?"

"Not at all."

Rupa turned to look at her son. "Oh. Well, I didn't meet anyone, did I?"

"But you have to look for people if you want to date," said Nina. "They don't just land in your lap. I met Nikhil through an app. Why don't you try online dating?"

Rupa shuddered as she chopped up a cassava for the mogo chips. "Absolutely not. I can't bear the thought of all those disgusting men judging my profile and looking at me. No. I don't want to date strangers. Terrifying. And I'm too old. I'm nearing sixty."

"You're not too old," said Nina. "You're such a catch. I mean, you *are* an obsessive clean freak. But you're really attractive, and you dress amazingly, and you're super healthy. That's the kind of stuff men love."

"Which is why you could benefit from just buying a few new clothes," said Rupa, looking beseechingly at her daughter. "I don't know why you won't just let me buy you some new dresses. Something pretty, and floral, maybe."

It was Nina's turn to shudder. She glared at Kal.

"Mum, you know it's not too late," he offered. "You could try online dating now. Me and Nina could help you."

Rupa stared at her son in shock. "What?"

"Yep," said Nina. "It would be nice for us to do it together. To help you."

Her mum looked from one child to the other. "You two? Both of you? Spending time together?" They nodded in unison.

"Well . . ." She turned back to the mogo and sprinkled the wedges with chili powder. "I only want to date an Indian man. And there won't be any on those sites. So it won't work anyway."

"There might be," said Nina.

"No there won't," stressed Rupa. "They're all married, aren't they? No one gets divorced. I'll be left with the dregs."

"What if we find someone white?" asked Kal.

"I just don't think it would work," said Rupa, shaking her head. "Culturally, they're so different. I need someone who understands our religion, like why I fast on Thursdays. Someone who can come to weddings and garba with me."

"Okay, firstly, no one understands why you fast on Thursdays — not even god," said Nina. "And white guys love Indian culture! Like Gareth. He was obsessed with the food, the clothes. Do you remember when we took him to Veeraswamy's? I swear he liked it more than we do. And he always used to talk about how cool it would be to get married and wear a pink turban and ride in on an elephant."

"It might be different for men in your generation," said Rupa. "I gave up hope for me a long time ago."

"No, Mum," cried Nina. "Don't give up hope. You deserve proper love. Right, Kal?"

"It's true. You do, Mum."

"Well, I'm not going to go looking for it," said Rupa.

"What if we go looking for it for you?" asked Nina. "If we find you an appropriate date, will you say yes?"

"Oh fine," said Rupa. "It's not like there are any appropriate men my age in Leicester anyway. So good luck."

14. I'm incredibly persuasive.

Nina closed her laptop and collapsed into bed. She'd been up since six a.m. writing articles, and now that it was midday, she was officially exhausted. But she was happy. It seemed that her actions in trying to help her family were already paying off; karma had rewarded her with a job. She was the newest employee for *Goss,* an American

229

celebrity magazine that paid her to write about red carpet fashion and what A-lister was shagging whom, while they all slept. It wasn't the world's most exciting or well-paid job, but Nina was still thrilled. It was regular work, they were happy for her to take on extra weekend and evening shifts, and best of all, they seemed to have no idea she'd gone viral as a racist all over the UK. Nina calculated that if she did a shift every single morning including weekends, she'd earn her *Raze* money back in two and a half months. If she took on extra evening work as well, she might even have enough to finally move out of her mum's house by Christmas.

The only downside was that she no longer had time for a social life. But considering her newly reinforced single status and the fact she'd been demoted from being a bridesmaid, this wasn't really an issue. She'd been taken out of Jo's hen do Whats-App group, Elsie had sent her an empowering meme but never replied to Nina's follow-up asking to hang, and the only thing she'd heard from Gayatri was when she asked if Nina minded her going on a double date with her husband and Nikhil and Karina. She hadn't replied. The only one who seemed to care that Nina was now

230

AWOL was Meera, who'd protested about her new hours when they'd caught up over cake — but they'd vowed to arrange their schedules to meet weekly and keep in touch with old-fashioned phone calls. In the meantime, Nina was devoting any spare time to her mum's love life.

She pulled on the fluffy pink dressing gown she'd demanded for her fourteenth birthday and crossed the corridor to Kal's room. The door was slightly ajar and she could see there was a light on. She released a breath she hadn't realized she'd been holding and knocked on the door. "Can I come in?"

"What do you want now?" asked Kal, closing a serious-looking book he'd been reading as his younger sister bounded into his room and climbed onto the bed. "To make me a dating profile too?"

"Ooh, good idea," cried Nina. "The whole Mistry family can get them. We can take advantage of the fact we're all single at the same time and go on triple dates."

Kal winced. "No thanks. Sounds like my idea of hell. And that is weird we're all single. Do you think there's a Mistry curse?"

"Do not say that. I'm already finding it hard enough to find Mum an appropriate date."

She opened up an app on her phone to show Kal their mum's profile. "This is weird," said Kal, shaking his head as Nina showed him a selection of photos of their mum looking glamorous.

"I think the photos are going well," said Nina. "She's getting a lot of comments on the one of her in her off-the-shoulder dress, and there's a lot of likes on the one of her at Sunil Mama's barbecue. But no one's responding to any of the written stuff, about her hobbies. Shall we change them?"

Kal looked at what Nina had written: "I love all things healthy, from cooking low-fat food to doing yoga. Appearance is really important to me, which means I love dressing up, and I'm a huge fan of Marie Kondo's tidying tricks."

"You're joking," said Kal. "Of course no one is replying to this; she sounds like Mary Poppins."

"Well, she's actually had fifty-five messages."

"That's loads," cried Kal. "Surely one of those will do?"

"Um, not really. That's the problem. Most of them are really gross-looking, and the only normal ones just want to shag her."

"Okay, I literally can't have this conversation," said Kal, pushing his sister out of the bed.

"Sorry, sorry, I'll rephrase. I think quite a few of the men on here are looking for something more casual. But that's not even the biggest problem. None of them are really, um, her caliber."

"In what way?"

Nina showed him the photos of their mum's suitors. "In every way. They're the same age as her, but they look about twenty years older. She's just . . . better than them."

"Why don't you try younger men?" suggested Kal. "They probably take care of themselves more. Go to the gym and stuff. Maybe even yoga."

"There's no way Mum will date a younger man."

"She would," said Kal, reaching for a Post-it note. "She wrote me a dating checklist: Decent job, over six feet, good teeth, no bald patches, Indian, aged forty-five to sixty-five. There you go."

Nina tried not to think about the fact that Alejandro fit into her mum's dating age range. "Um, why did she give you that checklist, not me?"

Kal shrugged. "I thought you just wanted her to be happy."

"Oh fine. Here we go, forty-five it is." She

started scrolling dubiously and then grinned happily. "Hey, the quality of men is already better. Good shout, Kal. What about this guy? Good job, good looks, and he likes doing yoga."

"Nice. But he's got crooked teeth."

"Oh, I didn't see that. This one? Oh no, wait, bald patch. Oh my god, Kal! Look at this one! He just messaged. Devon. He's a property developer — okay, nice, they can talk about houses if all else fails — he's attractive, tall, great teeth, brown, and I feel like he has good stepdad vibes. And he's . . . forty-five."

"It's only fourteen years younger than her. That would be nothing if it was a man with a younger woman."

"And look how cute his message is," cried Nina. "He says Marie Kondo revolutionized his sock drawer."

"I like that. It's better than a 'Hey, how are you?' anyway."

"True. Oh no, he's sent a photo. I can't look! What if it's a dick pic?"

"Then there is no way I am looking either," said Kal firmly. "It's even worse for me."

"No it's not, you have one," said Nina. "Let's just do it together on the count of three, okay?" Kal sighed in agreement, and the two siblings hunched up on the bed, hiding behind a duvet, and held up the phone.

"Okay," said Nina. "Here goes. One . . . two . . . Oh, thank god, it's just a photo of his sock drawer. Wow, he's color-coordinated them too. Do you think if he married Mum, he'd do mine?"

CHAPTER 15

"So as much as I'm loving hearing about your mum's dating life, I feel like we should talk about how everything's going for you," said Meera, as she dipped her carrot into hummus. "The last time we spoke about the, uh, incident that shall not be named, you were getting a lot of hate from other journalists of color. Is that still going on?"

Nina groaned loudly and rolled over on the grass. They were sunbathing in plain sight in Abbey Park, and — in spite of the fact that any old masi ba could see them — they'd stripped down to their bikinis. Nina didn't care; her reputation was already rock-bottom, and Meera's sexuality apparently meant no one was shocked by anything she did anymore. "Do we have to talk about it? I'm trying to pretend it's not happening."

"Hey, Nins, I know this is affecting you," said Meera, sitting up and causing an old lady in a sari and trainers to pause in shock at her bright blue sequined bikini top. "You're allowed to be struggling right now. I would not be okay if I was in your position and my fellow BAME colleagues hated me. Let alone with the kind of disgusting abuse you're getting."

"You're right," admitted Nina. "I fucking *hate* that I've alienated people I was trying to support. I feel horrible. But I don't know how to fix it. I've tried to apologize to some of them individually. But they keep saying that my apologies are meaningless and the damage is done."

Meera looked at her sympathetically. "I'm sorry, Nins. It sucks that everything is so — excuse my pun — black and white these days. There should be space for people to have complex conversations about things like race so people can question beliefs and not feel scared to talk about difficult issues in case they get canceled, like they've done to you."

"Yup," said Nina. "I've learned my lesson; never talk about race again."

"I don't think that is the lesson. Or at least it shouldn't be. I don't know, maybe you can use this as a chance to help others by admitting you got it wrong, but that you're learning? And that you still agree with your message about improving overall representation, but you messed up with the details? I think that being vulnerable and honest is the only way out of something like this."

Nina nodded thoughtfully. "Yeah, maybe you're right. I know I need to say something more than 'I'm sorry' to the people I've offended, but I guess I'm scared of putting more words out there in case I do it wrong again. It's so much safer to just write about celeb scandals for *Goss.*"

"Of course it's scary, but if anyone can face their fears, it's you," said Meera. "Especially now that you're finally off the diazepam."

Nina lifted up her sunglasses to squint at Meera. "God, they were so good. They made everything feel so much easier."

"Yes, which is why benzos are some of the most addictive drugs out there! Thank god you managed to stop taking them. They're really dangerous, Nins, and even people who are actually prescribed them are only meant to take them short-term. Why don't you try some ashwagandha root instead? Sarah swears by it."

"Um, maybe another time. But hey, thanks for the advice. No, not about the root, about the race stuff. I think I will say something online. I'm learning that there comes a point where you have to take responsibility for yourself, you know? I'm bored of blaming everyone else for my problems. It's like the book says — I need to be my own best friend and have my own back, because if not, who else will?"

"It's so true," said Meera. "You've got to be your own soul mate."

"Yep. I'm not totally there yet but, you know, work in progress." She rolled onto her front and picked her black bikini bottoms out of her bum. "So how are you and Sarah? Your Insta stories in Margate the other week were so cute."

"Yeah, it was fun. But if I'm honest, the passion is kind of going, Nins. I love Sarah, I really do, but I feel like we're growing further apart . . . I don't remember the last time we stayed up late just chatting, like we used to when we first got together."

"Oh, I didn't know you felt like that," said Nina, pulling herself up onto her forearms to look properly at Meera. "I'm sorry. Do you think it's fixable?"

"I don't know," said Meera uncertainly. "I always knew it would be hard when she has so much fire in her birth chart. But it's harder than I thought."

"I always thought relationships were meant to be hard. It's why I kept trying so much to make things work with Nikhil, even when I had doubts. But the self-love book says that things *can* be easy in relationships. You don't always have to choose the hard path."

"But is that feasible long-term?" asked Meera. "Don't they always get hard, no matter how 'right' they are?"

Nina shrugged helplessly. "I have no idea. The book didn't say. But from my experience, you normally know the answer deep inside. And if you don't know it yet, it's probably because you need more time. But if anyone will do the right thing, it's you, Meera."

Meera tilted the crisp packet into her mouth and sucked up the remnants. "Ah, you're right; I guess I need to get honest with myself."

"Welcome to the club."

Meera wiped the crisp dust off her mouth and then looked at Nina. "Also. Don't freak out, but I have a present for you. To cheer you up after the last few weeks."

"Ooh, what is it?" asked Nina. "Chocolate?"

"Better. It's a date. Or, to be more specific, a selection of dates."

"Um, what?"

"I got inspired by you setting your mum up. So I made you a dating profile."

"Oh my god," cried Nina. "You didn't! Show me!! Ooh, I have matches!"

"Obviously. You're a catch. Now you just need to say yes to one of them. How about Harveer? He's cute. And he's a Scorpio."

"Mm, he's five feet seven."

"So? You're only an inch taller."

"I know," said Nina. "But I am my mother's daughter, and she has a six-feet-plus rule."

"I thought you hated how judgmental your mum is, Nina. Come on. Imagine if someone was so dismissive of something you were born with that you couldn't control."

"But I prefer tall men," Nina said, shrugging. "Hey, what do you call a man under six feet?" Meera didn't respond, so Nina continued. "A friend!"

"That's not funny," said Meera, crossing her arms. "Imagine if someone was making that same joke right now about dating women of color, or larger-nosed women. It's discrimination, and it's unfair."

Nina opened her mouth to disagree, then looked down at the grass, chastened. "You're right, sorry."

"You don't need to apologize to me," said Meera. "I just think it's important to not perpetuate unfair beauty standards."

"Me too," agreed Nina. "I'm glad you said something. And you're right. I'm going to work on being less judgmental, and I will *never* make a heightist joke again."

"Cool. So how about Dylan? He's cute, he likes books, and most importantly, his message is grammatically correct."

"Oh, so we're allowed to be judgmental over grammar?" asked Nina as Meera threw her a withering look. "Okay, okay, let's say yes to Dylan. I like his man bun."

15. I'm always growing and learning. My
     life is the ultimate work in progress.

Nina and Rupa stood in the hallway putting on their jackets.

"You really do look amazing, Mum," said Nina. "If ever you get bored of that black dress, feel free to give it to me."

"You're sure it's not too dressy?" asked Rupa anxiously. "Trish chose it. I've tried to make it more casual with my heeled boots."

"Honestly, Mum, it's great. And you're going to a fancy wine bar. It's ideal."

"If you're sure," said Rupa. "God, I can't believe I'm doing this. And he's so young. Are you sure he knows how old I am? I feel sick."

"He's going to love you," said Nina firmly. "Trust me." She paused. "Also, I think it's really brave you're going on this date. I know it's a huge deal for you, and after being single for fifteen years, I mean . . . I think it's really great. That's all."

"Yes, well. It's just a glass of wine. We'll see how it goes," said Rupa, turning to look at her daughter. "Are you sure you want to wear jeans and trainers? Nina, you really should make more of an effort."

Nina rolled her eyes. "I'm fine. I'm only going to the pub; my date isn't as fancy as yours."

"Yes, it's a shame," said Rupa. "KAL, I'LL BE HOME AT NINE P.M. LATEST. BEETROOT BURGERS IN THE OVEN." She looked at Nina anxiously. "He's stopped shaving his beard lately. He's starting to look homeless."

"Hey, he'll be fine, Mum," said Nina firmly. "He's excited for you, remember? And he always seems a bit worse when they change his meds. You know the transition period isn't easy."

"I suppose so," sighed Rupa. "I just wish he was the one going on a date."

"I know," said Nina, slipping a black leather jacket on over her cream halter top. "But hey, two out of three Mistrys isn't bad.

And Kal will get there soon. I reckon his beard will help; he's got that hipster vibe going on."

"Maybe if he trimmed it. I'll see if I can convince him to go to the barber."

"Sure," said Nina. "But for now, try and just focus on your date, okay? You're allowed to have a child-free night."

"Oh, all right. Now, come on. I don't want to be late. I'll drop you off at your pub en route."

"Ah, I love that we have dates on the same night! Isn't it cute?"

Her mum shot her a look. "Cute is *not* the word I'd use."

"Oh, don't be so negative, Mum," said Nina, putting her arm around her. "We could be about to meet the loves of our lives."

It was patently obvious that Dylan was not the love of Nina's life. He was wearing some kind of leather loafer ensemble that looked like a school shoe, his loud floral shirt seemed completely at odds with his unassuming personality, and she was pretty sure he was missing one of his front incisors. Nina didn't want to be judgmental, but she couldn't deny that no part of her fancied him. And it wasn't like the conversation was

244

any better; he'd spent ten minutes telling her how difficult his journey to the pub was.

She desperately hoped her mum's date was going better than hers. She'd texted both her mum and Kal a series of ????s to ask how Devon was when Dylan had gone to the bar for her whiskey and his rosé, but neither had replied.

"Nina? What do you think?"

Nina jumped, realizing she'd been so engrossed in staring at his missing tooth that she'd stopped listening to him. Had he lost it in an accident? Was he going to get a new one? She had so many questions. "Sorry, I got distracted by, uh, nothing. What did you just say?"

"I asked about your work," said Dylan, leaning forward on the table. His floral shirt shifted to reveal a patch of sparse chest hair. "You're a journalist, right?"

"Oh, yes," she replied brightly, trying to make up for her rudeness. "I write about celeb news and pop culture for a website in the US. *Goss.* What about you?"

"I have to confess," said Dylan, smiling oddly at her as he ignored her question. Nina noticed curiously that the rest of his teeth were in perfect alignment; maybe the missing tooth was an orthodontal mistake? "I actually know who you are."

Nina's smile faded. "Oh? Because we have, um, mutual friends?"

"No, I've seen you on TV," said Dylan, with an apologetic grin. "And I used to read your columns on race. I've actually, uh, messaged you about them before."

Nina shut her eyes in shame. She should have known this would happen. Of course her date had seen her go viral. How humiliating. Then she opened her eyes. "Wait. Did you say you've messaged me? What do you mean?"

"Well." He laughed. "You never actually replied to me. But I messaged you some thoughts about your articles on Twitter. I did it back with your first one, before they all went viral, so you might have seen it? Then I sort of got in the habit and messaged you about the others as well."

"And . . . what kind of comments did you write?" asked Nina. "Positive ones?"

"Oh, you know, just general opinions. I don't always agree with you, so I'd explain that to you on social media."

"Oh my god, you've *trolled* me?" cried Nina.

"What, no! I'd never write, like, rape threats and shit. I'm not a psycho. I just explained to you what was wrong with your arguments. That's not trolling; it's debating."

Nina didn't know whether to laugh or cry. Instead, she downed her whiskey. "Look. This feels a bit weird."

"Don't be offended, please," said Dylan. "I matched with you because after you didn't reply to my messages I was really hoping to hear more about your views. I thought we could have a bit of a debate. You know, opposites attract and all that."

Nina stared at him in disbelief. How had she ended up on a date with one of her online haters? This was a complete, unmitigated disaster. She'd been through dozens of possible outcomes for this date — ranging from the bad (being catfished) to the even worse (being stood up) — but even she'd been unable to envisage something as grim as this.

"Um, I'm not sure I'm in the right headspace for a debate," she said finally. "I was more in a date mindset. I think I'm going to go."

"You've only been here twenty minutes," said Dylan, looking at the time on his phone. "Are you sick of me already?"

"No, of course not," cried Nina, inwardly berating herself for trying to protect his feelings when he clearly had no regard for hers.

She wondered just how bad his comments had been; was he one of the people calling her stupid? Ugly? A brown whore? "I'm just feeling a bit . . . dehydrated."

"Dehydrated?" He raised an eyebrow, and Nina wished she'd thought of a better excuse. "Maybe you should have some water or something. And didn't you say the next round is on you?"

Shit. This was why Nina hated men buying her drinks; she always felt indebted to them until she evened the score. "Fine. Do you want the same?" She looked at his glass and realized it was still half full.

"In a bit," he said. "So, were you serious when you came up with that brown girl magic shit?"

Nina winced. "It came out wrong. I am pro representation for all people of color, and that's it."

"But what about white people?" asked Dylan. "Surely true equality is where we don't have to go on about brown or Black people's rights, and we just talk about people as a whole?"

Nina's mouth dropped open. She'd presumed Dylan and his man bun were part of her left-wing haters who thought she was creating toxic divisions in the BAME community. But now she was starting to realize he was on the other side. The racist side.

Eventually she spoke. "No. True equality happens when you help the inequal parties first. The ones who are facing discrimination and bias and worse. It's like how we need feminism for equality, because for centuries women *haven't* been equal in this patriarchal world."

"But then shouldn't we call it equalism, not feminism?" asked Dylan. "Otherwise it creates divides and leaves men out."

"No," said Nina slowly, trying to process the fact they were actually having this conversation. "We need to lift up the people who've been marginalized first. And that's not men. Or white people."

"Well, not according to your article on yoga." He arched a brow. "You're marginalizing white people, saying they shouldn't teach yoga. And, just to play devil's advocate here, surely by making those divisions, you're paving the way for more groups to get discriminated against?"

"That's not what I was saying," said Nina, wishing she had more whiskey. "I was making a point about cultural appropriation. We need to be respectful about other cultures, especially those who've been treated badly in the past. It's not fair that white people can pick and choose the bits they like about other races, like — love bindis, love hip hop, hate that skin color."

"You say that now," said Dylan, taking a tiny sip from his wineglass. "But what about that article you wrote saying white people shouldn't fetishize people of color, saying they only fancy Asians? That's the exact opposite of cultural appropriation; they're appreciating people of color. So, why's it wrong?"

Nina stared at him in confusion. He was twisting her words and making no sense. "You can't fetishize races like that. It's ignoring the fact we're 3D humans and just making us into exotic stereotypes, or whatever. It's racist."

"Racist!" cried Dylan gleefully. "Racist for me to be here on a date with an Indian woman and fancy her? But it would also be racist for me to say I never date Indian women?"

Nina couldn't believe she'd spent fifteen minutes doing her makeup for this guy. He was probably an incel. "Look, I'm not in the mood for this," she said. "I've said everything I believe in my articles. If you don't agree, that's really not my problem."

"Hey, chill," said Dylan, raising his hands in the air. "It was just a friendly debate."

"Yeah, and I was hoping for a date, not a

debate. Just because I'm Asian and you've got questions about race, it doesn't mean I have to answer them, okay? Go read a book or something."

"I wasn't asking because you're Asian," said Dylan. "It was because you wrote about them. But point taken. I *promise* I'll stop talking about race. It's your round."

Nina sighed as she went off to buy her real-life troll a drink. This night was proving to be a serious waste of contact lenses.

Nina and Kal were slumped on the sofa watching *Friends* reruns when they heard a key in the door. "Finally," cried Nina, as their mum walked into the living room. "This is not nine p.m."

"Oh, don't be such a bore," said Rupa, breezily peeling off her camel trench coat and elegantly reclining back into the gray velvet armchair. Nina looked down at her own outfit. She'd immediately changed into a pair of her brother's pajamas bottoms, and they were covered in chocolate Hobnob crumbs. She brushed them into her hand before her mum noticed.

"So?" asked Nina, subtly swallowing the crumbs. "We need a full debrief. We've been waiting for hours. How was it?"

"I'm guessing you had a good time?"

251

asked Kal.

Rupa smiled. "Oh, yes. I mean, he was nothing to write home about. But he was a real gentleman. He paid for my champagne — it was a special organic one, really delicious — and he was tall. Good teeth. His shirt was Ralph Lauren."

"He sounds like your dream man," said Nina. "What was wrong with him?"

"Well, he's never been married," explained Rupa. "Even though he's forty-five. It's a bit strange. I expected him to be at least divorced, if not with kids. But he doesn't have any."

"There goes the stepsiblings dream," said Kal.

"He was very complimentary though," continued Rupa. "He couldn't believe that I'm fifty-nine. He thinks I look twenty years younger. I showed him a photo of you, Kal, and he's astounded I'd have a son as old as you."

"Why didn't you show him a photo of me?" asked Nina.

"I wasn't going to bore him with the entire family album," said Rupa. She looked at Nina, her eyes narrowing. "So, how was your date? It looks like you've been home for hours."

"Um. It's hard to explain."

Rupa waited expectantly.

"He . . . wanted to debate my articles," said Nina eventually. "He'd read them. And seen me on TV."

Rupa shook her head. "Well, that's what happens when you put your opinions everywhere. I've told you, Nina; men don't like such an opinionated woman."

"I think he actually wanted me to be more opinionated," said Nina. "I had to drown my sorrows in whiskey."

Rupa shuddered. "I don't know why you have to order such manly drinks. No wonder these men don't like you."

"So, Mum, are you going to see Devon again?" asked Kal, and Nina shot him a grateful look.

"I don't think so," said Rupa.

"What, why?" cried Nina. "He sounds amazing."

"He's only my first date," said Rupa. "I'm not going to settle for the first man who comes along in a Ralph Lauren shirt. Besides, as I said, never trust a man who's not married by forty."

Nina stared at her mum, speechless. Just then her phone vibrated. It was a text from Dylan. Hey. I had a good night, but I just wanted to let you know I don't really feel any chemistry between us. You're really great, but you're not for me. So best of luck on your romantic search. Happy to be friends though x.

"Wow," said Nina aloud. "My date just said he isn't into me, but he's happy to be friends."

"I guess you felt the same way though," said Kal. "So it's not so bad. Right?"

Nina sighed. "I just thought it would be me who rejects my trolls, not the other way around."

"Can you show me the message?" asked Rupa, putting on her glasses. "It sounds like just the thing I need to send to Devon."

CHAPTER 16

LIBRA SEASON

LIBRA
Season: September 23–October 23
Element: Air
Themes: Justice. Friendships. Beauty.
Best time to: Come up with balanced
  solutions to problems that seem impossible.

Nina sat on the pier, her legs dangling barefoot over the sea and the wind blowing her hair into tangled knots as she ate the last of her vinegar-drenched chips. She knew she shouldn't be grateful for global warming, but she loved that it was sunny enough to go to the beach in rolled-up Levi's and an old T-shirt in late September. It had been a last-minute decision to come to Margate, and the British seaside town was as cute as Meera had promised, with its vegan cafés, brightly painted wooden shop fronts, and wide beaches.

Like most good things in her life, she was there because of the book. She'd read a chapter all about guilt and realized just how much this feeling plagued her life. Whether it was about something big like her TV fuckup or just skipping Deepa's yoga class, a voice in her head constantly berated her for doing the wrong thing. Nina had always thought the pressure that had pervaded her whole life had come from her parents, but the truth was that most of it came from her own mind. She was her worst enemy.

"You can control your mind," said the book. "You don't have to let it continue these patterns or keep repeating unhelpful messages you received when you were growing up. Just tell your mind to shut up. Give it a name if you want. Call it Susan and tell her off whenever she starts criticizing you. Because you don't need to criticize yourself, ever. It's not helpful. Not when we already receive so many negative messages from the outside world. Instead, try to change your self-talk and let go of the guilt. It's in the past. Move on."

It had made Nina realize just how much she'd let Susan ruin her life. Even though she was trying to accept her mistakes, she still felt guilty that she'd lost so much money and caused so much stress for her family. Her mum was still dealing with the repercussions of her viral fuckup; the Lakhanis hadn't invited her to their dosa garden party, in what she was interpreting as a deliberate slight. Nina felt guilty for making her mum's life even harder, especially when Kal had spent the last week in the same gray tracksuit, shutting himself away just like their dad used to. Nina felt guilty about this too; why was it Kal who was so ill, when she wasn't?

But after rereading the relevant passages, Nina realized that feeling guilty all the time wasn't going to make anything easier. In fact, it did the exact opposite. So, in a burst of inspiration, she decided to do the most guilt-inducing thing she could think of: tell Susan to shut the fuck up and book herself a solo minibreak.

She didn't have the budget to go soul-searching in Southeast Asia, but she did have £12.50 for an off-peak train ticket to Margate. Well, she did after she asked Nikhil to pay her back for their TV license. But just because her first holiday alone was in England didn't mean she wasn't doing it properly. Nina had booked herself into a seafront Airbnb. It wasn't exactly luxury — she had a dusty pink floral room at the top of a house owned by an elderly couple who were sleeping in the room beneath her, which meant she wasn't allowed to make any noise post–nine p.m. — but she could smell the sea air from her bedroom window, and if she squinted, she could kind of see the sea. She'd immediately walked down to the beach after dumping her stuff (and eating the free cookies left out for her) and was now breathing in the salty sea air, telling Susan to stop panicking about her finances and just enjoy the present moment.

When she'd first lost all the money *Raze* owed her, Nina had felt it on every level. The acceptance practice had helped more than she could have imagined, but in the subsequent weeks she'd had to accept she wasn't just £6k down; she was now months away from moving out of her mum's house and finally achieving financial freedom. The job with *Goss* helped — it meant that with enough hard work, she could slowly increase the measly sum in her bank account — but the reality was that Nina was broke.

She knew she should try to love her reality like she'd chosen it, but this felt too hard. So instead, she'd found a chapter in the book that she could get on board with: "The Magic of the Abundance Mindset." It explained that for all too long Nina had been living in the "scarcity mindset," thinking there were limited opportunities, and feeling like she'd been punched in the stomach every time her peers won journalism awards. But now she knew that was wrong; there was space for all of them. She just had to get into the abundance mindset, spend some money, and start manifesting plenitude. The book explained that if Nina gave money to the universe, it would give it back to her. She had to trust the financial flow and not block it by hoarding her savings. Luckily, Nina now had no savings to hoard, and her love of food meant that she was spending plenty. All that was left for her to do was manifest money. She wiped her salty, vinegar-stained hands on her jeans and opened up the book.

"Close your eyes and focus on something you really, really want. Breathe through it and start visualizing what it will be like when you get it and how it will feel. Visualize it as a reality and send all your energy there. Smile and feel positive. Accept that you'll be okay if your desire doesn't come true. And then, let those thoughts go and have faith.

"To really enhance the manifestation, try masturbating while focusing on what it is you want to bring into your life. As you're climaxing, send every ounce of your concentration onto this one thing. Say it as an 'I am' rather than an 'I want.' For example, 'I am successful and loved.' If you have written this onto a piece of paper or a bay leaf, you might want to anoint it with the essence of your climax before you burn it."

Nina reread the last paragraph in horror. The self-love book wanted her to wipe her orgasm juices onto a leaf and burn it? She let out a short bark of laughter as she looked around at the groups of families and hand-holding couples on the beach around her. There was no way she was going to start climaxing on this beach. But the first bit sounded simple enough.

She closed her eyes, sat cross-legged, and focused hard on money. "I am rich. I have loads of money. I have earned back the money I lost from *Raze* — and then some. I am rich. Namaste." She repeated her new mantra several times, then let go and hesitantly opened her eyes, waiting to see if the universe would reward her. Nothing happened. But magic rarely happened instantly. Nina stood up, sliding her damp feet into her Birkenstocks, and went off to get an ice cream while she waited.

By the evening, Nina's positivity had worn

off. She felt bored, Susan was niggling at her for having spent £30 she didn't have on a pub dinner, and worst of all, she felt lonely. She'd managed to escape the dreaded loneliness all day, instead enjoying the freedom of solo travel as she spent hours wandering the aisles of M&S without Nikhil whining at her to hurry up and pick something as she reveled in the endless possibilities (supermarkets were to Nina what Tiffany's was to Holly Golightly), sipping her coffee happily on the train as she listened to the cloyingly sweet pop music she secretly loved and Nikhil not-so-secretly hated, then whiling away hours people-watching on the beach. But now that she was back in her floral abode at eight p.m., with no plans and no one to go for a drink with, Nina could feel the familiar restlessness creeping back in.

The elderly couple had already gone to sleep, so she couldn't even ease the loneliness by asking to look at their family albums. She scrolled listlessly through her phone, but there was nothing to look at. She could watch TV, but that felt like a waste of a weekend away with herself. There was always physical self-love as a backup, but Nina was too full of fish and chips to have sex, even if it was only with herself.

261

She flicked open the book again onto a random page. "How to Get Through the Agony of Loneliness." Nina's heart raced as she realized the book had given her exactly what she needed. It was apparently called "synchronicity," not coincidence, and it happened when someone was aligned with the universe. Which meant she was seriously aligned.

"Loneliness hurts," read the book. "It burns through your body and makes you restless. It makes you call your friends, people you barely know, people you don't like, and in extreme scenarios, turn to the likes of drugs and alcohol and unhealthy distractions — anything to escape it. But the answer to beating the hot loneliness doesn't lie in avoidance; it lies in letting it wash over you. Embrace it. Go into its center. That's where the true growth is. As Pema Chodron says, 'If the hot loneliness is there, and for 1.6 seconds we sit with that restlessness when yesterday we couldn't sit for even one, that's the journey of the warrior.' You are a warrior. Love yourself through that loneliness; love the loneliness."

Nina reread the passage five times. It felt like it was written exactly for her. She'd always thought the answer to loneliness lay in the practical, in finding new friends, a partner, a job; but the book was right — that might numb the loneliness, but it never made it disappear. If anything, it was just distracting her from the real problems. It was like how she'd tried to numb her pain after her TV disaster; it worked temporarily but it just prolonged the eventual agony.

She loved the thought that working on this made her a warrior. Her friends might be sitting law exams or organizing weddings and getting mortgages, but this was *her* big challenge. Okay, so she didn't have tangible external growth that she could Instagram, but she was a *motherfucking warrior* constantly overcoming the next internal battle. Her friends and family might not be able to see the constant self-doubt and anxiety she was battling — but it was real. And this Pema person got it.

Nina grabbed her hoodie and left the house (very quietly; she wasn't so selfish as to wake up her hosts). It was dark outside, but the sky was lit up by the large, glowing moon. She walked through the quiet streets, following the sound of the waves crashing against the shore, until she reached the beachfront. It was empty. She pulled her sleeves over her hands and sat down on the sand cross-legged. It was beautiful. There were streaks of light in the sea, and the rippling waves were lit up with the unearthly glow of the moon. Nina instinctively reached for her phone to take a photo to share on Instagram, then realized she'd left it in her room. She smiled at the workings of the universe and breathed in deeply, letting herself take in the surroundings with every single one of her senses.

After a while, Nina realized she felt high. Just staring at things and breathing made her feel like she'd smoked a massive joint. It was incredible. But she wasn't sure if that counted as sitting in the loneliness — she felt like it had to be more of an event than just sitting on a beach alone without her phone. Nina wasn't sure how to properly do this, considering the book hadn't given explicit instructions, but she instinctively shut her eyes, listening to the waves, ready to physically sit in the loneliness.

She began to visualize her loneliness inside her. She pictured it as big, black, angry, spiky, burning red at the edges — and then gasped out loud as she felt a wave of pain wash over her. It hurt. A lot. Just imagining this loneliness was painful, but this wasn't the end of it. She had to sit inside it too. With her eyes still shut, she imagined a tiny little Nina cartoon character climbing into the loneliness ball in her chest. At first she felt nothing, but as she focused on cartoon Nina sitting in the spiky ball, she realized that tears were streaming down her face. She could feel the intensity of the pain, and she was desperate for it to end. Out of fear that this would be a repeat of her prison breakdown, where her tears had lasted a solid four hours, Nina tried to resist the excruciating agony she was forcing herself into.

Then she remembered that she was meant to *embrace* the loneliness. Instead of fighting it, she was meant to make friends with it. So, feeling slightly ridiculous, she imagined cartoon Nina — she looked a bit like a brown Lizzie McGuire dressed like Kim Possible — hugging the loneliness ball. She had to adjust the image a bit to make it practically work; the ball shrank and became less spiky, while little Nina grew extra-long Spider-Man arms. The ball turned into a bright white light, and big Nina moved her hands to hold her chest. There were still tears streaming down her cheeks, but her sobs had calmed down and she could breathe again.

Big Nina wrapped her arms around herself and rocked herself gently as little Nina kept on emanating white light with her magic powers — until slowly, gradually, both

Ninas realized they weren't hurting now. The ball of loneliness was still there, but it wasn't black and spiky anymore; it was white, soft, and welcoming.

16. I'm a warrior. I don't run away from pain and loneliness (well, not anymore); I climb right inside. Literally.

When Nina got back to her bedroom, she felt lighter. She looked at her phone and realized she'd been out of the house for an entire hour. Even if she'd only sat with the loneliness for half of that time, it was still a hell of a lot more than 1.6 seconds. Pema would be proud. She pulled her T-shirt and bra off, then saw something small fall out of the fabric onto the floor. Nina bent down to pick it up and realized it was the rose quartz stone that Meera had slipped into the padding of her bra all those months ago after her astrology reading. Nina laughed. Maybe it was because of this little self-love crystal that she'd been able to sit in the hot loneliness for so long?

She grabbed her phone and typed out a message to Meera, knowing her friend would be thrilled to know that Nina had just sat alone on a beach for an hour, sitting in her pain and letting the pink crystal do its magic.

Meera replied almost instantly. Oh my actual god. You know it's a full moon tonight, and it's in Taurus? And you went out to the sea with a fully charged rose quartz next to your heart? This is insane. Rose quartz is the Taurean stone. No wonder you had such an intense visualization in your meditation!! You're inspiring me — I need to go and meditate on what to do with me and Sarah. Wish me luck.

Nina stared at her phone. Meera was right; she'd just meditated. And if that was possible, then, well, anything was. She rummaged through her bag for a pen, pulled out a receipt, and wrote on the back of it: "I love myself and have abundance everywhere in my life." It wasn't exactly a bay leaf, but it would have to do. Then, lying down on the bed, looking at her rose quartz for support, she slipped her hand into her panties, bathed the receipt in her female essence, and began to manifest her truest desires.

CHAPTER 17

"You're up early, dear. We thought you might want to have a lie-in."

Nina was sitting at the kitchen table with her laptop in front of her. She pulled her headphones out of her ears to reply to her elderly host. Sarah? Alison? Alice. "Oh, hi, Alice. Sorry, hope I didn't wake you."

"I'll put a pot of tea on for you," said Alice, bustling around the kitchen opening cupboards and taking out mugs. "You look busy."

"That would be amazing, thanks," said Nina gratefully. "I've been up since five a.m. working. But I've just finished, and now I'm . . . doing some personal work."

"Work! I wish our grandkids would do some of that," said Frank, walking in with a newspaper tucked under his arm. "But every time they're here, they just laze about, the lot of them. Millennials." He spat out the last word like he was talking about cockroaches.

Nina smiled politely. "Maybe they're just tired."

"Huh," said Frank, pulling out a chair and sitting down at the table. "This generation has it so easy, but they don't even realize it. Constantly whining. Didn't we see a story the other day, Alice, about one of them saying only her lot can do aerobics?"

Nina hoped this wasn't what she thought it was. "So, um, what's for breakfast? Can I help with anything?"

"It wasn't aerobics," tutted Alice. "It was *yoga*. I don't know what she means though; everyone's doing it down at the community center. People of all colors. I'll do eggs on toast, love. How do you like them?"

"Poached, please. Thank you so much."

"Poached? Are you sure? I was going to fry them. Frank likes them fried."

"Sunny-side up," said Frank. "Two a day every Sunday."

"Okay, fried works," said Nina. "Sorry, I hope you don't mind, I'm just going to zone out and quickly finish this bit of, um, work, if you don't mind?"

" 'Course not, love," said Frank. "Good to see one of your lot with such a strong work ethic."

"Frank!" cried Alice.

"What?" he asked. "I was talking about her being a millennial. God alive, you didn't think I meant her being *Asian*? They're the hardest-working people I know. Like Ali in the post office. Maybe that's why this one's working so hard."

Nina took her cue to slip her headphones back on and carry on writing. The self-love book had spoken about vulnerability, but in spite of her natural ability to overshare, Nina hadn't really made herself vulnerable since her TV disaster. She'd put herself out there — possibly too much, in hindsight — but she hadn't done a Brené Brown and spoken openly about her shame, her humiliation, and her failure. Until now.

Dear followers,

I don't know if you're reading this or if you even care. But I need to speak my truth.

I wrote my articles for *Raze* because I wanted to start conversations about what's appropriate and what's not when it comes to race. Most of all, I wanted to make a difference.

Things obviously didn't go to plan when I appeared on ITV last month, but it was never, ever my intention to offend anyone or make people feel alienated or uncomfortable. I do not support any of the racist views that have been attributed to me. I believe in true equality and always have.

At the same time, I know that what I said was wrong, so I want to truly apologize to everybody I hurt, especially the Black community. I made a mistake and I deserve to be called out for it and corrected. I'm grateful to everyone who has since shared their views with me, and I've learned a lot from all of your messages.

But I've also received endless amounts of abuse, and it's made me realize just how much the Internet disproportionately punishes not just me, but anyone who makes a mistake. I know I was wrong, but nobody's perfect. We all make mistakes, we all fail, and we will all need to apologize at some point in our lives. I just wish we allowed people the space to grow from that.

I know I have. I've learned to better educate myself on race, and the importance of using a public platform to spread positivity rather than negativity. But I've also learned a lot of personal lessons, like how to forgive myself for making a horrible mistake that has hurt so many people. It's been hard, but I think it's also been the most important thing I've ever had to do.

So again, I'm truly sorry to everyone I've hurt. I will do better by all of you. But I'll also do better by me. Because I get it now: nobody's perfect, especially not me.

Love, Nina

Nina couldn't bring herself to reread it. Not even to double-check her spelling. It all came completely from the heart, and she worried that if she read it again, she'd chicken out of posting it. So she quickly hit publish on her Twitter, her Instagram, and her Facebook (because if you're going to be honest on social media, you may as well do it on every platform) and then immediately logged out of all of them.

She'd put her more authentic, vulnerable self out there; she didn't need to hang around now to see people's reactions, because who cared? It was like that famous Theodore Roosevelt quote that Brené Brown loved: "It is not the critic who counts . . . The credit belongs to the man who is actually in the arena, whose face is marred by dust and sweat and blood."

From this moment, Nina no longer gave a shit about what any of the people outside of the arena thought about her life. If they weren't dripping in the dust of work failures, sweat of romantic shame, and blood of constant family drama, then their opinions were worthless to her. Obviously she still wanted them to know just how little she cared about their comments — hence her 343-word blog post — but that was it. She was officially moving forward, and from now on, she was going to stop hiding her failures; she was going to own them.

She ate the last of her fried egg and stood up. "Thank you for breakfast, and for everything. It was a lovely stay."

"Oh, not to worry, lovie," said Alice. "Do you want a bit more toast? There's some jam in the cupboard too, or did we have any cookies, Frank? I think —"

"I'm fine, thank you," interrupted Nina. "Honestly. But there is something else."

"What is it, pet?" asked Alice.

"I just wanted to say that — you know when you talked about that millennial Indian girl who didn't think white people should do yoga? Well, it's me. I'm her."

"Ah, I thought it was," said Frank. "But I didn't want to say anything in case I was wrong and got accused of thinking all you lot look the same. Have another slice of toast, go on, love. Alice made the jam herself."

"Yes, it's blackberry," said Alice. "Ooh, you know what, I might have a slice of fruitcake left in the cupboard. We can't send you back home without a full stomach, now, can we?"

17. I try really hard. Even if I fail, and fall
     flat on my dusty, sweaty, bloody face,
     I'm always trying.

"Oh my god, what have you done?" cried Rupa, staring aghast at Nina from the sofa with a glass of rosé in her hand.

Nina looked at her mum in confusion, trying to guess which of her latest fuckups her mum could be referring to. "I . . . don't know?"

"I mean, you needed to cut it," said Rupa. "That long hair was dragging you down. It gave you a very horsey face. But I don't know why you've gone so blonde, Nina. You look like you're on *Love Island.*"

"Well, I love it," said Nina, sinking down into the gray velvet armchair. She'd decided to cut all her hair off on a whim in Margate and now had what the hairdresser had called a "vibrant long bob." The blonde thing had been a risk; she'd always wanted to lighten up her hair, but Nikhil had said it would look ridiculous, so she'd never done it. But now she was single, there was nothing holding her back, and Nina didn't regret her choice. Her inner transformation was reflected in her physical appearance, and it made her feel light, sexy, and *cool.*

"I think it's fun," she told her mum. "The hairdresser said I look like a graphic designer. And that I'll save a fortune on shampoo and conditioner now it's short."

"Do you mean I'll save a fortune on shampoo and conditioner?" asked Rupa. "Because I can't remember the last time you contributed. And get off the armchair; you know it's only for guests."

Nina rolled her eyes as she slid down onto the floor. "Am I allowed to sit here, or would you like me to put a blanket down first? And where's Kal?"

"He's upstairs." Rupa looked down at her mauve manicure. "Sleeping. Couldn't you have taken him to Margate with you and Jo?"

"He wouldn't have come, Mum," said Nina. She'd lied to her mum about going away with Jo because she couldn't handle her comments about how pathetic it was to go on a solo minibreak, but now she was glad she had; it meant Rupa didn't have to worry about both of her children being lonely. "It's hard enough to get him out of the house, let alone Leicester."

Just then Auntie Trish walked into the

275

room holding the bottle of rosé. "Oh my god, Nina!" she cried, hugging her. "Look at you. It must feel so much freer and lighter. Do you feel better without it all dragging you down?"

"Okay, why did no one tell me my hair has been dragging me down all these years?"

"How was the lovely Margate?" asked Auntie Trish, topping up Rupa's glass.

"I ate everything," said Nina. "Manifested money. Found inner peace. All in all, a success, really."

"God, I'd love a minibreak," cried Auntie Trish. "Why don't we go away, Rups? It's been ages since we went to Santorini."

Rupa's smile flickered. "Well, I wouldn't want to leave Kal for too long. But we could go away for a weekend."

"If you've got a free one," said Auntie Trish. She turned to look at Nina. "Your mum's weekends are full up with dates."

"No way," cried Nina. "Who are they? And how was the one this weekend?"

Rupa shrugged nonchalantly. "Oh, you know. Very charming. A doctor. He took me for dinner at Bistro Pierre. His treat, of course. He's fifty. Divorced. Two kids."

"So, do you fancy him?" asked Nina. "Will there be a second date? Will I get along with my stepsiblings?"

"Calm down, Nina," said Rupa. "He was lovely, but I'm not sure how I feel about someone having an ex-wife on the scene. And he was wearing a brown shirt. It wasn't very flattering."

"Oh my god, how did you last the whole dinner?" asked Nina in mock horror.

"With great grace and patience," said Rupa, with a rare smile. "The fact is that I'm enjoying meeting new people. These apps are actually quite useful. Though I've changed the profile you made for me, Nina; it was far too dull."

Auntie Trish nodded. "Nothing wrong with taking it slow, Rups. You don't want to end up like me and accidentally stay with your rebound for five years. I ended up hating Gopal as much as I hated Dan."

"Auntie Trish, are you going to date too now?" asked Nina. "That would be so fun. You could keep Mum company."

"God, no," cried Auntie Trish. "I'm loving these years of singledom, especially now the kids are off at uni."

"Quite rightly," said Rupa. "But I've had fifteen years alone, so it's my time to enjoy myself now and let men spoil me."

"It's not very feminist, but I'm into it," said Nina. "You guys are giving me some serious inspo for my sixties."

"Sixties?" shrieked Auntie Trish. "We're both still in our fifties, thank you very much. Just."

"It's never too late to broaden your horizons," said Rupa. "I never would have thought I'd go on a date with someone like Paul the doctor, but there you go."

"Paul?" asked Nina. "Was your last date called Paul? As in . . . ?"

"As in, yes, he was white," said Rupa. "There's no need to be so shocked, Nina. It's not easy to find a brown man who meets my needs. I'm widening out."

"I think it's amazing," said Nina. "I just thought you were really anti-it."

"You've got to get with the times," said Rupa, waving her phone at Nina. "App dating is all about embracing the new. My date for next Friday night isn't even six feet."

"Oh my god," gasped Nina. "Who even are you?"

"He's five feet eleven," said Rupa proudly. "And he's a lawyer."

"Ooh," said Auntie Trish. "Show us a pic, go on."

Nina's phone vibrated with a message and she gasped out loud. "Oh my god!"

"What is it?" cried Rupa. "Is it Kal?"

"No, I thought you said he's upstairs?" replied Nina distractedly. "It's my friend

Meera. She just broke up with her long-term girlfriend. I need to go over. With ice cream."

Rupa sighed. "Don't scare me like that. And Nina, you've just got home, don't tell me you're leaving? You need to stop treating this place like a hotel."

"Sorry," said Nina, chucking her phone back into her bag. "But don't you always say that it's important to not let people down? I can't let Meera cry alone."

"Tell her she's better off being alone," advised Auntie Trish. "I wouldn't go back to being in a relationship if you paid me."

"Will do," said Nina. "Hey, you guys don't mind if I take the bottle of rosé you just opened, right? Thanks!"

"Oi!" cried Auntie Trish as Nina ran out of the room and Rupa raised her eyes to the ceiling, muttering in Gujarati.

CHAPTER 18

Nina stood naked in front of her full-length mirror, hoping no one would walk into her room. It was unlikely; her mum was at work, and Kal was still in bed. Nina blamed his new meds and wished he'd go back to his old ones — he'd still been depressed on them, but at least he'd gone for occasional walks and watched TV with her. Lately he didn't even come downstairs for *Bake Off.* When she'd barge into his room to force him to hang with her, he'd make up excuses to go back to sleep. Rupa had called his psychiatrist, but Dr. Fitzgerald had insisted they try the meds for another couple of months.

A breeze came in through the ajar window and made Nina shiver. She needed to focus. Trying not to look too closely at her naked body, with all its flaws very visible in the morning light, she picked up the book. Nina took a deep breath, told Susan to stop judging her, and started reading.

"You are a phenomenal woman, with a phenomenal body." That couldn't be further from the way she felt about herself — especially after she'd joined Meera in emotional comfort eating all weekend — but it was exactly how she wanted to feel, so she kept going. "It is important to feel beautiful. Let's not pretend that looks aren't relevant. But that doesn't mean you have to fit a narrow beauty standard to see yourself as beautiful. Society might have decided what constitutes beautiful, but you don't have to agree with its beauty standards. **You can pick your own.**

"Don't spend hours trying to make your beauty fit into a beauty definition you didn't choose yourself. Create your own instead, whether that means picking and choosing from ancient or global beauty standards or just flipping current ones on their head. Make a new beauty ideal that is conveniently made up of every single feature you already have — whether it's acne, rolls of fat, or stretch marks. Why not see them as beautiful? Why not see scars as stories? Spots as patterns? Fat as sexiness?"

Nina breathed deeply. She had never, ever, considered this before. Beauty was what she saw in magazines and movies. It was not what she saw in the mirror. Could she really turn her thirty-year-old definition of beauty on its head to match her own looks? Was she really capable of seeing big noses, brown skin, muffin tops, acne scars, and unwanted body hair as beautiful? Either way, it was time to follow the book's advice and find out. She was already naked. Now she just had to serenade herself.

She turned the page, cleared her throat, and began reading Maya Angelou's "Phenomenal Woman."

The poem began with Maya saying she wasn't "cute," nor did she have the body of a model, but that she still captivated men. Women — traditionally pretty women — didn't get it. And so, Maya tells them her secret lies "in the reach of my arms, the span of my hips, the stride of my step, the curl of my lips. I'm a woman. Phenomenally."

Nina allowed her eyes to glance at her full body. She'd never thought about having beauty in the span of her hips or the reach of her arms before. She looked back up to her eyes — small, almond-shaped things she was now unfortunately realizing for the first time were also completely asymmetrical — and kept on going.

The next bit was about Maya walking into

a room and all the men being drawn to her. This time she talked about her eyes, teeth, waist, feet — body parts Nina never really thought about. She spent so much time judging the ones she thought men were into instead. Maybe that was why Maya Angelou had so much confidence it was practically dripping off the page: she loved everything about her body, from her lips to her feet, and everything in between.

Slowly, Nina stopped avoiding the sight of her body in the mirror and allowed her gaze to travel down, from her not particularly pert boobs to her squishy stomach, her lack of thigh gap, and her cellulite-marked bum. She looked at it all without judgment, trying to see herself the way she would a painting in an art gallery or a sculpture from a previous century. As she did so, she kept on reciting the poem, feeling Maya's quiet, proud confidence start to move through her.

Nina smiled at her reflection, looking at all the things that Maya Angelou went on to talk about: her back, her smile, her healthy limbs. She began to veer off script, focusing on the shapes and slopes of her body that magazines never mentioned, like the graceful structure of her shoulders; her elegant, long neck; and her soft feet. Her cute new haircut. The more Nina looked at herself, the more she realized she might not have the perfect abs, boobs, or tummy that the media said women were meant to have, but she did have a whole collection of working body parts that weren't so bad. They could, à la Maya Angelou, even be described as phenomenal.

18. I'm a phenomenal woman.

Nina sat on her bedroom floor with her legs in full lotus, holding her vibrating phone. It was Jo. Nina hadn't heard from her since she'd been de-bridesmaided almost two months ago. Nina had sent a groveling apology and suggested they speak in person. But Jo had very formally declined. So why was she calling now? To yell at her? Or tell her she was no longer invited to the wedding? Nina hesitated, her finger hovering over "decline," and then remembered she was phenomenal and had nothing to fear. Not even a recently triggered bridezilla. She swallowed her nerves and pressed "accept."

"Nina, how's it going?" asked Jo brightly. "So glad you weren't too busy with work to pick up."

"Um, no . . . I was just meditating."

"Oh my god, I love that you're actually

meditating right now," cried Jo. "SO on-brand."

"Oh-kay. So, um, how are you?"

"I'm great, thanks. Just back from the hen. I'm sorry you couldn't make it — we all missed you."

"Um, yeah," said Nina, wondering why Jo was pretending everything was fine. "Well, I'm glad you had a good time."

"It was amazing, thanks. So fun. But I'm sure you saw it all on Insta. I know we went a bit overboard with the pics."

"I've actually been off social media for the last week," explained Nina. It had been hard at first to ignore the cravings to refresh her feeds and check her notifications. But after a couple of days, she'd practically forgotten Instagram even existed. And she'd felt so much calmer since. She didn't know how people were responding to her apology, and she didn't care. She'd spoken her truth; that was all she could do.

"What?" cried Jo. "Is that really a good idea?"

"Yes," said Nina defensively. "I feel so much better. Meera, uh, my friend, was right when she told me not to read the comments. It's so freeing."

"Why would you not want to read the comments? Nina, now's not the time for a digi detox. You're a self-love QUEEN."

"Sorry, what?"

"Are you telling me you don't actually know that the Internet is legit full-on obsessed with you right now?" demanded Jo.

"Um, no? The Internet hates me; I'm a millennial racist."

"You're also the person who started the #NobodysPerfect hashtag, which has gone completely viral. Even body-positivity influencers are posting them."

"Oh. My. God."

"Yes!" cried Jo. "Everyone is obsessed with your post. It's been written about on loads of websites, Nins. People are praising your honesty, and it's sparked all these other personal confessions where other journalists are admitting how tough it's been for them to be trolled. Like, actual serious journalists."

"Oh my god."

"Exactly. You need to get on Twitter right now and see. Also . . ." She paused. "I'm sorry. For de-bridesmaiding you. I shouldn't have done it. I think this wedding has gone to my head, and I maybe overreacted."

"It's okay," said Nina, still feeling dazed. "I'm . . . sorry too?"

"No worries, babe," said Jo happily. "It's

all in the past, and as you say, nobody's perfect!"

As Jo hung up, Nina sat staring at her phone, wondering what had just happened. She opened up her browser and typed her name into Google. Bracing herself, she waited for the millennial racist articles to pop up, but she couldn't see a single one. Instead, the top entries read "The Powerful Self-love Message Taking over Twitter," "Nina Mistry: How Going Viral Ruined My Life," and "Why We All Need to Remember that #NobodysPerfect." Jo was right. Her message had gone viral.

She clicked on the apostrophe-less hashtag and found herself on a Twitter page with over ten thousand entries. Nina stared in silence. People of all backgrounds were telling her they agreed, sharing their own stories, even praising her. Some of them still wanted her to "fuck off and stop trying to pretend you're not racist," but the majority were positive. Not negative. Positive.

High-profile figures had joined in too. The government tsar for mental health had responded to her post explaining the importance of cracking down on online abuse. Celebrities had written their own #NobodysPerfect tweets, complete with perfectly photoshopped selfies. And her favorite singer had retweeted her! It was crazy. Two weeks ago, Nina had been public enemy number one. Now, she was a full-blown self-love icon.

Nina scrolled in growing excitement. She knew she should go back to her calm, meditative breathing, but the truth was that she was no longer anything resembling calm. She was buzzing with adrenaline and desperate to log back on to social media, and then her emails, and maybe even re-install WhatsApp. Her apps ban had only been there to keep her safe from negative comments, but now that the abuse was being drowned out by positivity, there wasn't really any need to stay off them. Fuck it. Nina reached for her phone and clicked straight onto the app store. It was time to get all her socials back.

When Nina went to meet Meera at a pub quiz later that evening, she was radiating with excitement. She now had a total of twenty-five thousand followers. She had DMs from wellness brands asking her if they could send her free gifts in exchange for a promotional post. She had emails from national newspapers asking her if she'd send them quotes for articles they were writing about *her* post. And she had a text from

Nikhil saying he was proud of her.

She'd even received a message from Dylan, her troll date, saying that he'd read her post and hadn't realized how much all the publicity had affected her. He'd apologized for trying to make her talk about it on their date, and then, to Nina's complete surprise, he'd apologized for his deliberately provocative comments. It turned out he'd started dating someone else who'd opened his eyes and he was mortified by how he'd treated Nina. She'd forgiven him immediately — how could she not when so many people were giving her that very courtesy? They'd ended up messaging (it turned out he'd been born with a missing incisor) and exchanging funny feminist memes, so naturally Nina had invited him along to the pub quiz.

"Nins," cried Meera, waving to her from the back of the pub. Her bright pink hair was pulled into a topknot and she was wearing an oversized yellow jumper with denim shorts. She already had a pint in her hand and was at a table with a man and woman Nina had never met before and Deepa. "Look who I invited!"

Nina went over to slightly awkwardly hug her yoga teacher and Meera, followed by Jack, from Meera's astrology course, and

Alisa, Jack's sister. "I actually invited some-one as well," said Nina. "Do you remember Dylan?"

"Not the psychotic troll you went on a date with?" cried Meera. "You can't be seri-ous."

"It turns out he was only trolling me to get a reaction," explained Nina. "He's not actually sexist. Or racist."

"That's still fucked-up," said Meera. "Who pretends to be sexist to get someone to fancy them?"

"I know it's weird, but he really regrets it," replied Nina. "Besides, he's fallen in love with a feminist who sounds amazing, and he's got a really strong meme game."

"Sorry, you went on a date with a troll?" asked Deepa. "How does that work?"

"Yes, I think we need to hear this story," chimed in Alisa. "I have a lot of questions."

"Tell them the whole thing, Nins," said Meera. "While Jack and I pop out for a cigarette."

Nina raised her eyebrows at her friend; it was the first she'd heard of her smoking. But Meera shot her a pointed look, and Nina realized that Meera and Jack were shagging. *Already?* she mouthed at Meera in shock.

"I know it's quick," said Meera out loud.

"But things with Sarah were dead for a while. And" — she turned to smile at Jack — "it turns out me and Jack have secretly liked each other for ages." They walked out of the pub, with Jack's hand resting on Meera's back, leaving Nina speechless.

By the time Dylan walked in, the whole team knew about Nina's horrific date, her even more horrific experience as *Raze*'s first and last diversity correspondent, and her recent fame as a self-love goddess. Well, no one had actually used the word "goddess" to describe her yet, but Nina was sure it was only a matter of time. "So, is this as awkward as your last date?" asked Alisa, winking at Dylan as he returned from the bar.

"Alisa!" cried Nina. "It is now that you just said that."

But Dylan just grinned good-naturedly and turned to Nina. "How much did you tell them about me, then?"

"We know you have some pretty fucked-up views about women and race," said Alisa. "And that you're in love now."

"Also that you're really big on doing rounds," added Deepa. "If you feel like getting one in now."

"Huh," said Meera, coming back into the pub with Jack in tow. "Look who it is. The guy who thinks we should all be equalists, not feminists. And that it's okay to fetishize women of color."

Dylan looked sheepish. "I know I was a dick. I just thought it would be fun to debate about equality with Nina, considering her career and all. But Georgia — my new girlfriend — has made me realize how unfair it was of me. And also kind of sexist. She's really helped me see things from the perspective of a woman of color, rather than my own white male privilege."

"Oh, so you got a woman of color to educate you?" said Meera. "Like you tried to get Nina to do on your date. You know you could — shock, horror — educate yourself?"

"Hey, he is," interjected Nina. "He's spent the last couple of months reading Reni Eddo-Lodge and Audre Lorde. Haven't you?"

"Yep," said Dylan. "Thanks for the recommendation. And Georgia's lent me a few books. I've just finished Simone de Beauvoir's *The Second Sex,* and I was thinking of reading Naomi Wolf next."

Meera turned to stare at Nina with a raised eyebrow. "The misogynist has become a feminist."

"I wouldn't say I was a misogynist before,"

said Dylan. "But, yeah. I now identify as a feminist and an ally to POC."

"Okay, let's stop attacking Dylan," said Nina. "We all deserve a second chance, and it's time to start the picture round. You know how competitive I can get."

"Let's do this," said Deepa, rubbing her hands together. "And Dylan, I'll have a G&T please. A double."

The Ravenclaws came second to last in the quiz, but none of them — not even Nina — cared. They'd spent the evening realizing how embarrassingly little they knew about wildlife and bonding over how they all identified as the wittiest of the Hogwarts houses. Personally, Nina thought that Deepa was more of a Slytherin, but her yoga teacher had opened up so honestly about her recent breakup with the fiancé who'd been cheating on her with twenty-one-year-olds that Nina had been too impressed to be a bitch.

She'd thought that Deepa, who sat smiling sweetly at every Gujarati community event, subscribed to the same "Don't air your dirty laundry" and "You're a spinster if you're single at thirty" beliefs as most of the Indians she knew, but it turned out that she was a black sheep just like Nina and

Meera. Her family had been furious at her for becoming a full-time yoga teacher, and her mum was no longer speaking to her after her breakup with her paper-perfect fiancé. Nina could relate. They'd ended up having a long conversation alone, discussing the pros and cons of having a mother who cared more about appearances than her children's feelings, and had left with brunch plans.

Then there was Dylan. He'd proven himself to have more of a sense of humor than Nina could have ever imagined, and his knowledge of Tarantino films was impressive. Meera had taken her aside at one point and taken credit for bringing him into Nina's life via the dating app. "My gut instinct about people is never wrong," she'd said. "The universe wanted him to meet you so you could spark his journey to wokeness."

Nina had also realized how great Alisa was. She was a tall, skinny construction manager in her late thirties with a nose piercing and great hair who had endless hilarious stories about the everyday sexism she faced in her job managing burly men decades older than herself. She was so different from anyone Nina knew that hanging out with her was unimaginably refreshing.

"You know what," said Nina, linking arms with Meera as they walked home together, "I feel like tonight was proof that it's not too late to make new friends."

"Of course it's not. Why would it be?"

Nina shrugged. "I feel like most people's close friends are people they meet at school, uni, or work. So once you're in your late twenties or your thirties, it's too late to get new best mates. Unless you change jobs."

"Okay, that's complete rubbish," said Meera. "Especially for self-improvers like us who are constantly changing. As you get more spiritual, you vibrate on a higher frequency. So people around you who are vibrating at lower frequencies start to move away, and you don't vibe together so much. It's sad, obviously, especially when it means you're essentially growing away from people you've known your whole life. But you also start to attract people vibrating at higher frequencies, which is amazing."

"It's so true." Nina nodded emphatically — and a bit drunkenly. "I feel like I've manifested you, and the group tonight. Everyone was so great and *honest*. It didn't feel like anyone was trying to be cool or airbrush their lives. It was real."

"Yes, exactly. And sometimes you've got to lose the old to make space for the new."

"Like . . . you losing Sarah to make space for Jack?" asked Nina. "I can't believe how quickly you've found someone new. It's unreal."

Meera laughed. "I know, it's mad. We only hooked up this week for the first time, but I've known him for years, and Nins, I've always liked him — I just didn't realize it until I meditated with the full moon. He's super different from me, but he's just so open, and nothing is taboo for him. The other day he sent me a photo of a book he was reading. It's called *She Comes First.* Apparently it teaches men to be 'sexually cliterate.' "

"Marry him."

"I mean, you know I don't believe in the institution of marriage. But . . . I could totally see myself having a civil partnership with him one day." Meera grinned.

"Seriously?" asked Nina, stopping in midstep to face her friend. "You really like him?"

Meera nodded. "I think he might be the guy I'm supposed to try and make a life with."

"But you've barely spent any time with him. I mean, romantically. Maybe you should go slower. In case he hurts you."

"I know, but it just feels right," said Meera. "And I always liked him, but he didn't realize I date men, and I thought he wasn't interested. But . . . the chemistry is unreal. And I feel like I'm dating my best friend."

"That's amazing," said Nina. "Amazing." It was. Obviously. But inside she was panicking. Jack was great, but would this mean the end of her friendship with Meera? Was she going to lose her for months on end as she fell into the honeymoon period, and then, just as she came back, have to lose her to an engagement, and then wedding — sorry, civil partnership — planning?

"Hey," said Meera, as Nina felt the anxiety rising. "Don't worry. Our friendship won't change. I almost need my friends *more* when I'm in a relationship, because I need a break from the other person. Honestly, Nins, I know you're a bit sad about this, but it'll be okay. I promise."

"Oh my god, I'm not sad," cried Nina. "I'm super happy for you. I'm just . . . the tiniest bit scared."

Meera hugged her. "I know, babe. But you forget the difference is that you can tell me about this. It won't be like with your other friends when you had to hide your feelings. We can be honest with each other."

"Okay, thanks." Nina hugged her back tightly. "You can be honest with me too."

"I know. Which is why I want to tell you to be careful."

"With what?" asked Nina, peeling away from her friend's arms.

"Your self-love journey. You've worked so hard on yourself, and I just don't want you to lose any of it, or go backward."

"I wasn't planning on it," said Nina lightly.

"I just feel like this whole viral fame thing has the potential to be as damaging for you as when you had the viral hatred," explained Meera. "Just . . . don't get carried away. Remember that quote you screenshotted for me from your book: 'Be like a rock and be not moved by criticism or by praise.' You managed to get there with the criticism, but just — be careful with the praise stuff too."

"Christ," sighed Nina loudly. "That's such a Ravenclaw reaction to my viral self-love. But fine. I get it. I will channel the stationary rock. Promise."

"Good. Now can I show you the cutest message Jack sent me?"

CHAPTER 19

SCORPIO SEASON

SCORPIO
Season: October 24–November 21
Element: Water
Themes: Intuition. Perception. Honesty.
Best time to: Speak your truth.

The doorbell rang and Nina ran down the stairs to answer. She bumped into her mum in the hallway. "Why are you running through the house in a T-shirt and your brother's boxers?" asked Rupa in a pained voice.

"I was in bed," said Nina. "Also, my friend's coming over. I think this is him."

"A male friend? Who is he? Please tell me it's not the unhygienic old man with the beads. Nina, I will not have someone like that in my house."

"Oh my god, no. It's Dylan, the guy I went on a date with, who wanted to be friends?

He's my age. He's normal. And he has a girlfriend now. It's all good."

Her mum sighed. "Shame he's taken."

Nina stared at her mum. "You literally know nothing about him except for the fact he's a normal man of my age. How is that enough to make him an ideal boyfriend for me?"

Rupa shrugged and moved to open the door. "You are getting on a bit. You can't be as picky as you used to be."

The door opened to reveal a smiling Dylan wearing jeans, a black bomber jacket, and colorful Nikes, with his man bun chopped into a long bob like Nina's. It seemed Georgia had improved his dress sense as well as his views. "I reckon I am a pretty ideal boyfriend," he said. "Just maybe not for you, Nina."

Rupa smiled warmly at him. "Hello, I'm Rupa. Please come in. Do you want something to drink? I have some fresh watermelon juice in the fridge."

"That sounds amazing, thank you. And I'm Dylan."

"You told me I wasn't allowed to touch that juice," muttered Nina as she followed them into the kitchen. By the time she and Dylan were in her room with freshly squeezed juices and vegan, gluten-free "brownies" (Nina wasn't sure you could still call them brownies if they had no sugar or flour in them), it was obvious that Dylan was fully charmed by her mum.

"She's not normally like this," said Nina, when Rupa finally went to check on the Halloumi. "It's her guest persona. She does it in front of anyone new. She never stopped doing it in front of Jo — unless she saw us eating in the living room. Then it was back to 'GET THOSE FILTHY ADDITIVES OFF MY SOFA.' "

"I think she's great," said Dylan. "And she's *hot*. How is she still single?"

"I doubt she will be for long. But anyway, what did you want to talk to me about?"

Dylan's smiling face rearranged itself into an earnest expression. "I don't know how to tell you this. It's really hard for me, especially after just finishing *The Beauty Myth.* But I was talking it over with Georgia, and we agreed that it's better you know. So that you can keep yourself safe."

"You're scaring me," said Nina.

"So, back when I used to write things I'm not proud of on the Internet, I was part of this thread." Dylan looked nervously at his fingers. "It was a bit . . . anti-women, I suppose. And when you did your racism stuff, a few people shared quite a lot of negative

301

things about you on there. Not me — though, full disclosure, I did comment on some of their posts."

"It's fine, I've forgiven you. So long as you didn't do any gross sexual comments."

"No," said Dylan, his face contorted into a pained expression. "But I logged on the other day to close my account, and well, the same people are now saying different things about you. Sexual things."

"Ew," cried Nina. "What are they saying?"

"Just stuff about how they want to have sex with you. And that even though your opinions are pretty stupid, you're quite pretty."

Nina shook her head slowly. "Well, how times have changed. It wasn't so long ago they were telling me I'd die alone, eaten by stray cats."

"I'm sorry. I know it's shocking they're reducing you to a sexual object. It must be hard to hear. But I thought you should know in case you wanted to take any precautions."

"Um, I think the trolls finding me hot is actually quite a bit easier to hear than them telling me how disgusting I am," said Nina mildly.

"But they're objectifying you. And they still think you've got a big nose."

"I do though. A phenomenal nose."

"What?"

"Never mind," she said. "I guess . . . I don't care what they're saying. They've been saying I'm ugly for so long, and now they're saying I'm hot. It's bullshit."

"Oh-kay. This isn't how I thought you'd react."

Nina shrugged. "I probably wouldn't have been this chill a few weeks ago. But I'm learning to find myself beautiful the way I am. I don't really care what *anyone* thinks about the way I look anymore. It's my choice to see myself as hot, not theirs."

"That's really great, Nina. You don't need anyone's validation, especially not a bunch of incels. Not that they're all incels, but you know what I mean."

"Exactly. And you know what, this is actually a massive compliment. My trolls fancy me. And, oh my god, *maybe they always have.*" She sat up triumphantly in her chair. "You know that dumb shit about how boys on the playground pull the pigtails of girls they fancy; this is basically the equivalent. Maybe even when they were saying how much they hated me, they secretly fancied me."

"So . . . they trolled you to get your attention?"

"Why not? You trolled me, then matched with me."

Dylan stared at Nina, then shook his head laughing. "Wow. Maybe you have a point."

"I mean, obviously, I'm not 100 percent serious. But if my choices are to interpret their comments as something either negative or positive, then I'm going to pick the latter. Fuck it; my trolls are in love with me. And why shouldn't they be? I'm phenomenal."

Dylan laughed. "As coping mechanisms go, I guess it's pretty good."

"Yeah," said Nina, leaning back into her chair. "Wow, I can't believe I wasted so much time hating my trolls when they're basically my biggest fans. Though someone needs to teach them some new chat-up lines. 'Go kill yourself, bitch' isn't really doing it for me."

19. My ability to reframe things in a positive light.

"You'll be on air in sixty seconds," said a voice on the phone. Nina wiggled her toes in the warm bubble bath. This was it. Her first radio debut. BBC Asian Network had invited her to come onto the show to discuss her journey and self-love movement. She'd spent the last few weeks replying to endless messages from her followers, all asking her for advice in various self-esteem-related issues, so this time, she truly felt prepared for the interview. All she had to do was be herself, not say anything that could be taken horribly out of context, and convince the entire British Asian community to start opening up and breaking taboos.

"So with us today, we have Nina Mistry, the founder of the #NobodysPerfect hashtag sparking self-love journeys all over your social media," said the presenter, Saz. "You might remember her for going viral and being labeled a 'racist millennial' — a misunderstanding that cost her dearly. But since then, Nina has gone on to create the inspirational #NobodysPerfect movement. So, Nina, tell us — what exactly is your message?"

Nina sat upright in the tub with soap suds evaporating from her boobs. "It's all about self-love. I know it sounds a bit cringe, but actually, it's so important. We need to have our own backs, especially in a social media world where you're constantly being misunderstood, criticized, or even bullied, threatened, and abused. And what I've learned is that the more honest, authentic, and vulnerable I am, the less anyone can hurt me. If

I'm fully me, and someone doesn't like me, then that's their problem — not mine."

"Interesting," said Saz. "And how does that specifically relate to the Asian community? I know you're from Leicester, and you're Indian. Is this a message you think your community needs to hear?"

"Oh my god, like a million percent," cried Nina. "I've always grown up feeling so oppressed and judged. It just feels like there's this one acceptable path you have to go down, and if you deviate from it, that's it. You're canceled. You've brought shame on the entire family, and you're on the shelf forever. But I wish it wasn't this way. Why do we put so much pressure on everyone to live this one same life? Why do you have to be made to feel like a failure for not magically finding 'the one' by thirty? Why can't you mess up? And why does everything have to be so *secret*? If people weren't so scared to share their failures, then none of it would be this way. We could all be . . . happier."

"It's like that old joke about the F-word you can't use in an Asian home," said Saz. "Not the one we can't say on the radio, but failure. So any listeners out there, do you have any failures you want to share? Any imperfections you've been scared to say aloud until now? Message us your answers

306

or give us a call. And in the meantime, Nina will kick us off. Tell us some of your biggest failures. Anything imperfect about you that we don't already know?"

Nina hung up the phone feeling alive with adrenaline. The interview had gone better than she could have imagined. She'd felt so comfortable sharing about herself that she'd inspired a record number of messages and callers into the show. People had called to talk about having nose jobs, being divorced by thirty-one — one guy even came out as gay live on air. Nina had almost cried; she was moved by her message indirectly helping so many people.

"Nina, open up, now." There was a series of loud bangs on the bathroom door.

"Mum, I'm in the bath. Give me a second."

"How dare you," yelled Rupa, from outside the bathroom door. "You just told the entire community you've had a sexual disease."

"Oh my god," cried Nina, wrapping a towel around her and opening up the door. "HPV isn't an STI. I specifically said that. It's so common that 50 percent of people have it. You could even have it."

Her mum stared at her in horror. "What

is wrong with you? You can't talk about these things on the radio."

"But, Mum, I didn't share anything about you or Kal or Dad. I just shared my secrets. I deliberately didn't mention family stuff. Not even Uncle Sanjay's secret family."

"Thank god you didn't," cried Rupa. "Or no one would ever speak to us again. Though I doubt they will even now. People know you had THRUSH. You disgusting girl."

"Mum, thrush isn't my fault."

"Well, is it also not your fault that you stuck a garlic clove in there to try and remedy it and LOST IT IN THERE?" shouted Rupa. "Why, WHY did you think it was a good idea to tell that story live on the radio?"

Nina shrugged uneasily. "I got it out eventually. I just wanted to warn other people to be careful with homeopathic remedies. Don't you think it was cool that it inspired all those other people to share their failures too?"

"Cool? COOL?" Rupa looked so furious that Nina worried her blood vessels would burst. "Nina, you told the world you have anxiety. That you've had therapy. I thought it was bad enough when you were a racist, but this is even worse. People will think you're crazy and no one will ever marry you."

"Well, maybe I don't want to get married," said Nina, crossing her arms tightly. "Especially not to someone who judges me for having mental health issues. I just want to see what happens with my life without having a prescribed five-year plan."

Rupa shook her head. "I'm exhausted, Nina. As if I don't have enough to worry about with Kal right now. And then you're telling the world all these personal things, when you KNOW all it does is make people gossip. They don't blame you for all of this; they blame me, as your mother."

"And I'm really, really sorry about that," said Nina, putting a hand on her mum's shoulder, feeling her bony frame beneath the striped Breton top. "But it's not my fault they're so judgmental and narrow-minded. I haven't actually done anything wrong by sharing my own personal secrets. And you know what, Mum? I feel better for it. I'm not ashamed of who I am — even the thrush and HPV. I don't mind people knowing that I've been brokenhearted and that a Colombian man listed all my flaws while I sobbed in his van. It's just life. It's my life. And I'm proud of it, not ashamed."

Rupa broke away from Nina's grasp. "You

might not be, but I am. And I'd like you to find somewhere else to live. It's time you moved out."

CHAPTER 20

Nina had spent the last week in a feverish daze of hard work. She'd been taking on morning and evening shifts for *Goss,* as well as writing the odd self-love piece for newspapers. She'd even achieved her dream of being published in her symbolically favorite newspaper, *The Guardian,* with a double-page spread on "How I learned to love my so-called imperfections." It meant that she'd earned back half the money she'd lost and would soon be able to do what her mum wanted and move out.

For once, though it had hurt to be told, Nina actually agreed with her; she was too old to be living at home. She'd always thought that the Indian custom of grown children living with their parents until marriage was kind of tragic, but now she was proving to be just as bad. And unlike Kal, she didn't have a real reason for it. So she'd spent the last couple of weeks viewing flats, both in person and in her visualization meditations. The manifesting had paid off, and Nina had found a cute studio in town that achieved the holy trinity of being clean, affordable, and seconds away from her favorite coffee shop. All that was left for her to do was put down a deposit, pack her stuff, and become the independent woman that Destiny's Child had always known she could be.

"Nina, you left your phone in the kitchen," said Rupa, walking into the living room and raising her eyebrows at the packet of Hobnobs on Nina's lap. "You've got a call."

"You answered my phone?"

"I have no desire to answer your calls any more than you want me to, so next time don't leave your phone in the kitchen." She paused. "But this one looked important. It's a London number."

Nina picked up the phone in curiosity as Rupa settled down in the armchair to blatantly eavesdrop.

"Hello? Yep, I'm Nina. Mm-hmm. Oh my god!! Live on TV?"

Rupa's eyes widened.

"That's amazing. But . . . how would it work? Mmmm, okay. And, I wouldn't have to wear anything intense, would I?"

Rupa's face visibly tensed.

"And what would the fee be?"

Rupa frowned as Nina tried to swallow her squeal of excitement. "Okay, great. And there's no way you can go up on that? I mean, obviously spreading my message is really important to me, but it's quite a big ask. I imagine it'll provoke the trolls again, and it has been quite hard for me . . . Yep. Wow. No, that seems incredibly fair."

There was a pause as Nina nodded. "Great. Late November sounds good. Look forward to speaking. Thanks so much, bye."

She hung up the call and faced the steely glare of her mother.

"So," said Rupa in a tight voice. "They'd like you to go on and do something humiliating wearing something equally humiliating for a large sum of money. And, because it wasn't bad enough for you last time, you've decided to say yes."

"I wouldn't exactly call it humiliating," said Nina defensively. "It's actually a really lovely opportunity for me to talk about my self-love message on television." There was a long silence as Rupa stared down her daughter. "Okay fine, Channel 4 wants me to marry myself live on air."

Rupa's mouth fell open and she shook her head quickly. "No, Nina, how can you even consider it? That's mortifying. Oh, it's so tragic. You can't find a husband, so you're going to marry yourself instead?"

"It's got nothing to do with whether I can find a man or not. It's an act of self-love. To show that I support myself through thick and thin, no matter what."

"Yes, because no one else will," said Rupa, pacing the living room. "God, you're going to look pathetic. What will people say? Nina, how can you even think about this after what happened last time you went on TV?"

"It's different this time. And I won't look pathetic. They said they'll buy me a white suit. I'll look great."

"Yes, as you walk down the aisle to marry yourself like a complete nutjob," cried Rupa.

"It's not okay to say words like 'nutjob' anymore. Mental health, Mum."

"Well, I'm sorry, but it is the only word that describes a woman who goes on national television to marry herself," said Rupa, crossing her arms and standing in front of her daughter. "If you even think about doing this, Nina, I am going to have to ask you to leave this home immediately."

"Oh, do not worry. That is the first thing I plan on doing with the thousand pounds they're paying me. By the end of the month, I'll be out of here, in my new studio flat, eating greasy chips and dips on the sofa."

314

■ ■ ■ ■

Nina's mind should have been on her third eye, but she couldn't stop thinking about the fact her mum hadn't spoken to her for a week. This was getting close to the infamous Year Eleven record of ten days after Rupa had caught Nina smoking. She knew that it would pass; it always did. The Mistry way of resolving fights consisted of excessive silence eventually broken by a mundane comment like "What's for dinner?" when everything would go back to normal and they'd pretend it had never happened. But Nina hated the tense, silent period in between — especially when her mum was refusing to tell her about her latest dates. The curiosity was killing her, and Kal was too out of it to be of any help. He was still sleeping a lot, and whenever he went down to the kitchen to get food, he just grunted at Nina. She knew he was ill and everything, but she wished she could talk to him about their mum. She missed him being her brother.

"Just take a deep breath and let it all out," murmured Vaishali gently. "I'm going to start the energy work now. Try to calm your mind and just focus on your breathing.

Observe any changes."

The voice of the reiki practitioner suddenly reminded Nina she was meant to be in the middle of a spiritual energy exchange and not a stream of consciousness with herself. Meera had recommended she try reiki to "stay balanced and not get carried away with everything." It's why she was now sprawled out on a massage table in Vaishali's sage-cleansed, candle-lit garden shed with her eyes closed and a crystal placed on top of every single one of her seven chakras.

As Vaishali's hands rested on Nina's crown, she tried to shut down her thoughts and focus on the area Vaishali was sending positive energy to. She felt a slight fuzz of warmth, but she couldn't be sure if it was the actual body heat from Vaishali's hands or some magic reiki.

Her hands moved down to Nina's throat — the communication chakra — and, after a few minutes, moved on to her chest. Her heart chakra. Nina wondered if Vaishali would feel all the heartbreak there. She tried to connect with the energy to see if she could feel the reiki. She wasn't sure. She did, however, feel exhausted. There was a heaviness inside of her, and all of a sudden Nina felt really, really sad.

A memory popped into her head. It was

her sixteenth birthday — her first after her dad died. Nina was sitting alone at the kitchen table after school, in disbelief that her family had forgotten her birthday. She'd been crying hot, angry tears when her mum had rushed into the house, late from work, carrying a chocolate cake from the expensive bakery Nina had been begging her to visit for weeks. Kal had abandoned his insane studying schedule to give her a card he'd clearly spent hours making. It was a collage of Nina through the ages — moodily glaring at the camera in her teens, a toddler laughing naked in the garden with Kal, and a sleeping baby in the arms of her father.

Back in the reiki shed, Nina felt a pang of emotion and realized her eyes were starting to water. Oh god. She wanted to move her hands and dry off her tears, but then she remembered the only specific instruction for reiki: let her body do whatever it needed. She wasn't meant to resist it. She was meant to cry.

"Okay," murmured Vaishali. "We're coming to an end now. Take your time in slowly sitting up."

Nina woke up with a start. She'd fallen asleep and missed most of the session.

"How do you feel?"

"Um, okay, thanks," said Nina, slowly sitting up. "A bit tired, but relaxed."

"Good," said Vaishali, beaming at her. "I found that a really beautiful exchange. You have a wonderful energy, Nina. A very white aura."

"Thank you," said Nina, returning her smile even though she wasn't exactly sure what the compliment meant.

"The way I normally end a session is just by explaining a bit about what I noticed during the reiki, because I tend to pick up on a lot," said Vaishali. "So let me start with the crown. I found a lot of energy there. Your mind was going around in circles, really very active. I tried to quieten it down and bring some peace, so hopefully you'll feel that over the next few days."

Nina nodded; it was true — her mind did not want to shut up lately.

"But the place I really connected with was your third eye. It didn't want to open up at first, but then I kept on throwing reiki at it, and it finally opened. You've got a really strong intuition, but I get the sense you've been ignoring it a bit lately. Only after this, I think you're going to be much more aware of some home truths, and it'll help you with decision-making."

"Okay," said Nina. "That sounds . . .

318

important."

"Yes, I get the sense you have a few decisions coming up that this intuition will be really helpful for. So do try and go inward and listen to your gut instead of always making rational choices; some choices have to be made with the heart, not the head." Vaishali looked at Nina for a reaction, so she nodded obediently. Vaishali continued. "I felt your throat chakra was quite open, which is great. I think you must be communicating honestly already, so that will continue. But when I got to your heart, I felt a lot of pain. A lot of heartbreak. Your heart is very, very broken, Nina."

"Yeah, but it's okay," replied Nina uncomfortably. "Manageable."

"I found a lot of pain there," stressed Vaishali. "A lot. Your poor heart. It's been through so much, and you'll have more heartbreak over the years. But you have a very big heart, Nina, and it'll just get bigger the more it breaks. Remember that the cracks let the light in."

"Wonderful," said Nina faintly. "Can't wait."

"A lot of the pain and love, intertwined together, was linked to your family. You need to let yourself feel the pain and forgive yourself. You're carrying so much guilt here, but there's no need. The only way to heal is love — for yourself, but also for others."

Nina felt tears pricking her eyelids again. She hadn't been prepared for this to be so emotional. Vaishali smiled at her and kept going. "I also spoke to you in the other realm and asked you to choose a symbol to protect your heart with." Nina decided against asking any questions. "You weren't keen to pick a symbol, actually. You argued a fair bit. But you eventually chose the om symbol — even though you repeatedly stressed to me you aren't religious. So the om will be good to protect your heart from future pain."

"Oh-kay," Nina replied. This was starting to get a bit much.

"And then I moved on to your solar plexus. I called on Archangel Michael to guide me here, and I think you'll find a desire to explore new things in your career. Oh yes, I sometimes use angels to guide me. They don't always show up, but they did for you. When I got to your sacral chakra, Mother Mary came."

"Like the Virgin Mary?"

"Yes, exactly. She doesn't always come, but she made the effort for you."

"That's good of her, considering I'm not Christian."

"In the other realm, all spirits and gods are equal," said Vaishali calmly. "Mary helped you with your femininity, sensuality, and sexuality. She really focused on what it means to be a woman, sisterhood, and on women loving women. I'm not sure if you're a lesbian?"

"Uh, no," said Nina. "I've only ever dated guys, but I've definitely fancied women, although I've never had an opportunity to really explore that. I don't use labels; I just think of sexuality as a spectrum, you know? Wait — does Jesus's mum want me to date girls?"

Vaishali smiled. "It could mean anything; just wait and see. Anyway, in your root chakra, which is the base of everything, I moved the energy around. So I think you'll notice a lot of change and self-growth in the next few months."

"Thanks," said Nina. "That's . . . great."

"I'm glad it helps," said Vaishali warmly. "You're doing well. I felt a lot of self-love, but if I were you, I'd try and focus now on your intuition and heart, not your mind. Make decisions from your heart, not your head."

"But . . . surely I can't just make emotional decisions? I'll just end up poor and heart-broken and unhealthy from eating nonstop cake." She paused. "Okay, so it's not hugely different from where I am now, but you know what I mean. You have to be rational sometimes, don't you?"

"That's the problem with society today," sighed Vaishali, putting an arm around Nina's shoulders. "It's all about the mind, but that's just the ego. We need to go beyond the ego and be present in our consciousness."

"Um . . ."

"I know it sounds complicated, but really, the truth is always in your heart, your intuition, your soul, your light, whatever you want to call it. If you're stuck in a decision, don't use your head, climb into your heart and see what answer lies there."

20. My big, broken, healing heart.

Nina had just finished writing about the forty-nine best dressed at the BAFTAs when she noticed her social media blowing up more than usual. She absentmindedly clicked on her feed and froze in shock. There was a link to a crowdfunding page titled "Get Nina Mistry (and the other *Raze* journalists) the money they're owed." It was set up by a well-known journalist who'd read Nina's latest piece in the *Guardian,* and hundreds of people had already written messages on the page, expressing their support for #Nobodys-Perfect and making earnest comments about the unfair state of the media industry.

It had raised £3,000.

Nina stared at the page for what felt like hours. She couldn't really believe that it was real, but an email from the journalist proved that it was. Hundreds of people were donating to help her and a few other freelancers owed money by *Raze.* But as she was owed the most, the majority of the donations would go straight to her.

It was a miracle. An early Christmas miracle. Or an abundance miracle. Nina sat up straight as she suddenly realized that all of her self-love and financial success had come into her life ever since she'd gone and manifested via masturbation in Margate.

Nina knew that this wasn't the sort of monetary accrual skill she could put on her CV — or tell anyone who wasn't Meera — but it was life-changing. So long as she worked hard and kept on radiating an abundance mindset rather than a scarcity-based one, all whilst giving herself regular orgasms, then she'd always be financially okay. It was the kind of equation she wished she'd learned back in school:

(Meditation + Masturbation) × Faith = Abundance.

She knew it wasn't the most traditional financial plan, but if she enacted this equation daily, she'd be able to pay off her entire student loan by forty. With a heartfelt "namaste" to the universe, Nina sank into her bed, slipped off her knickers, and started to manifest more financial abundance into her life.

Chapter 21

SAGITTARIUS SEASON
SAGITTARIUS
Season: November 22–December 21
Element: Fire
Themes: Travel. Restlessness. Idealism.
Best time to: Face up to any disorder.

Nina looked nervously out of the train window as it left Leicester station and headed toward St. Pancras.

Everything was ready for her TV appearance the following morning.

The TV producers had bought her the promised white suit, and hair and makeup were primed to give her an "empowered bridal look." The idea was that the presenters would introduce her, and then "Here Comes the Bride" would play as she walked onto the set, where a nonreligious officiant would be waiting to perform the nonlegal — but very poignant — ceremony. She just had to prepare her vows, remember to bring her ring, and set her alarm for four a.m.

Rupa hadn't spoken to Nina when she'd left the house, but that was no surprise, considering she'd now officially broken the Year Eleven record. Nina had tried to talk to Kal about it before she left, but he'd been in one of his moods, silently staring into space until she'd felt so uncomfortable she'd left the room. And Auntie Trish, who normally always had Nina's back, had apologetically said she thought it "might be a bit tacky, love. Though I suppose at least if you don't ever have a proper wedding, you'll always have some lovely photos of yourself in white for the mantelpiece." Thank god Meera and Jack had told her she'd be amazing and promised to watch her live. She hadn't even told Jo she was doing it.

Nina was 99 percent sure she was doing the right thing. It was what she'd manifested from the universe, and it was a chance for her to talk about self-love in a public sphere. She knew it was admittedly great fodder for the trolls and had the potential to make her into a laughingstock. But really, what was more on-brand for self-love than a solo wedding? Hopefully, it would inspire other people out there to start their own self-love journeys, instead of letting Susan constantly berate them like she'd been doing to Nina for the last thirty years.

And if it didn't go to plan, Nina knew that this time she'd be okay. She wasn't exactly a stranger to public humiliation, and as the self-love book said, "Life is like a video game. It's good to try to do well, to get to the next level, but it's really not the end of the world if you mess up. You just try again. Don't take it too seriously. Our real life is what goes on in our inner selves — not this material world around us."

Nina was trying to be the kind of person who laughed at life rather than obsessing over it earnestly. She was sick of being a perfectionist; she wanted to live up to her white aura and make choices lightly. Which was why she was trying not to panic over practical issues like whether she'd be able to pay her rent after moving out of her mum's and was instead focusing all her energy on the promise she'd made to herself back in April: to finish her list of thirty things she loved about herself. And she still had a way to go. Getting to twenty wasn't bad, considering she'd started the journey from a cell in hummus-stained pajamas, but it felt a bit like cheating to marry herself already. Then again, no one knew about her challenge but Meera, and it wasn't like this ceremony was legal. What was the worst that could happen?

Nina groggily reached for her vibrating phone. How was it already four a.m.? It felt like she'd just gotten to her hotel room and collapsed into bed — after slipping every freebie she could find into her bag. She tried to turn her alarm off, but then realized it wasn't an alarm. It was a phone call from her mum, and it was only ten p.m.

"I thought we weren't speaking," she said sleepily, hoping this wouldn't be a last-ditch attempt from her mum to persuade her to come home.

"Nina. Have you heard from your brother?"

"I don't know," said Nina, confused. "I've been asleep."

"Well, check your phone!" cried her mother. "Hurry up."

Nina checked to see if she had any messages or missed calls. There were five from her mum, but that was it. "No, nothing from Kal," she yawned. "Why? What's wrong?"

"He's gone."

"What do you mean he's gone?"

"I don't know," cried Rupa hysterically. "I

think he's gone to, you know. Do something bad."

Nina froze. "What? Why do you think that?"

"He left the house at seven p.m. to go for a walk, which was unusual in itself. But I was just so happy he was getting some fresh air and exercise that I let myself believe everything was fine and went out." It felt like she was talking to herself more than to Nina. "Only when I came back a couple of hours later, he still wasn't back. Oh, why didn't I stop him? Why? I should have tried harder to help him. Oh god, *why didn't I do more*?"

"Hey, Mum, it's okay," said Nina, as gently as she could. She was now fully awake and quickly pulling her clothes on. "None of this is your fault, and we're going to find him. He's probably just lost track of time somewhere. When did you last hear from him?"

"He texted me half an hour ago. Just the word 'sorry.' I've been calling him nonstop ever since."

Nina felt the blood drain from her body as her legs started to give way beneath her. Fuck. This couldn't be happening. Fuck. No. She had to focus. She sat back on the edge of the bed and forced herself to

329

breathe. Now was not the time to start panicking. "Okay," she said slowly. "Okay. Where would he go? We need to think. Have you called his friends? The family?"

"He's not going to go to the family," said Rupa. "He's never turned to them before. And what friends? Hardly any of them speak to him ever since he got ill and stopped replying to them."

Nina felt her stomach sink as she realized her mum was right. It was so easy to let Kal's jokey attitude lull her into a false sense of everything being fine, but she *knew* things were more serious than he let on.

She pulled her trainers on and grabbed her overnight bag. "Okay, well, I'm on my way home. But in the meantime, keep calling people. Literally anyone we know, just in case. I'll try and think of where he could be. And I'll message him now."

"What about your TV thing?"

"It doesn't matter," said Nina firmly, ignoring the massive knot of tangled fear and panic in her stomach. "I'm on my way. And, Mum, try and be strong. It's going to be okay. I just know it. Trust me."

"Hurry," said Rupa, hanging up.

Nina spent the whole train journey feeling sick with anxiety. She'd been lucky; the

330

hotel was right by the station and there'd been a train scheduled fifteen minutes after her mum had called. She'd be back in Leicester in an hour, but that wasn't soon enough. She'd emailed the production company saying she had a family emergency, but she barely even registered their response. She had no idea where Kal could be. Why hadn't she made more of an effort to get him to open up lately, or even interrogated him if she had to? She'd taken him to paint a bloody dragon, but she hadn't forced him to reveal what was actually going on in his mind. What was *wrong* with her?

Nina shuddered as she imagined what his text might have meant. No. She couldn't think about it. She just couldn't. It was too terrifying to even consider. No. She had to focus on staying calm and trying to figure out where he could be. She refreshed her phone for the millionth time to see if he'd replied to her text, even though she knew he hadn't. She'd texted him immediately after getting off the phone to her mum, saying, I love you. Where are you? She didn't know if she should write another message. She didn't want to bombard him, but she also couldn't do nothing. She sent another.

Please, Kal. Just tell me where you are.

Silence. We'll fix it all. It'll be okay. Silence. Please. I love you.

She stared anxiously at her phone as the minutes passed by. Her mum called again. No one had heard from Kal. She'd even tried the relatives, but no luck. Nina sent texts to anyone she could think of who knew Kal, but none of them had seen him. She was starting to panic. She wrote another message. I promise, Kal. It'll be okay. A few minutes later, her phone vibrated.

It was Kal.

No, it won't.

Oh my god. He was alive.

Nina called her mum exuberantly. "Mum. He texted me back."

"Oh my god." Nina heard what sounded like her mum crumpling to the floor in relief.

"I'll be at Leicester station in thirty minutes. Will you come and get me? I'll keep trying to reach Kal in the meantime."

"I'll see you there."

Nina and Rupa were driving around bridges. They'd checked out the train station where Nina had arrived, but there was no sign of Kal, and then they'd spent an hour driving through the busy streets in town, looking in every restaurant and shop they passed. Auntie Trish was driving through the suburban streets of Newton Linford in case he was near their house. They were running out of places to look. Nina had tried to Google search for local suicide hot spots — much to her mum's horror — but nothing had come up. They had no idea where Kal could be. He hadn't replied to any more of Nina's texts, and both mother and daughter were tense with fear.

"Shall we try at home again?" asked Nina. "Just in case he came back."

Rupa sighed. For once she didn't look at all groomed. She had Nina's puffer coat on over her matching pajama twinset, her hair was pulled back in a bun, and her face, devoid of makeup, looked raw with vulnerability. Nina felt the pain on her mum's behalf. This was beyond horrific for her, but her mum was out looking for her *son*. The child she'd carried inside her. There was no way Nina could ever know what that must feel like.

Nina swallowed a lump of sadness and put her hand on top of her mum's. "Honestly, Mum, it's going to be okay. Let's go home. I'll drive."

"Don't be ridiculous, you're not insured on my car," snapped her mum, causing Nina to smile softly; it was comforting to see her mum return to her normal self, even if it only lasted a split second.

As they pulled up into Newton Linford, Nina turned to look at her mum. "I've just had a thought. What if he's in Bradgate Park?"

Rupa looked at her daughter in confusion. "But it's closed. He can't be."

"There's a way in at night," said Nina. "Don't make any *Crimewatch* comments, but I used to sneak in. Look, it's a long shot that he'll be there, but I think we should try."

"Okay. Let's go."

"You should go home in case he's come back," said Nina. "We've been gone for ages. I'll go to the park on my own."

"It's dark, Nina. I can't be worrying about you too."

"I'll be fine. You can come and join me if Kal isn't at home, and bring Auntie Trish. I'll . . . maybe I can text Meera to come help? If you don't mind me telling her?"

"Yes, call her," said Rupa. "You can't scour the whole park alone. It'll take too long."

"Should we, I don't know, call the police?

I know you don't like to involve them, but what if they can help?"

"I already tried," said Rupa quietly. "They can't help until it's been twenty-four hours, even with his history and the text. They advised me to call the local hospitals. I did. But they haven't heard anything."

"Fuck," exhaled Nina. "Okay. You go home. I'll go see if he's anywhere on the route we used to do as a family. I'll start with Old John."

Nina hiked her way up the hill she'd known since she was a child. The last time she'd come up here had been with Nikhil when he'd proposed to her at the top, with a bottle of champagne and a platter of M&S sandwiches. This time couldn't be more different. It was pitch-black, she was using her phone for light to stop her from stumbling over the uneven terrain, and she was so anxious she could barely breathe. She just couldn't stop thinking about the possibilities waiting for her at the top of the hill. What if Kal was there? What if he wasn't? Nina's blood was pumping with adrenaline as she forced herself to walk faster up the steep slope, yelling out Kal's name every time she caught her breath.

She still couldn't fully believe that she was

searching for her brother like this. This was *Kal.* The same person who had picked her up from Jo's sixteenth after she'd projectile vomited White Lightning everywhere. He'd washed her vomit-stained sheets for her so they could hide it from their mum — though Rupa had found out anyway after he'd used the wrong detergent. Kal had always been there for her. Even when he was just as broken as she was after their dad died, he'd still found the strength to watch *Die Hard* movies with her every night, teasing her for her inability to follow the plots. And when she'd had her heart broken for the first time at university, it had been Kal who'd picked her up in a cab and taken her back to his South London flat, where his flatmates were waiting with pizza.

Those same flatmates — Ben and Raj — had texted Nina back when she was on the train to say they hadn't heard from Kal in over a year. The crushing pain she'd felt on reading this made her realize how much hope she'd secretly been harboring that Kal would be with them. They'd been best friends since university, filling up the Mistry house with their football chat and loud laughter every holiday, but Nina hadn't seen them in almost two years. Not since she'd gone to their flat to help pack Kal's stuff after it became clear he wouldn't be going back to work anytime soon. None of them had known what to say to one another. They couldn't get their heads around the fact that the sensitive, slightly geeky, and very funny guy they all loved had transformed seemingly overnight into a shadow who just stared at them with sad eyes.

The doctors had attributed his breakdown to the nonstop pressure in his insane job with its thirteen-hour days and assured Nina and Rupa that after a proper rest, with the right therapy and medication, Kal would get better. And, in the first year, it really felt like they were right. His sense of humor had come back, along with his appetite. But in the last year, he'd plateaued. And in the last few months . . . With a horrible feeling of guilt mangled with anxiety, Nina realized just how much worse he'd been getting. And none of them had done anything about it.

She swallowed a sob as she forced herself to increase her pace. Why hadn't she found Kal yet? Where *was* he? She gasped as her stomach tightened with stitches, and for the first time in her adult life, she desperately wished she exercised regularly. Her phone vibrated and she unlocked it within seconds, her heart beating with hope. But it was just Meera. She was on her way to help look.

Nina's stomach sank in disappointment, but she forced herself to keep going. Her mum had already called to say he wasn't at home. She needed to hurry.

Her phone vibrated again. This time it was her mum. His pills are gone. He didn't have loads left, but he could have gotten more. Nina felt her stomach tighten in dread. What did that mean? Was her mum saying she thought Kal had taken all his pills? Fuck. Fuck. This couldn't be happening.

She started to run, ignoring the tight pain in the side of her stomach. Kal would be fine. And even if her mum's nightmares were true, it didn't mean anything. The character in *The Bell Jar* had tried to kill herself with pills, had tried hiding herself away until she died. But she was found days later and was still alive. Kal had only been missing for a few hours. That meant there was definitely still hope for him. Right?

Finally, Nina reached the summit. She shone her phone around the low stone wall and the crumbling ruins of the old brick tower that was Old John, as well as the grassy space surrounding it. There was no one there. Disappointment flooded her as she slumped onto the wall. She'd really thought she'd find Kal sitting there, raising his eyebrows at Nina's lack of fitness. But there was no sign of him. She wiped a tear from her eyes and pulled out her phone to send another text. Kal. Please just tell me where you are and I'll leave you alone. As she hit "send," she heard a pinging sound. Nina rushed up onto her feet and ran in the direction of the sound. It had to be his phone. It had to be.

She almost stumbled over him. He was lying in a crumpled heap on the other side of the stone tower, barely visible in the dark. Nina's phone light shone onto him, revealing his motionless body, clad in a black hoodie and tracksuit bottoms.

"Kal!" Nina shook her brother. But he didn't move.

She screamed his name again. "KAL! KAL!" There was no answer.

She grabbed his shoulders and shook him harder. His arm flinched and he made a strangled sound.

Thank god.

He was alive.

Nina didn't know what to do. In movies they always stuck their fingers down people's throats. Should she? She slipped her fingers into his mouth to see if it would work, but Kal choked and pushed her away. "Get off me," he mumbled.

Nina shoved her fingers in farther until he

gagged and threw up all over her hand. "What the fuck, Nina?" he cried.

"Sorry," she said, feeling nothing but relief. Now what? God. Hospital. Ambulance. Obviously. What was wrong with her? She wiped her vomit-covered hand on her jeans, pulled out her phone, and quickly dialed 999.

"It's my brother," she began in garbled panic. "He's overdosed. We're at the top of Old John in Bradgate Park by the stone tower thing. I just made him throw up. I don't know if that's the right thing to do. But he's conscious."

"Okay," said the voice on the phone calmly. "We're on our way."

As the operator gently talked Nina through what she needed to do, she sat in the pitch-black with Kal's head on her lap, stroking his head. He was groaning in discomfort and still lying curled up on the ground, but he was alive. And the ambulance was on its way.

21. How much I love my big brother.

CHAPTER 22

Nina and Rupa sat together in the hallway of Leicester Royal Infirmary's Emergency Department. They'd already been told that Kal was stable, but they were waiting anxiously for more information. They'd been sitting for hours on these plastic chairs, in the bright white corridor, staring into space. It was three a.m. and they were both exhausted.

"Mum. He's going to be okay, right?"

Rupa turned to face her daughter. She'd managed to change into jeans and a jumper, but she still looked nothing like her usual self. "Yes, he has to." Then her face fell and she bit her bottom lip. "I can't believe this happened, Nina. I knew things were bad, and that he'd had suicidal thoughts before, but I didn't think he'd take it this far. And I try to keep an eye on him all the time, just in case, but I was so exhausted, and I thought it would be okay to start going out more, because he said I should, but . . ." She burst into tears. "I just can't do this anymore."

Nina jumped up and put her arms around her mum. Rupa let her body collapse onto Nina's, and she sobbed quietly, without making a single remark about the musty smell of her daughter's faded blue hoodie. "He's my boy, and I don't know how to help him."

Nina rubbed her hand on her mum's back and held her tightly. "I know, Mum," she whispered. "I know. But he's okay. He's safe here."

Rupa continued crying quietly. A few minutes later, she dried her eyes and peeled herself out of Nina's arms. "But what about when we leave the hospital? What if he tries again? He's been taking medication for almost two years. He has therapy once a week. What else can we do? What's the answer?"

Nina didn't know what to say. "We'll get him even more help," she said eventually. "We'll get him into somewhere private, where they'll take care of him."

"I'm not sure I can afford it," admitted Rupa. "I've spent thousands on therapy courses for him, outside of what the NHS can provide, which just doesn't seem to be enough. And his City savings have almost dried up. Taking care of him is becoming a financial strain, Nina."

"I'll help."

"You can barely pay for yourself," Rupa said dismissively. "And now you've missed out on this TV money. You can't afford it."

"I've got, like, five thousand pounds savings you can have," said Nina, quickly calculating her earnings from *Goss* and the crowdfunding. "And if you don't mind me staying at home for a bit longer, then I can pay rent too." Rupa started to protest, but Nina spoke over her. "Mum. Honestly. I know you don't believe in kids helping their parents financially. But I want to help, and I'm earning regularly again now, so I can. And we need to take care of Kal together."

Rupa nodded weakly, and Nina felt a visceral shot of pain in her chest. It was the first time in years she'd seen her mum look this vulnerable. Nina had never thought of her mum in that way, but right now, with her son recovering from an attempted suicide in a hospital bed, fifteen years after her husband had taken his own life, her fragility was obvious. She looked frightened. Old. Still a good decade younger than her fifty-nine years, as Rupa would be glad to know, but older than she had looked before

Kal became ill. Nina felt a wave of compassion flood through her and finally understood what the self-love book meant when it talked about the definition of compassion being "suffering together."

"I'm sorry," she said, turning to look directly into her mum's eyes. "I'm so sorry you're dealing with all this, and for making life so much harder for you lately."

Rupa sighed. "It's okay, Nina. I just want the best for you. And I really thought you were finally okay with Nikhil. But when that ended . . . I was just so worried for you."

"But why? I know I was heartbroken, and I guess I still am, but, Mum, I'm getting stronger every day."

"Yes, and that's great, but I just thought that once you were married, I could finally stop worrying about you. You'd be safe with Nikhil, and . . . I don't know. I suppose I thought that's one child down, and then I could just worry about Kal."

"Oh, Mum," said Nina. "You don't need to worry about me. And I don't need a man to keep me safe or protect me. I can keep myself safe. Also, people get divorced. Or cheated on. Or . . . they get ill and die. Marriage isn't a guarantee for happiness; you know that."

Rupa nodded, her eyes tearing up again.

"But, Nina, it's so hard. I don't want you to go through what I went through, being alone all these years."

"It's not necessarily what I want either," acknowledged Nina. "But if it happens, I'll handle it. Honestly. You don't need to worry about me so much."

Rupa wiped tears away from her eyes. "Okay, beta," she said, reverting to the Indian pet name she rarely used. "I'm glad for you. I really am. I just think sometimes that you can be naive. You live in this dreamworld, and I don't think you realize how difficult it is out there. Like with your TV thing."

"Hey, Mum," said Nina, putting her hand on her mum's thin forearm. "I know I messed up, but I learned so much from it. If it hadn't happened, I never would have started #NobodysPerfect, and I wouldn't have figured out how to start loving myself. I'm just sorry I ruined your reputation in the community."

Rupa sighed again. "It's okay, Nina. I just . . . I never recovered from the humiliation of everything that happened with your father. It was all so public. Leicester's so small. Everyone found out he did it himself."

"But how can all these people judge you

for Dad being ill? It's no one's *fault.*"

"It was different back then," said Rupa. "People didn't understand mental health. Everyone blamed me. They said because I came from money and was so successful in my job that I'd disempowered him or, I don't know, drove him to it. It was all my fault."

"But that's ridiculous," cried Nina. "He was ill."

"I know. But I believed them, and it was devastating. Sometimes I still wonder if it was my fault. If I was an awful wife. And that's why he did it."

"Mum, that's not true at all," stressed Nina. "You know it's not. If anything, I used to wonder if it was *my* fault. I always felt if I was a better daughter, he wouldn't have done it."

"Don't be silly," said Rupa firmly. "Your dad loved you. He loved you both. He was just very unwell." She paused. "Like Kal."

Nina nodded quietly. "Mum. I know this sounds really bad, but a tiny part of me was . . . relieved when Dad died." Tears started to slide down her cheeks, and she hid her head in her hands. She didn't want to see the shocked expression on her mum's face.

She felt her mum's hand delicately rest on

346

her shoulder. "So was I."

Nina lifted her head. "What? Really?"

"Of course. I loved him, and I was heart-broken. But, Nina, he hadn't been himself for so long. And his illness made him hard to be around. I was relieved his pain was over. I pray to god he's at peace now."

Nina closed her eyes as she processed what her mum was saying. It had never occurred to her that she hadn't been the only one who'd been relieved that her dad was finally at peace. "I never knew you thought that. We never spoke about it."

Rupa let out another deep sigh. "I just didn't want to dwell on it. It was so hard afterward — I was just trying to focus on getting through it and raising you both. God, I was so scared. I had no idea what I was doing. And I couldn't cope with the fact that everyone knew, and was gossiping, excluding us, and judging us. Also, I missed the man I'd married."

"What was he like back then?" asked Nina curiously. "You guys always seemed so different. Like how he hated parties and was always so withdrawn."

"That was his illness," explained Rupa. "Back when we met, Rohan was much more sociable. He was also very kind and caring. He used to love eating out as much as you do. I married him because he seemed so stable."

They exchanged a sad glance.

"So what changed? I just don't get it."

"I have no idea," said Rupa. "I think maybe pressure at work. Pressure to be the perfect father and husband. I wonder sometimes if it was linked to his own childhood, but he never spoke about it, and your ba and bapuji were already dead when I met him. Or maybe it was just chemical."

Nina slumped back into the hospital chair. "Why is it all so hard, Mum?"

"It's life." Rupa shrugged. "All we can do is keep on going. I didn't think I'd cope when your dad died, but I did. And now we'll cope with Kal's illness."

Nina looked into her mum's eyes. "You're so strong. It's amazing you managed to be a single mum and have a full-time job and deal with all that pain — and still keep going. I don't even know how you did it."

"Oh, I had no choice. No one else was there to help. Even my family stayed away; they thought it was all my fault."

"What?" cried Nina. "I can't believe they thought that."

"Yes," said Rupa. "I had to be tough to get through it. But I think I . . . maybe became too tough. Especially on you and

Kal. And now I don't know how to be any other way."

Nina looked at her mum and saw her how she would have been back then, just a decade older than Nina was now, with two young kids, a husband of seventeen years who'd just killed himself — all alone with an entire community vilifying her.

"You did everything you could, and they can all fuck off," she said determinedly. "I am so proud of you, and I love you, Mum."

Rupa smiled at her daughter, smoothed her messy hair, and put an arm around her shoulders, picking fluff off her top. "I love you too, beta. But mind your language."

22. I'm my mother's daughter.

Nina nervously approached her brother's hospital bed. She hadn't seen him since he'd been rushed out of the ambulance on a stretcher, surrounded by glaring lights and the urgent shouts of paramedics. Even though the doctors had said he was out of the worst of it, Nina was scared to see him. She didn't know what to expect.

"Hey, Kal." She smiled hesitantly. "How are you feeling?"

Kal smiled back weakly. "Tired."

Nina looked down at her big brother. His

face was pale underneath his growing beard, there were bags under his eyes, and he looked skinnier than ever in his bright white hospital gown. He seemed so fragile she couldn't help but feel tears spring into her eyes.

"I'm so glad you're okay," she whispered. "I love you so much."

"Yeah." Kal didn't meet her eyes.

"You really scared me," said Nina, her voice breaking. Her mum had warned her not to get too emotional in case she upset Kal, but she didn't know how not to. He'd almost died. "I was so worried. But — I'm just . . . Thank god you're here." Kal's face tightened, and he looked away. Nina cleared her throat and wiped her tears away with the back of her hand. "Sorry. Sorry. I'm being too intense. You've been through so much; you don't need me making you feel bad about it. I'm just really glad you're okay, and I'm so sorry you're in so much pain."

"Thanks." Kal looked her in the eyes. "The pain just gets to be too much sometimes."

"I know." Nina reached out to grip his hand in hers. "I wish I could take the pain away for you, Kal. It's not fair you're dealing with this. It's fucking bullshit."

He gave his sister a small smile. "Yep. I just wish I was stronger."

"Hey, you are," cried Nina. "You're the strongest person I know. You're even stronger than Mum. You live with this pain daily, and you're still so kind, and funny, and wonderful."

Kal leaned back into the bed. "I don't feel like that. I . . . despise myself."

Nina blinked away tears. She knew her brother struggled with his self-esteem and the depression relentlessly ate away what was left of it. But to hear him talk about himself like that made her heart break. "Well, I love you," she said firmly. "I always have, always will. And when you get better, you'll be able to see just how amazing you really are."

"I don't think I'll ever get better," said Kal flatly. "There's no hope."

Nina clutched his arm tightly. "Listen to me, Kal. There is hope. You have an illness. It isn't who you are, and it isn't terminal. You're in a dark cave now, and you can't see a way out. But I promise there is one. There is a light, and I will help you to find it. I promise, Kal. We will find this light and get out of this motherfucking cave. Okay?"

Kal looked taken aback, and rubbed his sore arm. "Um. Okay. Do you . . . really believe that? The hope thing?"

"Yes," said Nina urgently. "I do. There is so much hope. And I will not give up until you feel it too. This depression is not forever, and when it goes, you'll still be there, stronger than ever. Okay?"

Kal blinked at her in response. "Uh, I don't know."

"Trust me," stressed Nina. "I love you, and I will do everything in my power to help you get out of this. It's not just you against depression. It's three Mistrys versus one mental health condition. Me and Mum are going to do everything we can to help you get better."

"Shit, maybe I would have been better off dying."

Nina let out a loud laugh. It felt unimaginably good to hear her brother crack a joke again. "We are not there yet," she said, gently hitting her brother's arm. "No suicide jokes. Do you mind if I sit a sec?" Without waiting for a response, she sat down on the edge of the hospital bed.

Kal winced. "And there's me thinking the hospital bed was for me, not you."

"Kal, I love you," said Nina, holding his hands in hers. "I just . . . really love you. No matter what. And I am so, so sorry you are hurting. But I need you to know that I am here for you no matter what. If you ever feel like doing something like this again, please just try and reach out. And call me. Okay?"

Kal's eyes watered. "I'll try. But . . . in those moments . . . I feel like you'd all be better off without me."

"That will never be true. *Never.*"

Kal coughed awkwardly and rubbed his eyes.

"Besides," added Nina, "you really can't kill yourself when Mum's around."

Kal's face clouded over. "I know. She looked so scared earlier."

"Forget that," cried Nina. "I'd be left to deal with her on my own!"

Kal laughed in relief. "You guys would kill each other so quickly, the Mistry line would be wiped out in days."

"Exactly," said Nina, leaning over the bed to put her arm around her brother. "So, young Kalpesh, I'm afraid you're going to have to stick around."

CHAPTER 23

CAPRICORN SEASON

CAPRICORN
Season: December 22–January 19
Element: Earth
Themes: Practicality. Determination. Hard
  work.
Best time to: Take stock of everything you've
  done over the past year.

"I know the answer! It's Handel!" cried Nina. "Definitely Handel."

"Handel? That's the wrong century," said Rupa.

"Nins, he would have been dead way before then," said Kal.

"Okay, fine. Then . . . I vote someone called Wilhelm. Or Wilfred. A Will of some sort."

On the television, Edinburgh University guessed Wilfred Josephs. "Correct," said Jeremy Paxman as Nina cried out in delight.

"That is definitely a point for me. A Wilfred."

"No," said Rupa. "It has to be the whole thing. Zero points."

"Half a point," amended Kal. "Which means you're still one whole point behind me."

Nina rolled her eyes and smiled to herself. She couldn't remember the last time her family had all sat down to watch TV together. Kal used to complain they always watched overly female TV shows — which was probably true, as both Nina and Rupa loved a cheesy rom-com or period drama, in spite of their serious lack of representation — and Nina could never sit through any of his boring political talk shows. But it turned out that the Mistry family were all quiz show fans, and to no one's surprise at all, Kal was currently the reigning *University Challenge* champion, with a record of 27.5 points.

The last few weeks had been some of the best and worst of Nina's life. She'd never felt so close to her family, spending hours with them without complaint and miraculously getting through an entire Christmas Day without a single argument. But at the same time, Nina had never felt so anxious. She tried to keep herself busy during the day, doing long shifts for *Goss* and hanging out with her mum and brother in the evenings. Yet every night, without fail, she dreamed about Kal's hoodie-clad body lying motionless on the top of the hill. It made her feel sick with terror, and she'd wake up gasping for air, her body damp and sticky — and not in the fun way. The only way she'd be able to fall asleep again was if she tiptoed down the corridor to Kal's room, to check he was safe in bed. He'd agreed to sleep with his door open for the time being.

He seemed to be doing okay. The doctors had finally changed his meds, so he wasn't sleeping as excessively as he used to. His mood swings were still severe; he could be joking with his mum and sister over dinner, then one of them would say the wrong thing — like Rupa tentatively inquiring if he was going to shave his unruly beard anytime soon, or Nina asking how he *really* felt — and he'd lapse into sullen silence or just leave the room. It meant mother and daughter were constantly walking on eggshells around him.

The doctors at the hospital had told them to keep an eye on Kal until he stopped showing signs of suicidal thoughts, and their crisis team had come round every day for the first week to check up on him. But Rupa had decided this wasn't enough and had taken time off work to dedicate herself solely to caring for Kal in spite of Nina's best efforts to share the responsibility with her. It meant Rupa was now always at home, cleaning excessively, cooking everything Kal had ever expressed a taste for, and constantly making excuses to check up on him. Nina could see her incessant attention was annoying Kal, but every time she suggested this to her mum, she'd stalk out of the room in deep offense, repeating, "I'm his mother; it's my *duty* to take care of him."

It was only when Nina came back from doing the food shop with nonorganic produce for the third time in a row that Rupa relented. She went back to leaving the house to do errands and go for walks with Auntie Trish, leaving Nina in charge of Kal Watch. This mainly consisted of Nina trying to give Kal space, then panicking that she'd given him too much space and inventing her own excuses to check on him. She now fully sympathized with her mum's plight, and to her surprise, they were getting on better than they had in at least a decade. Rupa had softened slightly, and when Nina had quoted the book's advice on play being the opposite of depression, she'd actually suggested ordering a Chinese takeaway, complete with MSG, which they'd eaten in the *living room* (on two entire newspapers laid out across the carpet, but still). Nina had invited Meera, who'd instantly won over Rupa by complimenting her decor and engaging in intellectual arguments about astrology with Kal. Being around people seemed to lift Kal's mood — even if it meant he'd sometimes be in worse spirits the following day — so Friday night take-aways feat. Meera and Auntie Trish had become a weekly occurrence. And in the meantime, the Mistrys were spending a lot of time yelling at each other over Monopoly and watching an unhealthy amount of television quiz shows.

"Lithium," said Kal. "I'm voting lithium."

Nina laughed. "You've guessed lithium for every single answer on the periodic table round. Do you even know any other elements?"

"Do you?" Kal shot back.

"Um, potassium. K," said Nina. "And, I don't know, iron?"

"He's right," cried Rupa with delight. "It's lithium. Well done, Kal."

"Well done? It was a lucky guess," said Nina. "That is blatant favoritism, Mother." She stopped herself from adding, "just because Kal tried to kill himself." While

Rupa laughed indulgently when Kal made suicide jokes, she'd hissed angrily at Nina for doing the same. She didn't even like it when Nina made fun of herself, jokingly referring to herself as the Runaway Bride after the *Daily Mail* captioned her as such in an article.

It was all because she hadn't turned up to marry herself on TV — and had declined to reschedule. The presenters had made a joke about her jilting herself at the altar and how it was lucky she hadn't gone through with it and ended up divorcing herself. Their comment had somehow made its way into the tabloids — with mocked-up images of Nina's face stuck on top of white wedding gowns — and had instantly become a social media meme.

But Nina didn't care. She had bigger things to worry about, and she no longer felt the need to be so public about her self-love journey. She'd always craved people's validation, but now she was too preoccupied to care what anyone but her loved ones thought. Besides, she knew that the universe would keep making her go viral until she fully learned the lesson of staying chill in the face of criticism or praise; only when she 100 percent became the equanimous rock would she stop being humiliated publicly. It was why she'd barely checked her phone since Jo had sent her the Runaway Bride memes. She had much more important things to do. Like watch TV with her family.

"Just so you know, we're all having dinner with Auntie Trish on Friday," said Rupa. "I presumed neither of you had plans."

"Oh, for New Year's Eve?" asked Nina. "Can we order Thai?"

"No, we're going out. To Veeraswamy's."

Nina looked at her mum, and then at Kal, who was engrossed in the show. "Out? I thought we'd just spend New Year's Eve like we did Christmas. Hanging out at home and eating."

"Why shouldn't we celebrate?" asked Rupa, lifting her chin defiantly. "We have as much right to go out as anyone else. Dinner's booked for nine p.m."

Veeraswamy's was buzzing. The tables were all full and there was an hour's wait for anyone without a reservation. That was not the case for the Mistry clan plus Auntie Trish, who had a table waiting. The women were all dressed up. Auntie Trish was wearing a black-and-white-patterned tunic over leather leggings with heels and turquoise hoop earrings. Rupa had gone for the dark green silk jumpsuit Nina had borrowed on her first date to Veeraswamy's, paired with black kitten heels and a neutral lipstick. And Nina was in her favorite black jeans with a soft black jumper that slipped off her shoulders and a dark red lipstick with gold hoops. When she'd walked downstairs, her mum had suggested she put on something a bit more colorful because black really wasn't doing her any favors. Nina had very maturely taken a deep breath, smiled brightly, and said no.

She'd been glad she hadn't started World War Three the second Kal had appeared in a tracksuit, looking withdrawn. A look of panic had come into her mum's eyes, especially when she'd kindly advised Kal to change into his jeans and the blue shirt that she'd ironed and he'd said no. Unlike Nina, he'd said it in a monotone voice whilst putting his headphones in. Nina could see the tense look of strain on her mum's face as she simultaneously tried to accept her son's depression and the fact that he was about to turn up to a packed Veeraswamy's in a navy tracksuit with dirty trainers.

"Yo. What can I get you?"

Oh god. It was the waiter with a diamond earring who'd laughed at Nina's rejection-by-receipt all those months ago. She tried to busy herself in the menu so he wouldn't recognize her.

"Shall we just get the usual?" asked Auntie Trish. "Peshwari. Saag paneer. Tarka dhal. Veg kofta. Pilau rice. Anything else?"

"Shall we do starters too?" asked Rupa.

"Um, yes," said Nina. "Chili paneer, crispy bhajia, mixed chaat. And bhel phuri if anyone's keen."

"How about the boss's number as well, mate?" said the waiter, snorting with laughter.

Rupa gave her daughter a dirty look, and Nina muttered, "There goes his tip."

"Oh, I heard about that." Auntie Trish winced. "So awkward. We thought you'd met Gita. But" — she turned to the waiter sternly — "at least she's making an effort to get a date. You know how worried your mum is about you. She keeps posting your bio in the parents' Whats-App group."

The waiter skulked away, looking annoyed.

"Sorry, what's this WhatsApp group?" asked Nina.

"Oh, it's just us local parents in the community," said Auntie Trish. "We post our kids' bios to see if we can get any matches going. That boy's hardly got any interest though — I mean, he's a full-time waiter.

Most of the girls on there are doctors and accountants."

"Jesus," said Nina.

"Kal, did you want to order anything special?" asked Rupa. "Maybe a chicken dish on the side?"

Kal shrugged, and Nina saw her mum's face drop.

"You love a bit of chicken," she said to Kal, nudging his arm. "Do you remember that time when we had our first McNuggets and never told Mum?"

"What, when?" asked Rupa. "I raised you as pescatarians until you were sixteen."

"Me and Kal decided we needed to try chicken way before then," said Nina. "So we got Ba to buy us chicken nuggets when she babysat. She had no idea what we were ordering, because she didn't speak English."

Kal begrudgingly smiled. "That was fun. And we used to get Happy Meal toys."

"Yes, the Hot Wheels cars," cried Nina. "Do you remember that racetrack we made?"

"That was sick," said Kal. "I wonder what happened to it."

"I cannot believe you both took advantage of your poor grandma like that," said Rupa. "You know she was strictly vegetarian. She would have been horrified if she'd known she was buying you two meat."

"She tried one once," laughed Nina. "We told her it was Quorn."

"Oh my god," cried Auntie Trish. "Don't look now, but isn't that Nikhil's sister over there with her husband?"

"How is his family always at this restaurant?" asked Nina in disbelief, turning around. "Well, at least he isn't here with Karina."

"They're actually in Morocco for New Year's," said Auntie Trish. "Oh, didn't you know? Sorry, love. I saw it on her Insta and just presumed you knew."

"You follow Nina's ex's girlfriend on Instagram?" asked Kal. "That's weird."

"Right!" cried Nina. "Weird!"

Auntie Trish shrugged. "We both go to the same beautician, so I've known her for ages. You know, she gets a Hollywood every two weeks?"

"Ugh, that is so typical of her to get everything off," moaned Nina. "I barely remember to shave my legs."

"Well," said Rupa, sipping on her salted lassi, "that could be why things didn't work out with you and Nikhil. Men do prefer a well-groomed woman."

I dumped him," cried Nina, as the tables near them — including Nikhil's sister and husband — turned to look. She lowered her voice. "Besides, people don't break up with each other over body hair."

"Don't be so naive, Nina," said Rupa. "Of course they do. I'm surprised Nikhil stayed with you when your washing machine broke."

"What? When I was flat-sharing with Jo three years ago?"

"I'll never forget that damp smell." Rupa shuddered. "Sometimes I think I can still smell it on your coats and jumpers. Maybe that's why you're still single."

"Mother, I am not single because of my clothes," said Nina. "They don't even smell!"

"How's your dating life going anyway, then, love?" asked Auntie Trish, tactfully moving the conversation on. "I haven't asked you about it for a while."

"It's nonexistent," said Nina. "I'm working on myself. I'm actively single."

"Oh good," said Rupa, leaning across the table. "Then you're free to go on dates. How about Mehul? He's recently single. His mum posted a very appealing bio in the WhatsApp group."

"Wait, Mehul Patel from my year?" asked Kal. "Isn't he a bodybuilder now? I cannot imagine him with Nina."

"Ew," said Nina. "He sounds gross."

"He is not gross," said Rupa in a loud whisper. "Can you please lower your voices. He's an accountant who is very into fitness."

"And health foods," added Auntie Trish, showing the table his Instagram account. "Look; he eats the same breakfast every day: granola with chia seeds and coconut milk. Then the same dinner: salmon and sweet potato."

"Every night?" asked Nina in horror. "The same meal? He doesn't get bored?"

"Not according to his Insta grid," said Auntie Trish.

"Ugh, he's like Deliciously Ella," said Nina. "Deliciously Mehul."

She started giggling at her own joke. Kal joined in loudly, and Auntie Trish did so quietly out of respect for Rupa, who was glaring at them with her arms crossed.

"Ah, that's funny," said Kal. "I'd love to see the boys from school hear that."

"I don't think it's funny," said Rupa. "But that's a good idea to reach out to the boys! I'm sure they'd love to hear from you after so long. Rishi and his wife are back in Leicester, you know."

The laugh dropped off Kal's face and he looked down at the table.

Auntie Trish tactfully interjected. "Rups,

it's funny because Deliciously Ella is one of those famous wellness bloggers. They're mocking him for being like her."

"No, I know who she is," snapped Rupa. "I have her cookbook. But what's wrong with this poor boy wanting to eat healthily and take care of himself?"

"Um, because it's not normal to eat the same thing every day," said Nina. "It's sad. Does he even eat dessert?"

"Well, I'm afraid that wasn't one of the things I asked his mum when I saw her at Pilates," retorted Rupa. "I know his height, his job, that he's Hindu, not Jain, he's not vegetarian, and for some reason, he thinks you're pretty. But I don't know his thoughts on crème brûlée."

"Wait, he thinks I'm pretty?" asked Nina. "Show me his pic."

"He does eat dessert," said Auntie Trish triumphantly as she held up her phone. "The same one every night."

"Oh my god, he's American Psycho," said Nina. "I don't care how hot he is; I'm not dating him." She squinted at the photo on Auntie Trish's phone. "What dessert is that? Tiramisu?"

"Strawberry cheesecake," said Auntie Trish. "Own brand."

Nina stared at her in horror, and Kal

smiled again. "Of all desserts," cried Nina. "Not even chocolate cheesecake! Who *is* this guy? And he buys the supermarket own brand?"

"So unnecessary." Auntie Trish shook her head. "The branded ones are always on offer, and they're much nicer."

"Exactly," said Nina. "Sorry, Mum, but there's no way he's for me."

Rupa sighed. "Maybe not. Though I suppose it depends on the supermarket. Waitrose? M&S?"

"Lidl," replied Auntie Trish.

Rupa put her cutlery down. "Right. Back to the drawing board."

By the time they were all mopping up the remnants of their curry with their second order of Peshwari naans, Kal was in a much better mood. Nina exchanged a smile with her mum as he joked with Auntie Trish about how the carb-heavy meal would be Deliciously Mehul's idea of hell. Neither of them was so naive as to think there'd been a breakthrough, but it was an immense relief to see Kal smiling and laughing.

"Okay, guys," said Nina. "I know this is very non-Mistry, and you'll probably hate it. But I thought that as it's New Year's Eve, it might be nice if we could go around the table and say something we love about ourselves. Or like about ourselves. Like an American Thanksgiving, but celebrating *ourselves,* not external things."

Rupa groaned. "Oh, Nina, really? It's so tacky."

Kal shrugged. "Okay."

"Oh, all right, then," said Rupa. "Fine. Well, I . . .." She paused, and then, with her voice wavering, said, "I know you might not think I'm the world's best mother, but you both mean everything to me. So I suppose the thing I love most about myself is that when it comes to you two, I'd do anything."

Nina sat back in surprise. She felt her eyes water and reached out to put her hand on top of her mum's while Kal leaned across the table to hug his mum.

"Oh stop, I'm going to spoil my makeup," cried Auntie Trish, dabbing the mascara under her eyes. "You're all so gorgeous it's killing me."

Nina laughed. "Okay, okay, Auntie Trish, why don't you go next?"

"Oh, all right. Well, I suppose I love that I'm an optimist. Not that I've had much choice with my own two being such brats, never coming home from uni and spending every summer with their dad and that bloody bitch in Marbella. But I do think I see the silver lining in things, and it's helped me live a happier life."

"Quite right," said Rupa, regaining her composure. "It's important to stay positive. It's one of my favorite things about you too. Well, that and your loyalty."

"Oh, Rups," said Auntie Trish, reaching out to hug her friend. "I don't know what I'd do without you."

Nina smiled, catching Kal's eye. She suddenly remembered him in the hospital bed saying how much he despised himself, and her smile faltered. "Do you . . . want to go, Kal?"

"I'll give it a go. Look, we all know I haven't had a good year. There's no point pretending otherwise. I definitely don't love myself. And it's pretty hard to even think of something I like about myself. But . . . when Nina took me to that pottery place back in September, it was cool to connect with my more creative side. So, I guess, that, yeah."

"You've always been creative, beta," said Rupa, discreetly blinking away tears. "Even as a child, your drawings were so much more inventive than Nina's. I think you must get it from me."

Nina rolled her eyes at her mum and downed the rest of her pinot. "Well, wherever you get it from, Kal, I love that you've

reconnected with your creativity, and we should totally go back to the pottery place. You've got a gift for it."

Kal smiled back at his sister.

"What about you, then, love?" asked Auntie Trish, looking at Nina. "Do yours."

Nina exhaled deeply as the table braced themselves for an inappropriate overshare. "I just feel like I've been discovering so many things I love about myself ever since my birthday. It's been such a journey, and honestly, there is no way I could have learned to love myself if it wasn't for you guys."

"All right, we didn't ask for a speech, Nina," said Rupa. "Get on with it."

"Okay, well, I guess I love that I'm fully living my life, the ups and the downs. It's all been so zigzag lately, and really, really hard at times, but I'd much rather that than just living a straight-line life."

"So that's two things you love about yourself?" said Kal. "The facts that you're fully living your life and that it's zigzag?"

"Sorry, I didn't realize we were being quite so semantically accurate," said Nina. "But yes. In the words of Ronan Keating, life is a roller coaster, and I am riding the shit out of it."

"Language," tutted Rupa. "Ronan

wouldn't swear."

"It's almost midnight," cried Auntie Trish. "Come on, everyone. Let's do the countdown. Hold hands. Okay, TEN . . ."

The Mistry family reluctantly held hands and followed Auntie Trish's lead in shouting out the numbers. As the rest of the restaurant joined in the countdown, Nina looked around the table and laughed. Last year, lying on the beach in Bali with Nikhil, there was no way she could have imagined spending the following new year in Leicester with her family. But right now, she knew there was nowhere else she'd rather be.

"THREE . . . TWO . . . ONE . . . Happy New Year!!!!"

23. My life is a roller coaster, and I'm riding the fucking shit out of it. Sorry, Ronan.

CHAPTER 24

Rupa was standing at the kitchen hob boiling a pot of chai, dressed in khaki trousers and a matching jumper. She turned to face her daughter when she walked into the kitchen, an old hoodie thrown over her pajama bottoms.

"Nice tracksuit," yawned Nina.

"It's not a tracksuit," said Rupa, clearly offended. "It's lounge-wear. And it's cashmere."

Nina rolled her eyes and started flicking through an open *Daily Mail.* "Can I have some of the chai you're making?"

"I suppose there's enough," said Rupa. "Though really, it would do you good to have hot water —"

"With lemon and a drop of apple cider vinegar," finished Nina. "I know. You have it before you do your daily morning poo."

"Nina," tutted her mum. "Can you not talk about it like that? But it is very good for your digestive system; you should try it."

Nina rolled her eyes and reached out to take the cup of warm chai her mum handed her. "Thanks. We should call you Deliciously Rupa. Maybe you should date Mehul."

"Don't be ridiculous," said Rupa, as she took her own mug and sat down next to Nina. She took the newspaper from her daughter. "I always read the paper with my chai. You'll have to wait. Seeing as I'm the one who pays for it."

Nina let her mum take the paper from her and sipped her tea. "Ooh, it's nice. I forgot how good chai is."

"I make it every day," said Rupa, without looking up from an article about Leonardo DiCaprio's inability to date women over twenty-five. "If you woke up earlier, you'd know that."

"All right, I'll come to the kitchen for homemade chai more regularly. But no way am I doing poo tea." She paused. "Hey, Mum. How come you've stopped dating lately?"

"I'm too busy."

"Really? You managed to do it quite regularly before."

"Well, that was before everything with your brother," said Rupa. "He's my priority now, not my love life."

"But, Mum, you can do both," said Nina. "I can help you take him to his therapy appointments if you insure me on your car. And his new meds seem to be, well, stable. You can have your own life, you know."

"It's not that easy," snapped Rupa, finally looking up at her daughter. "You wouldn't understand. I'm his *mother.* I need to be there for him, twenty-four seven."

"But I'm here too," pointed out Nina. "I watch Kal when you're out with Auntie Trish; why is it any different if you're on a date?"

"It just is. Leave it, Nina."

Nina finished the rest of her tea in silence, then turned to face her mum. "Mum, sorry if I'm completely wrong, but were you by any chance out on a date the night that Kal . . . you know."

"Yes, okay, yes," cried Rupa, slamming her cup down onto the table. "There you have it. Proof that I'm a terrible mother. It's what you've both thought all along, and now it's true."

Nina stared at her mum in shock. "What? I don't think you're terrible. I think the opposite. I didn't mean to . . . I'm sorry."

"Just . . . leave me alone, Nina. I don't need this right now."

"But nobody expects you to be around Kal all the time," said Nina gently. "That would be unhealthy. It's not a big deal that you were out when it happened."

"It might not be a big deal to you, but it is to me. He's my baby. And I wasn't there for him."

"Mum, it's okay," said Nina, hesitantly placing her hand onto her mum's cashmere-clad arm. "Nothing would have changed if you'd been at home."

Rupa picked up her mug of chai. "I just feel so guilty."

"It's not your fault," said Nina firmly. "Don't feel guilty. Please."

Rupa sighed again. "We'll see."

"Hey, so, how was that date?" asked Nina. "Did you like him?"

Rupa sniffed. "He wasn't bad."

"Ooh, high praise. Who is he?"

"Brian," said Rupa, raising her chin. "He's actually a very successful landscape developer. He's fifty-five. Loves yoga. And because of his job, he's in very good shape."

Nina started laughing. "Sorry. It's just . . . Rupa and Brian. I never imagined you with a man called Brian. A Balaraj, maybe. But not a Brian."

"It's not funny, Nina," said Rupa, suppressing a smile. "He's very handsome.

And . . . he's kind. His son had mental health problems too."

"Wait, you opened up to him about Kal? That's . . . amazing."

"Yes, well, it doesn't matter, because I will not be seeing him again," said Rupa, her expression serious once more.

"Why not? I could get on board with having a Brian as a stepdad."

"I told you — I'm done dating. Besides, I practically abandoned him in a wine bar. He won't want to see me again."

"But . . . he's texted you? In the last — how long has it been, since . . ."

"Five weeks," said Rupa. "He's messaged once or twice. I let him know Kal was okay."

"Give me your phone," said Nina, holding out her hand. "Give it to me."

"Don't be ridiculous, Nina. I'm the one in charge here."

Nina snatched her mum's phone off the table and danced around to the other side of the kitchen, typing in Kal's date of birth to unlock the phone. "Oh my god, Mum, he's messaged you, like, five times since then. Asking if you're free, and checking in about Kal. He seems lovely. And his picture is *cute*. Why haven't you replied?"

Rupa crossed her arms. "I can't. Kal's ill. Brian's white. Your father's dead. How many more reasons do you want?"

"Those aren't reasons — they're just random facts. I'm texting Brian back."

Rupa shrieked. "Nina Mistry. Give me that phone back now or . . . I'll disown you!"

Nina raised an eyebrow at her mum from across the kitchen. "Please. As if you could. You wouldn't be able to cut me off knowing I'm out there using non-eco-friendly cleaning products."

"Nina," shouted Rupa. "You cannot text Brian. And I have *told* you that the chemical products can affect your hormones."

"Sorry, too late." Nina grinned. "You've apologized to Brian for the silence because you had a lot going on with your family, but you'd love to see him again."

Rupa shook her head in stony silence.

"Mum, you don't need to be scared," said Nina kindly. "You're allowed to move on, and you're allowed to have your own life."

"But how can I do that when you and your brother can barely sort your own lives out?"

"Okay, I know my life doesn't look the way you imagine a thirty-year-old's should. But I think I might be happier than I've ever been. I'm finally learning to be okay alone."

"But I'm not okay with you being alone," said Rupa glumly. "Every function I go to, people always ask me, 'Oh, how are your two? Is Kal still working in the City? Nina's thirty, isn't she — is she married?' It's just so exhausting."

"But can't you just put a spin on it all? Like, 'Oh, Nina's soo busy with her amazing career that she has no time for a man!' "

"I do sometimes. But I get so tired of making things up all the time."

"Um, it's not a complete lie! I've done a few articles for the *Guardian* now, and I did one for the BBC. Which *everyone* reads. Also, Mum, everyone puts a spin on stuff. Like Kanta Masi with her kids? She acts so thrilled that her daughter married that guy, but he's just some guy she met in Spain after A-levels."

"I suppose so . . ."

"It's just the game, Mum. If you want to be in the Indian community — especially the aspirational middle-class one — this is just what you've got to do."

"All right," sighed Rupa. "But it would help if you would just be open to going on a few dates with some boys that Pooja Auntie has suggested for you?"

"I'm taking some time out from men, sorry! Can't you just appease them by bringing Brian along to an event instead? He's already texted back and can't wait to take you for dinner on Friday."

Rupa gave her daughter a dirty look. "This is the last time I let you join me for my morning tea."

24. I'm okay alone.

Nina couldn't wait to give her present to Kal. The idea had come to her ever since he'd told her how he despised himself. She knew that she couldn't magically make him love himself — her own life was proving self-love was not as simple as it sounded — but she could show her brother how loved he was. Which was why she had made Kal a love jar.

It had, naturally, been inspired by the book. There was a passage about how the best gift you could give anybody was to inspire them to start their own self-love journey. Nina had immediately thought of Kal and decided to give him a kick start by showing him all the things he could choose to love about himself. She'd thought about giving him a straightforward list but, after hearing him talk about his creativity, had decided to do something more inventive. So she'd bought a large glass jar and lots of colored paper that she was going to cut up into one hundred pieces, with something she loved about her brother written on each one.

Nina had worried it would be a challenge, given how she still hadn't found thirty things she truly loved about herself. But when it came to Kal, there was no shortage of things to love. His kindness, intelligence, love of science, sense of humor, weird obsession with painting fantasy figurines, gentleness with animals, comforting smell — it was all in there. Everything she'd come to love about her brother in thirty years of knowing him was in the jar, and had it been big enough, she could have gone on well past one hundred. But unfortunately the jar was smaller than it looked, so she'd only made it to seventy-two.

"Kal?" Nina knocked on his door and pushed it open. The curtains were open, but Kal was lying on the bed watching a video on his phone. "Are you busy?"

He shrugged. "Just watching a TED talk on depression. My therapist recommended it."

"Oh! I can come back."

"No, it's fine," said Kal, leaning up onto his elbows. He still looked thin, and his beard was now so out of control that he'd definitely get stopped at airport security, but he was freshly showered in a clean white

T-shirt. "He keeps talking about 'curing' depression, and it's annoying me."

"Oh. Okay. Well. I have a present for you."

"Bit late for Christmas, isn't it?"

"It's a self-love present to say how grateful I am for having you in my life." Nina revealed the jar from behind her back with a flourish. "It's seventy-two things I love about you."

Kal's eyes lit up as she handed it to him. "Wow, that's really cool. Thanks, Nins."

"I just thought maybe it could help you learn to love yourself," said Nina. "I don't know, maybe it's silly. I just really, *really* hate the thought of you despising yourself."

Kal unlocked the jar and pulled out a folded piece of purple paper. "Your comforting smell."

"Okay, that's a weird one. The others are better. But honestly, you do smell good."

"Your geeky vibes," he said, raising an eyebrow. "Thanks? What's this one . . . Your natural charm. Your loving heart."

"I'm going to let you read them alone," said Nina, as Kal's eyes began to water. "But, yeah. I love you a lot. And I hope one day you can learn to love yourself that much too. Oh, and be ready by four. I've booked us a slot at the pottery café."

Nina had already finished her mug. She'd kept it white and just drawn on the outlines of two boobs with a black pen. It had taken her ten minutes. She'd spent the last hour and fifty minutes watching Kal painstakingly paint his two-inch knight — because "you can't have a dragon without a knight." Watching him so engrossed in his creativity made Nina think of something she'd read recently in the book about the meditative state of being "in the flow."

"Being in the flow happens when you use your talents and are fully engrossed in them," said the book. "You're not thinking about the results or possible success of your actions; you're doing them purely because it feels right. When you're that fully aligned with the universe, time can fly by. It's something that many artists and creatives talk about, but it can happen even with cooking, cleaning, or doing daily tasks. The key is to focus fully and let your task absorb you."

Nina rarely felt in the flow when she was cooking or cleaning — but that could be because her mum was always there hovering in the kitchen, making sure Nina had used the right limescale remover. But she did get it when she read novels, and even when she wrote. It didn't happen all the time — especially not when she was writing about A-list breakups — but it did occasionally happen when she was writing about something she cared about. Like her recent self-love articles for the *Guardian,* BBC, and now *Glamour.* Or when she was taboo-breaking. Things that could *help* people. Nina made a mental note to keep pitching more ideas along these lines. *Goss* was keeping her busy, but she wanted to keep writing about things she truly loved, and now that editors from big publications were actually responding to her pitches, she needed to make the most of it.

"Nins, why do you keep staring at me?" asked Kal, without looking up. "You know I'm not going to try and kill myself in the pottery café."

"Kal," cried Nina. "You're the worst. Obviously that is not what I was thinking. I was just . . . being inspired by you being in the flow. You know, the meditative —"

"I know what it is," interrupted Kal, pausing to paint a tiny, intricate cross onto his knight's shield. "I've read about the flow in scientific books. And yeah, I guess I am. It's good to not think about anything except for what I'm doing. It makes me feel really calm afterward."

"Yes. Like meditation! I love that."

"It's cool. Who knew painting pottery would make me feel almost as good as my drugs do?"

Nina sat in silence for a while as her brother added the finishing touches to his art, then sat up straight, suddenly inspired. "Hey, Kal, do you know if there's an arts therapy group or anything like that for people with mental health problems? In Leicester I mean."

"I haven't come across anything. Why?"

"Because you should set one up! This seems to be helping you, and it could maybe help others too."

Kal looked up at his sister. "Seriously?"

"Yeah, it would be amazing. You could all come here and just spend a few hours every week or so painting. And chatting."

"It's a nice idea," said Kal. "But I don't think I could do it."

"I'd help you! We could set up a Facebook group to spread the word. And I could chat to the owner to see if they'd give us a discount and put a sign up."

"I don't know," said Kal hesitantly. "I'm not sure I'm well enough to lead a group for mentally ill people. I'm still one of them."

"Which is why it's perfect," said Nina. "You're not claiming to fix anyone, and it's not even to make money. It's just to . . . build a community. I think it could really help people. And you."

Kal looked at her doubtfully. "Do you really think that many people in Leicester have mental health issues? Or would want to be seen publicly attending a group for people with mental health issues?"

"I think you'd be surprised. I mean, one in four people will suffer from them at some point in their lives. Leicester isn't exempt from that."

"But would they actually come to an arts therapy support group? What if no one came?"

She shrugged. "We won't know unless we try."

"Yeah, maybe. I'll have a think about it."

"I'd do all the admin! My rising Virgo would love it."

"Well, I guess we could try . . ." said Kal. "But only if you promise that we go slow, and if it doesn't work, or if it stresses me out, we leave it. Nina. Nina, what are you — ?"

Nina let out a cry of excitement, and

before Kal had finished his sentence, she'd walked off to corner the boss of the café. Kal sighed wearily and began finishing off the silver tip of his knight's spear while his sister persuaded the owner to give their new venture a 25 percent discount. With free tea for all.

CHAPTER 25

AQUARIUS SEASON

AQUARIUS
Season: January 20–February 18
Element: Air
Themes: Individuality. Revolution. Change.
Best time to: Embrace the weird and just do
  you.

Nina was late for the pub quiz.

She'd spent the last week in a whirlwind. *Goss* had wanted her to work extra hours, so she'd been doing double shifts, and any spare moment had gone to organizing her brother's Mental Health Pottery Club. They now had a Facebook page with sixty-five members, half of whom were BAME, and eight people had already committed to coming to their first-ever session the following month. Kal had been shocked to find there were other people nearby going through something similar to him — especially when he saw the amount of brown faces. He'd started replying to people's queries in the private group, and it had somehow already turned into a forum for people to share and support one another.

Nina was so proud of him that it physically hurt. She'd helped with the practical side of things, but now she was bowing out, and Kal was taking ownership of what was always meant to be his. It was no surprise to Nina that her brother was a natural at speaking eloquently and honestly about his condition, to the point where others were inspired to do the same. The whole thing made her so happy. She couldn't believe it had taken her this long to realize just how fulfilling it was to help others instead of spending all her time thinking about herself.

Her mum also seemed a little happier. She'd begrudgingly gone on her date with Brian — after Nina had practically shoehorned her out the door in a cream silk shirt with tweed trousers — and returned after midnight, chauffeured to her front door in Brian's sparkling BMW. Nina had spied on them from her bedroom window, witnessed their good-night kiss, and squealed so loudly Kal had yelled at her to shut up. She knew she was being as creepy as dads of teen daughters in high school movies, but she didn't care. Watching her mum fall for someone was far more fun than doing it herself, and it had the added benefit of putting Rupa in such a good mood that she no longer berated her daughter for lying on the sofa.

"Nina, hey," cried Alisa from a table in the corner of the pub.

Nina waved eagerly as she walked over to the Ravenclaws' table. As much as she loved her brother, it felt really good to get out of the house and have a proper break from Kal Watch. Plus, she missed her friends and she was desperate to see Meera. She hadn't come to the last couple of Friday nights chez Mistry because of "work," and Nina was scared that she was losing her friend to her new relationship after all.

"How's it going?" asked Alisa, as Nina greeted her with a hug. "Dylan and Deepa are just getting more mulled wine. And this is Dylan's girlfriend, Georgia." She pointed to a serious-looking Black woman with cool pink glasses and a block fringe. Nina felt an irrational twinge of irritation at a new person being brought into their group, but then remembered: abundance not scarcity. There would still be space for her.

"So nice to meet you," she said, generously giving Georgia a hug.

"You too." Georgia smiled, no longer looking quite so serious. "Dylan's told me all about you — and how you met. It's so ridiculous I love it. Sometimes when we're in bed, I call him 'Troll.' "

Nina and Alisa laughed in shock. "That is a detail I did not need to know," said Nina. "Hey, where are Meera and Jack?"

"They canceled last minute," Alisa said, shrugging. "No idea why."

Nina's face fell in disappointment, but before she could fall into self-pity, Georgia's eyes widened in panic. "Oh my god, it's started. Quick: what's the capital of Bhutan?"

The Ravenclaws were losing. Again. It turned out that they were worse than ever without Jack's sports knowledge and Meera's unexpected geographical trivia skills. But Georgia's impressive literary knowledge was helping. And Nina didn't really care how badly they were losing, because she was having fun with her friends. She still couldn't really believe that her closest friends right now were people she'd known for less than a year, but she wasn't complaining; there was no way she'd be having conversations like these with her school friends.

"Can you guys stop talking about how moon cycles affect your periods and start trying to answer these questions?" asked Dylan. "You can't leave me to do the sports round alone. And I don't have anything to contribute when it comes to ovulation chat."

"Poor little privileged white man," said Georgia, affectionately ruffling his hair. "Is it hard for you to be in the minority? To not have a body that makes human life and is linked to the divine?"

"Oh my god, Dylan," cried Alisa. "Are you joking? Number five is obviously Michael Owen. Everyone remembers that hat trick."

As they began discussing the glory days of 1997 premier league football, Nina zoned out of the conversation and turned to Deepa. "Sorry I haven't been able to hang around after class for a chat lately. I've been so busy with work and family."

"Oh, don't worry about it," said Deepa. "I've also been quite busy; I've actually met someone."

Nina's eyes lit up. "No way! Tell me more."

"Well, he's into similar stuff to me. He's a few years older — well, quite a bit older. He teaches meditation, and he uses it in sex. We practice tantra together, and it's fucking mind-blowing."

The smile dropped off Nina's face. "He's

not called Alejandro, is he?"

"Yes!" cried Deepa. "Do you go to his meditation classes?"

Nina bit her bottom lip. "Kind of. In summer. I was also dating him, or sleeping with him — or, well, we never actually defined it, which ended up being a bit of an issue. But anyway. It ended with him listing all my flaws and telling me how awful I am."

"Fuck me," breathed out Deepa. "That's weird. When did it end with you guys?"

"Oh, way back in August. When did you start dating?"

"In November. Thank god we didn't overlap."

"That's a while. Four months. Is it . . . serious between you guys?"

"Maybe," said Deepa. "There's something about him. We both seem to get each other. And oh my god, the *sex.*"

Nina nodded. "I feel you, girl. The man is gifted."

"I know! The other day I did a headstand and he opened my legs and started going down on me." She paused, then cracked a grin. "I guess you could say he went up on me. Did you ever do that with him?"

Nina stared at her. "Um, no. I cannot do a headstand normally, let alone with someone going . . . up on me."

"Well, there's your incentive to keep going with your headstand practice." Deepa winked. "Coming upside down is life changing."

Nina went over to the bar alone. She needed a moment to process the fact that her yoga teacher was dating her former lover and meditation teacher. It wasn't really as shocking as it should be; the spiritual scene in Leicester wasn't exactly large, and considering Deepa had the body and mind Nina could only have if she actually did yoga daily, it made sense Alejandro was into her. But it did feel weird to know that her friend was now with her ex (if she was allowed to call Alejandro that), especially given the circumstances of their breakup (if she was allowed to call it that).

Nina sipped on her tap water and tried to figure out how she felt. Alejandro had really hurt her. But she wasn't angry at him anymore. At the time, she'd felt her only choice had been to either follow Meera's lead and label him as a complete fucking asshole or give in to her insecurities and agree with all the cruel things he'd said to her. But now she realized the truth was somewhere in the middle. They'd both been at fault. Alejandro had been so caught up in his narrative of Nina being just like a younger him that he'd ignored the reality. While Nina had been so caught up in her narrative with Alejandro as the hot but temporary Colombian lover who'd come into her life purely to help her move on that she hadn't gotten to know the real him. She'd been selfish, but so had he.

He had acted cruelly, but it had clearly come from a place of hurt rather than hatred. And his comments hadn't been fully right or fully wrong. They were somewhere in the middle, and it was up to Nina to decide how she interpreted it all. It was like her reframing with the trolls: she couldn't change the fact that people got off on being abusive and frightening, but she could change how she felt about it.

As Nina downed the rest of her water, she decided she felt okay. Alejandro wasn't a bad person — he was just human. And just because their romance had ended in negativity, it didn't mean the same would happen between him and Deepa. It was like the book said: "Life isn't black and white. Things are rarely awful or amazing; they're often somewhere in the middle. Learn to live in the gray."

25. I'm finally living in the gray.

■ ■ ■ ■

Nina stood outside Meera's crystal shop feeling oddly nervous. It wouldn't normally be a big deal for her to show up uninvited, but lately Meera had been noticeably distant. Nina was shit-scared she was already reneging on her promise not to disappear into her relationship. But she knew she owed her friend the benefit of the doubt, so with a deep breath, she pushed open the shop door.

"Hey!" she called out.

Meera emerged from behind the purple curtain looking shocked. "Oh my god, Nina. What are you doing here?"

"Oh, you know, just in the area," said Nina, trying not to read into the fact that Meera hadn't immediately walked over to hug her.

"Great! Though it is a bit of a busy day today. So I don't have much time to chat, sorry."

"No worries," said Nina. "It's fine. It's . . . Meera, is everything okay?"

"Fine. Why wouldn't it be?"

Nina's stomach sank. There was an awkward silence, and then she spoke quickly. "Okay, I feel like you're lying to me and something's up. I don't want to force you to talk about it, but you know you can tell me. I love you and I'll support you with anything. Promise."

Meera suddenly burst into tears.

"Oh my god, what is it?" cried Nina, rushing over to hug her. "What's wrong?"

"It's okay," sobbed Meera. "I mean, I don't know if it's okay. I'm just really emotional. I'm . . . I'm pregnant."

Nina's mouth fell open in shock. "What? I . . . What?"

"We've been using protection. Condoms, because I hate hormonal contraceptives. Only it broke. And then I started craving Coco Pops and I never eat Coco Pops. So I did a test a few days ago, and . . . I'm officially pregnant."

"Oh my god," said Nina, dazed. "Wow. This is huge. How do you feel? Are you okay? Do you . . . know what you're going to do?"

"We're having the baby," said Meera decisively. "I know it's mad. But I can't get rid of it; I just can't. And the truth is, I'm actually excited. I think . . . I'm happy about it? But I'm just so overwhelmed."

"Wow, just . . . congratulations," cried Nina. "God, you're going to be a mum!"

"I know," said Meera, giving her a watery

smile. "I'm really excited. But also beyond terrified. I haven't told anyone except Jack."

"How's Jack about it?"

"He's thrilled," said Meera, and Nina could see her love for him literally radiating out of her eyes. "He said we're going to be fine. He's got a pretty stable gig at the moment for that music production company he's working for — you know he just does astrology on the side as a hobby. So I think we're going to be all good. We'll probably move in together next year, before the baby comes, but obviously, no rush. It's not exactly what we imagined happening so soon."

Nina listened to her friend, trying not to freak out. Everything was going to change. They wouldn't be able to go on the holiday they'd been planning to Southeast Asia. Meera wouldn't be free for spontaneous park chills. Or Friday night takeaways. She'd be a mum. A real grown-up. While Nina was still a pathetic woman-child living in her mum's guest room.

Nina's heart quickened, and she took a deep breath. No. She refused to go down the path of self-doubt and insecurity. This was big news, and it would change their friendship. But it also meant there'd be an extra human in the world. A beautiful baby she'd have the privilege of getting to know. Abundance. Gratitude. Abundance. Gratitude.

"I'm so happy for you." She smiled. "I know it's scary and big news, but I know Jack loves you. And you love him. That's all that matters."

"Thank you. And I'm sorry I didn't tell you earlier. I was scared to tell you because that made it real."

"Hey, it doesn't matter at all. Honestly. I'm here you if you need me, but you don't owe me anything."

"Thanks, Nins," said Meera, starting to cry again as she hugged her friend. "I just feel really emotional and really lucky to have you in my life."

Nina laughed as her eyes teared up too. "Oh my god, don't. You're going to make me cry and I don't even have the hormonal excuse you do. You know I love you, and you're going to be an incredible mum. How pregnant are you?!"

"Two months. I think the baby's going to be a Cancer! I'm so scared though. I keep throwing up. I've had to cancel loads of work. But . . . I'm excited. I've been looking at the stars, and it's a good time for me to do this. Motherhood is in my chart."

Nina laughed. "Of course it is. God, if

your baby is anything like you, I cannot wait to meet them. Even if they're not. I love them already."

"Me too," cried Meera. "I just feel so much love it hurts. I can't cope."

"I guess that's just what it means to love your family," said Nina. "It's how I feel about my mum and brother. Well, sometimes. Like once a month maybe. Once a year for my mum."

"Oh my god, I forgot to tell you something," cried Meera. "I finally did your brother's chart for you. And it turns out he's an eleven in numerology."

"Which means . . . ?"

"It's the other master number. Eleven and twenty-two are both really special, spiritual, big-energy numbers. It's just really beautiful that you're both siblings with master numbers. It explains why you have this amazing bond."

Nina looked at her. "We both have special spiritual numbers?"

"Uh-huh," said Meera. "I feel like you could be really integral to his journey, Nins. And you know how you can reach a lot of people and make a difference? Well, he can too."

"Oh my god, I love that. Can I help him?"

"You already are. Honestly, you guys have

the sweetest relationship." Her face crumpled and she let out a loud sob. "I'm so sad my baby won't have a sibling to have a special, magical relationship with."

"Hey, hey, they might one day. And if not, I'll be their magic aunt. Okay? I promise."

CHAPTER 26

Nina wasn't sure she was in the right place. She looked down at the flyer in her hand saying "Joyful meditation: dance your way to inner peace" and checked the address. Yep, she was meant to be inside the Gothic church looming above her. This wasn't the first time she'd done something so outside her comfort zone, but her palms were sticky with sweat. The thought of dancing with strangers was seriously intimidating, but Nina knew she had to give it a try. Her mind had been so overactive lately with all the positive comments she was still receiving online, and meditating in silence felt impossible. So instead she'd decided to try a more active, fun meditation. One that also ticked off her cardio for the week.

She downed the chai latte she was holding and walked inside. The vast church was lit up with candles, and a handful of people were stretching on the floor. A DJ was standing at the altar with decks, playing techno-spiritual tunes, and a woman with an official-looking clipboard was sitting next to the pews. Nina wandered over to her uncertainly. "Hi, I'm here for the joyful, um, meditation?"

"Adult or concession?"

"Um . . ."

The woman sighed. "Adults pay £12. Seniors and under-eighteens pay seven pounds. Students pay nine pounds."

Nina decided it was unlikely she'd pass for a senior or child. "Student."

"£9."

She handed over her money, hoping it would be worth it, and then stood there awkwardly. "Sorry, it's my first time. I'm not quite sure what —"

"Just copy everyone else. DJ Ananda will tell you what to do."

Nina dumped her stuff on the side and self-consciously tried to imitate the people stretching. After several awkward minutes, DJ Ananda spoke.

"Welcome, souls of light and being. Thank you all for showing up today for this joyful active meditation. We're going to start by standing up, closing our eyes, and swaying. Then, throughout the practice, I'll give oc-casional words of guidance, but remember

— this is your meditation. You do what feels right for you. Now close your eyes and dance."

Nina tried to force her rigid body to sway to the beat. It was the kind of hippie-esque song she imagined Gap Yah backpackers playing round a fire as they strummed guitars and tripped on acid. She'd never been on a Gap Yah, and even if she had, she imagined she'd be the kind of person who didn't do any acid at all.

"Let the music fill your soul," said DJ Ananda. "Listen to the lyrics: 'Love is the fire, burning in the night. Your love is the fire in me.' "

As the music crescendoed, Nina found herself loosening up. She peeked one eye open and saw people dancing wildly, throwing their arms and legs into the air. She closed her eye again and tried to emulate what she'd seen. The others were now singing loudly: " 'Burning up. Burning up. I'm burning in your love.' "

Nina suddenly remembered this was meant to be a joyful meditation, and there was nothing joyful about panicking over whether people were judging you — just ask her mother. With an internal *Fuck it,* she started to sing along, waving her arms around, not thinking about how insane she must look.

"Let the love fill you," cried DJ Ananda. "Come on! Let go of negativity. Let go of whatever you've been holding on to."

Nikhil.

His name appeared in Nina's heart. But it didn't make sense; she'd already let him go. She'd dumped him.

"Be honest with yourself about what you need to let go of."

Nina felt a tear slide down her face. It was true. She hadn't fully let go of Nikhil. A very tiny part of her still hoped they'd one day fix their issues and magically get back together.

"It's okay," said DJ Ananda, making Nina feel he was talking directly to her. "Visualize yourself letting go. Send love to whatever you're letting go of. And breathe. Let love fix it all."

With a deep breath, Nina followed the instructions. She sent Nikhil love and smiled through her tears. Then Karina's face appeared in her mind. Nina felt a knot in her stomach tighten. She tried to send Karina love too, but it was just too hard.

"You can do it. Just let go. Trust it'll be okay."

Nina's face was now damp with tears, but she kept going, swaying as she visualized herself sending love to Nikhil and Karina. Slowly, it stopped hurting. In her mind's eye, she walked over to the couple and hugged them both. The knot tightened so much that she gasped out in pain, but then suddenly, it disappeared completely. She felt a wave of love spread through her body. She was free.

When the third song ended, Nina sat down panting. She was dripping in sweat and starting to realize how unfit she was. But this was the most fun she'd had all week. DJ Ananda — his name meant eternal bliss — had played nonstop hippie songs with powerful lyrics, and Nina had found herself dancing wildly around the room with bankers, artists, and everything in between. It was like being in a club, but in daylight with an athleisure dress code and free fruit. Nina kind of loved it.

"We're going to do a final song now to prepare us to go back into the outside world," said DJ Ananda. "Focus on the burning ball of love inside you, and think of someone who needs it."

Kal. Of course.

"Use all your energy to send this burning ball of love to that one person. And as you dance, let your loving energy transfer to them. Send them your positive vibes."

Nina focused every single bit of her energy on her brother. She let her body sway to the song — some kind of Ibiza remix of an Indian hymn called "Om Namah Shivaya" — and thought about Kal. She remembered him as a five-year-old naked in the paddling pool, beaming at her with a massive smile, and his enormous eyes with their unfairly long lashes. She saw him growing up, patiently teaching her how to ride a bike, letting her tag along with him and his friends to Bradgate Park.

She focused all her love on Kal, thinking about him lying sad and broken in his bed — she even let herself remember him slipping out of consciousness on the top of the hill on that awful night — and prayed to the universe that he'd find the happiness he deserved.

Nina felt more tears fall down her face as she danced and sang, but she didn't care. This was for her brother. She felt the loving energy fill her body, and as she cried, she knew she was smiling. Love. Kal. Love. Kal. She sent the massive burning ball of love inside her straight to her big brother, with her new mantra chanting loudly in her mind, praying for him to find love in all its forms in his own life. Love. Kal. Love. Kal.

When the session ended, she wandered over to her stuff, feeling lighter than ever, with a stupid smile on her face. She absent-mindedly checked her phone, then froze in shock. She had a message from Kal. He'd sent her a photo of the two of them in the paddling pool in the garden, with a five-year-old Kal splashing his little sister.

Just found this, he'd written. Love you, Nina.

26. How spiritual and hippie I've turned out to be.

Nina stood at the back of the pottery café, trying not to cry. There were fifteen people of different ages, ethnicities, and back-grounds all painting bits of pottery. Some were chatting. Some were laughing. And some were sitting in silence. Her brother was at the center of it all, painting a two-inch castle and leading a conversation about everyone's individual coping mechanisms. He looked at ease, but more importantly, he was putting everyone else at ease. As he leaned across the table to include a nervous-looking young woman into the conversa-tion, Nina felt her heart swell with pride.

"Nina, can you give me a hand, please?

Honestly, you'd think I wouldn't need to ask."

Rupa was standing in the doorway of the café, holding a stack of large Tupperware boxes.

"Mum, what are you doing here?"

"I came to support my son, of course. I brought sugar-free, gluten-free, dairy-free brownies for everyone. Healthy body, healthy mind."

Nina shook her head as she helped her mum unpack the snacks onto plates. "How did you even know about this?"

"It came up on my Facebook News Feed. God forbid I find out about these things from actual conversations with the children I share a house with."

"Sorry," said Nina. "We would have told you eventually, but we thought you wouldn't like it, because Kal's being so open about his mental health stuff."

"It's not 2015 anymore!" cried Rupa. "Even the royal family talks about mental health. There's no need to keep the taboo going."

Nina's mouth dropped open. "But . . . that's what I say."

"Brian agrees with me."

Nina hid a smile. "And how is the wonderful Brian? When do we get to meet him? I owe him a thank-you for getting you to finally listen to the things I've been telling you for years."

"Don't be so sanctimonious. It's unattractive. And I was thinking he could come for Friday night dinner one week."

"Oh my god," cried Nina, causing Kal to shoot her a glare.

"Nina, please lower your voice," tutted Rupa. "Is it really surprising that I'd introduce my partner to my children?"

"Oh my god, your partner!! Sorry. Sorry. That's just, yep, great idea. So, your last few dates have gone well, then?"

"Yes, thank you," said Rupa. "We had that lovely dinner you forced us into. Then we did a nice walk around Foxton Locks, followed by a pub lunch. And last week, we went to a delicious new Chinese place. We have dinner plans tomorrow for Valentine's Day, and he's going to take me on a minibreak to Bath for my birthday next month. To try out a restaurant he loves."

"Well, it sounds like you really love eating together. Do I get any details on his personality, or how the relationship's going?"

"Absolutely not," said Rupa. "I'm not going to gossip with you. I'm your mother, not your friend. Now, can you take these brownies over to the group? And why don't

410

you ask Kal who that lovely girl is?"

"Super healthy vegan brownies for every-one," said Nina, taking a tray over to the group. "Courtesy of my and Kal's mum."

There was a chorus of "Thank you" as people passed them around. She caught Kal's eye and they both smiled.

"Sorry, is this gluten-free?" asked the nervous-looking woman both Nina and Rupa had noticed. She was pretty up close, with curly brown hair and green eyes under her thick black glasses.

"Yep, it's everything-free. I like your, um, mermaid?"

She smiled. "Thank you. I thought I'd use the metallic paints to get an iridescent glow." A look of anxiety flashed across her face. "Though I'm not sure it's working. Oh god. Maybe I shouldn't have done two layers."

"It looks great," said Kal, and the woman's face relaxed into a smile again.

"Hey, I'm Nina. What's your name?"

"I'm Sita," she replied. "I'm a scientist. Well, I was. But then I had to take a break. Because, well, the . . ."

"You don't have to talk about it if you're not ready," said Kal. "Only if it feels right."

Sita flashed him a grateful glance. "Thank

411

you. Maybe later."

"Or maybe in private," suggested Nina. "As in, with Kal. Sounds like you two have a lot in common."

Kal shot her a furious look.

"Anyway, um, I'll leave you to it," said Nina. "Ignore me. Really, really great pottery, everyone. Oh my god, that bowl is absolutely stunning."

Its middle-aged male owner smiled at her. "Thanks. It's evoking the Japanese method of kintsugi, where you repair broken pottery with gold. To show the beauty in so-called imperfections."

"That is beautiful," cried Nina. "I love that."

"Good," said Kal. "Now would you mind leaving us to it? And if you wouldn't mind saying the same to Mum?"

Nina took the hint and wandered back to her mum.

"So, who is she?" asked Rupa. "She looks around his age. Possibly a couple of years older. She's not wearing a ring though, which is a good sign."

"Oh my god, Mum. Calm down."

"Nina Mistry," seethed Rupa. "Tell me who she is."

"I'll swap you one detail about Sita for one detail about Brian."

"Sita?" repeated Rupa. "Ooh, she might be Gujarati. What's her surname?"

"Brian detail first, please," said Nina, crossing her arms. "Ideally an emotional one."

"Oh, you are just so immature," hissed Rupa. "Fine. Well. I love him. Is that enough detail for you?"

Nina's mouth dropped open. "Oh my god. Mum. I didn't know. That's . . . Oh my god. I'm so happy for you."

"Yes, okay, Nina. Now do you think she could be a Pabari? Please tell me she is, because I know their daughter went to Oxford. Oh, she'd be ideal for Kal. I can't believe I didn't think of setting them up earlier."

CHAPTER 27

PISCES SEASON

PISCES
Season: February 19–March 20
Element: Water
Themes: Feelings. Connections. Empathy.
*Best time to: Tell your friends how much you
    love them.*

Nina sat on a fur-clad chair in the corner of
her favorite café, waiting for Meera. They
hadn't met for over a fortnight, and she
couldn't wait to see her. They'd been messaging nonstop, sharing their headline news
— Nina had told her all about her magic
meditation and Kal's pottery, while Meera
had sent relieved updates about how well
her parents had handled the pregnancy
news. The fact that they'd been speaking
like normal had reassured Nina their friendship wouldn't die just because Meera was
going to be a mum. It would simply change.

And as the book said, "Change is the only certainty in life." So if she wanted to enjoy life, then she'd need to learn to enjoy change.

"Just let things *be*. Stop trying to control things, and enjoy what you have. Be grateful." And Nina was grateful. For her family, her best friend, and naturally, for herself. She now had twenty-six things she loved about herself, and with two months to go until her birthday, she was no longer worried about reaching her goal. At this rate, she might even go over thirty.

"You look pleased with yourself," said Meera, greeting her with a hug.

"I am, actually." Nina smiled. "I'm feeling very, very grateful."

"Ah, that'll be the Virgo full moon," said Meera. "It's making me extra emotional about all this." She gestured to her tummy as she sat down.

"Tell me everything," said Nina, leaning across the table. "It's so great your parents have reacted so positively. Well, your mum and stepdad. Does your dad know yet?"

"Nope. I'll leave it to Mum to break it to him eventually. Might need to pretend me and Jack are married though."

"Do you think —"

"No," said Meera firmly. "We've barely

been together five months. There's no way we're getting civil partnered already. Having a baby together is definitely enough for now. And god knows what it's going to be like living together, though I don't think we're even going to cross that bridge until next year."

"That makes sense. Hey, are you going to find out if it's a boy or girl?"

"Definitely," said Meera, pouncing on the brownies that Nina had ordered. "Oh my god, you're a dream; I'm craving chocolate like mad." She shoved one into her mouth and carried on talking with her mouth full. "I need to know the sex, because I massively want a girl and am going to actually cry if it's a boy. God, I hope it's a girl."

"It's true," agreed Nina. "A girl would be so much better. And that second brownie was for me."

"Sorry," said Meera. "Let's get more. *Anyway.* I don't want all our conversations to just be about the baby from now on. How's your work going? I read the article you did for the *Guardian* interviewing CEOs about their failures. I loved it!"

"Thanks," beamed Nina. "I pitched it myself. I'm still doing the celeb stuff for *Goss,* but I'm starting to write more elsewhere too."

"Good for you! Oh my god, you should totally have your own column. Why don't you pitch one?"

"I couldn't," cried Nina. "That's for, like, celebrities. I can't just pitch an idea to, I don't know, *Vogue.* It's not that easy."

"Why not?" demanded Meera. "You have a fuckload of followers now. You're a big deal."

"Not that big a deal. And it's so competitive. Why would they pick me?"

"Why would they not?" countered Meera. "Just pitch an idea. What's the worst that can happen?"

"I actually did have an idea for a column," admitted Nina. "To interview people about things they love about themselves. Famous people, but also ordinary people."

"I love it!" cried Meera. "It's so you. Promise me you'll pitch it as soon as we say goodbye?"

"Oh fine," said Nina. "I get so scared of rejection, but I guess I've already hit rock bottom. I promise I'll try. Not that I'm holding out any hope."

Meera took a sip of her tea and smiled at Nina. "God, I am so proud of you, girl. I mean, like, how far have you come since we met?"

Nina pulled a face. "Stop, you sound like

you're in a movie. You've even got the same glowing skin that rom-com heroines have."

"Seriously, these hormones are insane," agreed Meera. "They need to bottle this shit. Also, I actually have one more baby thing I wanted to talk about . . ."

"Okay, cool." Nina forced her face into an encouraging expression. "What is it?"

"Do you want to be the godmother?"

Nina let out a high-pitched shriek.

"Okay, calm down. People are staring."

Nina ignored her and started tearing up. "I can't believe this. I mean YES, obviously. Oh my god, YES." She turned to face the odd handful of couples and solo readers around her. "She just asked me to be her baby's godmother!!"

No one replied, bar the waiter who was forced to smile politely. "Oh my god, Meera, this is possibly the most exciting thing that has happened to me this entire year."

Meera laughed but looked genuinely pleased. "I find that hard to believe, but I'm glad. I know I haven't known you long. But I feel like this baby is partly yours in a weird way. She — okay, maybe he — has come out of the last few months I spent with you."

"That is beautiful," said Nina, touching a hand to her heart.

"You have the same life philosophy and

energy as me," continued Meera. "I love Jack, but he isn't as spiritual as us. So it's really important you're there, especially in case something happens to me. To share our values with her, or him. You know?"

Nina clutched her hands to her heart. "Yes. Oh, Meera, I would love that. I can't wait to meet her, or him. So, when's your next doctor's appointment, and what time should I be there?"

Nina had just finished filing her morning's articles when her bedroom door burst open. It was Kal. He looked more animated than he had in months.

"Have you checked your Twitter?" he demanded.

Nina groaned. "No. What is it now? Actually, don't tell me; I don't want to know."

Kal looked at his sister sympathetically and sat on the edge of her bed before quickly standing up again. "Ugh, is that your dirty underwear?"

"Sorry," said Nina, pushing her knickers off the bed. "You can sit now."

"Uh, I'll stand. Nina, your account has been hacked."

"What? That . . . doesn't sound good."

"No," agreed Kal. "Especially because they've deleted your fifty thousand follow-

419

ers and all your tweets." He paused as his sister stared at him in shock. "They've gotten rid of your entire account, Nins, and I don't think there's any way of getting it back."

"But . . . but it took me months to build that up! It's my . . . my platform. My voice. They can't just take that away from me."

Kal gingerly sat down next to his sister. "I know. Sorry. I've tried to contact Twitter for you, but judging from previous stories online, they won't do anything."

Nina stared at him. "I can't believe they've just erased me. I've got followers. I've been helping people. It's where I launched #NobodysPerfect. They can't just get away with this."

Kal nodded. "I know. It's not fair. But there's still a chance Twitter might help, considering you've got such a big following."

"Oh my god," said Nina, lying flat on the bed. "I can't believe this. Why is it that every time things start to go right, they go completely wrong again? It's just so exhausting."

"They've, um, also been doing racist tweets."

"Oh fuck," cried Nina, sitting up. "The Internet's going to think I'm a racist again."

"Don't worry. They're so badly spelled that it's obvious it isn't you." He showed his sister her former account on his phone. The first tweet was anti-Muslim. The next was anti-Christian. The third was anti-Semitic.

"Oh look, they've just done a new one that's anti-Buddhist," said Kal. "They're really covering all their bases. It's good they're not discriminating with their discrimination."

Nina didn't know whether to laugh or cry. In the end she did both.

"Uh, are you okay? You look a bit mental. And it's fine for me to say that, because I actually am."

"Mmm, I'd say you're still not allowed. But, yeah, I am okay. I think I'm really okay."

"You don't look it . . ."

"No, I really am," said Nina. "If this was the first time I'd had some Internet-based crisis, then I probably wouldn't be. But I've had worse. And I think it's time to learn my lesson."

"Which lesson would that be?"

"To be an equanimous rock. Moved not by extreme trolling or extreme fangirling."

"Come again?"

"I'm not going to let it get to me. It's just

421

social media. There's more to life." She inhaled and exhaled deeply. "I'm just going to keep breathing through it. As my favorite pranic healing sleep meditation says, so be it."

"Um, are you sure you're okay?"

Nina grinned at Kal. "I actually think I am."

"Cool. Because, while I'm here, I wanted to ask your advice. About Sita."

"Oh my god!" Nina sat up and clutched her hand to her heart. "You've come to me for girl advice. *Finally.*"

"Make it weird and I leave," warned Kal. "It's just, we've been chatting and she's really cool. We have a lot in common. But I'm scared to suggest we become more than friends. Because I'm still so . . . you know. And she's got a personality disorder caused by trauma. Neither of us is okay."

"I think just take it slowly," suggested Nina. "See how it goes; it's still early days. And then ask her what she thinks. Just float it and see how she feels. But remember, the only way to stop yourself from being disappointed is to have zero expectations."

"Yeah. Okay. Thanks, Nins."

"It's what I'm here for. Love you!"

"Yeah, you too," said Kal, walking out of the room.

Nina collapsed onto her bed smiling. She'd been using her X-rated manifestations to bring more joy into the lives of her loved ones, and it seemed to be working for Kal. He still had days where he didn't speak to anyone and shut himself in his room, but the Mental Health Pottery Club seemed to be lifting his spirits. And now he actually *liked* someone!

It was almost as exciting as Rupa falling in love with Brian. Nina felt her own heart fill with love as she thought about her mum and brother. She was so happy for them that it outweighed how sad she was about her social media being hacked. God, she hoped it was just her Twitter. Quickly, she opened up her other accounts to check whether they were okay. They were fine. She opened up her email, and it looked fine too. Thank god. Then she froze. There was a reply to the message she'd sent to *Vogue* pitching her column.

Nina took a deep breath, preparing herself for the inevitable rejection as she opened it up. She scanned it quickly. The editor loved it, but there was no space in the print issue. Of course not. It had been naive of her to expect anything else, but at least she'd tried. And the editor had said she loved it! Nina was about to exit the email when she saw there was another paragraph below. The editor would love for her to write a weekly column online.

Nina screamed aloud. She, Nina Mistry, a brown, big-nosed, imperfect woman, was going to have a column in *Vogue* magazine! For the first time in her life, she'd be able to see a woman who looked like her in the pages of the hallowed fashion magazine — *and it would actually be her!!* The best part was that she'd be able to interview incredible people across the world to hear about the things they loved about themselves, and in doing so, she could inspire thousands of readers. She was basically Carrie Bradshaw, except her area of expertise was self-love, not sex.

Nina lay down on her bed in her favorite yoga pose, allowing her breathing to return to normal. This was amazing, but she wasn't going to lose her mind over it. She wasn't even going to tweet about it, because the universe had taken her account away from her. Instead, she was going to take a moment to savor this celebration, whilst accepting the loss of her followers. There was space for both of these things in her heart. All she had to do was stay calm and breathe.

27. I'm an equanimous rock, moved not

by extreme fangirling or even more extreme trolling.

So. Be. It.

CHAPTER 28

"What are you wearing?" cried Rupa as Nina walked into the dining room.

Nina looked down at her jeans and faded band T-shirt in confusion. "My . . . clothes?"

"But Brian's coming! Don't tell me you've forgotten."

"Of course I haven't," replied Nina. "I've been excited for weeks."

"Then why are you wearing that ratty old T-shirt?" shrieked Rupa.

"What's going on in here?" asked Auntie Trish, walking into the living room carrying two bottles of prosecco. Nina took in her bright makeup and flowing chiffon top, and then her mum's leather skirt and black shirt. "Oh, Nina, didn't you realize we were getting dressed up tonight?"

Nina sighed and walked back up to her room to get changed. She knocked on Kal's door. "We can't wear normal clothes. We have to look smart for Brian."

Kal opened the door wearing a clean shirt and black jeans. "I know. Mum laid this out for me."

"Bloody hell," said Nina, walking over to her mum's bedroom. She'd just finished putting on her favorite green silk jumpsuit when the doorbell rang. She ran downstairs to finally meet the man who had melted her mum's heart.

"And you must be Nina," said Brian, opening up his arms to hug her. He was tall, broad, and as any man of Rupa's needed to be, immaculately groomed, wearing a crisp linen shirt with the sleeves rolled up. He was even holding a bouquet of flowers that clearly wasn't from the supermarket.

"You're real," cried Nina. "Sorry, I just couldn't fully believe you existed."

Her mum shot her a look and then turned to Brian with a sugary smile. "Come through. Dinner's ready. I've made pan-fried salmon with seared asparagus, crispy kale, and sweet potato fries."

"So what do you think?" Nina whispered to Kal as they hovered in the hallway.

"He seems nice," Kal said, shrugging. "He has a kind face."

"Yeah, but Mum's being weird. Do you think she'll stop yelling at us in front of him? I don't want him to change her."

"Oi," said Auntie Trish, poking her head into the hallway. "Come and eat dinner before it gets cold. And isn't Brian cute? Nina, I might need you to make me a dating profile too. But," she added quietly, "I'm not sure I want to compromise on the brown thing like Rupa has. A full-blown Gujju for me, please."

"This is really delicious, Rups," said Brian, putting his arm around Rupa and squeezing tightly.

Nina stared in shock as her mum smiled up at him and let him kiss her cheek. Her mother despised public displays of affection. She thought they were tacky. Nina was about to verbalize this when she saw Auntie Trish shoot her a "Don't you dare" look. She sighed and speared a perfectly cooked asparagus instead.

"So," said Auntie Trish, "tell us more about yourself, Brian. Rups says you have your own landscape gardening business? Sounds fascinating."

"Oh, I don't know about fascinating." He smiled. "But it's my passion. I just really love nature. I need to be outside. It's good for my soul."

"Oh my god, are you an earth sign?" asked Nina. "You love nature. You love food. You have really good-quality clothes. Wait, are you a —"

"I'm a Taurus," said Brian.

Nina squealed in excitement. "Oh my god! This is just amazing. Do you know where your moon is?"

"No, he does not," snapped Rupa. Nina smiled in relief; her mum hadn't changed.

"I actually might do," said Brian apologetically as Rupa turned to him in blatant surprise.

"A friend did it for me once. Let me think. I'm pretty sure it's also Taurus. Or Virgo. No, my rising sign is Virgo and the moon's in Taurus. I'm not sure I fully believe it all, but it's pretty harmless. And I am very earthy."

"Shut. Up," cried Nina. "Oh my actual god. I can't believe this." She turned to look at her baffled family. "Mum's dating me."

"Um, what?" asked Kal.

"Brian is the exact same as me," said Nina. "Taurus sun, Taurus moon, and Virgo rising. Which means that Mum, a repressed Pisces who has basically become a Virgo, likes me so much that she's found a man who has the same birth chart as me."

Brian laughed good-naturedly, while Rupa looked horrified. "It can't be . . . It's not . . . Well, it's all mumbo jumbo anyway."

Auntie Trish shook her head, laughing. "Honestly, Nina, I haven't heard anyone talk about star signs since the seventies."

"Well, I'm honored to share astrology with you," said Brian. "Have I phrased that right? Although I don't know how we can be so similar star sign–wise when you're so much more successful than me. Your mum was telling me all about your new *Vogue* column. She's very proud of you. Congratulations."

Nina looked at her mum in surprise, but Rupa was studiously slicing a sweet potato fry. "Thank you," she said. "It's all thanks to the universe."

Kal rolled his eyes. "You sound like such a hippie these days. When did you get so spiritual?"

"Um, since I started my spiritual journey?" she retorted, before rearranging her face into a relaxed smile. "It's the best thing I ever did. Life just feels so much easier. Nothing's really an issue when you have a spiritual perspective."

"Honey, you're being a little bit too positive right now," said Rupa. "It's a bit off-putting."

Brian joined Nina and Kal in suppressing a smile, while Auntie Trish nodded. "Life isn't all sunshine and roses, my love."

"Thanks for the heads-up," said Nina. "But aren't you guys pleased I'm becoming more brown? India's, like, the original home of spirituality and wellness."

"Don't say 'brown' like that," said Rupa. "And I wish you'd connect with other parts of our culture first. Like listening to your elders, following your duty, and being more respectful."

"Well, astrology is a big Indian thing," volunteered Auntie Trish. "And what's that quote from the Bhagavad Gita? Bloody hell, I can never remember it. Wait, oh yep, 'It's better to live your own destiny imperfectly than to live another's perfectly.' That always reminds me of our Nins, doing her own thing in her own imperfect way."

Nina's mouth fell open. "That came from the Gita? Seriously? It's beautiful."

"Oh, there's so much more," cried Auntie Trish. "I don't know why your mum hasn't taught you these. Do you know the Gandhi one?"

" 'An eye for an eye and we'll all be blind'?" offered Kal.

" 'True happiness is when what you think, what you say, and what you do are in harmony,' " said Auntie Trish proudly.

"Who knew Hinduism was so woke?" asked Nina. "These quotes are so my vibe right now."

"Have you ever been to India?" asked Brian. Nina shook her head. "Oh, you should go, I think you'd really love it. Particularly Rishikesh — it's the birthplace of the yogic philosophy — and it's breathtaking with the Himalayas. I can't get enough of that mountain air, and the puja ceremonies on the Ganges are something else."

"You've been to India?" asked Kal, as Rupa beamed with pride at Brian.

"Oh yes, I've gone for yoga and meditation retreats." He turned to look at Kal. "Hey, Kal, your mum tells me there might be romance on the cards with a Sita?"

Kal blushed. "We're just friends. I didn't know anyone even knew we've hung out."

"I have my sources," said Rupa smugly. "You know I'm friends with Sita's mum. And it may just be that Sita keeps talking about you. A lot."

Kal blushed darker. "Really? Actually, don't tell me. It's not fair on Sita."

"Good on you," said Brian. "There's nothing like young love. As me and your mum will attest." He winked at Rupa.

"Oh, you two," cried Auntie Trish. "Honestly. Get a room."

"We just need Nina to find someone now,"

said Rupa. "At this rate she'll be the only single Mistry left."

They all turned to Nina expectantly, but she just looked at them blankly. "What?"

"Mum was being Mum," said Kal.

"Oh, right," said Nina, then she beamed at them all. "Guys, I've had an epiphany, and it's all thanks to Brian. I am going to go to India and embrace my roots."

"I'm . . . pretty sure that's not what Brian said," said Kal, as Rupa's mouth fell open, Brian coughed, and Auntie Trish clapped her hands together.

"How exciting," she said. "Let's all go. Vacay!"

"You won't last a day," cried Rupa. "India's difficult, Nina. It's dirty and polluted, and there's poverty." She paused and a dreamy expression came onto her face. "But oh, it was wonderful living in Hyderabad. We had a house full of servants, and they'd let us chew sugarcane for snacks, and oh, the wildlife!"

Nina rolled her eyes. "Yes, we know. The best year of your life was when you were ten and moved from Uganda to India. Leicester can never compare; we get it."

"It's just the most wonderful country," added Auntie Trish. "Every part of it is completely different, even in one region, like Rajasthan. There's deserts, cities, lakes . . . Oh, and the forts! Gopal and I found one that was abandoned and crawling with monkeys! They'd taken over the Moghul ruins. It was stunning. Though those buggers stole my sunglasses."

"I'm not sure it's for you though, Nina," said Rupa. "I can't imagine you haggling with rickshaw drivers; you don't even speak a word of Hindi. And it's not safe for a young woman alone."

Nina smiled, suddenly certain. "It's what I need to do, Mum. As Auntie Trish and the Gita say, my destiny is mine to live as imperfectly as I want, and I want to go to India. On my own. Sorry."

"But . . . when?" asked Rupa.

"Now," said Nina. "Well, once I've packed and stuff."

"And miss your oldest friend's wedding?" asked Rupa, her eyes narrowing. "Nina, you know how expensive weddings are. It's not polite to cancel."

"Oh god," said Nina. "Fine, well, right after Jo's wedding. Then I'll be going straight to India. Namaste, bitches! Sorry, sorry, language."

28. My life is my own.

To the surprise of the entire Mistry family, Nina's resolve to go to India had only increased since the dinner with Brian. She had already booked her tickets to go away for an entire month, leaving in a couple of weeks' time. It meant eating into her savings, but after so many months of working double shifts and staying with her mum to help look after Kal, Nina had decided it was worth it. Especially given the fact that her new column would add a considerable chunk to her monthly salary. It was time for her to celebrate with a spiritual pilgrimage to the motherland.

It did feel strange that she, an Indian woman, was making her first trip to India at age thirty. But she'd never had any reason to go before. Neither of her parents had any family there. Both of them were part of the generation who'd been born in Uganda after their parents went over to work for the British Empire, and it was only her mum who'd spent a short time living in India. Her stories had never particularly inspired Nina to want to visit, but the thought of inner growth did. She'd already spent the last year connecting with her country on various levels — from yoga to spirituality to chai lattes — and now she wanted to connect on a deeper level. Which was why she'd booked herself into a month's yoga retreat in the Himalayas, away from all the tourists in Goa. Nina was going to do her temporary adult Gap Yah authentically.

"You'll have to cover up, you know," said Rupa, emptying her entire wardrobe onto her bed, where Nina was sitting. "You can't go around half-naked like you do here. You can borrow all my kurta tops and linen trousers. In fact, you can have them. Leave them there for the locals."

"Oh that's nice of you. Thanks, Mum."

"It gives me an excuse to buy new ones," said Rupa brightly. "Right. You can have all these. But do be careful, Nina. India's dangerous. Yes, I know you've been to Thailand and whatnot, but it's not the same. There's a lot of thieving in India. Lying. Manipulating. Bribery. Rape. Murder."

"Okay, Mum, you're not really selling the homeland to me. But I get it. I'll be careful. Promise."

"Honestly," sighed Rupa. "I don't know what the masis and masas will say when they find out you're going alone."

"Loads of girls I know have traveled there alone," Nina said with a shrug. "It's not a big deal."

"*White* girls," said Rupa. "It's different for them." She pulled a pale pink pastel dress out of the wardrobe and held it against her. "What do you think of this?"

"Um, isn't it a bit dressy for India? And it's strappy."

"It's for Jo's wedding," cried Rupa. "It's next week and you still don't have an outfit. No, do not even think of wearing that shapeless black sack to your best friend's wedding. Yes, yes, I know you're going to accessorize it with big earrings and heels, but it's too casual for black-tie."

Nina sighed. "Isn't that a bit ruffly? What are you wearing?"

"Oh, I still can't believe Jo invited Trish and me. She's such a lovely girl."

"Calm down. She's only invited you guys to the ceremony."

"Actually, we're allowed to come back later for dessert and dancing too," said Rupa. "Not that we will. We're going out afterward."

"Okay, but what are you wearing?"

Her mum held up a long, black, structured halter-top dress.

Nina gasped. "It's incredible. I want it. Please can we swap? Please?"

"Absolutely not. I need to wear it for when Trish and I go clubbing afterward. It's an early birthday treat."

Nina looked unhappily at the pink chiffon

dress. "Why is my fifty-nine-year-old mum's life better than mine?"

"Because I've been working my entire life and raising two kids alone, and it's time for me to have fun."

"I hate it when you're right," sighed Nina. "Okay. I'll wear this pink thing. Even though it's seriously un-me."

"Good. And be careful with it. No stains, please. I know what you're like when you see free dessert."

CHAPTER 29

Nina was lying in bed journaling. It had been a while since she'd written in her journal — she had a bad habit of only turning to it when things in her life were disastrous — but now that practicing gratitude was a key part of her life, Nina was making an active effort to record the good stuff too. She'd just covered her new column, Things We Love About Ourselves, being a godmother, and potentially getting a stepdad, when she heard her mum shouting her name.

"What?" she asked, opening her bedroom door. "I thought we weren't allowed to shout in this household."

"Nina, come downstairs. It's important."

Nina reluctantly trudged down the stairs in her fluffy pink dressing gown and bumped straight into a teary, red-eyed Jo.

"Oh my god, Jo! What are you doing here? You're getting married tomorrow!"

Jo burst into tears, and Nina wrapped her arms around her. She mouthed to her mum for help over Jo's shoulder, but Rupa just narrowed her eyes as if to say "Don't fuck this up" and retreated into the living room. Nina carefully led Jo up the stairs into her bedroom and sat her down on the bed.

"Jo, what's going on? Tell me everything."

"I'm . . . sorry," wept Jo. "To just, turn up like this after such a long time. But . . ."

"Do not be sorry," said Nina firmly. "This is what we do best. We've been crying on each other's beds since 2003, and there is no need to stop now. In fact, I wonder how many of our tears this very duvet has seen? God, that's a depressing thought."

Jo smiled through her tears. "More tears than orgasms, that's for sure."

"Hey," cried Nina. "That's . . . probably true, unless we count self-love ones."

"Oh yeah, you definitely win the prize for that," sniffled Jo. "Ah, god. Sorry for this, Nins. I know we haven't spoken properly in ages, and it's really weird of me to show up like this. But I just needed to talk to someone, and the truth is, I'm starting to realize I can't talk to the people I thought were my closest friends."

"I know that feeling," said Nina softly.

"I thought you'd get it. It's why I wanted

to talk to you. You're so honest about how shit your life is, and it makes me feel like I can do the same."

"Um, thanks?"

"Also because, well, you are a bit of an expert at abandoning weddings," Jo said, grinning weakly.

"So you've just come to me because I couldn't commit to Nikhil or to myself?" asked Nina in mock annoyance, before her expression suddenly became serious. "Wait, does this mean you want to abandon your wedding?"

Jo sighed. "I honestly don't know. I love him, Nins, but things have been so bad lately. We can't stop arguing. And I'm being such a bitch, constantly yelling at him to choose between salmon and sea bass."

"Sea bass, obviously," said Nina. "But isn't that just what it's like organizing a wedding? It doesn't mean there's anything wrong with your actual relationship."

"I don't know," said Jo miserably. "I just . . . How can I know for sure that Jaz is the one? Is it normal to have doubts?"

"I think so. But people just don't talk about them. I know I'm never 100 percent sure about anything — even sea bass, actually — so why wouldn't it be the same with a relationship?"

"I guess I just don't know if Jaz truly loves me," said Jo. "He's always out with his friends, and it seems like he'd rather be with anyone but me."

Nina frowned. "Do you think you're maybe being a bit of an unreliable narrator right now? Tell me all the facts and let's figure things out."

It didn't take Nina long to sift through Jo's insecurities and projections to get to the core problem: Jo was worried she was losing herself in the relationship. She'd made Jaz into the key source of all her happiness and was starting to irrationally resent him for having a life when she was losing hers.

The answer was easy. It was, like most things in Nina's life, right there in the self-love book, with her favorite title yet: "The Spice Girls Are Wrong; It's Two Become Three." It went on to explain: "It is very easy to fall into unhealthy traps with relationships. Our societal idea is that two become one. That a relationship is a union. We refer to the other person as 'our other half' and use 'we' instead of 'I.' But this isn't right. It should be two become three. Think of it as a triangle rather than a straight line. Instead of person A and person B becoming AB, they should stay as A and

B whilst creating C — their relationship. That way you all equally prioritize yourselves, as well as your relationship, rather than losing yourselves."

Jo immediately agreed, reminding Nina of what their friendship had been like when they were teenagers who saw the world the same way, and went on to admit that she'd turned into the kind of girlfriend she'd never wanted to be. She'd befriended her fiancé's friends, seamlessly fitting into his world, all at the cost of her own.

"I just felt like my world was a bit shittier than his and my friends weren't that bothered to see me go," Jo said with a shrug, breaking Nina's heart.

"Don't think that," cried Nina. "You're amazing. And *I* was sorry to see you go. I thought you wanted better friends than me. Like Gayatri, and all your couple friends with Jaz. And this conversation is making me realize just how much I've missed you." She paused. "Jo, I'm sorry that I wasn't excited enough about your wedding."

"Don't be," said Jo instantly. "I'm sorry I turned into bridezilla. I don't know how you put up with me. And, Nina, you know that no matter how close I am with Gayatri, you'll always be special to me."

Nina smiled. "Thanks, Jo. But I do have

to apologize. I was a bit of a grinch about it all, I think because I was jealous. Your life seemed so shiny and perfect, while mine was completely falling apart. With Nikhil, and then the Colombian guy, and work stuff. I'll fill you in on it all another day. But basically, I felt like there wasn't any space for me in your perfect world, and I felt lonely."

"But *I* was lonely," wailed Jo. "I missed you so much. I just didn't realize it, and then it was too late because I was so busy with this wedding crap, and I didn't want to come crawling to you because of my bloody pride." She paused. "And also, Nins, I was jealous of you too."

Nina stared at her. "I'm sorry, what?"

"You've got all these new friends, and you're a self-love queen, and I only ever hear about it all on Insta. I feel like my life is so stale and meh in comparison."

"That's only because you've abandoned it to become a 'we,' not an 'I.' You can get it back." Suddenly Nina sat up straight. "Oh my god, I can help you. I basically know the entire book by heart, so I can give it to you. And you can start *your* self-love journey."

"Um, what are you on about?"

Nina produced the self-love bible with a flourish. "You just need to read this. And write a list."

"A list?" asked Jo dubiously.

"Yup," said Nina. "Of all the things you love about yourself. So that you can find yourself again and start having a life that's separate from your life with Jaz. I mean, I'm sure he'll be on your list in some way. But you'll have another twenty-nine things on there too."

"Thirty?" cried Jo. "I couldn't think of five."

"I know, my love," said Nina, putting her arm around her oldest friend. "I've been there too. But you can do it, I promise."

"How?"

"The book will help, but in short, you need to start leaving your comfort zone. Speak your truth. Sign up for classes. Haven't you always wanted to do salsa? And if you feel you can't talk to your current friends, it's never too late to make new ones — or reconnect with old ones."

"I guess so," said Jo slowly. "You do sound like you know the book by heart. This isn't the worst idea you've ever had, Nins. Does it mean you still think I should marry Jaz?"

"Just follow your heart. Not your head. Do not think a single rational thought. Just . . . listen to your intuition, and make sure that you make your decision out of love, not fear."

Jo stared at Nina in confusion for several seconds, then her face broke into a beaming smile. "I guess I'm getting married tomorrow!"

29. I'm actually quite good at giving advice.

It was one a.m. when Jo left Nina's house in a taxi. They'd spent another four hours lying on Nina's bed eating chocolate, repeatedly adding hot water to the same mint tea bags until they were just drinking hot water, and talking about everything that had happened in the last eleven months. Jo had begged Nina to explain the story of her own list, so Nina had told her all the ups and downs of the last eleven months. Jo had shrieked with excitement at all of Nina's recent good news. And, like a true friend, she'd paled with horror at the reality of the online abuse Nina had experienced, as well as the Alejandro breakup. She'd tearfully apologized for de-bridesmaiding Nina and for not being there when she'd really needed a friend — though she'd drawn the line at apologizing for not helping Nina get out of jail, because in Jo's opinion, that was really the catalyst for her self-love journey.

They'd wept together when Nina relived

the night with Kal in the hospital, and then spent an hour and a half stalking Brian on social media. It had all been so easy and comfortable opening up to Jo that Nina realized how much she'd missed spending time with someone she'd known her whole life. She didn't have as much in common anymore with Jo as she did with Meera, in terms of life values and the way they saw the world, but they did have twenty years of friendship behind them, filled with twenty years of memories. Bar her family, there was no one who knew her so well.

They could have gone on talking until dawn, but Rupa quietly knocked on the door at midnight, reminding them that Jo needed to go to sleep four hours ago if she wanted to look like the fresh-eyed dewy bride she'd spent thousands of pounds and even more hours planning to be. Jo had decided an extra hour of friendship bonding was worth the bags under her eyes — "Why the fuck am I paying so much for hair and makeup if they can't fix this?" — which Nina had interpreted as much more of an honor than being a bridesmaid. She'd definitely rather be the person the bride cried on before going down the aisle than the one who had to carry a bouquet and wear an unflattering dress. Though, unfortu-

nately, it seemed like she'd be doing the latter anyway.

CHAPTER 30

ARIES SEASON

ARIES
Season: March 21–April 19
Element: Fire
Themes: New beginnings. Physicality.
  Confidence.
Best time to: Use your power to create the
  life you want.

"Congratulations," cried an elderly white lady in a large pink hat to Nina. "You did wonderfully out there. Beautiful, all of you."

Nina smiled politely and nodded. "Thanks so much. Though, I'm not actually a bridesmaid. Just dressed like them."

The elderly lady looked at Nina in confusion until she blushed. "Oh, I'm so sorry. Gosh. Well, you look lovely all the same."

"Thanks," said Nina, pouring the rest of the prosecco down her throat. This was the fifth variation of a conversation she'd been

449

having ever since Jaz had smashed a glass under his foot. It turned out that pale pink chiffon strappy dresses were the official bridesmaid uniform of Jaz and Jo's Jindu wedding and Nina was a walking faux pas.

She was mortified — so much so that she'd spent a good hour hiding behind a naked statue in the stately garden, drinking prosecco straight from the bottle. She'd only rejoined the celebrations when her mum and Auntie Trish had dragged her out. Not that they'd been much help. Rupa had refused to swap outfits with her, on the grounds that her new size eight dress wouldn't fit Nina, and Auntie Trish had just laughed merrily and told Nina to own her humiliation.

The two women were now basking in compliments on their chic outfits and causing guests to howl with shock when they revealed their ages (there were actual howls; Nina could hear them), while Nina was trying to take Auntie Trish's advice and rise above her shame. She slowly made her way across the large lawn toward Jo and Jaz, who were being photographed by a tree. She gave her former-but-maybe-actually-current-again best friend a big hug. "Congratulations, Jo, you look incredible."

"Nina," cried Jo. "I missed you. I mean,

it's been a whole ten hours since we last hung."

"Thanks for convincing Jo not to abandon me," said Jaz, giving Nina a hug.

"My pleasure," she said, hugging him back tightly. "I'm so glad we're all being so normal with each other and not pretending last night didn't happen. I was scared we'd go back to fake niceness."

"Absolutely not," said Jo firmly, putting her arm around Nina and leading her away from Jaz. "I would never do that to you. Although I do need to apologize in advance. I made the seating plan when I was pissed off with you. So you're not at the fun singles' table, sorry."

"Not the kids' table?"

"Couples," said Jo apologetically. "With Nikhil and Karina — sorry! I was being a bitch. Please don't hate me."

"Oh, it's fine," said Nina, looking down at her outfit glumly. "I deserve it for dressing like this."

Jo burst into laughter. "Oh my god! I didn't even realize!"

"I'm so sorry. It was a total accident. My mum thought it would make me look prettier and more weddingy. It's so embarrassing. I'm this close to ordering a cab to go home and change."

"I love it," said Jo. "It's like you were destined to be a bridesmaid all along."

"Really? You're not mad?"

"Of course not. We need to get you a bouquet."

"No need; people are already congratulating me on being such a lovely bridesmaid."

They both started laughing, stopping only when they heard a loud click behind them. "Sorry," said the photographer. "I just wanted to get a photo of the bride and her favorite bridesmaid sharing a candid moment."

Jo and Nina burst into laughter again. "How do the others feel about me being your fave bridesmaid?"

"They can like it or lump it," said Jo, linking arms with her. "Come on. Let's go eat tandoori sea bass."

It wasn't till the dessert course that Nina managed to speak to Nikhil alone. "Hey, so you and Karina seem happy."

"We are, thanks, Nins. I wouldn't have predicted it, but I really love her."

Nina smiled bravely. "I'm glad. I probably wouldn't have been if you'd said that to me a month ago, but I did a dancing meditation thing recently, and it really helped."

Nikhil raised an eyebrow. "Do I want to

know more?"

"Let's just say it involved me realizing I was still holding out a bit of hope for you and I. And I finally let go of it."

"That's great!"

"It really was," said Nina. "I fully accepted you and Karina, and I sent you both loving energy — not sure if you felt it? Nope? Sure. Well, it made me realize I'll always love you, but it doesn't have to be in a romantic way."

Nikhil smiled. "I feel the same about you, Nins. You were my best friend, and I'm always going to care about you. Those feelings will never fully disappear."

"Oh my god," cried Nina. "You're the Chris to my Gwyneth."

"What?" asked Nikhil, as the rest of the table suddenly fell silent.

"When they broke up, they said they wanted to redirect the love so it wasn't romantic, but would be platonic instead," explained Nina, oblivious to their audience. "That's what we're doing; we're keeping the love, just channeling it in different ways."

"What are you trying to say?" Karina leaned across the table.

"Just that Nikhil and I didn't split up; we consciously uncoupled."

"We . . . did?" he asked.

"Yes," cried Nina. "And, if I remember

correctly, this week is the official one-year anniversary of our conscious uncoupling. Congrats!"

She reached out to hug a baffled-looking Nikhil and a suspicious Karina, closing her eyes and feeling a very, very tiny knot in her stomach disintegrate as a wave of loving kindness flooded her body.

Nina was a wedding convert. She was five proseccos and four lychee martinis in, having the time of her life. She was obsessed with the mash-up of Bollywood-meets-Israeli music and had been so excited by the Jewish custom of dancing in the middle of a large white sheet that she'd spent an hour with Jo inside it — long after everyone else had stopped holding on. No wonder Jo had become such a bridezilla; weddings were incredible.

She only stopped dancing when Jaz clinked his knife against his glass to do his speech. The night before, Nina had tried to convince Jo to break patriarchal traditions and do the big speech herself, but Jo had refused on the grounds that it meant she wouldn't be able to get shit-faced. Nina's feminist arguments had fallen flat in the face of such faultless logic.

"Thank you, everyone," said Jaz. "I just

want to say a few words today about my beautiful, amazing wife. I never thought I'd find someone like Jo. I honestly didn't think I was deserving enough. She's so intelligent, hilarious, kind, caring — and I think you can all agree that she's also bloody gorgeous."

The guests all cheered and clapped. Nina felt several emotions stirring within her. She knew exactly how Jaz felt — his words about Jo were exactly how Nina had started to feel about . . . herself.

"I feel so lucky to be with someone so undeniably talented and strong," said Jaz, and Nina beamed as she thought about Jo's, Meera's, and her own strength and talents. "Jo is one of the most wonderful people I've had the privilege to meet, and I fully plan to continue appreciating her every day for the rest of my life." Nina felt tears prick her eyelids as she thought about her own self-love vows. It no longer felt like a chore to appreciate herself; she loved herself without thinking.

"Jo has helped me become a better person. She inspires me every day to make better choices, to be kinder, more compassionate, more understanding, and more resilient. I wouldn't be who I am today if it wasn't for her."

Nina realized tears were sliding out of her eyes. If she just changed the word "Jo" to "Nina," it was precisely how she felt. She had helped herself become a better person, growing daily, and constantly trying to improve herself. She wasn't perfect — as the Internet now knew — nobody was, but she was a fucking decent work in progress, and she was so *proud* of all the hard work she'd done. The results might not be obvious to anyone but herself, but she knew how far she'd come. She wouldn't be who she was today if it hadn't been for all the tears and failures.

"I am so lucky to have this much love in my life," said Jaz, as Nina nodded heartily in agreement. "It is a gift that I remember to be grateful for every day, and no matter what happens or what life brings us, I know that I will never, ever stop loving my wife the way I do now — because yes, people, she's my wife now!"

Nina stood up with the rest of the guests and raised her glass to Jo and Jaz. But though her lips were saying the names of her friend and husband, on the inside, she was toasting herself. She was her own plus-one, the Jaz to her Jo, for better for worse, for richer for poorer, in sickness and in health, to love and to cherish. She, Nina

Mistry, was completely and utterly in love with herself.

It didn't matter that she wasn't engaged or that she was still living at home with her family, single with a deteriorating womb. These things didn't define her. She was Nina Mistry, and as of right now, she had thirty things she truly loved about herself. She had no idea what the future held, but she knew that whatever it was would be exactly what was meant to be. Finally, she had the courage to live her own life on her own terms, starting with a solo soul-searching trip to India. Nina had no idea what would happen next, but if she thought about her life like a book, she couldn't fucking wait to read the next chapter.

Because Nina had Nina, and no matter what happened, there was no way she'd ever stop loving her.

30. I am unashamedly, proudly, 100 percent in love with myself.

Epilogue

Taurus Season

TAURUS
Season: April 20–May 20
Element: Earth
Themes: Self-care. Sensuality. Pleasure.
Best time to: Set goals to make your dreams
  come true.

Nina walked out of the "Nothing to Declare" door at Heathrow airport, scanning the crowd of excited faces for her mum's less-excited face. She walked up and down the corridor twice, weighed down by her large backpack, repeatedly trying to call her mum as people gave her pitying looks. Eventually, she slumped down in a corner and checked her phone again. Her mum had sent a text.

Sorry, running late; Trish and I had afternoon tea first. Meet us in pickup area. Be quick.

There was a second text. Hurry up. If you're late we have to pay £5.

Nina sighed and hauled her bag back up onto her sore shoulders, rearranging her top so it didn't crumple the plastic wrap protecting her brand-new tattoo, and walked out of the airport to find her mum's car.

"There she is," cried Auntie Trish, emerging out of the car in a floral maxi dress with large sunglasses. "Welcome home, darling. And happy birthday."

Rupa stayed in the car and called out of the window. "Nina, bag in the back. We've got three minutes before we need to pay."

Auntie Trish quickly jumped back into the car, and Nina slid into the back seat. Her mum sped off, just making it through the barriers without paying, and then turned around to look at Nina.

"Happy birthday, honey. You look like you need a shower."

"Who doesn't look like they need a shower after they get off a flight?" replied Nina. "And thank you. But I'm super tired; do you mind if I nap? I want to be on good form for tonight."

"Honestly, I have no idea why you felt the

459

need to organize a surprise birthday for yourself tonight," said Rupa, speeding onto the motorway.

"Oh, it'll be fun," cried Auntie Trish. "You just rest, my love. You can tell us all about India tonight."

"Thanks," said Nina gratefully.

"But just give us a few highlights first," said Auntie Trish. "Was the retreat as magical as you expected?"

"Um, so it wasn't exactly a retreat in the end. Turns out it was a yoga teacher training course."

"What?" cried Rupa.

"Yeah . . . There were five a.m. starts every day. Thirteen-hour days. And nonstop yoga and meditating. Not exactly the relaxing break I was hoping for."

"God, it sounds like hell," said Auntie Trish. "Did you find time to connect with your roots?"

"Oh yes," said Nina. "I'm officially proud to be Indian. I'm also a qualified yoga teacher. They gave me a certificate."

Rupa turned around to gape at her daughter. "You? You're a yoga teacher?"

"Uh-huh," said Nina. "I mean, namaste."

"I can't believe it," said Rupa. "How did you keep up fitness-wise? I just . . . Nina. A yoga teacher."

"Well, I'm very proud of you, Nins," said Auntie Trish. "Now let's get to the good bit — did you meet a cute boy?"

"Uh, not really," said Nina, biting her lip. "I'll tell you guys another time."

"Oh no," cried Rupa. "You met another man in beads, didn't you?"

Nina paused. "Um. I kind of met a woman in beads."

The car jerked wildly as Rupa slammed on the brakes. "You always have to be different, don't you, Nina? It's not enough for you to be thirty-one and unmarried, chasing yoga and spirituality, and getting a tattoo — oh, don't think I didn't see that plastic wrap peeking out of your top. You need to be a lesbian too."

"I'm actually not putting labels on it," said Nina. "I still like men. I just like women too. I always have, I just never got the chance to act on it before." She shrugged. "It's not a big deal; it just means more options."

Auntie Trish shook her head in confusion. "Your generation is too much for me with all this fluid sexuality."

"I don't know why you have to do this to me," cried Rupa. "After I ordered you a cake from Sona's as well."

"Oh my god, the white chocolate one with

strawberries? Mum, you're the best."

"And this is how you repay me?" asked Rupa, shaking her head. "It's bad enough at dinner parties having to explain you're single. How am I meant to say you like women too?"

"You never know," said Nina. "I might still end up with a wealthy doctor. She just could be a woman."

Rupa moaned dramatically, and Auntie Trish turned to look threateningly at the back seat. "How about you take that nap now, Nina?"

Nina woke up an hour before she needed to be at Veeraswamy's. Her mum and Auntie Trish had already gone over to sort out decorations and food — they were going all out for this birthday, considering her thirtieth had been canceled — so Kal and Nina could have more time to get ready before getting a taxi.

"Come in," Nina yawned as Kal tapped on her bedroom door.

"Hey, how are you feeling?" he asked, coming to sit down on her bed.

"Better, thanks. How are you? Sorry we didn't speak much earlier — I just needed to pass out."

"It's okay. But yeah, things are . . . better." Kal smiled. "Sita and I are officially a couple now."

"Oh my god! That's so exciting. She'll be there tonight, right?"

"Yep. I hope you don't mind; I also invited the Mental Health Pottery Club."

" 'Course I don't. I'm so excited it's still going strong."

"Thanks, Nins. You know, it's nominated for a local charity award for providing support to those in need."

Nina shrieked and flung her arms around her older brother. "OH MY GOD. I'm so proud of you."

"You and Mum. Turns out mental health isn't something to be embarrassed about when you've been nominated for an award. Her latest line is 'Oh, we're so proud of Kal for leaving his City job to give back.' "

Nina burst into laughter at his impression of their mum. "Looks like she's finally learned how to spin her kids' lives to make them more palatable for the community. Does that mean she's boasting about me too?"

"Um, not yet . . . But I'm sure she'll get there."

Nina stood in the hallway of Veeraswamy's practicing her surprised face for Kal. But he was too busy staring at her outfit. She'd borrowed Jo's wedding dress — a simple cream silk slip — and it fit her perfectly, especially after her month of nonstop yoga and diarrhea.

"Are you sure you're not a bit overdressed?"

"If I can't wear a wedding dress to my thirty-first surprise birthday, when can I?" replied Nina.

"Um, your wedding?" asked Kal.

Nina grinned and then looked down at her phone. "Oh my god, they're ready for us. Wait, I've got to look more shocked."

Kal pushed open the door. It was pitch-black, but as they walked in, the lights came on and a crowd of fifty-odd people shouted, "SURPRISE." There were so many people that Nina didn't have to fake her look of surprise after all. Her friends were there grinning and waving wildly, but so were dozens of people she'd never met before.

"What are you wearing?" cried Rupa, as Brian waved apologetically at her side.

"Jo's dress," said Nina. "Who are all these people?"

"My guests, because I'm the one paying for this," said Rupa. "Nina, you look ridiculous."

"NINA," shrieked Meera, running up to

hug her. "Happy birthday!"

Nina hugged her hard as a tight-lipped Rupa was swallowed into a crowd of well-dressed Indians. "You look amazing." She crouched down and put her face next to Meera's belly. "And so do you. Hello, darling. It's me, your godmother. Again. I missed you while I was away. I have SO much to tell you." She looked up at Meera's raised eyebrows. "And your wonderful mum, of course."

"Nina," cried Jo, holding up the folds of her pink chiffon dress so she didn't trip. "The dress looks incredible."

"Are you wearing one of your bridesmaid dresses?" asked Nina.

"Yep, moral support." Jo beamed. "I made Gayatri give me hers. She's here somewhere too."

"What's going on?" asked Nikhil, sidling up to the group with Karina and her two besties trailing behind him. "No one told me it was a black-tie dress code. But you look great, Nina." He put his arm around her, and hastily dropped it as Karina's friends stared him down.

"So do you," said Nina, giving him a bear hug. She turned to Karina and co. and enveloped them into a group hug. "As do you guys, as always."

"Ew," said one of the girls, as she pulled away. "Okay."

Meera snorted. "So, are you going to tell us why you're wearing a wedding dress, then?"

"Everyone's started drinking, right?" asked Nina.

"Yes, thank god," said Deepa, appearing out of nowhere and raising her glass in greeting to Nina.

"Okay. Here goes."

Nina stood up on the raised platform next to the huge birthday cake. She shouted, "Excuse me." No one heard her, so she fiddled with the speakers until the music stopped and the room went quiet.

"Hi, everyone," she called out, ignoring her mum loudly muttering, "Oh dear god."

"I know it's a bit early for speeches, but I just wanted to say thank you to everyone for coming. Some of you . . . I don't know very well. Or at all. But some of you are the people I love most in the world. You know who you are. So, first of all, can I just say a massive thank-you to you all for existing and for always being there for me."

There was a polite scattering of applause, with a large cheer from Meera. Nina smiled at her gratefully.

"The reason I'm standing up here today is because it is exactly a year since I spent a night in jail." There were loud gasps in the room, and Nina could feel the hot fury of her mum's gaze. "Don't worry, I was innocent. But that was one of the best nights of my life, because it was the start of my self-love journey. It forced me to go inward, to make my peace with who I am, and ultimately, to fall in love. With myself."

Nina saw her mum drop her head into her hands and watched Brian put his arm around her in consoling support.

"It's why I want to do something today that I almost did on national TV last year. It wasn't the right time or place then, but it is now. I am ready to take the ultimate step of self-love commitment. And marry myself."

Rupa made a strangled noise, and Nina mouthed *Sorry, Mum* to her, while everyone else started talking loudly.

"Okay, can we quiet down, please," she called out. "I did think there would only be about fifteen people here today, and this is a bit of a surprise, so if there's anyone who can't send me loving kindness right now, please leave."

No one moved, apart from Rupa, who tried to turn around — but Auntie Trish and Brian firmly clutched onto her arms to stop her from leaving.

Nina beamed. "Wow. Thank you. I am going to take your presence here today as a sign of unequivocal support. So, here goes. I, Nina Mistry, take myself to be my unlawfully wedded wife. And before I pronounce myself to be my own soul mate, I'm going to read out my vows: Thirty Things I Love About Myself.

1. I love how honest I am.
2. My sense of humor.
3. I'm brave as hell.
4. I'm a doer. Thanks, Mum.
5. My relentless determination.
6. I'm not afraid to break taboos.
7. My spontaneity.
8. I can put myself out there and be vulnerable enough to make new connections.
9. I'm living my life fully in the present.
10. I always try to speak my truth. Even when people don't listen.
11. I keep going.
12. I'm learning to accept things the way they are — good or bad.
13. I'm stronger than I ever realized.
14. I'm incredibly persuasive.
15. I'm always growing and learning.

My life is the ultimate work in progress.

16. I'm a warrior. I don't run away from pain and loneliness (well, not anymore); I climb right inside. Literally.
17. I try really hard. Even if I fail, and fall flat on my dusty, sweaty, bloody face, I'm always trying.
18. I'm a phenomenal woman.
19. My ability to reframe things in a positive light.
20. My big, broken, healing heart.
21. How much I love my big brother.
22. I'm my mother's daughter.
23. My life is a roller coaster, and I'm riding the fucking shit out of it. Sorry, Ronan.
24. I'm okay alone.
25. I'm finally living in the gray.
26. How spiritual and hippie I've turned out to be.
27. I'm an equanimous rock, moved not by extreme fangirling or even more extreme trolling.
28. My life is my own.
29. I'm actually quite good at giving advice.
30. I am unashamedly, proudly, 100 percent in love with myself."

Nina looked up at the crowd of confused faces, searching for her friends and family. Meera was weeping loudly, as were Auntie Trish, Brian, and Dylan. Nikhil gave her a massive thumbs-up. Jo blew her a kiss. Alisa and Deepa cheered. Kal had his arm around Sita and winked supportively at her. Rupa glared at her and pointed her finger at her watch.

Nina laughed. "Okay, that's it. Thanks, everyone. I didn't want to get myself a ring — because patriarchal symbol, et cetera — so I got a tattoo instead. Wait a second. Let me just adjust my dress so I can show you," she said, slipping the strap down and covering her boobs with one hand while she tried to reveal a tattoo on the side of her ribs without flashing her guests. "It's an om!" she said, pointing to an espresso-sized replica of the Hindu symbol. "I've gone back to my roots!" Rupa gave Nina a murderous look.

"So, with this self-love spiritual tattoo, I officially declare myself my one true love and lifelong partner. For ever and ever, amen. Through better and worse, through richer and poorer, through thick and thin. Oh, and sickness and good health. I think that's it. Right?"

After an awkward pause, the audience

470

clapped and cheered. Nina walked past the people she'd never met and went straight to hug her friends and family.

"You're an absolute nutter, but I love you," said Auntie Trish, hugging her tightly.

"I don't know why you always have to be the center of attention," said Rupa, shaking her head. "And it really is tacky to be so into yourself."

"So you liked it, then?" asked Nina.

"Oh, it wasn't as bad as it could have been," said Rupa.

"Your mum means she's proud of you," said Brian, wrapping his arm around her waist. Rupa looked at him in surprise and then laughed.

"Wow, he can contradict Mum and make her laugh in the same sentence," said Kal. "I didn't know that was possible."

Brian put his other arm around Kal's shoulders. "Well done, Nina. It was very . . . original."

"It's the most you thing ever," said Meera. "Jupiter in seventh house."

"I presume that denotes being melodramatic and self-obsessed?" asked Rupa, arching her eyebrows.

"Something like that," said Meera. "Very self-confident, talented, and lucky. Just a bit much sometimes. Oh, and a tendency to be lazy," she added as Rupa nodded in agreement.

"Sorry, can you please stop dissecting my personality?" said Nina. "I think you'll find I just did it quite concisely for all of you in just thirty bullet points."

"You know it's why we love you," said Jo, putting her arm around her former bridesmaid. "You wouldn't be who you are without your flaws."

"Mmm," said Karina dryly. "Apparently nobody's perfect."

Rupa let out a bark of laughter, and Nina was reminded that Karina was the daughter her mum had always dreamed of.

"It's true," said Nina. "But more importantly — when are we going to eat the cake?"

Rupa tutted as Auntie Trish squealed and ran to find candles.

"Ooh, I love that Sona's cake," said Alisa, and Rupa's eyes widened at the sight of her nose ring.

"Who are you?" she asked. "You didn't meet Nina in India, did you?"

Alisa shook her head. "Nope, why?"

"Mum," cried Nina. "Alisa already has a girlfriend. I'm not going to try and steal her away just because I had a thing with a girl in India."

"You had a thing with a girl?" cried Jo and Meera at the same time.

"I'm actually single as of last month," Alisa said with a grin, as Nina cocked her head. This was new information.

"So, uh, how about this pan-ear, then?" asked Brian.

"I think it might actually be cake time," said Kal. "If Auntie Trish doesn't collapse under it."

They all turned to see Auntie Trish carrying the huge rectangular cake over to Nina, lit with thirty-one blazing candles.

"Fuck me, it's huge," cried Nina as Rupa said, "Language!"

"I meant it in a good way," said Nina. "I can't believe you love me enough to pay for the extra-large cake."

Rupa's response was drowned out by Auntie Trish now loudly singing her own version of "Happy Birthday" with the rest of the guests trying and failing to join in. "Happy Birthday — and WEDDING DAY — to Nina. Happy b— Oh bugger, it's melting! Happy birthday to you."

Nina put her hands into a prayer position at her heart and looked around at the roomful of guests. "Thank you. I won't do another speech, because I'm not sure my mum can handle it. But all I want to say is I

love you all so, so much." She paused and
grinned. "Almost as much as I love myself."

31. I'll never stop being me.

ACKNOWLEDGMENTS

I am so grateful to everyone who believed in *30 Things I Love About Myself* and who helped this book become a reality.

The first person I want to thank is Ella Schierenberg. I told you about *30 Things* back at the very beginning, on one of our Heath walks, and you were so excited about it that I shared the Google Doc with you right then. You were the very first person to read Nina's story, pretty much in real time, as I wrote it, and your love for her (okay, mainly Rupa) motivated me to keep going. Thank you, El. Your support for all my writing means so much to me.

None of this would have happened without my agent, Maddy Milburn. Thank you so much for encouraging me to turn a vague idea that I emailed to you into an actual book. I have loved working with you on *30 Things* and you've made the entire process so seamless and joyful. Thank you for believing so much in this book, and for finding me the most wonderful editors to work with!

Which brings me to Eli Dryden, my editor at Headline Review in the UK, and Kate Seaver, my editor at Berkley, Penguin Random House. I have loved working with you both and feel so incredibly lucky to have not just one editor I can always turn to for support or advice, but two!

Eli, I will never forget my first meeting with you and the Headline team. It was so special it made me cry. I still can't believe you all made me my own love jar, filled with things you love about both yourselves and this very book. I knew I would love working with you from that moment (also because you all told me your star signs). I've learned so much from working with you. You've helped make *30 Things* so much stronger and you've been such a champion for it. I had a feeling we'd end up working together ever since I read your first email to me and Maddy, where you were so honest about Nina inspiring you on your own journey, and I'm so glad we did!

And Kate, thank you so much for being such a wonderful editor. I've loved our Zoom chats discussing so many elements of this book (especially because we seem to always agree with each other!!), and I love that I've been able to work with Berkley again after publishing *Virgin* and *Not That Easy* with you. I can't wait to work with you on the next book, and I'm so grateful for all your support.

There are now way too many people to name, but thank you so much to everyone on the Headline and Berkley teams and at the Madeleine Milburn Literary Agency, who have helped this book come out into the world. To publicity, marketing, sales, audio, and all the other teams — your hard work has been amazing. Thank you.

I am very lucky to have so many wonderful friends and loved ones in my life who are ultimate +2s — whether I've known you for decades or only just met you this year. You all know who you are. Thank you so much for all of your support and for helping me to manifest so much magic. Also, for accepting how much I talk about magic. A special thanks also to the other early readers of *30 Things,* particularly Sarah Walker for always being happy to talk through plot changes with me on the phone.

So many of the lessons in this book — and also in the imaginary book within this book: *How To Love Yourself (and Fix Your Shitty Life in the Process)* — are not of my own creation. I've learned them from my wise soul sisters in Barcelona (Cristina Gómez Felip, Laura Nieto, Alba Alonso. Me encanta aprender de — y con — vosotras. Os quiero mucho!), from strangers I've met along the way, and from the endless podcasts and books I've devoured over the years.

I've tried to credit ideas and theories where I can, but a lot of them have just become a part of me and I can no longer remember exactly where I first heard them all. . . . Still, I would like to say thank you to some of my favorite writers/speakers/ general sage souls for always inspiring me: Elizabeth Gilbert, Brené Brown, Byron Katie, Martha Beck, Eckhart Tolle, and pretty much all the guests on Oprah's *Super Soul* podcasts. I love that you exist. Thank you.

Lastly — and obviously — I want to say a big thank-you to myself. For pushing past all the anxieties and insecurities to get this book to where it is today, for making me laugh so much whilst writing it (yes, I laugh at all my own jokes), and for going on the self-love journey that inspired Nina's story. I love you!

■ ■ ■ ■

READERS GUIDE
30 THINGS I LOVE
ABOUT MYSELF

RADHIKA SANGHANI

■ ■ ■ ■

QUESTIONS FOR DISCUSSION

1. At the start of the book, Nina can barely think of six things she loves about herself. Could you write a list of things you love about yourself? Do you think it's important to love yourself?

2. Something Nina really struggles with is loneliness — within her former relationship and with her friends — whilst solitude seems to help her heal. Do you think there is a difference between being alone and being lonely?

3. Nina gets canceled for her views on race. What are your thoughts on how she handled the situation?

4. Alejandro is incredibly harsh to Nina when they break up. Do you think his reaction was justifiable?

5. Nina's family takes up a big part of her life. How do you feel about her attempts to help Rupa and Kal? What do you think of Auntie Trish?

6. Rupa doesn't think a mother and daughter should be friends and she stresses that while she loves her daughter, she doesn't always like her. Is this an unusual depiction of a mother-daughter relationship? How does it compare to other mothers and daughters in popular culture?

7. Spirituality plays a huge role in Nina's journey toward loving herself. Are there any particular messages that really resonated with you that you'd like to incorporate into your own life?

8. Nina also goes on a journey to create new friends as an adult (as well as heal an old friendship). Can you relate to any of her friendship struggles? Which of her friends did you like the most?

9. Rupa and Nina both date at the same time. What do you think about their different approaches to dating? Do you think they show anything about generational differences in attitude?

10. Nina's journalism is focused on tackling complex topics and raising awareness. What did you think about the articles she wrote and the messages behind them?

11. *30 Things I Love About Myself* doesn't finish with a traditional romantic happy ending. What did you think of this ending for Nina's story? What do you imagine her going on to do in the future?

ABOUT THE AUTHOR

Radhika Sanghani is an award-winning journalist and author based in London. She writes features for publications like the *Daily Mail,* the *Daily Telegraph,* the *Guardian,* and *Grazia.* Her two previous novels, *Virgin* and *Not That Easy,* were published in thirteen countries worldwide, with *Virgin* made into an online TV series. Radhika is also a body-positive campaigner and founded the #SideProfileSelfie movement to celebrate big noses. *30 Things I Love About Myself* is her third novel.

The employees of Thorndike Press hope you have enjoyed this Large Print book. All our Thorndike, Wheeler, and Kennebec Large Print titles are designed for easy reading, and all our books are made to last. Other Thorndike Press Large Print books are available at your library, through selected bookstores, or directly from us.

For information about titles, please call:
(800) 223-1244

or visit our website at:
gale.com/thorndike

To share your comments, please write:
Publisher
Thorndike Press
10 Water St., Suite 310
Waterville, ME 04901

CPSIA information can be obtained
at www.ICGtesting.com
Printed in the USA
BVHW060351210422
634917BV00004B/7

9 781432 898342